THE FAG IS NOT FOR BURNING

THE FAG IS NOT FOR BURNING

A MYSTERY NOVEL

by

WILLIAM MALTESE

The Borgo Press
An Imprint of Wildside Press

MMVII

CONTENTS

CHAPTER ONE

MORGAN

"WAS I SURPRISED?" Morgan G. Kent asked, rephrasing Detective Cord Maxwell's question and pouring himself the drink the policeman declined. The *Chevas Regal* formed an immediate stripe of pale amber that glistened through the refracting lead crystal of the tumbler. Morgan drank the booze English-warm while Lake Union dock lights and attending flotilla offered him and his Seattle penthouse a dazzling backdrop through two-story-high picture windows. "As early as two years ago, an acquaintance of mine commented that Horton Lendland would undoubtedly die violently. I was possibly surprised by the suggestion, but probably not."

"This acquaintance?" Cord asked, looking up from his notebook and its seemingly illegible scrawl. He wrote only to look official in the presence of someone he found unacceptably disconcerting. It was more than Morgan being gay. If Morgan *were* gay. Cord was unable to find anyone to verify that on a first-hand basis, although the handsome and successful writer was always mentioned in any *who's-who-within-the-gay-community* conversations.

"I'm reluctant to give you a name," Morgan said with a wide smile that dimpled his cheeks; those attractive concaves perfectly offset the small cleft couched in his chin, "because his comment was one anyone might have deduced from the evidence. By now, even you must have enough of an overview of Horton Lendland's lifestyle to be less than shocked by his manner of dying."

Whether Cord was shocked or not, he was interested in anyone who could read aloud the writing on the wall as early as two years before. "I would like to know who said it," he persisted, remaining embarrassedly distracted by this man whom, at close to forty years of age, looked no more than twenty-five. Morgan either had a body miraculously resistant to the wear and tear of middle age, or he had one he was able to camouflage perfectly within the expensively cut pewter-grey Brioni.

"Gary Green," Morgan said finally, Cord having almost forgotten the triggering question, "but you'll be wasting your time. Gary and Horton only met a few times in passing. They certainly didn't run in the same social circles, as enemies, friends, lovers, *or* tricks. Gary wasn't Horton's type and vice versa."

"That's Gary Green, the schoolteacher?" Cord asked. He'd always been acutely aware of any gay-oriented news breaking within the Seattle area. Gary Green, schoolteacher, had received more than his fair share of press.

"One and the same," Morgan confirmed. "Gary Green, molester of young boys, the greedy gobbler of adolescent dick." Morgan's boyish good looks (God, how *did* the man manage to look boyish at forty!?), seemed out of place with his x-rated comments. But Cord had it from those *who professed to know* that it had been just Morgan's devil-angelic paradox, complete with wit and intellect, which had been his entrée into mansions and back rooms, his key to acceptance by kinks, socialites, and literary scions alike. On *his* terms, not theirs. "Although I would be careful about accusing Gary of his misdeeds in any public forum," Morgan added, "in the face of his total acquittal, I mean."

"You're the one who's calling him a pederast," Cord reminded defensively.

"Am I?" Morgan asked, all practiced innocence that came across surprisingly unaffected. "Surely not! Gary is a *dear friend*, as I'm sure he'll be the very first to tell you."

Cord's uncomfortable feeling of being mind-fucked by a pro seemed to be confirmed by Morgan's radiated sense of amusement at finding himself in the presence of the young policeman whose muscles and guts, at twenty-six, obviously needed far more attention than Detective Cord Maxwell had recently been able to give them. "Do you really find this as amusing as you're coming across?" Cord accused. "I find it unusual from someone purporting to have been Horton Lendland's friend—if not his *best* friend."

"Am I purporting to have been Horton's *best* friend?" Morgan asked, his accompanying laugh refusing any chastisement. "Funny, but I don't recall purporting any such thing."

"He left you over one-hundred-thousand dollars worth of paintings," Cord said, consciously willing himself to stay calm and cool. He suspected Morgan was baiting him, and he refused to play faggot games. Goddamn it, he was a police officer on an official investigation of a man brutally murdered and burned to a fucking crisp, and there was nothing even vaguely amusing about it.

"Haven't you heard? My so-called inheritance went up in the same smoke Horton did," Morgan reminded, pouring himself another drink. On the lake behind him, a yacht jockeyed for mooring, masts bedecked with glimmering lights like ornaments on a Christmas tree.

"Which doesn't negate the fact of his leaving them to you," Cord rebutted.

"It *does* remove any motive for murder, though, doesn't it?" Morgan reasoned. "Not that I knew he was planning on leaving me such a bonanza. When he made me executor of his will, I assumed the fees he knew I'd milk from my executorship would be adequate compensation. Disappointed?"

The question took Cord by surprise. "Disappointed?" he echoed.

"About my motive for murder having been flushed down the toilet?" Morgan elucidated. He cocked his head, his silky black hair moving in an hypnotically fluid motion. He had a scar almost lost within the arch of his left eyebrow. "Although that's possibly not an apropos analogy," he said, "considering we're talking fire here. *Gone up in a puff of smoke* might be better. Yes?"

"There's the insurance," Cord said, wishing he hadn't refused a drink, because he could sure as hell use one. "I'm sure you'll *make out like Flynt* once the estate is settled."

"Horton wasn't much for insurance," Morgan said. "Once you see the final figures, you'll agree my share wouldn't have warranted sticking a spear up my friend's ass and barbecuing him in a fire made from his gallery and its (my) paintings. Besides, I'm not exactly so poor that I have to go around murdering people, friends, associates, or enemies, to supplement my income."

All of which Cord had verified, wondering now how he'd been maneuvered into the role of recalcitrant schoolboy getting run over the coals by *a know-it-all* teacher.

"What about Jim Holdsett?" Cord asked, deciding to take the conversation elsewhere.

"*Jim* Holdsett of *Lendland/Holdsett Gallery*?" Morgan asked, as if he knew several Jim Holdsetts and needed specifics to sort one from the other. "What about him?"

"Could *he* have murdered Horton?"

"Why not?" Morgan said with a shrug. "He gets the gallery."

"Now burned to the ground."

"And the insurance does only cover a fraction," Morgan agreed.

9

"He might not have known that."

"Oh, yes, he *would* have known," Morgan contradicted. "Jim might be just twenty-one, but he's not stupid. How many other young men do you know who became partners in a lucrative gallery at age sixteen? Now, he might have done his share of initial bargaining beneath the sheets, for a foothold, but he didn't hang in there for all of these years without *some* smarts. I don't think Jim would have murdered Horton and burned down the gallery when he was far better off with Horton as a respected figurehead; not to mention all the advantages of having a few paintings to sell."

"Lendland and Holdsett were lovers?"

"That *is* what I insinuated, isn't it?" Morgan said, as if that admission surprised him. He moved across the room from wet bar to black leather easy chair and sat down, resting his right calf on his left knee and balancing his glass on the former. He wore *Gucci* loafers. Cord decided the lighting, or absence thereof, was what kept Morgan looking so young. Once the man got out in the sunlight....

"And I do suspect the two did *play around*," Morgan said, interrupting Cord's reverie. "After all, one never gets something for nothing (at least that's been my experience), and Jim has certainly chocked up his fair share of *somethings,* hasn't he?"

"But you don't know for a fact that the two were lovers?" Cord pressed. It was a facet of the investigation he would like clarified. Jim Holdsett denied any sexual involvement with Horton Lendland. However, Morgan wasn't the first to insinuate otherwise.

"Lovers?" Morgan asked, his expression denoting disappointment at Cord's use of, or misuse of, the hackneyed term. "What a catch-all *lovers* has become," he bemoaned. "Are you referring to a *man-man-equals-husband-wife* relationship? To a *man-man-equals-husband-mistress* relationship? To a *man-man-equals-husband-prostitute* relationship? To any of the hundred-and-one other gradients?"

"Did Horton Lendland and Jim Holdsett fuck each other?" Cord asked in mounting frustration. He wanted a simple yes or no from this bastard instead of this verbal diarrhea he *should* have expected from a writer. At least Morgan's income *presently* derived from his writing. He'd supposedly gotten it from far more interesting sources in the past, but Cord was still checking to verify those rumors.

"I was never there when Jim dropped his pants and bared his cock and ass for Horton, if that's what you mean," Morgan admitted. "Horton was never into group scenes, except in back rooms so dark he couldn't see who belonged to whatever the cock he was sucking. And when he was sober, he wasn't always one-hundred percent truthful about such things. I remember him telling me once that he'd seen (platonically, mind you), Grey Matthews (a local weight-lifter, AKA *Mr. Northwest Muscle*—since mainlined to the big gymnasium in the sky), without clothes on. Horton insisted Grey was hung like an ant. Later, of course, I caught a glimpse of Grey naked on one of those gay greeting cards, and *hung like a horse* would have been more like it. As for Jim, he certainly wouldn't have done any confiding in me about Horton and his clandestine sexual life. He was too busy trying to convince me, him, his psychiatrist, and everyone else that he was the only straight in the whole Seattle art community. Then again…."

"Then again, what?" Cord asked, knowing Morgan's pause was for effect. Cord didn't like feeling, as he did, that he was being merrily led down some garden path.

"There might, once upon a time, have been an incriminating photo."

"Might?" Cord responded. By Christ, there either *was* a photo or there *wasn't*. What was all of this *might* bullshit?

"I was very drunk at the time," Morgan resumed. "Horton must have been very drunk, too—" According to Cord's sources, Horton had been drunk *most* of the time "—because he was really quite shy and not at all flamboyant in his sexual activities as he was in other areas. But I do vaguely recall a photo of Jim looking very un-straightsman-like with his trousers bunched around his ankles and Horton's hungry mouth burrowing deeply over Jim's crotch."

"You wouldn't know where this photo is now?" Cord asked. There had been photos galore, a whole sack of them, which Darold Keshmont, Horton's house mate, had dubbed *Horton's Bag of Dirty Tricks*. However, there had been no photo of Darold or Jim among the lot, just a rogues' gallery of other men, in one form of undress or another, including the gay greeting card of well-hung Grey (Mr. Northwest Muscle) Matthews.

"Horton had a whole collection of photographs that he kept in a bag somewhere," Morgan confirmed. "Ask Darold to dig them out for you. Darold knew far more about Horton's sex life than Horton suspected. He certainly knows more about it than I do, or ever did."

Darold Keshmont was another subject Cord wanted to cover extensively with Morgan, but first—"You only saw the photo of Jim and Horton that once?"

"It wasn't a viewing experience that warranted a concentrated effort in ever repeating," Morgan said with a grimace. "Jim has never been my type and, at the time, he was covered with enough baby fat to make him positively cherubic. More Gary Green's type than mine."

Cord would not ask Morgan what type he *did* prefer, because the answer was geared more to Cord's personal, rather than to his professional, curiosity. "So, what was Lendland's relationship with Keshmont?" he asked instead.

"Why don't you ask Darold?" Morgan suggested.

"Why don't you let me decide what questions to ask, to whom, and when to ask them?" Cord suggested in miffed alternative.

"You seem awfully young to be a homicide detective, Detective Maxwell," Morgan threw at him from left field, as if having intuitively waited for that moment. Cord's youth was a personal sore point, as tender for the young policeman as was the rumor that he'd risen so far so fast in the force because his father's father and his father (both retired police officers), were friends and poker buddies of the present police commissioner.

"I'm not the youngest to have made detective grade," Cord volunteered, trying not to sound defensive. There had been a guy two months his junior who had made detective on the Seattle force. So what if it had happened in 1915? "And if you have any questions about my qualifications, let me assure you that overcoming looking young has in no way hindered my excellent results in the field."

"I do believe that's the first time I've heard someone boast of *overcoming looking young,*" Morgan said, mock awe oozing over. He took another swallow of his drink. An emerald-and-diamond ring on his right pinkie finger caught what little light there was and sent it back in a sunburst of glitter. The ring was another item about which Cord would have liked asking, except he wasn't certain how the gift, reportedly from a woman many years Morgan's senior and now dead, could relate to the present case.

"Maybe your surprise comes from too long running with a youth-worshipping crowd," Cord criticized. "Youth and good looks aren't everything. In fact, they're a damned superficial way to judge any one."

"They don't judge a man by his age in the police force, then?" Morgan asked. The knife was in and given a twist.

"Let me remind you, once again, that I'm asking the questions," Cord said, refusing to surrender control. "If you'd rather we conduct this at the station, I'd be more than happy to oblige, as well as arrange for you to be interviewed by someone associated with this case who's more to your liking."

"Not likely," Morgan countered, and Cord read all sorts of innuendo. The policeman blushed. Not something he enjoyed doing, because it tainted his peaches-and-cream complexion and said too much that was better left unsaid about the state of his emotions. "There are others assigned to the case, are there?" Morgan asked. If he'd seen the evidence of Cord's blushed discomfort in the dim lighting, he'd had the good grace not to capitalize upon it.

"This is a murder and arson," Cord reminded, thankful for something to say. He'd just realized he'd probably been turning pink for nothing. Morgan's *not likely* comment likely had no sexual connotation. This left Cord relieved but curious and uneasy by whatever had triggered *his* misinterpretation.

"Mmmmmm," Morgan hummed, sounding very much a man who'd just been offered the Brooklyn Bridge for $1.50 and was only pretending to consider the sincerity of the offer until the cops arrived. "I'd just assumed that everyone else *but you* was presently assigned to the *Dint Slough* murders." The *Dint Slough* murders had occurred over the last five years. It had taken so long for the public to become incensed by them because the killer concentrated on whores, whom he brutally fucked, fore and aft, with myriad inanimate objects, then killed (suffocation being his primary *modus operandi*), and then unceremoniously dumped somewhere within the forty-square mile boundaries of the wetland known locally as *Dint Slough*. What had caused the present glaring focus of attention on them had been the recent discovery of Karen Reinstick's discarded corpse by a cub scout out with his father collecting insects for a merit badge. As it turned out, Karen *wasn't* a prostitute, and that was what raised the outcry that eventually rattled the very doors of city hall. That Karen had been killed not by the *Dint Slough* killer but by her *found-another-love* husband (as later came out), still emphasized to John Q. Seattleite that someone had been dropping bodies at *Dint Slough* for over five years without getting caught or punished for it. Maybe it was only prostitutes now, but it could soon enough spill over to include someone *like* Karen Reinstick. So, a special task force was formed, its progress (consistently next to nothing), daily condemned by the news media and an increasingly irate public. The death of twenty-two whores suddenly held precedence over most everything, especially over the death of one (albeit socially prominent) faggot. Queers invariably killed their own, didn't they? While a killer of prostitutes more closely skirted the heterosexual norm. First things first.

"The Seattle Police Department is geared for the successful investigation of more than one murder at a time," Cord assured, knowing he was assigned to the Lendland case because he was the only detective the chief figured he could spare. Cord would have pre-

13

ferred being back on the *Dint Slough* task force. Gay murders in general—gays in particular—were *not* his cup of tea. Male whores were forever on the make, and it was small wonder more weren't iced each year by the straights they accosted. The other day, in the men's rest room at Alki, Cord had been propositioned by a kid young enough to be Cord's son (and *that* was pretty damned young). Cord had been so taken aback that he hadn't thought to arrest him. What he should have done was turn the little shit over his knee and give him a good spanking. But he'd been too taken back for that. Besides, the kid would have probably liked it.

"I hold out little hope of you getting to the bottom of this, you know?" Morgan said. "Especially in the face of the gay hustler murdered two months ago, and the gay lawyer murdered just last month. Your department isn't exactly batting a hundred on gay murders, is it?" Detectives Sudlow and Hillock had been working on those, but they'd since been assigned to the *Dint Slough* task force. The cases, though, were still officially open, if getting colder by the day, probably to be stone cold by the time Sudlow and Hillock got back to them —if they *ever* got back to them. Even Cord believed all that was expected on this one was that he go through the motions. To appease the more militant and political gay groups, Cord had been assigned, as liaison with the gay community, a young lawyer named George Genlic who was gay and, what's more, looked and acted it.

"I hope you're not insinuating the police haven't done, and are not doing, everything that might be expected of them as regards this case," Cord challenged. It was all right for Cord, secretly or otherwise, to criticize his own, because he was on the inside and a certified member of the offending fraternity. It was *not* okay for Morgan to criticize.

"And if I were?" Morgan countered, not backing down as Cord had expected and wanted him to. "Would you attempt to persuade me otherwise by using your phallic billy club? Where does a plainclothesman, by the way, hide it?"

"If you were so insinuating, I'd assure you that we're doing the best job we possibly can under the circumstances," Cord said, refusing to comment upon where he did or didn't keep his billy club. He only hoped Morgan's remark hadn't been a double entendre referring to the unsightly bulge Cord's mysteriously swollen cock was making in his pants. "Hampered," he continued, "by wise-ass faggots, like you, who think it's a joke when one of your own gets skewered up his ass by a spear and roasted over a bonfire."

"*Touché*," Morgan conceded, sounding not in the least repentant. "So, let's get on with this, shall we?" He checked his watch, a

Piaget Polo that Cord couldn't have afforded after a lifetime of foregoing lunches at McDonald's.

CHAPTER TWO

ROCKY

"OH, JESUS, MAN!" Samuel (*"Rocky"—because-of-his-big-balls*) Bennuti said and groaned, having turned toward the tap on his left shoulder and seen who was there. "I'm bothering no one, waiting for a bus."

"Yeah?" Cord asked mockingly. "And I'm the tooth fairy. Come on. I want a few minutes of your time."

"I'm going to miss my ride," Rocky whined. "My mother is going to be pissed."

"Your mother would be more pissed if you surprised her to death by showing up on her doorstep at all. Now, get that ass you're peddling in gear before I pull you in for soliciting."

"Fuck!" Rocky bemoaned, falling into step beside the policeman, all the while enviously eyeing the drivers of the steady stream of cars passing him by. "Where are we going?" he asked after they'd reached Cord's unmarked car, the cop motioning him inside. "Change your mind about a blow-job?"

"You watch your faggot mouth!" Cord warned, sliding behind the wheel. "Or you're going to find it too fist-punched sore for sucking."

"There's always my firm young ass," Rocky reminded rebelliously.

"And who's paying to fuck a hole that could take on Amtrak and feel no friction?" Cord retorted with a grunt. He eased them away from the curb and into the hustler-cruising traffic.

"I ain't done nothing!" Rocky assured; Cord didn't bother to explain the *what* of a double negative.

"Don't be so fucking paranoid," Cord said. "I just want you to come somewhere with me."

"*Come* where with you?" Rocky asked, emphasizing the sexual connotations by cupping his crotch with his right hand and giving an obscene squeeze.

"You fucking little pervert!" Cord accused, shaking his head in real and feigned disgust. "Just sit there and shut up."

Cord knew Rocky from when Cord worked vice three years before. At the time, Rocky was new enough to selling himself on the streets to make the mistake of propositioning Cord, a vice decoy at the time. Cord had hauled Rocky's ass on in, booked him, and called Rocky's mother to get *her* ass downtown to pick her kid up. Rocky had been back on First Avenue two days later, wise enough to give Cord a wide berth. He'd been a young (thirteen), fresh-faced kid from Ballard, at the time. Now, he was sixteen and looking twenty. Whatever it was that kept Morgan Kent young, Rocky hadn't been made privy to the secret. Not that the kid wasn't still attractive, in a hardened, much-used sort of way. His military haircut, black eyes, pouty mouth, super-thin body, big cock, and bigger-than-most balls, still appealed to a few; although he was on a fast track heading nowhere and was beginning to look it.

Cord drove to the University District, wondering if Rocky looked at the college kids with any jealous resentment. What Rocky *looked* was ticked off that Cord had yanked him off First Avenue during the busiest and most lucrative part of any hustler's evening.

Cord located a parking spot across the street from the *University Cinemas*. "What now?" Rocky wanted to know.

"We sit and wait for the ten-to-twelve feature to let out," Cord said, checking his watch, a *Timex* not anywhere nearly as expensive as Morgan's sleek *Piaget*. He thought a lot about Morgan, telling himself he did so only because the guy was not easy to figure. Thought gay by gays, and by most straights, Morgan didn't seem to have bedded anyone who was willing to kiss and tell. Anyone who thought he or she knew someone with whom Morgan had supposedly tricked was always wrong. The majority, men and women, just *wanted* to go to bed with him. Why not? Morgan was handsome as hell, and he came complete with enough celebrity for any famefucker. Who else had gone from writing fuck books to writing Harlequin SuperRomances to writing a best-selling nonfiction account of a downed U.S. bomber crew behind German lines in World War II, the latter book having been developed into a rating-breaker twelve-hour miniseries starring sexy newcomer, Daley Moore? What's more, Morgan had appeared on Jay Leno not once but twice.

"We waiting for anyone in particular?" Rocky asked, sounding and looking bored. The audience from the last show was finally exiting the theater.

"At the moment, we're just waiting," Cord parried vaguely.

Cord hadn't discarded the possibility that Morgan was a heterosexual in homosexual disguise. Just because the guy was exceptionally handsome didn't make him queer. Hell, Cord had been mistaken often enough for a gay, especially when working vice, to know that for a fact. Nor did associating with queers, as Morgan did, mean queerness rubbed off. If the latter were the case, all of the literary and theatrical set in Seattle would be confirmed nellies by now.

So, did Morgan fuck women? Whether women, or men, or dogs, Cord had drawn a complete blank. There had been a heterosexual fruit-fly Morgan ran around with in his early days of pounding out two fuck-books (one gay, one straight) a month for a San Diego smut publisher, but Sandra Wheems hadn't been seen for ages. There was the eighty-three-year-old woman who had been Morgan's sugar-momma and had literally shown him the world on a series of mind-expanding and expensive cruises, but had he actually fucked Mary Bjorn or ever offered her anything but companionship? Cord couldn't ask Mary; she was dead. Of natural causes, after an operation for gallstones; the operation had succeeded, the patient had died of heart failure. Leaving Morgan rich as Midas and wearing the *big-dollar-value-emerald-and-diamond* pinkie ring that had become his trademark, as well as the *Brioni,* as well as the *Piaget.*

"The theater is shutting down," Rocky said, bringing Cord out of his reverie. The marquee had just gone dark.

Cord opened the car door and got out, motioning Rocky to do the same.

"The last show is over and done," Rocky reminded; Cord certainly didn't need to be told the obvious.

"Well, you and I are VIP's," Cord argued, jaywalking to the theater and knocking on its locked door.

"We're closed!" came a none-too-courteous response from within.

"Well, *un*close, please," Cord said. "It's Detective Maxwell from Seattle Police, and I want to talk with Miss Taylor."

"Hold a sec." The voice was more respectful, this time, but not accompanied by any sounds of an unlocking door.

Rocky examined the promo poster for *Spinal Tap,* a movie about a rock-and-roll band that was one of the oldies-but-goodies playing inside.

"Detective Maxwell?" a muffled query came through the closed door.

"Miss Taylor?" Cord replied. There was a click, and the door opened a crack, then farther. "Sorry about this," Cord apologized with a wide grin, "but I'm hoping I can impose upon your good graces once again."

Sharon Taylor was in her early twenties, a graduate student in psychology at the *University of Washington*. She managed the *University Cinemas* for pocket money to supplement the scholarship that made her life easier but not carefree. She had naturally blonde hair, a *pretty-rather-than-beautiful* face, *sufficient-but-not-Dolly-Parton* tits, and legs that started at the floor and seemed to go on forever. She'd been one of two theater employees who had positively identified Morgan Kent, from his photograph, as having been in the audience on the night of Horton Lendland's murder. "Come in, please," she invited, sounding pleased to see Cord, despite the lateness and inconvenience of the hour. Her sparkling smile of welcome was only slightly dimmed when Cord called Rocky over to lead the way in.

"I'd like to see that movie once again," Cord said. "I tried to get here for the last scheduled showing, but...." He let Sharon add her own ending, hoping she could come up with something better than he could manage. Actually, he was there purely on an impulse, after having spotted Rocky on the street corner. "If it's too much brother, though...." Again, he paused.

"Well," Sharon said, checking her watch; it was neither *Piaget* nor *Timex,* "Sid has a test tomorrow, but I can stick around and run the projector. Why don't you go on in, and I'll manage the film?" She still managed a nice smile: pink lips pulled back over seed-pearl teeth. She smelled of lily of the valley.

Cord mumbled his thanks and steered Rocky into the auditorium.

"That babe is hot-hot-hot for your body," Rocky chanted, selecting an aisle seat and plopping down in it. Cord climbed over him, leaving an empty seat in between. "She has excellent taste in men," Rocky added.

"Don't start!" Cord warned.

"Stud, I know what I'm saying," Rocky persisted. "I deal in passion, remember?"

"You deal in hurried cock-sucks and ass-fucks, blow-jobs and hand-jobs," Cord clarified.

"You couldn't see her little pink tongue hanging out all of the way to her little pink clit?" Rocky asked in a *don't-feed-me-that-line-of-bullshit* voice.

"Keep it down, you little prick!" Cord hissed. He could hear Sharon in the projection booth and didn't know how much she heard in return.

"Hey, guy, my prick *isn't* little," Rocky protested. "Want to see?"

"What I want is for you to shut up," Cord warned. He didn't have the time, the patience, or the inclination to listen to Rocky's inept run-on come-ons.

"Don't knock what you haven't tried," Rocky said, looking far less rebuffed than Cord thought he should be. Though, he apparently sensed the negative vibes, because he settled down in his seat and changed the subject. "So, why are we at a private screening of an old rock-and-roll movie?" He propped his feet on the back of the chair in front of him.

"We're not seeing the rock-and-roll movie," Cord surprised. "We're seeing the one being shown in Cinema II."

"Which is?"

"Another Country."

"What other country?"

"Just watch the movie and find out, damn it!"

"Ready?" Sharon called.

"Yes, thanks!" Cord called back.

The house lights dimmed. "Think I could have some popcorn?" Rocky asked. "Or how about you share your hot-candy balls?"

"Shhhhh!" Cord hissed, not pleased by Rocky's responding chuckle.

Cord expected Sharon to come on down and join them. She later admitted that she'd been tempted but had used the time for extra study. Cord gave her a lift home to her boarding house waffled between sorority and fraternity houses on frat row. Rocky had the wherewithal to keep his comments to himself until Sharon was out of the car and, more importantly, out of earshot.

"So, what'd you bring me along for?" Rocky asked finally. "As the chaperone who would keep you from having to fuck the bitch?"

"You are genuinely one sick puppy, you know that?" Cord informed, made uneasy by the perceptiveness of the sixteen-year-old queer, because Sharon likely *would* have invited Cord in if— "Tell me what you thought of the movie," Cord ordered.

"I couldn't understand half of it," Rocky complained. "What in the hell language were they speaking, anyway?"

"English," Cord informed. Some of the upper-class English diction *had* been hard to follow, but he'd managed better this time. He still wondered what appeal the film offered Morgan Kent that the man had seen it five times. Beautifully photographed in Rembrandt-dark sequences, it was a slick presentation of the gay aspects of English *public* school in the 1930s and had won several awards after its initial release in the theaters. If its basic purpose was an attempt at explaining the eventual betrayal of country by spies like Kim Philby, a product of the English public school system, *Another Country,* on the surface, remained a tender love story between two young men. And Cord had met only one person who had thought Morgan Kent a romantic, and that was Edna Potts. Edna was eighty-six, and she'd been Mary Bjorn's best friend and confident until business tycoon Robert Lasalo had introduced Mary to Morgan Kent at a party, *magic* striking. Edna, though, insisted Morgan was *the best thing that could have happened to Mary.* "They were both such romantics, you know?" she said. "Morgan made Mary's last days very happy and exciting, indeed."

Morgan Kent a romantic? *Cynic* was the most popular description, followed closely, if not in dead-heat, by *jaded.* Even Rose Westphal (AKA Rose White, Rosalind Cary, Rosemary Wine), someone who knew Morgan (AKA Morgana Kent) quite well from their Harlequin days, didn't say he was a romantic. Romantic, yes, but *a romantic? "A cynic, like I am,"* was what she actually said. *"But with so much charm that you could miss the cynicism if you weren't damned careful."*

"What did *you* think of the movie?" Rocky asked Cord and rolled down the car widow to let in surprisingly damp-free air for Seattle. "Enough, I guess, to have come back to see it a second time, huh?"

"I know *my* opinion," Cord said. "At the present, I want to hear *yours.*" After all, Rocky was gay, and Cord wanted a gay perspective. Although it seemed ludicrous to think Morgan and Rocky's thought processes could ever operate along one and the same line.

"Well, I wouldn't be all that hot to see it for a second go-round," Rocky judged, although the butt-warming scene was kind of a turn-on."

"The disciplinary caning?"

"The what?"

"The butt-warming," Cord reverted, finding it easier to sink to Rocky's level than try bringing the hustler up to his.

"Yeah," Rocky confirmed. "At least I could get off on that."

"Because your parents beat you, you mean?" Cord ventured. How many kids were on the streets because abuse in the home had driven them there?

"Hell, if my parents had whacked my ass once or twice more often, it might have been better for all of us," Rocky defended, shattering Cord's theory all to hell. "I was talking about how many johns are into B&D, these days."

"You mean, there are customers of yours who spank your ass, or vice versa?" Cord asked. There was no reason he should be shocked. He'd worked vice. He'd seen and heard worse.

"Some get turned on by that, yeah," Rocky admitted, obviously knowing more about B&D activities in Seattle than about disciplinary caning in the English public school system. "And they're not *just* into spanking either. There's this really butch number out of Canada who always wants me to tie him up and fist-fuck him."

"So, I suppose, you tie him up and give him what he wants?" Cord asked, unable to control a shiver from head to toes and back again. "And do these johns ever want to tie *you* up?" he asked, without a pause.

"Some of them," Rocky admitted. "One guy uses electrical tape...."

"Do you know that three gays have been murdered in this town during the last four months?" Cord interrupted. His glance toward Rocky, if looks could kill, would have done the job. "All three tied before being murdered."

"I don't make it with freaks," Rocky objected. "I can spot the sick ones right off."

"Like you spotted me for vice the time you asked if I wanted to suck off your big cock or vice versa for ten bucks?" Cord argued facetiously.

"Hey, I've come a long way, since then, baby!" Rocky assured. "There have been lots of cocks, mouths, and assholes under the bridge since I tried to slap the make on you and yours that first time."

"Don't you think those three dead gays once thought that *they* could spot the sickies, too?" Cord asked. This kid really wasn't all there. Rocky's common sense had been sucked out of his exploding cock by one too many queer who'd paid ten dollars for the meal.

"Hey, you're worried about me, aren't you?" Rocky said. "Ain't that sweet. Real sweet. But I can take care of myself, see. There ain't no goon going to fool me into letting him kill me. Right? Right!"

Horton Lendland had not been a fool, yet someone had gotten to him. And if that someone could get to Lendland, Rocky—brave talk or not—wouldn't stand a chance. "I'm taking you to the station, Rocky," Cord said. "I'm telling them you asked to suck my cock. Then, I'm calling your mother and telling her if she lets you back out at night, ever again, she'll have bloody hell to pay."

Rocky's laugh wasn't what Cord expected. It said more than words how long Cord's warnings to Rocky, or to the kid's mother, would keep Rocky from hustling. Selling his body was Rocky's karma, his fate, his place in a *some-people-are-shat-upon-and-some-people-do-the-shitting* world. "Drop me where you picked me up, will you, Maxwell?" Rocky asked, still smiling and shaking his head.

"You aren't likely to turn a trick this late at night," Cord protested feebly. "Why don't you let me drive you home?"

"Not unless you're planning to come on in with me," Rocky said. "And you aren't about to do that, are you, stud? So, do the next best thing, and stop worrying about me."

Despite the hour, the street wasn't deserted. There were warm bodies on display, lined up against buildings like targets in a shooting gallery, a constant stream of slow-moving traffic circling around them like hunters on the hunt.

"Here!" Rocky announced, and Cord robot-like turned the car to the curb and stopped. Rocky hopped out and shut the door behind him, slapping the roof in friendly farewell.

A young kid emerged from the attending shadows. Nine years old? Ten? Closer to nine. No more than a baby, glancing toward the car, saying something to Rocky. Rocky laughed, his voice clear and painfully youthful as he called back to Cord, "Hey, Maxwell, little Timmy, here, wants to know if you'd like to fuck his tight virgin asshole."

Cord eased the car away from the curb. In his rearview mirror, he caught a parting glimpse of the very young kid who would, in three short years, or in less, look older than Rocky, maybe even older than Cord. Life on the streets drained more than the cum from young hustlers. It drained much, much, much more than just the cum.

CHAPTER THREE

DAROLD

"**GODDAMN IT,** will both of you quit making such a fuss!" Darold Keshmont yelled just before opening the door and letting Cord inside. "The damned dogs," he explained, "are about to drive me crazy." He led the way through the dining room and into the recreation room of the impressive Tudor house. From behind the closed door of an adjacent room came muffled barks and scratches, echoed by similar sounds from behind the door leading to yet another room. If the dogs were driving Darold crazy, Cord had it from several sources that the dogs, themselves, were *out of their fucking minds*. Every dog introduced into that particular household had supposedly degenerated into one or another category of *crazy* that would have left even Barbara Woodhouse throwing up her hands in dismay. "Don't mind the clutter," Darold apologized, motioning Cord to an empty seat. "Morgan, as Horton's executor, has had people in, taking inventory, these last few days, and I've been pulling things out of closets that haven't seen the light of day in decades. Drink?"

"No, thank you," Cord declined, hoping he wouldn't regret that decision.

Darold, a well-preserved older man whose expertly dyed hair made him seem younger, was five-foot-nine and neatly dressed in slacks, an *open-at-the-collar-to-show-naturally-gray-chest-hair* shirt, and a Ralph Lauren sports jacket. He chose a chair opposite the one into which he'd motioned Cord and sat down. "Making progress?" he asked; something about his asking said he already had his answer and was merely making conversation.

"It's a difficult case," Cord said. "Horton knew so many—shall we say, interesting?—people."

"You might as well go whole hog and call them what they really were and are—crazies!" Darold insisted. "Certainly, don't think you're saving my sensibilities by painting the picture rosier than it was."

24

"Horton did seem to have a preference for...." Cord's pause, this time, was purposeful.

Darold obliged by filling the missing space without missing a beat: *"Trade,"* he identified. "Yes, Horton *did* have a penchant *for trade.*"

"Yet, Morgan Kent was his best friend, or am I wrong about that?"

"One doesn't necessarily suck or fuck one's friends," Darold reminded. Which Cord wanted clarified farther.

"Horton and Morgan weren't sexually involved, then?"

"Hmmmmm," Darold considered, sitting farther back and folding his arms over his chest. "I'm not sure I can say for sure. Horton confided very little in me about his sexual assignations. He labored under the misconception that I cared and would be hurt if he spent his nights sucking some young man's brains out."

"When, in fact, you *didn't* mind?" Cord injected, wanting to keep the conversation rolling.

"Horton and I ceased being sexually interested in one another over twenty years ago," Darold said with no evident embarrassment. "Naturally, I assumed he was getting *it* in the interim, despite his often elaborate and ridiculous denials."

"But why would or should he deny it?" Cord protested. "I mean, if you and he were no longer sexually involved with one another...."

"He thought I viewed his tricks as rivals for gallery profits I believed rightfully mine," Darold said candidly. "I've always been frugal in my outlook towards money, Detective Maxwell. It was a characteristic which proved useful in those earlier years of getting Horton and me through some very lean times. *Before the gallery* times. *Before-super-success* times. *Before-Horton-fell-into-art-dealing-because-he-was-so-ill-suited-for-anything-else* times. Horton thought *I thought* he was squandering money on his young men. He thought *I thought* they would become trophy studs to see me soon relegated to the trash heap, like some poor wife no longer useful or desirable after having slaved away her better years to put her husband through medical school."

"None of which you really felt?" Cord suggested.

"Oh, let's *do* be realistic!" Darold protested, crossing his legs, and pyramiding his index fingers to rest their resulting point against his chin. "Where there's smoke, there's usually fire and, of course, I resented the money he spent on them. And the money he spent on himself, I might add. I mean, he took his tricks with him to Hawaii. He took them with him to Tahiti. He took them with him to Europe. He lavished expensive gifts and clothes on them and on himself. All of which cost money that, if invested properly, could have reaped far greater returns, in my humble estimation, and certainly more long-lasting returns, by anyone's estimation. And when Horton began giving his tricks jobs, more than *just* menial, at the gallery, well, is it any wonder I, at times, questioned whether the business would survive? Those young men never heard of Mark Toby, or Karl and Hilda Morris, or Paul Horiuchi, or Kenneth Callahan, yet were suddenly expected to deal successfully with a buying public far more knowledgeable than they were. I had every right to feel put upon, considering it was my paycheck in the early days that allowed Horton to survive for the success in an art business that was supposed to see me through my old age."

"Your income, at the time of his death, remained entirely dependent upon the gallery?"

"That's really a statement, isn't it?" Darold said, a wry smile curling the corners of his thin lips. "I've no doubt but that you've checked my present financial position."

"Merely double-checking," Cord assured.

"Figuring to get it from the horse's mouth, or thinking I might, for some reason, pretend I was less dependent than I was upon the *Lendland/Holdsett Gallery* at the time of Horton's death?" Darold ventured.

"Let me assure you...."

"Oh, you needn't bother offering assurances of anything," Darold said with a dismissing wave of his hands. "Feel free to play all the little tricks of your trade on me, or on anyone else, if it will help you get to the bottom of Horton's murder. We were together a long time, Horton and I. Over thirty years. And our relationship, placid and stormy, was made of sterner stuff than what did or didn't happen in some bedroom."

"In the end, he left you well-provided for," Cord observed carefully.

"My inheritance looks even greater in the face of poor Jim's legacy, the gallery going up in poorly-insured smoke," Darold acknowledged with a sad little shake of his head. "Poor Jim! He has worked so hard to have ended up on the short end of the stick. Granted, he's not a horribly polished individual, even now. But even Morgan will agree that Jim appeared at a time when someone was badly needed. Horton, you see, had become quite bored by the art business. This was why, I suppose, he kept hoping one of his tricks would exhibit the same wherewithal *he* had managed in making something of *himself*. Unfortunately, most of his young men were on the streets because they didn't have any real talent for succeeding anywhere else, Jim the pleasant exception."

"Your relationship with Jim Holdsett is congenial?"

"Oh, yes. Although, admittedly, it wasn't nearly so congenial in the beginning," Darold confessed. "Frankly, I wasn't too impressed by his business potential when I first met him. Judging him, I guess, by *his-brother-who-had-been-there-before-him.*"

"His brother?"

"Surely, I'm not the first to tell you about Rolin?" Darold asked, and his left eyebrow arched. "I didn't think so," he answered his own question. "Rolin having been the first of Mr. and Mrs. Hold-sett's twelve children to enter the Lendland fold. And it might all have been Rolin's—the gallery, the partnership, the whole ball of wax—if he'd had the least aptitude for business. But Rolin—a far more likeable and enjoyable person than his brother, as Morgan will verify—remains one of those carefree people who prefers to wile away life in the guise of perpetual schoolboy. Even now, he's attending the *University of California*, majoring in basket-weaving or something equally esoteric. I can only wonder how Horton's death, and the gallery fire, will affect Rolin's *gotten-accustomed-to* lifestyle. Jim always says Rolin is *on a lifetime gallery scholarship.*"

"Not much love lost between the brothers?"

"Oh, Rolin loves *everyone,*" Darold insisted, following Cord's cue. "When Rolin realized Horton was looking for someone to take over the gallery, Rolin hardly up to it, he generously brought Jim around. Jim now… Well, admittedly, he loves less and is, in turn, less lovable. He remains piqued that he came by his good fortune by default. Salt rubbed into the sibling rivalry wound by Jim having needed Rolin to get an intro to Horton. And, of course, Rolin was around long enough for those inevitable comparisons between him and *his-brother-who-came—*" Darold's wide smile and suggestive pause added the insinuated sexual connotation. "—later. Comparisons in which Jim, despite his superior business acumen, comes out the perpetual loser. Undeniably a blow to his ego: those unfavorable comparisons with someone he considers one of life's biggest losers."

"Horton was less than discreet in such comparisons, was he?"

"Oh, Horton was certainly far more discreet than some I could mention," Darold defended. "He was never so much putting Jim down as he was crying Rolin's virtues to the treetops. You know: Rolin's good looks, his politeness, his athletic prowess, and etcetera. All of which is admittedly true. Morgan took Horton's lead and picked on Jim the same way. The one who was really undiplomatic, though, was Harley-Gransen Davis who always managed to come across a bit crude in spite of all those private and big-named schools he supposedly attended. He spent one whole evening over dinner, Jim at the table, arguing that Jim had to be one of the ugliest things on two legs. Of course, such bitter grapes were only because Jim was *so much* Harley's type and wouldn't give the man the time of day. Still, it couldn't have been pleasant for Jim that night, even when Morgan white-knightishly surprised everyone by insisting Jim wasn't *all that bad.*"

"You say, though, that Horton and Morgan both liked Rolin better?" Cord reiterated, drawn to a possible piece of the jigsaw puzzle that was Morgan Kent. "Do you think Morgan and Rolin were ever involved?"

"Of course, you mean *sexually* involved," Darold intuited. He paused for a long moment—waiting for Cord to deny it?—seeming to consider, simultaneously eyeing Cord with a look the policeman found unsettling. "Tell me," Darold said, having apparently decided to ask his own question, rather than answer Cord's, "have you ever come across anyone who admitted having sex with Morgan Kent?"

"No," Cord admitted.

"Well, if Rolin had sex with Morgan, and there were admittedly more than a few chances for that happening, Rolin never confided it to me, nor to anyone else I know. As for Horton having sex with Morgan, I only remember one time I thought the evidence spoke for itself." The ensuing pause had Cord wondering if Darold would proceed. "It was Morgan's belt," Darold said finally, Cord thankful he wasn't going to have to coax the information out. "I came back to the house one evening and found Morgan and Horton waiting to take me to dinner. There, plain as the nose on your face, was Morgan's *Gucci* belt dangling the top of the television. The buckle, mind you, is quite distinctive, Horton having bought it for him when the two were in the Orient for an art show some while back. So, I picked up the belt and, I must confess, made quite a little production number out of wondering aloud how it possibly got off Morgan's pants and on top of the television. Morgan, though, didn't look, or act like someone caught in the act. He said he'd borrowed a sweater from Horton, and his belt buckle had caused an unwanted bulge at his waist, so he'd removed his belt to solve the problem. More than a plausible explanation, considering I've had similar experiences in dressing."

"You must have known Horton well enough, though, to *know* the truth, didn't you?" Cord persisted. Why was it so damned important for him to put proof-positive to Morgan's sexuality?

"My gut-feeling, you mean?" Darold defined, his faint air of amusement hinting more knowledge than Cord would have preferred his having of the motivation behind the policeman's question.

"Yes, your gut feeling," Cord agreed. "An educated guess from someone who lived with Horton Lendland for over thirty years, through good times and bad. Who had to know him better than anyone."

"Frankly, I don't think they had sex, then, or ever," Darold confessed. "Something else bound those two together besides hanky-panky in some bedroom, back room, or in the gallery after closing. And whatever that something was, I can only guess at it, because Morgan Kent remains as much an enigma to me as I suspect he does to you. And that, itself, is possibly part of the attraction he offered for Horton."

"But only *part* of the attraction he offered?" Cord wanted insights and was desperate to have them.

"You would have had to ask Horton," Darold parried, "and I truly doubt he could have told you. Except that Morgan seemed to leave Horton forever feeling, whether skillful illusion or not, that even the usually most terribly mundane experiences were totally new and exciting. But then, Horton, as worldly-wise as he liked to think himself, had really seen life only from a very narrow perspective. While Morgan...."

He paused and, this time, Cord knew he wasn't planning to continue. This didn't stop Cord from trying to get from Darold a more definitive commitment. "Was what?" he asked. "Jaded?"

"Oh, but jadedness insinuates a certain dullness brought on by excess, doesn't it?" Darold argued, momentarily consenting to continue. "Tell me, does Morgan Kent strike you as in anyway dull, or of having been dulled by excess, or dulled by anything else? Besides which, he *does* have an innate way of making the old seem somehow new. This offers a definite attraction to anyone thinking everything has been seen or experienced. Or to someone growing old but desperately not wanting to feel that way.

"Was Horton beginning to feel his age?"

"Aren't we all?" Darold answered obliquely. "As for Horton, well... To the end, he thought he'd found his fountain of youth by hungrily sucking magic elixir from young men's cocks as desperately as Dracula would have sucked their blood to survive. If Horton sometimes doubted the effectiveness of those youth-generating juices, he saw Morgan as providing some kind of possible alternative. You know what Horton called Morgan, don't you? His nickname for him, I mean? Dorian Gray. Why? Because, at times, I think Horton really believed there was a portrait in some attic, somewhere, growing old while Morgan stayed pretty much the same. Even I have to agree that Morgan looks little different from when I first set eyes on him several years ago. Of course, it's all a matter of his genes, but that's not anywhere nearly as romantic as that portrait oozing corruption in some attic, is it? And Horton *was* a romantic, pure and simple, beneath it all. His constant stream of young men was nothing, more nor less, than his desperate search for love in a world notoriously stingy with it."

"And Morgan? A romantic, too, would you say?"

"Morgan, a romantic?" Darold asked, punctuating with a raucous *you-have-to-be-kidding* laugh. "My God, no! Morgan is a diehard cynic, through and through. It's only that he comes across in so many other fascinating guises that truly makes him as deliciously hypnotic and enticing as *something* beckoning from a forbidden swamp of quicksand."

"You see him as dangerous, then?" Cord asked; the question was more automatic than the result of careful thought.

"That depends," Darold answered with a smile, "on how anxious some of us are for change and challenge."

Cord embarrassedly knew Darold's perceptive comment had less to do with the death of Horton Lendland than with the future well-being of Detective Cord Maxwell.

CHAPTER FOUR

JIM

"HE NEVER HAS LIKED ME," Jim Holdsett said, plopping loose-limbed into the seat opposite Cord. "Horton, of course, assured me that Morgan liked hardly anybody, so I needn't be offended. It wasn't anything personal. It was just that Morgan decided, somewhere down the line, that he had one too many friends and one too many acquaintances, and he was no longer anxious to add numbers to either."

"Did you care?"

"Why in the hell should I care?" Jim answered; Cord thought the young man did so a mite too quickly. "Morgan bought paintings from Horton, whether he liked me or not, and that's *all* I cared about. Besides which, Horton found him amusing."

"I see," Cord said, wondering if he *saw* anything. The weave of relationships wasn't getting any easier to untangle. "Could you tell me just *how* Horton found him amusing?"

"How?" Jim asked, as if the question confused him.

"Horton had quite a few friends, didn't he?" Cord encouraged. "Did you ever wonder why Morgan Kent had been elevated by Horton above all of the rest of them?"

"Yeah, special," Jim admitted, albeit with seeming reluctance.

"Do you think his *specialness* for Horton was a sexual thing?"

"How in the hell would I know?" Jim exploded. Again too quickly. Way too vehemently. "Horton and my relationship was a business one. I paid no attention to his personal life."

"But you knew he was gay?"

"And he knew I was straight," Jim countered. "Neither of which had anything to do with business."

"Of course," Cord agreed, once again telling himself that looks didn't necessarily identify underlying sexual preferences. There were plenty of teeny-bopper sex idols around, with the same androgynous kind of pretty-boy looks that Jim Holdsett packed into his

31

five-foot-ten-inch frame, who fucked every female groupie who came begging after a rock concert. Besides, unlike in the case of Morgan, Cord had found several young ladies who'd admitted to having shared Jim's bed. Granted, they remained unanimously unimpressed by his *fuck-them-and-then-kick-them-out* performances, but Cord, as with Morgan Kent, had found no *man* ready to step forward with equal *kiss-and-tell* exposés. Although enough men admitted to *suspecting* Jim, like they suspected Morgan, was gay.

"About this angel?" some old man asked, appearing suddenly in the doorway. In his right hand, he upheld a small wooden sculpture from which most of the original paint had weathered.

"It belongs to Father Margaux," Jim said. He sounded defensive and became more so. "If you don't believe me, call the *Retreat St. Julian* and ask." The man disappeared with the angel, and Jim shot a disgruntled glance in Cord's direction. "Horton wouldn't have approved of his shit!" Jim vented in obvious anger. "I'm not a goddamned thief."

"I was at his house earlier," Cord said, trying for an *I'm-on-your-side-but* attitude, "and they're taking inventory there, too."

"Oh, yeah?" Jim responded, obviously not impressed. "Well, I'd bet you money that, even with all the bedrooms in that house, including the one now empty upstairs, Morgan didn't insist that any inventory-taker move into the place to keep Darold company, did he?" He answered his own question: "Hell, no! But Mr. Colbert, in there, has taken up residence in *my* only spare bedroom. Why? Because little Jim here just might walk off with one of the pictures on the wall, or walk away with one of the sculptures on the coffee table, all of which have suddenly become part of the Lendland estate. I suppose I should be grateful Morgan is letting me stay on here until he sells the place right out from under me."

"None of this is yours, then?" Cord asked, his nod including the condominium and its contents.

"Sure as hell it's mine!" Jim insisted. "Oh, not the fucking expensive knickknacks and paintings. But the condo is mine, all right, and I have half a mind to sue the estate to get it. Horton told me, time after time, it was mine. No matter, he insisted, that he was officially making the payments for me; that was only because it was easier for him to get credit. He sure as hell deducted from my salary whenever condo-payment time came around. Though Morgan will want proof of that, you can bet your ass. And there isn't any paperwork, because who in the hell expected Horton to get killed?"

"I met someone the other day who said *he* wasn't surprised," Cord said, remembering Morgan's reference to Gary Green. Jim was strangely silent. "But *you* apparently remain surprised," Cord injected.

"So what that Horton knew some kooks?" Jim asked, casting a disapproving look toward the bedroom where it sounded as if Mr. Colbert was moving something heavy away from one wall. "Horton wanted to help every last one of them. He thought they, each one, had unseen potential that Horton alone could recognize and bring to flower. The truth was, they were all a bunch of fucking losers!"

"Any one of whom might have killed him?" Cord asked.

"Shit, most of them were just scared kids," Jim argued. "Kids growing old too fast on the streets and looking for that quick pot of gold at the end of the rainbow. At first glance, Horton appeared to be that pot. Just because they found out later that he was more interested in helping them help themselves than in giving them everything they wanted on a silver platter, you honestly think that was motive enough to kill him? Shit, those guys' whole lives were filled with less well-meaning johns than Horton. If they killed every Tom, Dick, and Harry who promised them the moon, sucked them silly, fucked their asses raw, then left them high and dry, there'd be dead bodies three feet deep all of the way between here and Canada."

"How about, maybe, one or two real loonies in the bunch?" Cord suggested. "Granted, most were probably harmless, but Horton knew an awfully lot of street people, didn't he? The law of averages says there must have been at least one or two rotten apples in that barrel."

"I didn't monitor Horton's sex life!" Jim reminded, reverting to his previous line of defense. "You want answers like that, ask Darold Keshmont. Ask Morgan Kent, for that matter. I dealt with customers buying and selling paintings not flesh."

"How about Bobby Jordan?" Cord asked. "Darold said Bobby called the house and the gallery several times during the week Horton was killed."

"We didn't know for sure it was Bobby," Jim said. "The phone would just ring and nobody was ever there."

"But Horton *assumed* it was Bobby. Darold *assumed* it was Bobby. *You* assumed it was Bobby."

"Bobby had done that type of thing before, that's all," Jim admitted. "Then, he'd show up, and Horton would ask him why he never said anything when the phone was answered."

"To which Bobby replied?"

"*I just wanted to make sure you were safe,*" is what he said. Then, they'd both laugh at some seemingly private joke and go out for lunch or something."

"Or *something?*"

"They usually went out for lunch," Jim edited, his look indicating little amusement at any attempts Cord was making to attribute to him more insight into Horton's sex life than Jim was admitting.

"You've met Bobby, then?"

"You hearing me deny it?" Jim asked, squirming in his seat.

"He once worked at the gallery, didn't he?" Cord progressed.

"A lot of guys worked at the gallery before I did."

"Like your brother Rolin?"

"Yeah, if you could call what Rolin did *work.*"

"Do *you* think Horton and Bobby had a thing going? Do *you* think that was why Horton hired him to work at the gallery?"

"If you're insinuating that because Bobby worked at the gallery and had sex with Horton that I...."

"I'm insinuating only that I've been led to believe that Bobby Jordan was not your ordinary kid off the street," Cord interrupted, thinking *the gentleman,* once again, possibly did protest too much. "And you're in a good position to give me insight on Bobby Jordan that I might not pick up elsewhere. Did you know, for instance, that he'd once robbed a grocery store, holding a pregnant woman at knife-point for three hours?"

"Yeah, that's part of the Bobby Jordan legend, isn't it?"

"The story isn't true, then?"

"Oh, I suspect it's true enough, all right," Jim confirmed. "It was in juvenile hall that Bobby got fucked up the ass—for the very first time—to hear him tell it. What I'm saying is that he was a helluva lot more fucked up in those days than he is now. Horton paid for him to see a shrink, and Bobby hasn't robbed a store in ages."

"But he has beaten up a few people, right?"

"Horton was Bobby's babysitter, not me," Jim protested.

"Bobby is into drugs, too," Cord informed. "Did you know that?"

"All the Bobbys of the world are on one kind of drug or another," Jim lumped with a shrug. "That doesn't make them killers."

"You don't think Bobby Jordan killed Horton?"

"You're the cop," Jim said, screwing his too-pretty mouth into a disgruntled pout. "You tell me."

"I hear Bobby is manic-depressive."

"Heard from whom? His shrink?"

"Dr. Riley is reluctant to discuss him," Cord admitted. "Something to do with doctor-patient privilege."

"Well, don't ask me to make a diagnosis when the good doctor isn't even willing to make a commitment."

"I just thought.… Well, you do have a certain expertise as far as…."

"Shrinks go?" Jim added for him. "Specifically, as far as Dr. Riley goes?"

"Could I ask why Dr. Riley is treating you?"

"Maybe you should ask Dr. Riley," Jim suggested evasively.

"I asked her, but…."

"More doctor-patient privilege?" Jim surmised.

"Right," Cord confirmed. "However, she said if I got the information from you it would be another matter."

"Well, if I thought it had any bearing whatsoever on the case, I'd air my dirty psychological linen for you. But it doesn't."

"Anything to do, you suppose, with your occasional…ah…fits of…ah…temper?"

"What in the hell *ah…fits of…ah…temper* would those be?" Jim came to a rigid sitting position.

"Well, even before Horton, I understand that you beat up a classmate. Then, there was some complete stranger in a public rest room," Cord reminded.

"Both were fucking queers who wanted to suck my cock," Jim defended.

"And it wouldn't have been easier to give them a simple, *no thanks*?"

"You ever know a queer to take a simple *no* for an answer?" Jim argued.

"Yes," Cord admitted. "You're not, after all, the first attractive young man ever to be propositioned by one." *That* Cord knew from first-hand experience.

"Yeah, well…." Jim looked as if he were going to say more on the subject then apparently decided not to. He settled back in the chair, assuming a less defensive posture. "I've matured a good deal since then," he said finally.

"You've not beaten up any queers lately?" Jim asked, all innocence.

"I've admitted to beating up those two when I was younger," Jim insisted.

"I know," Cord admitted. "Now, I'm talking about more recently. Say as recently as last month."

"I didn't beat up anyone last month," Jim assured.

"You and Bobby didn't park outside *The Playground* and harass a few queers, shortly before Bobby dropped out of sight the last time?"

"I didn't beat up anybody!" Jim repeated.

"Did Bobby beat up anybody that evening?"

"Not exactly."

"Not exactly?" Cord echoed but made it a question; definitely he wanted clarification on this one.

"A couple of shoves isn't beating someone up," Jim rationalized.

"And you didn't call encouragement to Bobby all the while he was *shoving around* this queer?" Cord questioned.

"Look, as I remember it, the faggot made some wise-ass comment about how Bobby should drop his pants and get himself fucked, since that was the only reason anyone came down to play at *The Playground*."

"And was that the reason Bobby and you *had* gone down there?" Cord asked, and Jim came to his feet.

Apparently, though, Jim *had* matured to where he was better able to abort his temper's spontaneity before it got the better of him. He walked over to the window, looked out, walked back to his chair and sat down again. He smiled, whether to congratulate himself on his self-control, or because he found something amusing, Cord couldn't tell. "I like to dance," Jim said. "A lot of straights do. So, we go to *The Playground,* because the music is first-rate."

"And who, I wonder, were you planning on dancing with that night?" Cord pondered. "With Bobby?"

"What in the fuck is *that* supposed to mean?"

"It means, I don't recall hearing you had a girl along that evening."

The smile wasn't on Jim's face any longer. "There are usually girls at *The Playground*," he said after a reflective pause.

"Gay girls? Lesbians? Dykes? Cord asked. "All of whom welcome dancing with homophobic straights?"

"Look, there are plenty of straight girls there, too," Jim protested. "I told you, the place is popular and pulls in a mixed bag."

"You ever dance with another man, Jim?" Cord asked. To cut off any indignant outburst, he quickly added, "Remembering that it's unlikely you could ever do so in a place like *The Playground* without causing talk among the inquisitive faggots."

"Bobby and I danced together *once,*" Jim admitted reluctantly, looking extremely ill at ease. "We did it as a lark. Okay? We'd both had a little too much to drink, you know? It was nothing…. Well, you know…."

"And you did it *just once*?" Cord queried, giving Jim the opportunity to reconsider and be mistaken.

"Hell, maybe it was a couple of times," Jim revised, sounding nervous.

"Do you get a hard-on whenever you dance with Bobby?" Cord asked.

"Fuck, no, I don't get a hard-on!" Jim responded loudly, once again on his feet. "I've told you once, I've told you twice, and I'll tell you yet again: I am not gay. Okay?! My dick gets hard when I dance with women, not with men. You want more names and addresses of the broads I've screwed?"

"That won't be necessary," Jim said, staying right where he was, leaning deeper into the cushions of his chair and looking up at the young man standing belligerently over him. Jim didn't look as if he could fight his way out of a paper bag. Maybe that was why he'd taken up karate. "In fact, I've already interviewed several such women," Cord admitted.

"Well, then!" Jim proclaimed triumphantly. He apparently felt vindicated and resumed his seat, again appearing relaxed.

"To a one, they think you a somewhat cold, mechanical fuck," Cord observed nonchalantly.

"Yeah, well, that's probably because they expect more from me than a good screw."

"What kind of *more?* Love, for instance?"

"Yeah, now that you mention it."

"And you could never love *a woman,* right?"

Morgan had been right: the kid wasn't stupid. At least, Jim wasn't stupid enough to fall into *that* one. "I'll fall in love when the right lady comes my way," he assured cannily. "Until then, I'll enjoy myself. If the broads don't like it, they don't have to come back for seconds, do they?"

"Do you remember a *broad* called Sally West?" Cord asked offhandedly. Although Jim obviously knew by now that nothing the policeman asked was all that offhanded.

"Yeah, I remember Sally West," Jim said. "We didn't hit it off all that well, as I recall."

"She says that it was *okay* until you insisted you were going to fuck her in her ass."

"The bitch is fucking crazy!" Jim proclaimed loud enough for Mr. Colbert to stick his head around the bedroom doorway, only to remove it when Jim gave him *the finger*.

"Of course, there's nothing all that wrong, I guess, in fucking a girl's ass," Cord conceded, "if both parties are willing. I mean, this is the age of sexual enlightenment, isn't it?"

"I did *not* want to fuck her ass!" Jim insisted. "If she says that I did, she's lying."

"She said you roughed her up when she said no."

"She's a lying sack of shit!"

"She said you really got upset when she suggested that *you should do it with boys* if you wanted asshole so badly."

"That crazy, lying cunt!" Jim exclaimed, once again on his feet, this time pacing the floor at full-throttle. "She's full of shit up to her brown eyes."

"You left her with one *black* eye, remember?" Cord reminded, watching Jim stop pacing and give him an *if-looks-could-kill-you-would-be-dead* look. Did you tell her that you should kill her, right then and there?" Cord asked.

"Look," Jim said, all persuasive reasonableness; Cord, for the first time, imagined how the kid might well sell a painting. "Sally likes it rough, okay? And, maybe, I *did* get carried away a bit and hit her too hard. But as far as my supposedly wanting to fuck her ass... hell...it was when *she* started begging me to brown my dick up her butt, and *I* said no, that the trouble started. *I* told *her* that *if I wanted asshole I'd get a man*, and she came unhinged. If I threatened her, why didn't she go to someone about it before now, huh? I'll tell you why. I *didn't* threaten her, that's why."

"Did you ever crack one of Horton Lendland's ribs?" Cord asked, purposely throwing the question in from left field. He hoped for an automatic response, one more candid than with-forethought. He was disappointed.

"Jim faced him for a good thirty seconds before coming up with a thoroughly noncommittal answer: "Cracked his rib, how?"

"By hitting him, I suppose," Cord ventured with a shrug. "Anyway, that *was* the insinuation."

"Insinuated by whom?" Jim asked. "By Darold? By Morgan?"

"Would you believe by one of the guys who works in packing and delivery in this very building?" Cord offered in alternative. "Seems he was working late one evening when you and Horton had some kind of a shouting match in the garage, leading to you literally chasing Horton down."

"Horton running? From me?" Jim added with a laugh. Once again, he walked over to the window and looked out to where the condo's veranda merged with the gray flagstone surrounding a deserted pool. "Horton was about six-feet tall and weighed in at close to 200 pounds."

"Maybe he knew you were a karate expert," Cord suggested.

"Maybe, but I don't remember the incident," Jim amended, turning back from the window. "We had our fights, like any other friends and business partners."

"Fights that occurred whenever Horton put the make on you?" Cord suggested.

"Fights over *business-related* matters," Jim countered.

"Surely he must have, at least once, suggested you might be sexually appreciative for the opportunities he'd dropped in your lap? He made you a partner when you were only sixteen, didn't he?"

"He made me a partner, because I sold paintings," Jim insisted. He wiped his forehead with the corner of a sleeve. "If sex were the criterion for promotion, there would have been plenty more partners ahead of me, yet none of my predecessors made the grade."

"Horton never propositioned you—even once?" Jim persisted. "I mean, Horton was gay, and you're not exactly a dog, are you? The two of you were together every workday, Horton not known for any particular reluctance to mix business with pleasure."

"Maybe he did proposition me a time or two," Jim conceded, sounding as if those times had been blocked from his memory if, in fact, they had ever occurred. "But when I said, *no,* Horton respected that. Why? He was tired of selling paintings, and I could sell them for him. He'd been waiting for someone like me to come along for a long time. You think he was going to blow it by blowing it?" He smiled widely at his own clever play on words.

"How about your brother and Horton?" Cord asked. "From what I hear, Rolin wasn't so good at selling paintings.

"Rolin isn't much good at anything," Jim said, frowning. "But, in answer to your question, I suggest you ask Rolin. Not that I wouldn't tell you if I knew, but I don't know. I didn't *want* to know at the time, and I'm not all that hot to know now. I figure what people do in bed, my brother and Horton included, is their business."

"Which is why you beat up queers?" Cord asked facetiously. When he didn't get any immediate response, he added, "Considering the nature of this murder, do you blame me for being curious about Horton's sex life?"

"And would you be quite so curious if Horton had been straight?"

"That he had a spear rammed up his ass and was set ablaze would have made me as curious on any count," Cord defended.

"Well, I didn't spear Harold's ass, and I didn't put a match to him. Nor, you can bet *your* ass, did I burn down our gallery," Jim stated with firm finality.

"Do you think Morgan might have done it?" Cord asked on impulse.

"Whatever for?" Jim asked. "What in the hell would Morgan have had to gain by doing either?"

CHAPTER FIVE

JOHN

"I'VE AN ALIBI, you know?" John Berd said, motioning Cord to a chair on the patio overlooking manicured grounds.

"Who said anything about you needing an alibi?" Cord asked.

"You are here about Horton Lendland's murder, are you not?" John asked, sitting across from him.

"Yep."

"Well, depending upon to whom you talked before you made your trip out here, I was either grateful that Horton arranged for me to check in here, my first time at rehab, or I remained jealous of Horton and Bobby to the end."

"Which is closer to the truth, do you think?"

"Well, since I do have an alibi.... They have told you, haven't they? I mean, I may have had to check myself into this place, but they do keep tabs on me once I'm here. I was being monitored 24/7 the night Horton was murdered. As I remember it, I spent most of that night vomiting up a storm."

"So, I've been told," Cord confirmed.

"Then, I can be candid and admit that, as usual, the truth exists somewhere between the extremes. I appreciated Horton taking the time and bother to get me to one side and explain how I was shooting everything down the tube by going through life a sloppy drunk; Bobby, likewise, finding my drunkenness distasteful. On the other hand, it was difficult for me not to be jealous of Horton and Bobby."

"It was sexual between them?"

"Oh, I'm sure!" John said, sounding not the least doubtful. "Bobby's body is the only thing he has to sell. On the other hand, his relationship with Horton was more than the sex, and that's where I had trouble adjusting. I could handle Bobby's promiscuity, because that's just the way he is. Even I, on occasion, want more variety than Bobby's big cock up my mouth or asshole."

Cord blushed and did his best to abort it. "So, what was it between Horton and Bobby that went beyond the sex?"

"I think it was Horton being the first person who not only truly cared Bobby had gotten one of life's raw deals, but who tried to do something about it. Firsts, like that, you always remember, like the first guy you made it with." John smiled, and Cord knew it was probably in response to the policeman's obvious embarrassment. "Or, the first woman you ever made it with," John added in amused concession. "That I care about Bobby, probably a helluva lot more than Horton did... That I gave him more material things... Well, those mean something, sure. But Horton was the first to do more than take what Bobby had to offer and toss the kid to one side. That Bobby was no salesman and couldn't take full advantage of the opportunity Horton offered at the gallery was no fault of Horton."

"Bobby is now living with you, though, so the Horton-Bobby relationship soured somewhere along the way," Cord reminded.

"Soured?" John asked, as if mulling over the definition of that one. "Possibly too strong a word to describe what happened."

"If you've a better word, I'd be willing to hear it."

"It's difficult to sum it up in a word," John said. "As is my relationship with Bobby. As was my relationship with Horton. As was Horton's relationship with...."

"Morgan Kent?" Cord heard himself automatically inject.

"Oh, by all means!" John agreed. "*That* relationship surely requires more than a one-word explanation. However, I was thinking more along the lines of Horton's relationship with Darold and/or Jim."

"Would you at least make the attempt to tell me what Bobby saw in Horton and vice versa?" Cord asked. He was more interested in John's opinions on Morgan, but those would have to wait. It was important he keep prerogatives in order.

"Father-son, mentor-*protégé*, priest-acolyte?" John suggested. "Certainly those and more. Horton and Bobby touched base on all sots of psychological levels, and that's probably the main source of my jealousy all of these years."

"How many years has it been?"

"Five," John said. "Five years of heaven and hell."

"Tell me about the hell," Cord encouraged.

"No one is ever interested in the heaven, are they?" John observed with a wry smile. "But, then, bliss doesn't make for murder, does it?"

"Whoever killed Horton didn't love him," Cord refreshed. "He was still alive when he was skewered up the ass, and he was probably alive when someone set him on fire."

"It *was* a spear, then?" John asked, seeming genuinely surprised. "The Seattle papers are so puritanically vague about such sexually explicit details. The local gay rag would, of course, have been more edifying, I don't doubt, but I don't have an easy access to it here as I would at my bar."

"You haven't discussed the murder with Bobby?" Cord asked, knowing the answer. He'd flashed Bobby's picture at reception, having rescued a clipping from an old newspaper account of an art show being prepared by Horton Lendland and *his new assistant.*

"Have *you* discussed the murder with Bobby?" John asked, his tone saying he knew the answer.

"He seems to have dropped out of sight," Cord confessed.

"Yes, he does that on occasion," John admitted, offering no farther explanation.

"I was hoping you might give me a clue as to where I might find him. Considering you and he have such a close live-in relationship."

"Well, if I could, I would certainly think seriously about telling you," John said. He obviously hadn't recovered from the regimen of this latest expelling of alcohol from his system. He looked tired and had the loose, colorless skin of someone who'd lost too much weight without any accompanying exercise program. "However," he continued, "Bobby pulled his last disappearing act a couple of weeks before Horton's murder. Normally, I'd say he was about due for a reappearance, but if he's heard about Horton's death—and who in Seattle's gay community hasn't—he's probably decided to keep a very low profile. I mean, *he is* a prime suspect, isn't he?"

"Without an alibi, he will be," Cord admitted.

"And if Bobby is running true to form, he won't have an alibi. He never seems to be in the right place at the right time. However, if you want my personal opinion, alibi or not, Bobby didn't kill Horton. It would have been too much like patricide, mentor-cide, priest-a-cide—or whatever."

"Bobby's background is, you'll admit, violent for a young man his age. How old is he, by the way?"

"Twenty-one," John said. "Part of his trouble, you know, being his age. For, on the streets, twenty-one isn't just old, you understand, but *old*-old. He's lasted longer than most, but it can't go on forever. Youth is the chief commodity bartered out there, and when you lose it, you lose your position in the marketplace. Twenty-one is a man, and there's a tendency toward tenderer and tenderer meat nowadays, if you know what I mean." Cord knew, still remembering the kid who'd come out of the shadows when Cord had returned Rocky to the street corner. Then, there was the kid who'd come up to Cord in the can out at Alki.

"So many younger boys flooding the marketplace," John continued. "Where *do* they all come from? From wherever, they're responsible, aren't they, for making pre-pubescence such a major commodity? It's become *de rigueur* sampling even for those who've had to make it an acquired taste. Even Bobby likes the young ones."

Cord was somewhat surprised. Horton had been no spring chicken, and John, while in his thirties, didn't even give an illusion of brand-new merchandise. Cord doubted John would, even after a few months of heavy workout in a gymnasium, look all that much better. "Bobby likes the young ones, though, for different reasons than he liked Horton or likes me," John said. Having read Cord's mind? "They make him feel particularly desirable and less old when he doesn't have to pay them."

"Did you know he was calling the gallery the week Horton was murdered?" Cord asked, deciding not to mention there'd been no positive I.D.

"Ring up and, then, not say anything, you mean?" John divined. "That's what he does whenever he returns after one of his disappearing acts. Call Horton, first thing."

"Why?"

John shrugged. "He says it's to be sure Horton is still alive. I suppose that's as good an excuse for it as any. Bobby is never very good at keeping hold of people who care about him, and vice versa. He's sometimes not the most lovable person, you know? But then, how many of us are?" He laughed. "I've been told I'm masochistic to put up with him, but I always consider the source of such comments. Usually they come from those who would give anything o go to bed with him, knowing there's not a chance in hell of it ever happening."

"He has beaten you up on occasion," Cord said, and it wasn't a question

"Usually only when I deserved it," John rationalized. "It's not been easy for Bobby living with a drunk, as anyone who has lived with a drunk will tell you."

"Still," Cord objected, not about to concede there were ever logical reasons for that particular brand of physical violence, "he hospitalized you at least once, didn't he?"

"Did he?" John asked, all innocence.

"I know what you told them at the emergency room at Swedish," Cord said, "but I've talked to a few people who tell it differently."

"People gossip," John said with a dismissing sigh. "When the truth doesn't suit them, they make up lies."

"Rumor has it happening after a dinner party at a fancy restaurant in Bellevue. *Noah's Whale,* was it?"

"Jonah's Whale," John amended. "And I'm telling you this, off the record, you understand, only to illustrate how Bobby didn't beat on me indiscriminately. Also, of course, because I'm sure you've heard who was in attendance that evening and won't leave it alone. Right?"

"You, Bobby, Horton, and Morgan Kent."

"You *have* heard!" John exclaimed in mock surprise. "Have you heard the rest of the story and, if you have, does it warrant repeating?"

"I'd certainly like to hear your version, if you don't mind."

"The dinner was Bobby's idea. He said it was because he wanted an evening with two of his favorite people."

"Meaning, you and Horton?"

"Who else?" John asked curiously, and then realized the third possibility. "Morgan, you mean?"

"Morgan wasn't included on Bobby's list of favorite people?"

"Oh, I wouldn't begin to try unraveling Morgan Kent or his relationship with various people, including his relationship with Bobby or me. That maze is *way* too complicated."

"Why complicated?" Cord asked. He wasn't the only one who would have liked answers.

"Would that you could find someone to tell us both why," John said. "Morgan Kent is a veritable mixture of hatefulness and liability. Besides being way too fucking handsome for someone his age."

"He seems pleasant enough to me," Cord defended.

"Example: After my first visit here to Chesterfield, I went out into the big wide world, got depressed, and slipped off the wagon. I was having drinks in the bar of the *Sheraton,* never having believed it good policy to get sloppy drunk in my own gay establishment, you understand. Anyway, who should come in but Horton, Jim, and Morgan. Spotting me, of course. They had reservations at *Fuller's,* but Horton and Jim detoured to come over. Not Morgan. Without a nod of hello, he went into the restaurant. Horton gave me a verbal tongue-lashing about being drunk after all I'd gone through to get sober. You know what Morgan gave me?"

"No, what?" Cord asked, realizing John expected his response.

"Two bottles of Scotch, delivered to my table. Not exactly the most sympathetic thing for him to do, was it? On the other hand, the statement made by the sudden arrival of those two bottles on my table did more to get me back here a second time than did all of Horton's disappointed moaning and groaning. The question, of course, being: did Morgan send me Scotch with hopes I would see the light, or with hopes I would progress deeper and faster into alcoholic oblivion?"

"What do *you* think?"

"The whole purpose behind that little story, Detective, is to illustrate that I don't know what to think about Morgan Kent, and I never have. God knows, it would help me, if I did know, to put into perspective my own disjoined feelings about him. Bobby says Morgan *really* doesn't give a damn for me, or for most people, one way or another."

"Why does Bobby think that, do you suppose?" Cord prodded.

"You'd have to ask Bobby," John parried. "But it does make a sort of sense. Morgan being so selective somehow makes a helluva lot of people anxious to be included among the select few. Possibly for the same reasons someone wants to join *the Equus Riding Academy and Country Club,* or the *University Club,* or the *Tennis Club:* just because there's a restricted membership. And, surprisingly, it's not just because Morgan is a celebrity, because he wasn't always one, you know, but he *always* drew people like nectar draws bees. Of course, when he began writing and publishing fuck books, that was an additional draw. Have you ever read any of his porno?" Cord shook his head. "I have several in my collection," John informed, "if you should ever become the least bit curious. They're quite good, most of them, depending, of course, upon your tastes. After all, gay sex has as many nuances as straight sex, and Morgan's books seem to have covered the whole spectrum: S&M, B&D, water sports, rubber, chicken, you name it. Even bestiality and necrophilia. Not to mention his straight fuck books which you'd probably find more interesting, but none of which, unfortunately, I have on hand."

"You've seen his straight fuck books, though?" Cord asked to keep John talking.

"Some of them. There are plenty of switch-hitters in gay life to get off on Morgan's imagery of cock fucking pussy. Pardon me while I gag, but it was his straight fuck books, even more than his gay ones, that contributed to Morgan's early mystique. It all made him tremendously interesting, exotic, and excitingly multi-faceted. It made you wonder how he would *be* in bed, quite aside from you already having wondered the same thing because of his looking like Adonis personified."

"Did he go to bed with very many guys?" Cord asked.

John laughed, shaking his head. "The *real* question, Detective Maxwell: Did he—does he—go to bed with guys *at all*?"

"I don't understand," Cord replied, trying to sound as if it was only the first time the subject had come up.

"You've undoubtedly talked to more than a few gays during the course of your investigation," John said, sounding unconvinced that Cord could possibly be as surprised as the policeman seemed. "How many have been to bed with Morgan Kent? How many known anyone who has?"

"I'm not sure the question ever came up," Cord lied. "I'm investigating the murder of Horton Lendland, not the sex life of Morgan Kent."

This didn't keep John from continuing right along. Did he intuitively sense Cord's interest in what Morgan did in bed? "Well, I own *The Playground* and have for years, as you already obviously know," John said. "I suspect every gay in Seattle has been to *The Playground* at least once in his life, but I've only met one kid, name of Russ Tompson, who ever sounded at all convincing when he said he'd been fucked by and had blown Morgan Kent. Bobby got around, too, before and after I met him, and he can only come up with a couple other likely candidates. Some broad this Russ Tompson *and* Morgan Kent were supposedly messing around with. And some fruit fly name of Sandra Wheems, who is long since 'gone with the wind.' Aside from the possibilities of those, and the lot who'd like to *think* they'd had the pleasure, Morgan Kent's sex life remains purely conjecture."

"Do you think he makes it with women, then?"

"There *are* all of those straight fuck books he was so prodigiously pumping out," John reminded, "although rumor has it he once put a heroine's clitoris in the wrong place. Not a rumor to be taken seriously, however, since even *I* know where a woman's *little man in a boat* is located. Anyway, if he's in to girls—and he sure spends a lot of time with us faggots if he's all that turned on to pussy—I can't help you there. Getting within ten feet of a woman is twenty feet too close for me, as far as I'm concerned."

"You never heard if Horton and Morgan were sexually involved?"

"Bobby says, no, and Bobby is someone who has made it a point to find out. Horton, after all, was someone close to Bobby. And Bobby is admittedly still fascinated by Morgan Kent."

"Fascinated?"

"Oh, for ever so long. They'd met before Horton Lendland or I came into the picture," John confessed. "Back when Bobby first came out and was living with Tony France. You know Tony France?"

"Owner of the *1006,* the *942,* and the *716,*" Cord identified.

"The same," John confirmed. "And, at the time, Morgan had some kind of business relationship with this gay photographer, Scott Jesse. Scott is now big-time in Los Angeles, doing coffee-table *all-male* books and greeting cards. Some of his stuff even regularly appears in *Playgirl.* But back then, he was just a horny guy running around town getting other guys to strip down for photographs that Morgan used to accompany short stories he wrote for *Blueboy* and *Numbers.*"

"Bobby posed?"

"Oh, he might have if Morgan had asked personally," John said, his voice surprisingly absent of emotion. "Morgan used to show up regularly at the *942,* polish off a bottle of champagne at a sitting, talking to no one in the process, except maybe to Scott or Tony. Morgan and Tony were on speaking terms, probably I'd guess because Tony owned the place. Morgan, though, didn't talk to Bobby, and it wasn't for Bobby's lack of trying. Being the owner's lover apparently just didn't cut the muster, as far as Morgan's *who's who in Seattle's gay bar scene* was concerned."

"So, if Bobby didn't pose, where's the connection?" Cord asked, hoping John hadn't lost him.

"At the time, Scott was not a cool dude, you understand. I suppose he had recognizable talent, even then, or Morgan wouldn't have bothered, but, as I remember him, he was usually falling-down drunk. I mean, I would have had more sympathy for him these days, but then I was sober enough to find him obnoxious. But, Jesus, could he, sober or drunk, talk the pants off most anyone, literally and figuratively, and his pictures were good enough so that Morgan loaned him one of those professional cameras—Bronica? Hassleblad? Whatever?"

"This is all going to come together is it?" Cord asked, beginning to wonder.

"To make a long story shorter," John obliged, obviously sensing Cord's growing impatience, "Scott remained interested in Bobby's body. Bobby, though, had better taste. Rather, Bobby was living with Tony at the time and would have been crazy to endanger *that* by letting some fag photographer suck and photograph his cock."

"Which boils down to what?" Cord encouraged, wanting to hear the punch line, if there was one.

"To one evening in the *942,*" John said, "when this expensive camera just happened to go off, flash and all, Bobby thinking Scott had taken an unauthorized picture of him. Result: one broken camera; and one equally broken photographer's nose; the photographer bemoaning more the fact that the camera was officially Morgan Kent's personal property."

"And Morgan didn't take kindly to his property being broken?" Cord suggested, seeing it finally coming together.

"Why Bobby should have gotten so upset by it being Morgan's camera has always escaped me, you know?" John admitted. "No one has any business taking pictures in a gay bar and, even then, Bobby had a record of doing worse things than beating up a fag photographer. The truth, most likely, is that Bobby had the hots for Morgan and suspected the camera incident would squelch his chances. So, Bobby ran to Tony. Tony got Bobby and Morgan together, and Bobby apologized. I still find his apology an occurrence bordering on mind-boggling. All the time I've known Bobby, he's never apologized to anybody. But he's the one who told me this story, so that somehow makes the unbelievable at least conceivable. Anyway, *as a favor to Tony*, mind you, Morgan magnanimously took the camera loss as an income tax write-off. Plus, I guess, he'd already published his first non-gay adventure novel and was about to set Scott up on his own in Los Angeles, anyway."

"So, Morgan and Bobby go back quite a ways."

"Except, Bobby is the only one of the two who remembers it being all that long. Shortly after the camera thing, Morgan heads off on a ship of some kind with, the way I hear it, some very rich old gal with whom he ends up moving in with. He only shows up at the gay bars infrequently and, by the time he walks into Horton's gallery, a few years later, finding Bobby the new assistant, he doesn't seem to remember Bobby from beans."

"Doesn't remember, or *pretends* not to remember?"

"Bobby's convinced Morgan just doesn't flat-out remember. Smashing blow to the kid's ego, you know? Especially since Morgan remains as attractive and, I suspect, as desirable to Bobby as ever. Have you heard that Morgan has a portrait somewhere that gets old instead of him?"

"I heard Horton referred to him, on more than one occasion, as Dorian Gray," Cord said.

"Just exactly like Dorian Gray," John agreed. "Morgan Kent stays the same, and the rest of us get older. If Bobby, in his prime, wasn't able to entice Morgan, what chance does he have *on-the-verge-of-over-the-hill?*"

"You think that matters to Bobby?" Cord asked, wondering, once again, what there was about Morgan Kent that…

"Have you ever wanted someone," John asked. "I mean, *really* wanted, all the while knowing you didn't have a chance of a snow-ball in hell? Well, knowing you can't have doesn't mean your want-ing gets any the easier to bear."

"And do *you have* Bobby as completely as *you want* him?" Cord asked. "As much as you might have *had* him if he didn't have this thing for Morgan? If he hadn't kept returning, time and time again, to Horton?"

"And we've come full circle, haven't we?" John said with a wry smile. "Here we are back to Horton, back to my being jealous of him. A jealousy to which I, once again, freely admit. Because I have an iron-clad alibi for the night of his murder, don't I?"

"So, go back and tell me about the dinner at *Jonah's Whale.*"

"The night I ended up in the emergency room at Swedish?"

"One and the same."

"I never did get around to telling you about it, did I?"

"Maybe we can rectify that now."

"Admittedly, I made an ass of myself that evening," John pre-fixed. "In front of Horton *and* in front of Morgan Kent. It was natu-ral for Bobby to get upset."

"Upset enough to put you in the hospital with a concussion, two cracked ribs, and a broken arm?"

"Hardly!" John denied. "That had nothing to do with Bobby, remember? I fell down a flight of stairs, never having been the most coordinated person around. Especially when drunk."

CHAPTER SIX

JACK

"YOU THINK YOU have problems?" said Jack Sudlow, unfastening the towel to release a flood of flabby flesh that completely overhung his sizable cock and balls. He jockeyed for a more comfortable position in his corner of the sauna and pulled the release mechanism to squirt water onto the nearby pile of hot stones. There was the hiss of raw steam and a wave of overheated air that collided with Cord in the opposite corner. "They just found us another body," Jack elucidated, his usually white skin turned pink beneath its blanketing of coarse black hair.

"Jesus!" Cord said with an accompanying shake of his head. "I didn't hear anything." He modestly rearranged his towel over his genitals. Ordinarily, he wouldn't have bothered, but it was a protective response to having spent so much time lately with faggots who put such a high stock in other men's bodies, making Cord acutely aware of his own. Nor was he pleased at the layer of unwanted fat around his middle that hadn't been there the other day. If he was still a long ways from possessing the beer belly Jack did, the latter having caused an ultimatum from on high that Jack would either *take off some of that blubber or risk suspension*, Cord wasn't the prime-conditioned jock he'd once been. Shit, Morgan Kent was probably in better shape and years older.

"We hope we can keep it under wraps a few more hours," Jack said, moving a large leg to reveal the large sweat mark he'd made on the wood underneath. "Hopefully long enough to come up with an official statement that isn't going to make us look like complete idiots." He closed his eyes, his feminine eyelashes incongruous on his otherwise masculine face. "Of course, this isn't one of our man's, but it *is* a Caucasian female and, what with all the dead Caucasian females turning up lately, courtesy of the *Dint Slough* killer, I'll bet my next piece of ass that the newspapers will indiscriminately lump this one with the others."

51

"You're sure she's *not* yours?" Cord asked, simultaneously thinking it was too long since he'd been to a gym. There had been a time when he could have sat forever in sauna rooms hotter than this one without the sensation of suffocation he was now feeling.

"Forensics, of course, will have the final say," Jack admitted, "but this one wasn't even found near *Dint Slough*. And she was neatly wrapped and tied in garbage bags. Double-duty *Hefty's*, I might add. Our man hasn't been that meticulous with anyone. Open the car door and give the body a shove has been his M.O."

"And you've had no real breaks, then?" Cord asked, knowing he would have heard. Also knowing it wasn't going to be long before he would have to excuse himself for a cold shower; the heat was getting to him, and he was soaked with sweat. Jack, after several such nightly stops at the *Y*, was surviving far better.

"Not one fucking new clue," Jack confirmed, nonchalantly scratching his balls, giving the illusion that he'd sunk his hand and forearm into his belly and lost them there. His navel, too, had been devoured by one of the several folds that tiered his midsection. "But you didn't come here to discuss the *Dint Slough* murders, did you? Nor to work off fat you obviously don't have." Unfortunately, Cord was the better judge of the latter than the ballooned cop was. "However, as I've said," Jack continued, using his towel to wipe away the sweat beaded on his forehead, "I doubt there's anything I can give you that isn't in my reports."

"I'm trying to connect *those* gay killings to the Lendland murder," Cord said, as if that weren't obvious. If he could prove the deaths of three gay men were somehow connected, it might give him more leverage in an agency almost one hundred percent geared to solving the *Dint Slough* murders. "Both you and Hillock speculated on a drug-related motive behind *both* the lawyer and the hustler's deaths, right?"

"Pure speculation was all it was, too, buddy," Jack apologized. "We were grabbing at straws."

"But there were drugs connected with both killings," Cord insisted.

"The hustler was in possession of a bag of grass," Jack admitted. "Not very good stuff, either. We found a couple grams of some very good coke stashed in a fake head of lettuce in the lawyer's refrigerator. Cheap grass and good coke aren't exactly natural bedfellows, are they? Your guy, Lendland, a user?"

"Horton talked about snorting at time or two, but the guy he lived with said it was all talk. However, Horton knew an awfully lot of people who *did* indulge."

"Says his roommate, who should know?" Jack asked, opening his eyes and arching an eyebrow. He looked like the offspring of a cuddly panda and a beneficent Buddha.

"They'd been together over thirty years," Cord qualified.

"Well, I'll put my money on the roommate as the killer," Jack said with a silly grin. "I can think of nothing worse than thirty years with the same man, unless it's thirty years with the same woman." Jack had been through two stormy marriages, neither having lasted anywhere near thirty years. Hell, *together* they didn't even add up to five.

"The roommate came out prime beneficiary," Cord admitted, "but he's got an alibi. He was in Ballard, having supper with his mother."

"What parent wouldn't lie to protect a son?" Jack wanted to know. Whenever he'd had one beer too many, he'd bemoan his not being a parent. He blamed his wives, of course, but there was the consistent rumor that his impressive *plumbing* had been damaged by a severe kick to the balls sustained when, as a rookie, he'd been single-handedly trying to subdue a recalcitrant black man, on crack, in a dark alley.

"The mother might lie, but how about the hostess, two waiters, and a water boy at the restaurant?" Cord argued.

"So, who else you got?" Jack asked, scratching his back against the wall like a lazy bear rubbing the trunk of a tree.

"We'd melt in this oven before I listed half of them," Cord said, a river of perspiration draining his bared chest along his serrated pectoral cleavage.

"I'd say it's about time for a cold shower," Jack suggested. "What do you say?"

The shower helped, the sauna nowhere as claustrophobic when they returned to it.

"Okay, back to your suspects," Jack invited, again pulling the release mechanism to evaporate water on hot rocks.

"A hustler with a record of violence; he's conveniently missing. A business partner with a record of violence; he has no alibi, but he was better off with Lendland alive and kicking. A best friend with no apparent motive and no alibi; he was at a movie in the *U-District* earlier that evening, drove by the gallery afterwards, and saw the victim's car out front; he didn't go in, figuring Lendland was *busy*. A once-successful painter with whom Lendland had a stormy parting; he insists he didn't set foot outside his apartment between Lendland's throwing him out of the gallery and my stopping to question him. By the look and smell of him and his apartment, I can easily believe him. And, would you believe, a Catholic priest who might have been having an affair with Lendland's partner while spending a fortune in unauthorized church funds on Northwest art? Sundry street urchins from here to Canada; all of whom Horton had taken to bed. Any one of whom could have done him in because of broken promises, or for the sheer fun of it. A gay bar owner who might have taken revenge on Lendland and on Lendland's partner, both of whom might have been fucking, or been fucked by, the owner's sadistic lover."

"Jesus!" Jack mumbled. "You've got them coming out your ass, and we can't even drum up one suspect for the *Dint Slough* murders. In this business, it's feast or famine."

"I didn't mention the millionaire-now-bankrupt; Horton's testimony helped the prosecution in a hearing that proved embezzlement. Another guy who sued Lendland and lost, getting stuck with a fortune in judgment and court costs. A landscape gardener Lendland bad-mouthed all over town after a landscaping job on Lendland's yard took six months longer and $25,000 more than it should have. Nor...."

"Enough, enough!" Jack protested with a wave of a ham-sized and sweaty hand. "No wonder you had hopes of simplifying things with a drug tie-in."

"Aside from which, I'm not getting much help from the front office. There are a helluva lot of bases to cover in this game, just me to cover them."

"Are you *really* expected, though, to cover them?" Jack asked, putting into words what a lot of people, in and out of the gay community, in and out of the police department, Cord included, had wondered all along.

"Do you see anybody assigned to this but me?" Cord reasoned, deciding to take the high ground.

"Well, *Dint Slough* has pretty much tied up the police force, hasn't it?" Jack said. It was unnecessary to spell out how one dead queer, more or less, wasn't likely to get too many people excited.

"You know how Lendland was killed," Cord reminded.

"You know how the *Dint Slough* killer takes care of his?" Jack countered, just in case they were in a pissing contest. "And look how long it took people to get worked up over the death of a few prostitutes. You're hoping for miracles if you expect any quick dander up over one more faggot biting the dust."

"He was a man, and he was murdered," Cord reminded.

"And I wish you luck in coming up with his killer," Jack said, preparing to exit for another cold shower. "But you'll weather it a helluva lot better, emotionally and physically, if you accept you've got a no-win situation, my good man. It's not your fault, it's not my fault, it's not the department's fault."

"Then whose fault is it?" Cord wanted to know, feeling frustrated and sweaty.

"It's Horton Lendland's fault for not being a little more selective in regard to whom he went home with," Jack said, pushing open the sauna door and standing stark naked in the resulting rush of escaping hot air.

CHAPTER SEVEN

CURTIS

"I SEE," CURTIS HURT SAID to his companion, obviously relieved by the interruption afforded by the arrival of the cocktail waitress. He ordered a *Tom Collins* and asked Cord if he'd like something. Cord refused. If he'd accepted every drink offered since starting this case, he would be a candidate for admission to Chesterfield with John Berd.

"You seem unsure," Cord confronted Curtis, once the waitress had left the table to maneuver her way through the surrounding tables and black leather chairs of the bar at the posh *Equus Country Club and Riding Academy*. "Possibly my source was mistaken."

""No," Curtis assured quickly, punctuating with a pause. "It's just that...."

"Just what?" Cord prodded, not up to twenty questions. What he wanted was a very simple yes or no. Harley-Gransen Davis, recently picked up in Los Angeles on Cord's request, insisted that he'd been with Curtis the night of the murder.

"It won't have to go any farther than here, will it? I know it'll go into reports at the police station, but it needn't be made public."

"Mr. Hurt, it's not exactly any big secret that you're gay." Cord looked around the bar of the private club and added, "Nor has it seemed to have hindered you socially." It was no secret, either, that the likely only reason Curtis *was* a member was because he'd been in on the ground floor, having gotten together the real-estate and financial package that had made the *Equus* a reality.

"It's not people, in general, that I'm concerned with," Curtis parried. "I'm thinking more of one person in particular."

Cord wished the attractive bastard would get to the point. Cord gave not one goddamn iota about anyone who might be disturbed by Curtis's fucking Harley-Gransen Davis. Cord was out to get to the bottom of a murder, and Davis was a prime suspect. If the man did or didn't have an alibi was something Cord had all intentions of finding out, here and now.

Progress was frustrated, once again, by the waitress, decked out in her abbreviated English riding habit that kept with the place's horsy theme. She left Curtis's drink on a napkin embossed with the *Equus*'s double-horse-head logo which looked surprisingly similar to the *Gucci* belt buckle once laid on a Lendland television console when the buckle, and its attending belt, possibly should have been on Morgan Kent's pants.

"I would appreciate it if none of this gets back to Morgan Kent," Curtis said, bringing Cord back from a reverie with suspicions that Curtis was reading his mind. "There's no reason to tell Morgan, is there?" Curtis hurried on. Cord didn't answer. It was sometimes better to hang back and let someone talk himself into a hole. "I mean," Curtis argued, "all Morgan need ever know is that Harley *does* have an alibi."

"Why in the hell do you care what Morgan Kent thinks?" Cord couldn't help asking. It was Curtis who'd pulled the strings to get Morgan membership at the *Equus,* not the other way around.

"It's a little complicated," Curtis said, after draining half his glass in a couple fast swallows.

"Why don't you try to sort it out for me?" Cord suggested. What was one more complicated relationship that included Morgan Kent? Cord already had a file full of them.

"First, I *was* with Harley that night. *All night*. He couldn't have killed Lendland." Which was all Cord had come to hear. So, why was Curtis so fucking paranoid about Morgan finding out? Hearing the *why* was possibly going to be a bonus.

"I thought you and Harley were on the outs," Cord said when Curtis became more intent upon finishing his drink than finishing his explanation.

"Harley and I were together for six years," Curtis said, no more liquor immediately on hand for him to swallow. He motioned for a refill, not waiting for the waitress to come any nearer. Cord was amazed by how much liquor gays appeared to consume. "Ties formed during a six-year relationship are hard to break," Curtis said. "Understand?"

"Sure," Cord said, and he wasn't entirely feeding the guy a line of bullshit, either. Cord and Cheryl had gone together for over five years when they'd realized they were going nowhere, just treading water. However, if they remained good friends—and they did—their breakup wasn't orchestrated by a scandal that had one of them spending a couple of million bucks that wasn't his or hers to spend.

"*Most* people *could* understand," Curtis said, sounding relieved. "However, Morgan isn't *most* people, having never liked Harley from the get-go."

"Why didn't he like Harley?" Cord asked, as curious as ever to pinpoint what it was or wasn't that allowed someone through the barriers Morgan erected. Why Horton and not Harley-Gransen Davis? Why Curtis, for that matter, and not Harley-Gransen Davis? Harley had been a big wheel when Morgan first met him, no suspicions, yet, of the embezzlement and bankruptcy to follow.

"Something about my screwed-up potential," Curtis said, trying to drain nonexistent liquor from his empty glass. "Morgan, also, looked upon Harley as an excruciating bore."

"Let's start with *screwed-up potential*, shall we?" Cord suggested. "Morgan intuitively sensed the problems your ex-lover was about to have?"

"Oh, not specifically, I'm sure. But there was writing on the wall for all of us to read. Morgan just tuned in first. Horton followed suit and promptly yanked Harley as chief executor of his will. It took a while longer for me to catch on, because I refused to accept the facts. I was little *Miss Pollyanna*, thinking everything would turn out all right. Well, it did, but certainly not the way I expected."

"What *was* the writing on the wall?" Cord asked. What information had Morgan deciding Harley wasn't worth the time and/or the effort?

"Harley had several business failures about that time," Curtis said, "that Morgan saw as poor business acumen on Harley's part. And, he was right. Haley would meet someone one night and set him up in business the next. There was a restaurant in Carmel, a dry-cleaning business in Tacoma, a record company in Los Angeles, and a radio station in San Francisco. Anyone smart would have invested more wisely. For instance, Horton was looking for something to do, because he'd become bored with selling paintings. And God knows, Horton had proved his profit-making potential. All he needed was the right vehicle. Then, there was me. I'd been a successful real estate agent when I met Harley, but did he tap into that potential? Hell, no! He let me pick up commissions on the sales of a couple Harley-Gransen Davis buildings, but he was more anxious to tie me, as *Hausfrau,* to *his* house. I was his live-in wife, maid, and bottle-washer, taking care of domestic chores while Harley began going elsewhere for fun and games. Morgan said Harley only gravitated toward losers, unable to cope with the success of people like Horton or me who came from lower-class backgrounds. Harley was more at ease with failures, so busy feeling superior that he usually forgot those sinking ships were taking his money—or, as it turned out, the Davis's *family* money—right along with them."

"But you and Harley split before the embezzlement shit hit the fan," Cord reminded. At the hearings, Curtis had denied knowing anything. For which Harley should probably have been forever grateful.

"And you know who persuaded me to bail out?"

"Morgan?" Cord ventured. He needn't have made a question of something so obvious.

"Morgan. And Horton, of course," Curtis amended. "But you're right, it was mainly Morgan. He said I had potential, and I'd blown it. I'd literally fucked away the best years of my life and was ending up with nothing from that sizable investment but an empty bank account and dish-pan hands. I was still young and could make it, yet, if I'd get out from under the heel of someone holding me down, because I obviously had more brains than Harley did. You know what I said?" Curtis asked with a laugh of embarrassment. "Hell, I was insecure in those days!" His drink finally arrived, and he finished off half of it in one gulp. "I listened to Morgan persuading me to retrieve my balls from wherever I'd left them, and I whined that, after having lived amid and around beautiful things for six years, I couldn't possibly go back to paintings from *J. C. Penney's* hanging on my walls. Can you imagine? Harley had converted me, pure and simple, into a pampered lady of the harem, a captive of the opulence of the *seraglio*." He shook his head in obvious disbelief.

"To which Morgan said…?" Cord prodded.

"He said, Y*ou want beautiful things, I've plenty of extras; borrow them until you get your own*." Curtis laughed, reminding Cord of some television star he couldn't quite place. "About that time," Curtis continued, "I was approached about putting together the package for this place, and I decided to dump Harley and take the chance."

"And why was Morgan so concerned with you?" Cord asked cruelly. "What was his expected return on *his* investment of time and effort?"

"Membership here, for one."

"But he couldn't know you'd be asked to take on this project, could he?"

"No, but he always assured me there'd be *some* opportunity. He made it quite clear he made time for me, not only because he liked me, but because he saw my potential. He'd been impressed by the way I'd handled the Klevertons in Osaka."

"The Klevertons of Kleverton Lumber?" Cord asked.

"They were in Osaka for an art show the Japanese were giving for Pacific Northwest artists. Several works by artists Horton handled had been included in the show. Judd Kleverton and I hit it right off. It was he who suggested me for this project."

"Doesn't Morgan having put a price tag on his friendship strike you as a bit mercenary?" Cord asked. Certainly, Cord saw it that way.

"Maybe," Curtis admitted. "However, I've always been a better player when I'm aware of the rules. I told Morgan that in Osaka when Horton and I had a falling out that left me confused, and Morgan pulled me aside to explain some of the ground rules for any relationship with Horton."

"With Horton?" Cord asked, trying to keep things straight. Why were all these people so involved in such Machiavellian relationships?

"Horton never spelled out the rules of his games," Curtis said. "This often saw players leaving the playing field out of general confusion."

"Like how *didn't* Horton explain the rules?" Cord queried. Anything he could learn about Horton would help. Although Curtis was the last person he'd figured to give him any such insights.

"Horton was generous," Curtis said, sitting back in his chair, finally relaxed enough to leave the remaining liquor in his glass. "He genuinely liked giving his time and money, and he often made it seem that was all there was to it. The trip to the Orient was my first time out of the country, my first time experiencing the thrills of a strange place with two thoroughly exciting and sophisticated men. And, oh, by the way, Jim *was* along, too," he added as an obvious afterthought. "Anyway, I couldn't have been happier. Then, all of a sudden, Horton gets mad as hell one evening, and I didn't have the foggiest notion why."

"But Morgan told you why?"

"And I thanked him for doing so. And I told him I always played a game better when someone told me the rules. Can I dislike him for coming back later and spelling out the rules of *his* game? After all, he was there when I needed someone, and no one gets anything without paying the piper. It's not as if he asked the impossible. In fact, he would have probably gotten membership here without me. He's liked by some very important people in this town. The Klevertons weren't just impressed by *me* in Osaka."

"I'd think Morgan's background made him less than acceptable in polite society," Cord threw out for comment.

"His porno, you mean?" Curtis asked and flashed a wide smile. "But does he *look* or *act* like a dirty old man, Detective? Certainly he doesn't, in the stereotypically accepted kind of way. In fact, he can come across as quite shy and innocent. And there's no question he comes across as someone with more and better breeding than Harley who, with his private schools and a million-dollar inheritance, was born with a silver spoon in his mouth. Morgan *is* cultivated, *is* charming, *is* traveled, *is* witty, *is* intelligent, *is* successful, *is* rich, *is* colorful, *is* unique, *is* handsome. Those attributes can get anyone far in today's society. And it certainly helped that he didn't *just* write boy-boy fuck books. What's more, I think he always calculatingly knew the advantages to be had in adding boy-girl books to his literary repertoire. Most of the world *is* straight, isn't it? And Morgan remains one of the few people I've ever met who knows where he's been, where he's at, and where he's going, in control every step of the way."

CHAPTER EIGHT

STEVE

"MAYBE I SHOULD call my lawyer?" Steve Footer suggested.

"A strange response from someone whose relationship with Horton Lendland has been called *minuscule at best*," Cord accused.

"So minuscule as to be just about nonexistent," Steve assured.

"Which is how I understood it," Cord agreed. Steve wasn't an easy nut to crack. The vice-president of an import-export firm, he'd come through the ranks by dealing with obnoxious bureaucrats.

"I just find your question a little strange," Steve argued.

"The circumstances surrounding Horton Lendland's murder have sexual connotations," Cord explained. "Isn't it, therefore, logical that I might pursue a sexual line of inquiry?"

"It was my understanding that Morgan doesn't have a motive," Steve said.

"If motives were always obvious, we'd solve more murders a lot faster than we do," Cord pointed out.

"This is, I suppose, your rationalization as to why your department doesn't have much of an arrest and conviction record as far as murderers are concerned," Steve said. He hadn't asked Cord to sit down, or (surprise!) offered him a drink. In fact, he'd let him get no farther than the front porch.

"We can't solve murders without cooperation," Cord said. What was there about Steve Footer that allowed *him* such staying power in Morgan's life? He was the only friend Morgan retained from junior high school. No one remained from high school or college, and only one—now living in Los Angeles—was a holdover from Morgan's Army days.

"Well, why ask *me?*" Steve challenged. "Why not ask Morgan?"

That struck home! Of all the people Cord had asked, Morgan—the horse's mouth—hadn't been one of them. "Police work is a system of checks and double-checks," Cord explained. He had a hostile witness here, but hostile about what? Witness to what?

"I'm hardly qualified to fill you in," Steve said. "Morgan and I don't exchange data on sexual conquests. Anyway, *Morgan* doesn't. When *I* get a few drinks in me, I'm liable to ramble on, but Morgan gets silent when he gets drunk."

"Is he gay, though?" Cord asked, determined to get something out of this bastard.

"You mean, does he fuck men and boys?"

"*Gay* has some other definition nowadays, does it?" Cord asked, wondering if this were worth it. Steve was Morgan's friend, and his connection with Horton was tenuous at best.

"I never saw Morgan fuck any man or boy," Steve said.

"Take an educated guess about what went on when you weren't there to see it," Cord suggested.

"You deal in supposition, do you?" Steve dodged again.

"This isn't a court of law," Cord reminded. "Morgan Kent isn't on trial."

"So, maybe he's fucked a few guys," Steve admitted. "Now, if that's all, you...."

"Can you give me any names?" Morgan interrupted.

"No; I can't give you any names," Steve said indignantly. "In fact, I can't be one-hundred percent sure he's fucked *anybody*. He *has* talked about a couple of back rooms in Canada..."

"With Horton?" Cord interrupted.

"You want to hear this from me?" Steve asked, leaning against the balustrade and crossing his arms. "Or, do you want to tell it yourself?"

"He went to Canada with Horton?" Cord repeated, not about to be brow-beaten by this prick.

"Yeah, with Horton," Steve confirmed. "Even, once or twice, with me."

"With you? Yet you, not once, recall seeing him making it in a back room?"

"*I'm* the shy one," Steve argued. "It was always the notion that Morgan might see *me* making it in a back room that got me all embarrassed. Besides, I don't go to bars to mind-fuck."

"And Morgan does?" Cord pressed.

"Some people can cruise when they're out with friends, but I can't," Steve said. "Friends cramp my style. That's all I mean."

Cord didn't get the connection, but he left it at that. "What does Morgan find so fascinating about back rooms?" he asked instead. He was too far into this to stop now.

"Who in the hell knows?" Steve replied, obviously not impressed with Cord's question. "What do *any* of us find so fascinating about them? They're dark. You don't have to worry about making conversation. It's impersonal. You want your cock serviced, you pull it out, and there's always a mouth to suck it, or an ass to squat over it, or a hand to beat it off. Neither mouth, nor ass, nor hand has a name—thank God!"

"And that kind of uninvolved sex appeals to Morgan?"

"Hell, it appeals to me. It appeals to a lot of people. It would appeal to you, too, if you gave it a try." Cord had a quick reply to that, but he contained it. There was something about any too-quick response that always seemed to insinuate guilt. And, by God, *he* was guilty of nothing! "You might be surprised," Steve continued, his *I'm-not-impressed-by-your-butch-cop-routine* smile growing wider, "by how many heterosexual men stop by back rooms when the little lady is on the rag. What happens in the dark isn't *really* the same as doing it with a guy in the daylight, is it? I mean, how does anyone know who or what is really going down on him?" Cord thought he'd have no difficulty whatsoever in making the distinction. "So, are we finished?" Steve asked.

"What about women?" Cord asked.

"Good God, what about them?" Steve asked, obviously none too pleased by the continuation.

"Does Morgan fuck them?"

"I'm an expert on fucking women, especially on Morgan fucking them, am I?"

"It's rumored you might be more expert than most," Cord said candidly. "Not necessarily on Morgan's fucking them, but on fucking women in general."

"All of that mishmash you just sprouted means something, does it?" Steve challenged, his arms folding tighter.

"Maybe I was misinformed," Cord offered in alternative.

"Yeah, maybe you were," Steve agreed, not giving an inch.

"So, *was* I misinformed?" Cord challenged, getting damned tired of prying for every bit of information.

"*My* sex life has something to do with this?"

"Your sex life doesn't interest me in the least," Cord assured. "Except that, as someone reported to like men *and* women, you might know another bisexual when you saw one. Especially if he happens to be someone you've known since junior high school."

"So, *maybe,* he's fucked some women," Steve admitted grudgingly. "We haven't exactly run in the same social circles, gay or straight, men or women, these last few years."

"Why do you only say *maybe* he's fucked some?"

"Because I've no more seen him fucking them than I've ever seen him fucking men," Steve said. "And he's never come out and said he's fucked them, either. But...."

Here we go again, Cord thought, waiting long enough to be sure Steve wasn't willingly going to resume where he'd left off. "But *what?*" Cord prodded.

"I hate conjecture!" Steve exploded; for a moment, Cord thought the man was about to go back inside and slam the door between them. "And that's all this bloody is," Steve insisted. "Conjecture, pure and simple. And I don't want Morgan getting his tail in a kink because I've shot off my mouth when I shouldn't have."

"Look—" Cord assured, again amazed at so many people seemingly so reluctant to be on Morgan Kent's shit list. Whatever the hell were they so concerned about? "—why should Morgan get upset by having you suggest he *might* fuck women?" Cord asked. "*Normal* is fucking women, isn't it?"

"Is it?" Steve challenged with a smirk. "How nice it must be for you to go through life so one-hundred percent certain."

"Morgan is part of that straight world, isn't he?" Cord argued, deciding to ignore Steve's sarcasm. "He belongs to its posh clubs. He eats at its posh tables. His books, at least the ones he writes nowadays, are aimed at a straight readership. It couldn't hurt him if it got around he'd banged a little pussy in his time."

"*You* think he banged Horton Lendland, right?"

"If I do, everyone else seems to think otherwise."

"Well, I agree with everyone else."

"Why?"

"Horton wasn't Morgan's type."

"Morgan's type being?"

"Attractive and well-built. In a word: perfection."

"And young?" Cord queried. There *was* a preponderance of *tender meat* offered on the marketplace.

"No way!" Steve said with a shake of his head. "For Morgan, young isn't perfection. In fact, that's where he and...."

"Cord waited, finally figuring—for not the first time—that he could wait forever and get no completion. "Where Morgan and Gary Green disagree?" he suggested, adding his own fill-in.

"Gary was acquitted," Steve reminded. "And I'm saying no more about *his* sex life without my lawyer present."

"Morgan doesn't like them young, then?" Cord asked, backtracking.

"He's into the Greco-Roman ideal. Prepubescent boys look like girls to him. Morgan says *there's no sense fucking second best.*"

"Meaning, why fuck boys who look like girls, when you can fuck women?"

"Or, *why fuck boys who look like girls, when you can fuck men?*"

"Did he ever mention Grey Matthews?" Cord asked.

"The body-builder?"

"He did know him, then?"

"Hell, we *all* knew Grey Matthews."

"Attractive and well-built," Cord noted.

"Yeah, wasn't he?" Steve agreed. "Before he got so strung out on dope, anyway."

"Cocaine, was it?"

"Who knows? I don't. Grey might have been my type, but I sure as hell wasn't his."

"Was he Morgan's type?" Cord asked.

"Wouldn't it be more to the point to ask if he was *Horton's* type?" Steve asked, a decided downward curl to the corners of his thin lips.

"*Was* he Horton's type?" Cord revised, making neither apology nor explanation for not having taken that route in the first place.

"Morgan said Horton and Grey were making it. Morgan was amused when Horton attended some Mr. Northwest contest and presented the trophy. The only weight-lifting Horton ever did was Grey's big cock and balls."

"Morgan said Grey's cock was big?"

"Morgan didn't have to *say* anything," Steve contradicted. "There was this gay greeting card, photographed by some big-time photographer of male nudes in Los Angeles. Captioned something like, *Who says you can't take it with you?* A naked Grey being ushered into a Rolls Royce by a dirty old man."

"Back to Morgan and Grey," Cord said, "and please don't ask me why. I've my official reasons, I assure you."

"Grey wasn't Morgan's type," Steve said. Cord's surprise was written all over his face, and Steve laughed in apparent recognition of it. "Oh, I see," Steve said. "You say: *attractive and well-built.* I say, *Oh, I agree.* And you presume what you and I believe is attractive and well-built is Morgan's idea of attractive and well-built. Wrong! Grey was too bulky for Morgan. Cute enough, mind you, before he went to pot—or coke—but his body wasn't *where it should be* by Morgan's standards. According to Morgan, *no guy is perfect if he only looks good out of his clothes.* You ever see Grey in a suit? No? Well, take it from someone who has: he looked like a simian dressed up like a human being. All he needed was an organ grinder. Not that he didn't always have a few volunteers lined up to grind *his* organ." He smiled widely.

"Morgan must have pointed out someone to you, somewhere along the line, who he thought was perfect."

"Not in Seattle, he didn't," Steve begged to differ. "He did once comment on Mel Gibson, *in that actor's younger days*, looking good. That said, he once got from Horton, by way of a little gift, this guy from Vancouver, Canada, who was supposed to be some kind of Mel-Gibson look-alike, but Morgan passed."

CHAPTER NINE

TONY

"SURE I DO," Tony France said, eyeing the activity at the bar—*his* bar. Cord and he were at one of the back tables at the *942*. "He fucked Sue Parring," Tony said. "And he gave her one helluva ride. She was convinced she was the female Messiah who had led Morgan to blessed straighthood, but I suspect she wasn't the first broad he'd ever screwed. She'd been fucked by too many cocksmen to have been put on cloud nine by someone who'd gotten *all* his practice fucking male mouth and asshole."

"Sue Parring lives in Seattle?" Cord asked, trying to sound nonchalant. It was to Sue he now wanted to talk.

"She used to," Tony said. "Hung around the bars quite a lot, usually with Russ."

"Russ?"

"Russ Tompson. A lover of mine. One of many. Might still be if not for some bastard behind the wheel of a hit-and-run."

"You wouldn't know how Morgan and Sue Parring met?" Cord cajoled, reminding himself this was the man who'd been Bobby Jordan's lover when Morgan's expensive camera, on loan to a *gay-photographer-now-famous-in-Los-Angeles,* met its early end in this very bar.

"I always presumed Russ introduced them," Tony said, drinking *Coke*. "Russ was bi, and he fucked Sue on and off. She was always after him to line her up with some die-hard gay boys to whom she could *show the way.*"

"You mean, Russ walked up to Morgan one day and says, *There's a woman available for fucking if you're interested?*"

Tony laughed, looking way too clean-cut for the Mafia connections he was purported to have. Despite an Italian first name, his graying blond hair looked more Holland than Sicily. "Pardon that outburst," Tony apologized. "It's just that I heard Russ march up to so many people so many times and deliver that very same line.

However, with Morgan his approach was probably a little more circumspect."

"Why, do you think, so many people are so anxious to tip-toe around Morgan?" Cord wondered aloud.

"If you have to ask, you've never met Morgan," Tony suggested, having apparently assumed the question had been for him.

"Goddamn right I've meet him!" Cord insisted.

"Right." Tony sounded apologetic but didn't look it. "Maybe, though, you've only met him in your official capacity."

"Why don't you fill me in on what I'm missing," Cord suggested.

"He's one of the really fun people I know," Tony obliged. "I never sit down with him, for even a few minutes, without enjoying myself. Not that he ever seems consciously out to entertain me or anyone else, but he's definitely a sun around whom revolves this fascinating array of human flotsam and jetsam, all standing attendance. No person turned on by people-watching is disappointed by Morgan. He's a consummate manipulator, never appearing to be."

"I'll see if I can't catch his act one of these nights," Cord said, oozing sarcasm.

"Do," Tony agreed. "When he's with people, you can really see what he's all about. Even people who know better can still become addicted."

"I hear he comes down to the bars less often than he used to."

"I know *I* haven't seen him in a long time," Tony confirmed. "The last few times he was with Horton Lendland."

"Which is why I'm here, now," Cord explained, not wanting any of his questions to come across as anything *but* official.

"Of course," Tony agreed.

"Tell me about Lendland," Cord said.

"A loud-mouthed faggot," Tony obliged. "No finesse. Of course, that's only my humble opinion," he qualified. "Certainly, he had all the right social connections, and Morgan was definitely upward mobile. Eventually, Morgan surpassed Horton on that score, didn't he?"

"Did he?"

"You don't get much snootier these days than the *Equus,*" Tony observed. "You never saw Horton on the club membership list."

"Maybe Horton wasn't into joining."

"Don't believe it," Tony argued. "Curtis Hurt put his name up, and it got blackballed right off."

"I would have thought Horton more socially acceptable than Morgan," Cord said.

"I don't begin to understand that level of society who flocks to places like the *Equus*," Tony said. The way Cord heard it, Tony was on very good terms with several *Equus* members who had probable underworld connections. "But people like Morgan have a certain *savoir faire* that often sneaks them through doors slammed shut upon the more *rough-around-the-edges* types. As in most things, in society it's often the façade that's most important. Horton Lendland had a way of rubbing people the wrong way."

"Like whom?" Cord asked, wondering if Tony were about to unload several more suspects. If there was anything Cord didn't need, it was even one more of those.

"I'm speaking in generalities," Tony insisted. "Of social abrasiveness as a mere irritant, not as a motive for murder. Just because Mr. Lasalo, for instance, thought Lendland a loud-mouth didn't mean he was going to kill him for being one, does it?"

"Did Mr. Lasalo think Horton a loud-mouth?" Cord asked. Robert Lasalo was one member of the *Equus* who wouldn't have been nearly as socially acceptable if some of the rumors about him were ever proved true. Maybe he felt comfortable around Morgan because they'd both had rumors bantered around about them but had survived, socially and otherwise, in spite of them.

"Lasalo was just a person whose name I picked out of the society-page hat," Tony said. "It might as easily have been Judd Kleverton." He smiled. "I doubt very much if either man even knows who Horton Lendland was."

You could bet your ass Cord would be checking, especially on any Lasalo-Lendland connections. "So, what about Sue Parring?" Cord asked, wanting those specifics and having been waylaid.

"Oh, Horton never fucked Sue," Tony assured. "His preference was cock-sucking, usually as the suck*er*. And Sue preferred getting hard cock stuffed in her cunt, although she had nice things to say about Morgan's experienced tongue being there as well."

"Your lover introduced Sue and Morgan," Cord backtracked.

"Russ was into local theater and wanted a portfolio of pictures for his agent to show around. He'd seen some stuff done by Scott Jesse and liked them. Scott has since moved on to bigger and better things, from which Morgan still gets a fat percentage. Leave it to Morgan to recognize potential in a guy I remember only as an obnoxious drunk more interested in sitting on cock than photographing it."

"So, Russ got Scott to do the portfolio pictures?"

"Scott would have had to clear it with Morgan. Contractually, Scott isn't free to shit without Morgan getting a piece of the action."

"Morgan gave permission?"

"Oh, Morgan and Russ always seemed to hit it off. But, then, they had several things in common."

"Sue Parring, for one?"

"Oh, certainly, there was Sue," Tony agreed. "And they liked leather, Russ having had quite a collection."

"Leather?"

"A lot of people are *into* leather," Tony assured. "It's nothing too horribly perverse, as these things go. And Morgan still indulges, although his tastes have graduated to *Gucci*. He wore a leather jacket to *Gaddi's* that had Gaddi himself joking about *motorcycles waiting outside.* That's what I mean by *savoir faire,* by the way. Few people would have had the panache to get away with wearing leather in *Gaddi's*. No matter that Morgan was, also, wearing tuxedo pants, a dress shirt with gold studs and cufflinks, and a bow tie at the time."

"*Gaddi's?*" Cord asked. He wasn't surprised he hadn't heard of that particular gay bar. He'd never eaten at *Canlis,* either.

"A very posh restaurant at the *Peninsula Hotel* in Hong Kong," Tony sad, apparently figuring, and rightly so, it was necessary to explain further or have Cord miss the point entirely.

"He was in Hong Kong with Lendland?" Cord asked, figuring he had the answer.

"Yes," Tony confirmed. "Curtis Hurt, now in real estate, was there, too. Possibly Horton's partner, as well. They'd gone to Japan for an art show, then on to Hong Kong. You might check with Morgan about their itinerary. Most of what I know is only second- or third-hand, filtered through the gossip mills of the bars."

"You seem to have kept up with Morgan's whereabouts," Cord commented. How many people—Tony?—had Cord interviewed who might have been to bed with Morgan but, for whatever the reason, weren't saying?

"Most people are so fucking boring, you know?" Tony observed and drained his *Coke* in obvious signal that, as far as he was concerned, the interview was over. Cord wasn't that anxious to extend it, either, since the bar was filling, and there was an air of attending sexuality that the cop found disturbing. "Morgan may be many things, but he's *never* boring," Tony suffixed. "If Horton were alive, he'd tell you his last days were more exciting with Morgan having been a part of them."

"I'd like to talk to Miss Parring," Cord said. "Could you give me an address where she can be reached?"

"Sue dropped out of sight," Tony informed. "Nor did she leave explanations with Russ or Morgan. Which we all found a bit strange at the time."

CHAPTER TEN

GARY

"JESUS, NOT YOU AGAIN!" Gary Green exclaimed. Not that Cord blamed him. Green had had more than his share of cop problems. "I hardly knew Horton Lendland, remember?" Gary insisted. "I must have met him a grand total of twice. We went over all of that, didn't we?"

"This is merely a routine follow-up," Cord assured, wondering how Green had gotten so fat. "Your friend Morgan Kent was a friend of Lendland, and I want to go back over a few things and, maybe, cover a few new ones."

"I still don't have an alibi," Gary admitted, biting his plump lower lip. "I mean, I still have one, *but* my computer still isn't talking. I was at my computer until two the next morning, working on the story of my infamous trial. Morgan and I are collaborating on a book," he said, sounding nervous. "Shall I call my lawyer?" he added in punctuation.

"You didn't need one last time, did you?" Cord reminded. "But if you'd like one present, please, feel free."

"I've had enough of lawyers *and cops*," Gary said but seemed less nervous.

"Yes," Cord agreed, attempting to sound sympathetic. He would have been less successful if Gary had been convicted of pederasty. But Gary had been acquitted on all counts: a pretty good indication of innocence in the face of raging public paranoia brought on by the widely publicized child abuse cases in a California daycare center. Not to mention a supposedly child porno ring operating out of a private elementary school in Georgia.

"Coffee?" Gary asked.

"Please," Cord replied; Gary had already pulled down two ceramic mugs from the cupboard. "Black," Cord instructed.

Gary handed Cord his coffee and carried his own steaming mug into the living room. "Horton wasn't one of my favorite people,"

Gary admitted. "I met him twice, and each time he threw a tantrum of some kind, the causes for which I was never able to grasp. I get nervous around people who are that unpredictably volatile."

"Morgan Ken seems to have survived his association with Horton," Cord commented, sipping his coffee.

"Yes…well…it did have somewhat rocky beginnings, didn't it?" Gary said. Cord didn't know about *rocky beginnings*, but he wasn't saying so. If he were lucky, Gary would assume Cord knew and take it from there. Cord *was* lucky. "And it would have been short-lived if Horton hadn't towed the line," Gary said, looking too big for his chair; he *was* too big for his chair. "Morgan hates scenes, especially in public places, which was where Horton seemed to perform his best. Usually some shouting match with his *latest-queer-in-residence.*"

"Horton toned down his act for Morgan, did he?" Cord asked, sampling more coffee. If Cord had had Green's troubles, he might have turned to drinking something stronger. Gays were really queer.

"It was either that or a parting of the ways," Gary agreed, "and Morgan would have been content with the parting. Horton had to work his buns off to bring Morgan back around." Cord figured that had been no easy chore. John Berd's abysmal behavior at *Jonah's Whale* had put him and Morgan on non-speaking terms. What's more, Cord suspected Morgan's gift to recovering alcoholic John of two bottles of Scotch had been less than any good-will gesture. "But, then, Horton wasn't used to meeting anyone in a gay bar who could care less about Horton Lendland," Gary said.

"*Morgan* could have cared less about Horton Lendland?" Cord asked. The way he'd heard it, Morgan had used Horton as a social stepladder. If Horton hadn't been totally acceptable to a good section of Seattle society, he was the major conduit for paintings by great Northwest masters like Mark Toby and Kenneth Callahan; most of the Seattle rich were collectors.

"Horton threw one of his tantrums at a restaurant in Carmel," Gary said, seeming to warm to the subject. A smile seemed to linger somewhere within the folds of his jowly face. "A real screaming match with his latest play-thing. Don't bother asking me for a name, because not even Morgan could keep up with them."

"This happened in, Carmel—California—did you say?"

"Horton, Darold, Morgan, and Horton's *latest-in-a-long-long-line-of* had gone down for the *Bach Festival.*

"And Horton threw a tantrum in a restaurant, to which Morgan took offense? Throwing a tantrum of his own?"

"Hardly!" Gary protested. "Tantrums aren't now, nor have they ever been, Morgan's style."

"But he wasn't pleased," Cord ventured.

"To say the least," Gary agreed. He finished his coffee, asking whether Cord would like a refill. Cord did.

"I'm presuming Morgan let Horton know," Cord said, once they were resettled.

"In San Francisco," Gary confirmed. "They went there after Carmel. Horton used to have a gallery there, you know?"

"In San Francisco?" Cord asked. His other choice was Carmel.

"Oh, yes. Quite successful, too. San Francisco's prissy gay set was into art collection, big-time, and considered Horton one of their own. Not taking it too kindly, though, when he returned to Seattle and left the gallery in charge of some jerk who thought *art* was some hustler on Polk Street. Not that I can't see Horton's reasons for leaving. He was more comfortable being a kingpin in Seattle than just being another successful art dealer in San Francisco. I guess Darold wasn't too pleased, but Darold is more *San Francisco* than *Seattle,* don't you think?"

"So, what happened between Morgan and Horton in San Francisco?" Cord asked.

"At the *Top of the Mark*...rather, in the elevator *en route....* Morgan somehow—and don't ask *me* how, because *only* Morgan could have managed it!—picked up a prostitute." Gary laughed a full-blown belly-laugh that put all sixteen layers of his sizable stomach into motion. Cord had visions of Gary being beaten to death in the resulting whiplashes of roiling flab. "Horton was furious," Gary said with a giggle. "More so when Morgan brought the prostitute to their table, plied her with champagne, and then went off with her, leaving Horton just sitting."

"Morgan and this prostitute had sex?" Cord asked, that being the reasonable assumption.

Gary, though, didn't agree. "Oh, I hardly think so!" he protested. "It was the illusion that counted, don't you see? He was letting Horton know that the company of a prostitute was preferable to that of a loud-mouthed drunken art dealer."

"Morgan doesn't like women, then?" Cord asked, trying to sound as if he were asking the question for the very first time.

"Oh, he *pretends,*" Gary admitted, leaning forward, as if to include Cord in a private confidence. "For some reason, gays are often turned on by guys who swing both ways, so Morgan pretends in order to make himself more desirable."

"He's sexually attracted to men, then?"

"Morgan has never been what you call oversexed," Gary explained, "but when the urge strikes him, I'd say, yes, it is men who end up on the receiving end, if you know what I mean."

"He never went to bed with Sarah...." Cord paused, as if trying to recall the name. "...Robinson?"

"Who?" Gary asked. If he knew the name, it didn't sound that way. Cord pulled his notebook out of his pocket, thumbed through its pages to his scribbling from his Steve Footer interview.

"Sarah Robinson," Cord said. Steve had only guessed at the first name, but he was sure of the last. Something about a song from some movie about a *Mrs. Robinson*.

"I don't know any Sarah Robinson, but I doubt Morgan ever went to bed with her," Gary said.

"She was apparently someone Morgan knew from Portland, Oregon, when he was stationed there at the *Armed Forces Enlistment and Examination Station*," Cord added to refresh Gary's memory. According to Steve, the incident wasn't one Gary was likely to have forgotten. "She visited him in Seattle when he, Steve, and you were rooming together on Capital Hill."

"That would have been on Twelfth Avenue East," Gary pinpointed.

"Right," Cord confirmed with another check of his notes.

"That *does* go back a ways," Gary excused. "You say her name was Robinson?"

"She drove up with a girlfriend. Tess someone-or-other. They arrived unexpectedly one evening, bringing Chinese food. Steve was on his way out. He was seeing an awfully lot of—" Again he checked his notes. "—someone called Lenard Powell. They were going to a movie. He stayed at Powell's that night and came back the next morning to find you furious."

"Why furious?" Gary asked. He shook his head as if it were all news to him.

"It seems Morgan had spent the night upstairs with Sarah, leaving you downstairs to entertain Tess."

"Oh, God, *yes*!" Gary erupted with a shudder that vibrated him like *Jell-O*. "*That* Tess! *That* Sarah Robinson! All planned by Morgan, of course, but how was I to know at the time? It was all quite traumatic for someone like me who's nauseated by the very idea of sex with a woman. All night beset upon by a supposed nymphomaniac who supposedly wasn't going to take *no* for an answer." Gary had never denied being gay. What he had denied was *liking children*.

"But it was a practical joke?" Cord probed. "Something Morgan had arranged?"

"I'd criticized this gay book he'd written. His very first. I'd said it was unrealistic. Christ, he had a guy fucking a goat on the edge of a cliff, if you can believe. Tess was his way of paying me back for that. He got even more revenge, of course, when the publisher scooped up the manuscript as if it was some rare treasure. Morgan said it just proved I *didn't know shit about what was or wasn't a turn-on for gays*. This did seem to be the case, considering all his books that came after."

"Including more than a few straight ones," Cord reminded.

"Yes. Well, in one of his books, do you know he had the main character fuck a crocodile?" Gary asked with a chuckle. His rolls of shaking flesh made *Jack-Sudlow-in-a-sauna* look like Steve Reeves.

"Meaning, he didn't have to fuck women to write about it?" Cord divined.

"Exactly!" Gary agreed, wedging his lower body more securely into his chair, if that were possible, and looking as if it would take TNT to dislodge him. "Besides, would someone who'd fucked women put a clitoris in the wrong place? Which Morgan did in one of his books. I even remember the one: *Glenda's Forbidden Daddy*. I would have laughed up a storm, except I wasn't up to another night of fighting off another Tess."

"Morgan eventually fessed up to siccing Tess on you, did he?"

"Not in so many words," Gary admitted, "but he did it, nevertheless. He knew my physical aversion to the very thought of sex with a woman, and he used it. It was his way, from start to finish: recognizing a weakness and capitalizing on it. You knew, of course, that Horton was deathly afraid of fire?"

"No, I...."

"Oh!" Gary interrupted with a squeal of apparent dismay. "But that comes out sounding as if I were somehow insinuating a connection between Horton's death by fire and Morgan's penchant for playing on weaknesses. And there is *no* such connection, of course."

"Who said Horton was afraid of fire?" Cord asked.

"Everyone knew it," Gary said with a shrug. "It was how Horton rationalized always having to travel with someone. Of course, his traveling companions were undoubtedly used for more than just fire alarms."

"Horton and Morgan had sex, then?"

"Oh, I should think not!" Gary disagreed immediately, shaking his head in earnest emphasis.

"They traveled together," Cord reminded. "And Horton *was* a man."

"Yes, well...." Gary said, rolling his eyes. "Except, *that* particular one and one doesn't necessarily add up to two, does it?" Cord wondered why, but he let it ride. "When I said Morgan preferred men, I didn't mean any specific man," Gary corrected. "His fucking a Bob, a Dick, a Harry, or a Horton would be too personal for his tastes. No, he's more into the anonymity of back-room sex. Where he knows he's got a man's mouth, hand, or asshole wrapped around his cock, but he doesn't have to be bothered with to whom it belongs. Besides, the darkness allows him to fantasize perfection he'll never find. If he waited around for a Mr. Right to fit his specifications, he'd be celibate forever. Except, of course," Gary added with a coy tilt of his head that looked absolutely ludicrous on a man that fat, "for a very few times Morgan *thought* he'd found perfection." He screwed up his face into a grotesque mask. "But was wrong." He smiled slyly. "Morgan's ideal man is too fucking perfect to be real."

Cord thought he'd detected what Gary may have insinuated, but he had to be sure. "Have *you* and Morgan had sex, then?" he asked, the notion almost too fantastic to be put into words.

"Oh, my goodness!" Gary responded, and Cord literally expected a peal of girlish giggles. "Morgan isn't a chubby-chaser," Gary explained, sighing. He sipped his coffee and eyed Cord coquettishly over the rim of his mug. "On the other hand," he added, "I wasn't always this fat. In fact, I was considered quite a catch in my time." Cord couldn't begin to imagine what *time,* in what long-distant past, that might have been.

"Would you know if Morgan likes young boys?" Cord asked, knowing the question was the wrong one even before he got it out. The sudden stiffening of Gary's flesh into the semblance of solid mass, and the accompanying hardening of Gary's facial features confirmed that the man found Cord's question inappropriate.

"I'm overly sensitive, I suppose," Gary said, his hostile posturing melting with surprising quickness. "On the other hand, your question *was* ill-advised, quite aside from my past legal problem."

"Yes," Cord agreed, feeling like an ass.

"Then, again, I could have calmly asked how young you considered *young,* couldn't I have?" Gary reminded. "You could have said, *Oh, boys above the age of consent,* and I would have known I'd been confused and upset by a misunderstanding in semantics. However, by young, I assumed you were referring to the merchandise most available these days on city streets." Cord didn't confirm, and it was apparent, from the shortness of the pause Gary gave him, that Gary didn't expect him to. "Merchandise which, though readily available, remains technically illegal game," Gary reminded. "So, I'm a little piqued that you might have thought me stupid enough to incriminate a friend at your casual dropping of such a leading question. And I'd be even more upset, except the answer to your question is a resounding *NO*. Not only does Morgan find pre-pubescence anathema to ideal physical perfection but, more importantly, he finds it boring. Young men, of the age to which you refer, simply haven't the mental dexterity to keep Morgan interested. I should have simply said all of that without my hackles rising."

"My motive in asking wasn't to remind you of your previous legal problem, or to trick you into incriminating Morgan. It was merely to get to the bottom of a murder," Cord assured. "I realize the question might not seem relative, but…."

"Oh, Horton's murder was bound to be tied up with something sexual," Gary surprised. "Like most of us gays, he was too highly sexed for his own good. Morgan is merely an exception to the rule."

"Well, thanks for your time," Cord said, standing. He looked for a place to put his empty mug, and Gary took it.

Gary walked him to the door. "I suppose you've talked to Nelton," Gary called out, having waited until Cord was at the elevator down the hallway.

"Nelton?" Cord called back, the name ringing no bells.

"Nelton Manson," Gary filled in. "A friend of mine. A friend of Steve. An *acquaintance* of Morgan."

"*Should* I talk to him?" Cord asked.

"It'll probably do you little good," Gary admitted, as if suddenly sorry for the suggestion. "Except he was closer to Horton than I was, and he had the black eye to prove it."

"A black eye, how?"

"I guess Horton got a little rough one night," Gary said. "But, then, for whatever the reason, Horton wasn't the first person to get Nelton in bed and proceed to beat the shit out of him."

CHAPTER ELEVEN

NELTON

"WHO TOLD YOU THAT?" Nelton Manson demanded.

"People talk," Cord consoled, not about to reveal his source. "You know that."

"It was Gary Green!" Nelton divined on his very own. "Who'd be thrilled through each and every fatty pustule if I were somehow implicated in Horton's murder."

"Why would he want you implicated?"

"Because he blames me for his horrid little problem with the law."

"Does he have reason?"

"It's hardly important, is it?" Nelton asked, heading down the hallway and leaving Cord to follow after. In the living room, a large picture window looked out over Puget Sound. A ferry moved slowly across the backdrop of impressive Seattle skyline.

"Why don't you let me be judge and jury of what's important?" Cord suggested.

Nelton had gone directly to the wet bar and was pouring himself a drink. As much as gays seemed to drink, Cord wondered why they didn't all fall over dead from sclerosis of the liver before they reached the ripe old age of thirty. "Drink?" Nelton offered.

"I'll pass," Cord replied. Hell, it wasn't even noon!

"Gary thinks I told a counselor at camp that Gary was fucking around with some little kid assigned him through *Big Cousins*. The counselor supposedly told somebody else, who supposedly let it slip to somebody else, who made an anonymous call of complaint to the *Big Cousins'* offices, who contacted the mother, who thought she could blackmail Gary, who would have none of that so ended up being prosecuted for pederasty instead." He took a deep breath.

"But you never told the counselor?"

"Isn't that what I said at the trial?" Nelton asked, refreshing his drink before carrying it to a chair. Cord sat without being invited. "I was the best character witness Gary had, which he assumes was because of my guilty conscience. But what's all of this shit about Horton and me?"

"My source says Horton gave you a black eye."

"*Your source*," Nelton said, his emphasis making it sound as if he'd just uttered *shit*, "is right."

"Why did Horton give you a black eye?" Cord asked.

"Because *his* source told him I was turned on by B&D."

"*His* source being…?"

"If I knew that, you can bet your ass I'd have done some butt-kicking," Nelton promised, taking a slug of liquor and tossing it back without a pause. "I would guess Morgan Kent, except I ran into a few other misinformed people before either Morgan or Horton came into my life."

"Why might you guess Morgan Kent?"

"He introduced me to Horton, didn't he?" Nelton said, draining his glass.

"Did he?"

"Yes," Nelton said, getting up for a refill and, this time, not bothering to offer Cord any. "Said Horton was tired of vacuous street people and wanted to meet someone who could talk to him in more than one-syllable words. Morgan thought of me. *I* thought it might be interesting. Granted, Horton wasn't the easiest guy to look at, but he knew how to show a trick a good time. For which, I was assured, he'd never want anything more from me than conversation and, maybe, just maybe, a chance to suck off my cock on occasion. That was easy duty. I could always shut my eyes and imagine I was getting sucked off by a young Richard Gere. Movies are a hobby of mine, and the young Richard Gere is my present fantasy figure for jacking off."

"I see," Cord replied, deciding he now had another movie star, besides Mel Gibson in the story-line.

"Don't you ever jack off, imagining you're with someone?" Nelton asked. It sounded accusatory, as if he were expecting Cord to deny it.

"I'm asking the questions," Cord reminded. He hadn't jacked off in awhile, thinking he was with someone or not, and not because of any permanent loss of a hard-on, either.

"So, what else do you want to know about Horton and me?" Nelton asked, staying at the bar where he could apparently refill his glass with less time and effort.

"Anything you can tell me."

"Morgan came around afterwards and apologized for Horton."

"Morgan apologized for Horton?"

"Yeah. He said Horton was sorry. Said it wouldn't happen again. So, I saw Horton, and Horton said it wouldn't happen again. Fucking liars, the both of them!"

"It happened again?"

"Damned right it did! And wasn't Horton surprised when I ended up exiting with a swift kick to his balls?"

"Which ended the relationship?"

"You would have thought so, huh?" Nelton said, shaking his head. "But the next time I see Morgan, he says Horton is again sorry. Horton won't do it again. Did I want to go to Tahiti? Horton was going to Tahiti and was looking for a traveling companion. Would I like to see Horton and talk over the possibilities?"

"You said you weren't interested," Cord ventured and didn't make it a question.

"Damned right I was interested. I'd risk more than a black eye for a trip to Tahiti. Wouldn't you?" Cord's answer to that was a firm, *NO,* and his expression said it all. "Yeah?" Nelton mocked, having gotten the message. "Well, some of us have a higher pain threshold."

"But you've never *really* been *seriously* into B&D?" Cord encouraged.

"Only dabbled," Nelton admitted. "But who hasn't dabbled? You're not going to know if you like something or not if you don't give it a try, at least once, are you? But I was never into any of the hard-core stuff. And I never did it with someone I didn't know and trust."

"What's your definition of hard-core?" Cord asked.

"Read Morgan's books," Nelton suggested. "They define it better than I can."

"Morgan is into B&D?"

"You read Morgan's books and tell me if there's *anything* he's *not* into, or *been* into at one time or another."

"I hear one of his characters fucked a crocodile," Cord reminded.

"Another fucked a goat. You think I'd be surprised to hear Morgan had fucked any and all God's creatures?" Nelton asked. "Well, guess again."

"Would you be surprised to hear he fucked women?"

"Is the Pope Jewish?"

"The notion of Morgan fucking women sure surprises Gary Green."

"Yeah? Well, Gary thinks Morgan is Jesus Christ, Buddha, Adonis, and Confucius incarnate. Something that perfect, in Gary's estimation, could *never* fuck a woman."

"Gary hates women?"

"Who said anything about his hating them?" Nelton asked, shaking his head, rolling his eyes, and taking another swallow of his drink. "You straights all think alike. I *like* women but would never think of fucking one. I've women who are my best friends. It's the same with Gary."

"So, what's Morgan? Bisexual?"

"Jesus, a Pigeonhole Queen!" Nelton exclaimed facetiously. "Well, don't ask me to come up with a convenient compartmentalization for you. Morgan fucks men, women, probably crocodiles, goats, and—by his own admission—a cantaloupe or two. *You* tell *me* if that makes him bisexual, multi-sexual, or a fucking fruit-sexual."

"Could you give me some names of people he's been to bed with?"

"Jesus, now he wants names," Nelton said with an accompanying groan that turned to a gargle with the addition of booze. "I'm not, nor have I ever been, Morgan's social secretary, or a voyeur he invites to watch him in performance."

"I only asked because so few seem to have names."

"That's not because Morgan is a saint," Nelton assured. "That's because he's super discreet and chooses his tricks accordingly."

"Why haven't I found such discretion all that prevalent elsewhere among gays?"

"Probably because you've met the wrong gays," Nelton suggested. He lifted the bottle to pour more from it but changed his mind. He left the bottle and his empty glass on the bar and came back to the chair he'd deserted earlier. "Cops make me nervous," he said without any trace of a smile. "Ever since I got picked up by a nasty one on a DUI. What he did to my face made Horton's efforts look like child's play."

There were plenty of replies Cord might have made, but he made none of them. Cops were no more perfect than anyone else, but society would have a helluva hard time working without them.

"How about Gary?" Cord asked, wanting the conversation brought back to more comfortable categories. "Do you think Morgan and he ever made it?"

"Doesn't Gary wish?" Nelton answered. "You've seen Gary. You've seen Morgan. Do you think Morgan would ever, in anyone's wildest dreams—except maybe in Gary's—find that sea of blubber attractive?"

"Has Gary always been heavy?"

"He's *not* heavy," Nelton begged to disagree. "He's one-hundred percent, certifiable elephantine. Has he always been? Oh, there was a time before elephantine, before fat, before heavy, before chunky, before big-boned, when he didn't look half bad. I knew him then; Morgan didn't."

"So," Cord said, hands on his thighs and pushing himself to a standing position, "I guess that does it, then."

"I don't think so," Nelton contradicted. Cord realized his mouth was hanging open and shut it. "So, you might as well sit down and hear the rest," Nelton said, momentarily eyeing the bourbon while Cord resumed his seat. "I have no desire to find you back here any time soon, so let's get it all out of the way now," Nelton added.

"Anything you say," Cord agreed.

"For starters, I did *not* go to Tahiti with Horton. I was *considering* the trip when someone came into my life. One of many Mr. Rights who turned out to be Mr. Wrong, but who seemed enough of a Mr. Right at the time that any notion of going anywhere with the likes of Horton became paramount to lunacy. Horton ended up going with Jim Holdsett, his partner. *Business* partner, ha, ha!" he offered as an aside. "And while we're on the subject of Jim Holdsett, I confess there was a time, after Mr. Right-Gone-Wrong revealed his true colors, and after Horton and Jim were back from Tahiti, at a time in my life when Horton once again began to look not half bad, that Horton, Jim, and I went out to dinner. Jim was obviously along to make me feel safer with him as chaperone. I got drunk, realized Jim was a thousand times sexier than Horton, and I turned my full attention toward seducing Jim. This pleased neither Jim nor Horton. This resulted in the shit hitting the fan. Or, rather, in this case, it was Horton hitting me. Luckily, I was so drunk that I didn't know what hit me. We were in a restaurant where Horton knew the staff, so it was all glossed over, me ending up dumped unceremoniously on my doorstep, wondering if it was the first day of the end of the world. After which, I was on Horton's shit list, and he was no favorite of mine. Morgan and I talked about it, and Morgan remained unsympathetic, as hard as I tried to milk from him a bit of human kindness. It seems that, when I put the make on Jim, I broke one of the cardinal rules of game-play. Don't ask me how. I mean, Horton and Jim weren't lovers, and hadn't I heard *that* enough times?" He succumbed to temptation, got up, went to the bar, and filled his glass. "Life is too fucking short to play games," he said, holding the liquor to the light but not drinking it. Finally, he took a swallow and turned back to Cord. "Some people get off on playing games," he said. "Morgan, Horton, Jim. Not me! To hell with them and their games." He was obviously more than a little tipsy.

"Anything more?" Cord injected into the pregnant pause that followed.

"Only for you to ask me where I was the night of Horton's murder."

"So, where were you?" Cord obliged.

Drink in hand, Nelton left the bar and crossed to the stairway leading to the second floor. He supported his free hand on the banister and leaned toward the stairs. "Russel, get your ass down here for a minute!" he yelled.

"What the hell?" came a muffled reply.

"Russel, damn it, do it *now*! It's important."

"What in the hell are you screaming about?" Russel asked, materializing at the top of the stairs. His robe was unfastened, revealing a muscled but hairy chest, and abdominals like Cord used to have but had no longer. Russel's big cock was hard as a rock. "Who in the hell is he?" Russel asked, trying to tie his robe closed while nodding in Cord's direction.

"Detective Cord Maxwell," Nelton informed, "come to see where I was the night of Horton Lendland's murder. Would you be kind enough to tell him?" Russel still looked half asleep. The awkward dangling of his arms was a feeble attempt to conceal the large tenting his hard cock made in the silk of his robe. "Come on, Russel," Nelton insisted. "No need to be shy around Detective Maxwell. He knows I'm gay. He knows you're gay. Gary has filled him in on every little detail of our relationship. So, admit that while Horton Lendland was being fucked with a spear and baked to a crisp, I was blissfully being stabbed by your fleshy spear and broiling in the ecstasy of your love-making."

"For Christ's sake, Nelton!" Russel protested, sounding embarrassed. He looked embarrassed, too, but not any more so than Cord.

"Was he here, or wasn't he?" Cord asked. It was information he might as well get now as later.

"Yeah," Russel admitted. "I got a raise at the plant, and we were celebrating with a night off. I usually work nights," he added in obvious attempt to explain why he was in his present state of undress at that hour of the morning.

"And where do you work, Mr...?"

"Russel Havelock," Nelton supplied. "He works in the maintenance department of the *Boeing* plant at Burien."

"Why do you need to know that?" Russel asked, looking very ill at ease. His erection had obviously softened somewhat, but Cord was still aware of it being there, shielded only by a wisp of slippery and clinging material.

"Merely to confirm you had that night off," Cord assured, anxious to get the hell out of there.

"Ah...Mr. Hendrix, my boss, he, ah...," Russel began but didn't finish.

"What Russel is trying his damnedest to tell you," Nelton rushed to the rescue, "is that he is still in the closet, and everyone at *Boeing*, Mr. Hendrix included, thinks my man here is straight as a nail."

"There'll likely be no reason for me to tell them differently," Cord assured. Russel looked unconvinced.

"Then, it's *a wrap*, as they say in the movie industry," Nelton announced. "This calls for a wrap party. Shall we all go upstairs to bed and suck and fuck our brains out?"

"Jesus Christ, Nelton, are you crazy!" Russel bellowed.

"I'm *only* drunk," Nelton insisted.

"He's only drunk," Cord confirmed.

"It's not even noon," Russel said with a condemning frown.

"Policemen make him nervous," Cord explained, wondering why he was making excuses for the obnoxious little shit. He smiled an embarrassed and silly grin, noticing how events had finally diminished Russel's cock to a hardly discernable bump. Cord excused himself. "I can find my way out," he assured, little pleased when he had one more question to ask before being safely out the door. "Oh, Mr. Manson?" he asked, turning. The two residents were where he'd left them, Russel looking angry and confused, Nelton looking pie-eyed. "Did you ever hear anything about Horton being afraid of fire?" Cord asked.

"Everyone knew he was afraid of fire, didn't they?" Nelton asked, his words slurred as his hasty consumption of alcohol began to take an even heavier toll. "His grandmother or some other family member got burned up when Horton was a kid. He was in the house at the time, and the firemen had to knock down three walls to get to him and get him out. Ask Darold Keshmont, Horton's roommate. Or, ask Morgan, since he's the one who told me."

Cord made a very unmilitary about-face and left. Fresh air never tasted so sweet.

CHAPTER TWELVE

BORIS

"WELL?" BORIS COUSEL ASKED, stepping back from a possibly completed painting. "What do you think?"

Cord thought the man and the room were a vast improvement over the last time Cord had been there. It made no difference that Boris still looked like death warmed over, or that there was probably a year's accumulation of dirt swept underneath the rug. As for the paint on canvas? It would be a cold day in hell before Cord would have paid money to own it. He'd found a lot of the fortune in artwork in Morgan's penthouse pretty wretched, too. He'd found a god-awful lot of the stuff hanging in the house Darold now could call his own. So…. "I don't know that much about art," Cord alibied.

"Well, take it from someone who does, it's good," Boris bragged, putting down paintbrush and palette and going to the refrigerator. He pulled out a couple cans of beer and popped their lids. He handed one to Cord who, not having been asked if he wanted one, decided to take it. Cord needed something to clear his throat of the paint, alcohol, linseed oil, piss, vomit, and sweat, which permeated the room. "As a matter of fact," Boris said, heading back to the canvas, "it's possibly one of my very best. Of course, whether the buying public agrees is yet to be seen, isn't it?"

"So, I'm to understand the *Lendland/Holdsett Gallery*, or what's left of it, is giving you a one-man show sometime soon?" Cord said, enjoying another swallow of cold beer. He belched silently when it reached his stomach.

"You mean the *Holdsett* Gallery, don't you?" Boris corrected, leading the way through the clutter to two director chairs by the window. "But I suppose you, more than anyone, are aware that Mr. Lendland is no longer with us."

"Holdsett is getting his shit together, is he?" Cord asked. His impression had been that there hadn't been enough paintings salvaged or insurance coverage to warrant picking up the pieces.

"Oh, it will take awhile," Boris admitted. "He's pretty much starting from scratch, you know? But a few of us are working hard so he'll have something to show within the next few weeks."

"That's good of you," Cord complimented. He wished Holdsett luck in trying to palm off this particular canvas. Besides, from what Cord had heard, Boris Cousel's paintings weren't exactly the hot have-to-have items they once were. This, went the rumor, was one of the reasons Lendland had dumped Boris shortly before the dealer's murder.

"I always did prefer Jim to Horton," Boris admitted. "Not that I didn't remain appreciative of all Horton did for me, mind you. Not that Horton ever did much more than recognize genuine talent when he saw it," he amended. "But Horton wasn't the easiest man in the world to work for. As a dealer, he had a flawed perception of artistic temperament."

"Meaning, *your* artistic temperament?"

"He was jealous of me, of course," Boris said by way of confirmation. "Most art dealers are frustrated painters. Since *they* can't produce, they're forced to live vicariously through real talent. How frustrating that must be for them, don't you agree?"

Cord shrugged. He couldn't imagine being envious of the haphazard splashes of color Boris had applied to the canvas on the easel. That would have been like envying the artwork resulting from a monkey turned loose in a paint store. "I understand you were quite famous at one time," Cord said, deciding to keep his opinions to himself and to flatter Boris into more conversation. It was surprising what tidbits might drop while someone was rambling on.

"There's a Cousel in the *Vatican Museum*," Boris informed. He had a disconcerting way of lapsing into an affected English accent. "There's one in the *Metropolitan*," he added. "Oh, yes, I *was* quite famous at one time. My work would still be in demand if Horton had had any real perception of my creative needs." His accent had become so pronounced that Cord was having trouble understanding. "Oh, everything was fine as long as I was producing paintings by the truckload. But when I had a severe blow in my private life that left me too distraught to continue, for however short a time, where was Horton then?"

"You're referring to your separation from Wayne Garotte?" Cord asked.

"God, yes," Boris said, looking genuinely surprised. His surprise, though, soon faded. "But, of course, it's your business to know such things, isn't it?"

"Actually, it is," Cord agreed.

"So, you have all the details?"

"Second-hand information is often distorted," Cord reminded, encouraging him to go on.

"I met Wayne in Paris," Boris obliged. "Very romantic city. Very romantic time for me. I was being wined and dined by celebrities, counts, duchesses, and the very rich, all of whom simply *had to have* a Cousel in their collections. Heady times, you understand, for a boy from Seattle. I was ripe for love, and Wayne was there."

"Wayne was a painter, like you?" Cord asked, out to verify his facts.

"Let's just say he was *a* painter," Boris amended, "for he had really very little talent. And that's not sour grapes. Ask anyone. Someone with even a modicum of talent would have made it with the opportunities Wayne had dropped in his lap. Oh, he had some small success after he left me. But had Horton spent half as much time and energy promoting me and my work as he did promoting Wayne and Wayne's work, we'd have all been richer men."

"It was my understanding that you weren't producing much art work in those days," Cord injected. What he'd heard was: *Boris was too fucking drunk on his ass to make it to a toilet to piss, let alone make it to a canvas to paint.*

Boris waved that off, as if it were an irritating gnat buzzing his head. "What I needed—*all* I needed—was rest. Even soldiers take R&R, don't they? In fact, it's mandatory for their good health. I'd given Horton the paintings he'd wanted for years, and he just wanted more, especially with his new gallery in San Francisco. But I was tired. A couple of months rest, and I would have been back as good as new, but Horton wouldn't have that. He got Wayne to pester me until I was fit to be tied. I would have done anything for Wayne, you understand, except I was tapped out and needed time to get the creative juice flowing again. Horton didn't have the time or patience. As it turned out, neither did Wayne." He sighed, finished his beer, and examined the empty can without going for a replacement. "Of course, by that time, Horton had quite convinced himself *and Wayne* that Wayne was the new Boris Cousel. They were both horribly deluded, of course."

"Was Horton getting more from Wayne than paintings?"

"Like sex, you mean?" Boris asked, squeezing his beer can and watching its collapse. "Of course. No doubt about it. Even *I* had to pull down my pants for Horton in order to get my first show. Proving that even genius, these days, has to make certain concessions for making it to the top. And Wayne was no genius."

"Do you know where Wayne is now?"

"Good God, no. Nor have I any desire to know. Last I heard, he'd run off with a size-queen to Los Angeles or New York, Wayne's big cock all he had left that was selling. By then, Horton had, at long last, realized his passion for Wayne's twelve inches had distorted his perception of that young man's far lesser talents as a painter."

"But you *have* had other shows at the *Lendland/Holdsett Gallery* since then," Cord reminded.

"Oh, yes," Boris agreed. "None very successful. For which, Horton blamed me. For which, I blamed him."

"Couldn't you have shown your work elsewhere?" Cord suggested.

"Oh, but you do have a lot to learn about the politics of art if you believe that," Boris countered. "An artist only has full access to other galleries when he's on top, or when he's well on his way up. Once word gets around that he's on his way down, nobody wants to hitch their wagon to his falling star. When I quit producing, Horton wasted no time making clear to everyone that my *day in the sun* was over."

"But you began painting again, didn't you?"

"Let me tell you a little about this business," Boris said, placing the crushed beer can on the stand by his chair. "The commodity is produced by artistic people often too consumed by their passion to create to pay much attention to the nitty-gritty nickel-and-dime stuff. That's why there are dealers to handle all of that. And most dealers are lucky if they know good art from a hole in the ground, though they pretend otherwise. What they *really* do is to grab haphazardly from the artwork available, hoping to hit eventually. Their reputations are built on luck of the draw, their failures usually forgotten. Since Horton Lendland had more luck than most, he *had* an excellent reputation. Not just in the Pacific Northwest, either. So, if he said I was on my way down, you can bet your ass that dealers, less lucky than he, weren't about to risk taking on this has-been."

"Which doesn't explain why Lendland kept showing your work, does it?" Cord asked, insinuating Cord's naiveté might have allowed him to miss something.

"He did it for several reasons," Boris patiently explained. "He liked to promote the illusion that he stuck with his artists through thick and thin, because *that* was good business. He continued to blame me for my failure, and he periodically wanted to prove it wasn't *his* fault my work wasn't selling. He, also, felt guilty for having stolen Wayne from me, knowing we would have all been better off if he'd controlled his runaway passions just that once. And he liked me around to inflate his ego, seeing me as an example of genius gone awry while he, less talented and less brilliant, retained his success. Oh, I could go on and on."

"But if you painted, and he was showing your paintings in his gallery, wasn't it the buyer who made the final decision to buy or not to buy?"

"My dear Detective Maxwell, the buyer of art, in the big wide world out there, is, more often than not, less knowledgeable than the dealers. Oh, not all of them are dilettantes, but the majority of them certainly are. They buy art because it's *the thing to do,* or because it's a tax write off, or because it's budgeted, or because Mr. and Mrs. Kleverton buy art, or because Morgan Kent buys art, or because any *cultured* person is *expected* to buy art. They rely heavily on dealers to tell them what's *in,* what's *out,* because they don't know shit and are too busy making their money to find out anything for themselves. Someone walks into a gallery specifically to purchase a Cousel, and do you know how easy it is for any dealer to persuade him to pay out that same amount, instead, for another painting, by some other artist, that'll be *a far better investment*? Ask Jim how many times Horton pulled *that* stunt over the years."

"You obviously get along better with Holdsett than you did with Lendland, yes?"

"It's just too bad Jim didn't show up years ago, that's all. Do you know that he wanted to give me a major show last year, but Horton vetoed the idea? Horton said I'd never sober up long enough to produce enough quality work. Well, I hope Horton's ghost is sticking around long enough to see that I *can* produce if given half the chance."

"You know all of this could be construed as a feasible motive for murder?" Cord said, frankly surprised by a man with no alibi being so candid.

"Except that Horton, no matter our less-than-perfect relationship, was my only source of income. Regularly, if begrudgingly, he advanced me a few dollars—for old-time's sake. On which I managed to keep myself amply stocked with booze. Anyone who knows anything about a die-hard drunk can tell you he's not about to cut off his nose to spite his face, where his drink is concerned. If ever forced to make the choice, it'll be the booze every time."

"But you not only seem to have survived without Lendland, but you're giving a damned good act of being stone-cold sober," Cord reminded. One can of beer did not an alcoholic make, and there was no evidence of any other empty cans or bottles around the room.

"I'm sober, because Jim has faith in me and needs my help. Something I could have never foretold before Horton's murder. Like everyone, I had to assume the fire was the last of the *Lendland/Holdsett Gallery*. After all, Horton was never one for adequate insurance coverage, as I had to verify, in the past, when he *misplaced* several of my paintings. And whatever the present inventory went up in smoke with him. I certainly couldn't have known Morgan Kent would step in to give Jim backing, when even Jim remains surprised by that turn of events."

"Morgan Kent stepped in? When? How?"

"With money, how else?" Boris said. "But, then, he's always been quick to see potential. He has several Cousels, you know? He was one of the very few people who bought them in spite of Horton's recommendations to the contrary. As for his financing Jim, well, no one knows better than Morgan that it's been Jim carrying the gallery workload these last few years. As for Jim accepting, well, he's ambitious and has enough sense to fall into line. There's still plenty of time for him to branch out some day with a gallery of his very own, and Morgan has agreed to give him star billing on this one." He smiled. "Morgan does seem to have the knack for knowing just what bait is right for cinching what deal. Jim might have been reluctant to settle for the *Kent/Holdsett Gallery*, or even for the *Holdsett/Kent Gallery*, but do you think he could turn down the magic sound of the *Holdsett Gallery,* even with a silent majority partner? Besides which, Morgan will be less of a taskmaster as far as making sexual demands."

"Why's that?" Cord injected, wondering how Boris could be so certain.

"Morgan likes his men to look butch," Boris said. "Jim, as sweet as he is, comes off a bit nellie at times, yes?"

"What makes you think Morgan prefers his men butch?" Cord asked, irresistibly drawn to asking the question.

"He likes them to *look* butch," Boris reminded. "*Looking* and *being* are not necessarily one and the same. Or, maybe, you didn't know that." He waited, but Cord made no commitment, either way. "Some of the nelliest queers around are only top men," Boris said, apparently deciding an explanation, in this case, was necessary. "And some of the studliest hunks in leather bars only like it up the ass."

"What makes you think Morgan prefers men who *look* butch?" Cord amended.

"Because, as a painter, I observe," Boris said. "Watch Morgan in a crowded room and tell me on whom his gaze usually lingers longest. In fact, Jim can't understand that Morgan doesn't dislike him, per se, but merely doesn't like Jim's physical type. Obviously, Morgan has paid enough *non-sexual* attention to Jim to know the guy will work his butt off for a chance of speedy resurrection in the art world. But Jim, sexually desired by so many gays, can't understand why one gay, particularly one to whom Jim is *so* sexually attracted, doesn't find him any more attractive than a wet noodle."

"Jim is sexually attracted to Morgan?"

"Isn't everyone?" Boris asked with a laugh. "Not, mind you, because Morgan is the handsomest thing around. Which he very well may be. Not because he's a celebrity, or sexy. Which he is. Certainly not because he's the youngest stud you'll meet on any city block. Which he's not. But because, among other attractive qualities, he gives the illusion that he's so goddamned unattainable. And exclusivity can be a powerful aphrodisiac. Ask the snobs lined up to join the *Equus*."

"But it's merely illusion? His unattainability, I mean?"

"Why? Are you interested?" Boris asked, arching a brow quizzically and flashing a smile which he soon got under control. "*Do* forgive me!" he apologized with an irritating trace of heavily English-accented mockery. "I'm forever talking to queers and forgetting there are men out there who prefer women and get downright upset if anyone even hints at questioning their manhood."

"I'm not upset," Cord assured, wanting to convince himself as well as Boris. No matter his gnawing suspicion that he *was* somehow drawn to Morgan Kent; he refused to believe his attraction, though, was in anyway sexual.

"Too bad you're so straight," Boris observed, crossing his legs and leaning back, "because you, at least, *might* stand a chance with Morgan. If, of course, you were up to spending some heavy-workout time in a gym." Cord flushed, little pleased that his *slipped* physical condition was so easily noted by someone other than himself. "But poor Jim!" Boris bemoaned. "He could spend every day and night working out, and his musculature would still keep him short of Morgan's expectations. Jim's so small-boned, yes? Just like a sparrow."

"What about Rolin?"

"Jim's brother, Rolin, you mean?" Boris asked, his brown eyes lighting with apparent insight. "Ah, you mean Rolin and Morgan *doing the dirty-do,* don't you?" He didn't wait for confirmation.

"Well, who knows about those two?" he mused. "Rolin certainly has the appropriate build and looks, and Jim certainly thinks the two *have done it* together. This is one more reason why there's friction between brothers. Have you met Rolin?"

"He's flying in tomorrow."

"Is he now?" Boris asked. "Strange Jim didn't mention it. But, then, he knows I've always been turned on to Rolin myself. Alas, unlike Morgan, *I* usually end up having to settle for second or third best."

"If we could regress a moment," Cord requested, welcoming a chance to veer from the sexual.

"Why not?" Boris agreed. "Anything to help the police."

"It's about your motive or lack thereof."

"What about it?"

"You weren't apt to kill Horton because his largesse was keeping you financially afloat?"

"Sad but true."

"But at the time of his murder, he'd kicked you out of the gallery, saying that he never wanted to see you again."

"If you're confused, that's because you don't know how many times Horton has thrown me out with those very same words," Boris reasoned; oh, Cord knew all right; it was one of the reasons Boris wasn't in jail, right now, up on the murder charge. "We had these blowups whenever I came asking for money," Boris explained. "Horton always resisted but relented. When Jim entered the picture, *he* came around to mend fences. In fact, the day before Horton was killed, Jim stopped by to say how sorry Horton was for that last blow-up. As a peace offering, Horton even sent Jim with six bottles of vodka. This was why I was passed out right here when Horton was so horribly murdered."

CHAPTER THIRTEEN

ROLIN

"**EVEN IF I'D GONE TO BED WITH HIM,** I wouldn't tell you!" Rolin Holdsett guaranteed, pushing blond-blond hair leftward across his tanned forehead. Unlike his brother, he had the body of an athlete, muscles making his shirt and pants seem attractively second-skin.

"Why's that?" Cord asked, deciding Rolin *looked* butch, with a well-defined physique that appeared mighty good in clothes (and out?).

"Because Morgan isn't the type to appreciate kiss-and-tell tricks," Rolin said. "He doesn't blab about anyone's performance in bed and rightly figures he deserves the same courtesy."

"You haven't been to bed with him, though?"

"No," Rolin said. His hair flopped forward again, and he again pushed it to one side. "Isn't that what I already said?"

"From all I've heard, you certainly *seem* his type," Cord observed.

"Yeah? What type is that?" Rolin asked, immediately raising a hand to nullify the need for an answer. "Nah, don't tell me!" he insisted. "It sounds too much as if I'm fishing for compliments. Besides which, I always figured I was Morgan's type, too."

"But?"

"I think his keeping his distance had something to do with Horton," Rolin said. "I had a thing with Horton once, you know?"

"A *thing?*" Cord attempted to sound ignorant and nonjudgmental but came across as neither.

"He used to suck my cock," Rolin said, surprising Cord with his frankness. It was more of a jolt, coming from someone who looked so masculine when Jim, the androgynous brother, continually boasted of fucking pussy and beating up queers. "Even when Horton was no longer sucking my dick, I think Morgan steered clear, figuring Horton *might* exhibit residual jealousy," Rolin analyzed.

"And *would* Horton have gotten jealous?"

"Maybe," Rolin admitted. "Horton was funny that way. One of his casual tricks once put the make on Jim, and shit *really* hit the fan. At the time, though, Horton was gaga over some kid up in Canada, so you tell me why he got so frigging hot and bothered. Jealousy?"

"Was Horton sucking your brother's cock?" Cord asked, congratulating himself on the ease with which he got that out with nary a stumble. A mere few days before, he would have been blushing from head to toe at calling that particular spade a spade.

"You can ask me anything you want about *my* sex with Horton," Rolin said, "and I'll probably tell you. If only because I'm presuming you're not asking for prurient reasons but because you genuinely think my answers will somehow help you find Horton's killer." Cord wished even half the other people he'd interviewed would have had the smarts Rolin had in seeing that. "But don't," Rolin warned, "expect me to speak for Jim, or be equally candid about anyone else's sex life. What other people do in bed is their business; if they want to keep it their business, *that's* their business."

"Horton did have a tendency toward sexual involvement with the young men he brought to work at the gallery," Cord said, taking only a slightly different tack.

"Maybe he did, and maybe he didn't," Rolin said, not about to be sucked into that one. "I don't know what he did with anyone else. I do know what he did with me. He sucked my cock. And so what if he did? We were both above the age of consent at the time."

"Never anal sex?" Cord asked, marveling at how he got that question out with nary a sputter.

"Horton wasn't into anal sex," Rolin said. "He wasn't into getting sucked off, either. His shrink told him he'd never progressed beyond oral fixation, and who knows but that she was right?"

"And you let him suck you off because it was enjoyable?"

"Well, it was no hardship, let me tell you?" Rolin assured. "Horton was an expert at it, having put in a lot of practice."

"And that's all you got in return: sexual pleasure?"

"Surely you can ask a more direct question than that?" Rolin criticized with a condescending smirk. Obviously, Rolin was no dummy. Having spent so many years in one college or another, some smarts had to have rubbed off. "Why not just ask what I got for dropping my pants on occasion?"

"What did you get for dropping your pants on occasion?"

"Trips. To Europe three times. To New York more times than I can count. To New Orleans. To the Caribbean. Nice clothes, nice restaurants, interesting people. An education. Pretty good return for a bit of wear and tear on my dick, plus a few quarts of my cum, wouldn't you agree, especially for a kid from a family of twelve who didn't have too many prospects before Horton Lendland came into his life?"

"Just exactly how *did* he come into your life?"

"A guy by the name of Bobby Jordan introduced us. Bobby and I met while hanging around on First Avenue." Cord, who had worked vice, didn't have to ask what Bobby and Rolin were likely doing on First Avenue. "Bobby said he'd introduce me to a guy who would make standing on street corners seem like picking up chicken feed," Rolin elucidated.

"Bobby didn't happen to tell you why he was doing you this favor, did he?"

"He and Horton were making it. I wouldn't tell you that, except Bobby and Horton's relationship was never a big secret, neither of them hiding it. Nor was it a secret that Horton wanted sex more often than Bobby was in the mood to give it. As a result, Bobby pimped to get himself off the hook."

"And after you and Horton made it, he offered you a job at the gallery?"

"Yeah. And I was always showing up in shorts and a T-shirt, when Horton wanted me dolled up in a suit. He bought me three suits, and I never wore any of them more than once. I gave them to Jim. Jim was the kind of guy Horton needed all along. Me, I'm too easy going. Like my father. Jim takes after mom. Her aggressiveness. Her looks."

"So, you introduced your brother to Horton?" Cord was careful not to use the verb *pimped*.

"Horton was looking for someone to take charge. I couldn't. I saw, right off, that Jim was more qualified than I was."

Cord didn't ask how Rolin knew Horton would find Jim suitable, considering the different physical types of the two brothers. Likely, Rolin, like Cord, found out early that Horton's tastes were definitely smorgasbord compared to Morgan Kent's more selective gourmet appetite. As long as a guy didn't look half bad and had a cock, the bigger the better, Horton was apparently interested.

"So, Jim took over the gallery, and you went off to school?"

"Right."

"Tuition paid by the gallery?"

"Right again."

"Jim putting up no objections?"

"Oh, my brother bitched a lot," Rolin admitted. "Down deep, he's more of a miser than Scrooge ever was. But I'd helped him, hadn't I, giving him his big break? He knew an obligation when he saw one. Besides, Horton was all for it, always ready to be generous to past tricks. He liked to think he was elevating us to higher plains, giving us a chance to come out of nowhere, like he did, and make something of ourselves, like he did. I certainly wouldn't have come this far without his backing and blowing. And look at Jim. When he started out at the gallery, he was just a wise-ass little prick making his pocket money by peddling dope to fellow teeny-boppers."

"Dope?"

"Purely penny-ante stuff," Rolin assured. "He grew some weed and then cut it with so much oregano it was more suited for cooking than for smoking."

"What about Bobby Jordan?" Cord asked. To make the question clearer, he added, "Rumor is that he's into hard drugs."

"You'll have to ask Bobby," Rolin parried. "I was never into anything heavier than smoking my brother's oregano."

"Horton into dope?"

"Not that I know of, and I seriously doubt that he was. He wasn't that experimental in anything, unless someone was leading him around by the nose. And only a few people ever managed to do that. Come to think of it, he might have snorted a couple of lines with a weight-lifter, Grey Matthews. Then, again, probably not. *Said* he snorted a couple of lines, is more like it. He never had sex unless it was to suck cock. He never ate anything more adventuresome than meat and potatoes. Once our cruise ship docked in Piraeus, but Horton didn't get off to go the few miles to the Acropolis. He later just *said* he went to the Acropolis."

"Did you know Grey Matthews died while mainlining cocaine?"

"I heard he died," Rolin confirmed. "Heard it was drug-related, but no specifics."

"Do you have any idea where I can reach Bobby Jordan?"

"Not now. Not ever. Bobby was always here today, gone tomorrow. The only time I ever had a clue was when I worked at the gallery. Whenever he'd get back into town, he'd start calling and, then, hang up without saying a word. That was usually our official notice that he'd been showing up in person in a few days. Usually to buy Horton lunch."

"Bobby did the buying?"

"No one had any staying power with Horton if they didn't put out with more than just hard cock on occasion," Rolin said. "It was

98

part of Horton's game plan; if you caught on, you got bonus points. I guess it helped him to believe his relationships were more than just one-sided *dirty-old-man-wants-to-suck-young-boys'-cocks* affairs. You'd be surprised by how many gifts he got from his tricks. Some downright expensive. Undoubtedly ripped off poor suckers mugged in dark alleys, but expensive nevertheless. A Dunhill lighter. Gold rings. A classical Greek coin. Hell, even the spear that killed him. Of course, the givers always got back ten times more than they gave. It was the *thought* that counted, although the more costly the thought, the greater the rewards."

"Was Morgan Kent a good game player?"

"Morgan? Why?"

"He had exceptional staying power in Lendland's circle of friends."

"Yeah, he did, didn't he?"

"Because Horton sucked his cock?" Cord suggested.

"I doubt it," Rolin said.

"Well, that was *my* suggestion. Why don't you tell me yours?"

"*Morgan* made *Horton* feel like the hustler," Rolin said. "That's the way I figure it."

"You mean, *Morgan* sucked *Horton's* cock?"

"Sweet Jesus!" Rolin exclaimed, his blue eyes sparkling amid the deeply masculine rumble of his full-bodied laugh. "If you can picture Morgan sucking Horton's cock, you've more imagination than I do," he said, shaking his head.

"So, why don't you explain what you *do* mean?"

"Well, what if Horton always picked up kids from the street because he secretly wanted to be picked up himself? What if he took them on trips, bought them clothes and expensive gifts because he secretly wanted someone to take *him* on trips, buy *him* clothes and expensive gifts? What if he introduced street kids to new environments because *he* secretly wanted to be introduced to new environments?"

"Morgan introduced him to new environments?"

"Let me tell you a little story my brother told me about Horton getting restless and wanting to go to Canada, Horton always heading for Vancouver whenever he felt restless. He knew a lot of the street people up there, and he had a thing going with one of them at the time. Anyway, he asked Morgan to go with him, saying the gallery would foot the bill. As an extra incentive, he booked them into *The Mandarin*, purely for Morgan's benefit. Horton came from a middle-class background and, while he was generous on some fronts, he preferred less expensive hotels. As it turned out, the room at *The*

Mandarin was as small as it was expensive. So small, even Horton's street friend, who was supposed to be impressed by the address, commented on its niggardly size. So, *Morgan* trotted down to the front desk, without asking Horton, and booked them all into the Orchid Suite *and*, most importantly here, paid the three-day bill in advance. No way would Horton have ever paid out fifteen hundred dollars a day for a hotel room! On the other hand, he'd always *wanted* to stay in a suite with two bedrooms, three bathrooms, two Jacuzzis, two bars, a kitchen, a formal dining room, a plush living room, a stupendous balcony. He always *wanted* a hotel manager personally to escort him to his room, complimentary champagne and chocolates, guest privileges at *Richard's on Richards*. He's always *wanted* clerks, waitresses, bellmen, doormen, and the concierge saying, *Hello, Mr. Lendland. How are you today, Mr. Lendland? Enjoying your stay, Mr. Lendland?* Morgan made that all happen for him. What's more, he did it without even asking Horton. He took charge completely, and Horton was usually the one who *had* to take charge in his relationships, and not because he always wanted to. And you wonder why Morgan had such staying power. Who wants to lose someone who intuitively knows what you want and, nine times out of ten, gives it to you?"

"The tenth time being sex?" Morgan injected.

"When I was attending *Columbia,* Horton and Morgan came to New York for a week," Rolin said. Apparently undaunted by the interruption, he'd easily made the transition. "We went to this place where you watched naked boys dance on the stage and, then, went off to a side room to join them for cookies and punch."

"Cookies and punch?" Cord asked incredulously, unable to help himself.

"Literally," Rolin assured with a wide smile that revealed white and perfect teeth. "Of course, no one touched the food for fear of ptomaine. It was merely there as the excuse for getting the prospective clients together with the naked dancers who, for one hundred dollars a pop, would go home with you for an evening. Needless to say, Horton would never have paid one hundred dollars for a male prostitute. Not cash on the barrel head, anyway. He didn't operate that way. If he usually ended up putting out more on even a common street kid, after he'd wined and dined him, that was okay. As much as Horton might have been turned on by this one particular dancer, it would have gotten no farther than that if Morgan hadn't calmly pulled out a hundred dollar bill and settled the matter, right then and there. Horton got his prostitute."

"And Morgan got one, too?"

"No way, and I *would* have known," Rolin assured, "because we all went directly back to the hotel. Horton and the kid went into one bedroom, Morgan went into the other, and I slept on the couch in the sitting room. I'm a light sleeper, and Morgan slept alone, unless he brought someone up the side of the building. This chocked up all kinds of points with Horton, because it gave the impression that Morgan was only concerned with Horton's welfare, that Morgan's sole purpose for coming had been to assure *Horton* had fun. Powerful stuff: that kind of attention! Ask any Japanese man who relishes the nonsexual services of a geisha."

"And what was Morgan getting out of this?" Cord wanted to know. At least a geisha got money. It sounded as if Morgan was the only one putting out the personal service *and* the cash.

"Ask most people, and they'll say *social connections*. He certainly got those, manipulating them to far better advantage than Horton ever did. But if you want to see even more tangible evidence, take a look at Morgan's extensive collection of Northwest art. I don't just mean the stuff in his penthouse, either. There are other pieces on loan to several museums, in the States and abroad: Tobys, Callahans, Horiuchis, Morrises, Havases, *you-name-the-Northwest-artist*; and all the pieces are the best money can buy. There are even more in storage, and Horton got them all for Morgan at bargain prices, seldom even bothering to add the gallery's commission on the sales, much to Jim's chagrin, although Jim's not apt to admit *that* now that Morgan's holding the purse strings."

"What exactly is your opinion of your brother and Morgan's present business relationship?"

"Why should my opinion be of interest?"

"I suppose it's a matter of perspective," Cord said. "Not all that long ago, I asked your brother about Morgan and him, and he said he was sure Morgan didn't like him and never had. Suddenly, though, Morgan is financing the *Holdsett Gallery*. I'm trying to understand."

"And understanding is going to help you find whomever killed Horton?" Rolin asked dubiously.

"Until I, or someone else, put all the pieces together, who's to say?"

"Mmmmm," Rolin hummed, as if he weren't quite convinced. He ran his fingers through silky hair that caught the light and held it. Cord watched, fascinated as razor-cut strands fell, one after the other, back into place. "For Morgan, I'm sure the relationship is purely business," Rolin said finally. "He's a smart businessman, and he's quick to see Jim's potential. Let's face it, Jim's run the gallery at a profit for years, Horton merely a figurehead. From my brother's standpoint, it's business, too, Morgan offering the money Jim needs for opportunities lost when Horton died. Unfortunately, Jim may be hoping for more."

"Unfortunately?"

Suddenly, Rolin looked very much as if he were in water deeper than was comfortable to tread. He folded his arms over his well-developed chest, a posture Cord had come to recognize as a *the-wall-is-going-up* signal. "For someone struggling to make heads or tails out of his sexuality, my brother really should give Morgan Kent a wide berth," Rolin said. "At least in this one man's humble opinion. Morgan has no patience for those less sure of themselves than he is."

CHAPTER FOURTEEN

CORD

THERE WERE WAYS to rationalize what Cord had done. He applied them as he washed most of the evidence down the drain, cleaned the remainder off his cock and fingers, and washed his hands. His cheeks remained attractively flushed, as did a *V* extending from the top of his chest to a point just above his sexily knotted navel.

For one, he was no longer going with Cheryl and had been getting less sex than he'd become used to. For two, he'd been the casual pickup route (there were always cop groupies at *The Galloping Pig,* a popular law-enforcement hangout), but casual sex had never really been his bag. Which made any quickie with a prostitute less an attractive alternative than for some cops. Jack Sudlow, after two unsuccessful marriages, swore that uninvolved sex with a hooker was the *only* way to go. Cord didn't agree.

Finally, Morgan Kent's *Glenda's Forbidden Daddy* had been a very sexy read. Granted, its incestuous theme and accompanying aspects of female degradation were disturbing, but it was all pure fantasy, and fantasy seldom—if ever—hurt anybody.

Cord checked his reflection in the mirror, consciously sucking in his gut to minimize the circumference of his midsection. He still didn't like *the love-handles-materialized-out-of-nowhere*, or the *once-scalloped-but-no-more* abdominals which now portrayed non-delineated smoothness. He really *did* need a few days in a gym.

He turned off the bathroom light and padded barefoot and naked across the carpet to his bed. The bedsprings squeaked protest beneath his weight, yet another reminder that he was carrying around more excess poundage than he cared to.

He reached for *Glenda's Forbidden Daddy*, critically eyeing the lascivious cover graphic that portrayed Glenda, a supposedly Lolita-like teenager nymph, dressed in black-lace panties, black-lace bra, black stiletto-heeled shoes, black stockings, and a black garter belt.

Did women still wear garter belts in the current age of panty hose? Did teenage girls even know what a garter belt was? The getup was obviously for the titillation and enjoyment of the rather plump and balding older man (who else but Glenda's father?) who was stripped down to his underclothes and was unabashedly leering on the cover with her.

In present retrospect, Cord couldn't understand how he'd allowed himself to get turned on by pure porn held together by a plot so thin as to be nonexistent. His passion spent, embarrassed by having beaten his dick off over the sink like a horny schoolboy, he tossed the offending paperback into a far corner, missing the wastepaper basket for which he'd aimed. So much for an aging fat man's coordination!

He did know one thing that wasn't two: there were no clitorises misplaced on any of that book's 160 pages of smut. Morgan Kent had lovingly detailed each and every one with anatomical precision. And Gary Green was wrong on another point, too, because there seemed little doubt, at least in Cord's mind, that the author knew far more about fucking women than could have been fantasized or picked up from locker-room conversations. No virgin at fucking cunt could have convinced jaded readers, let alone convinced Cord, that they were reading the genuine stuff. Not for as long as Morgan had managed it.

Cord stretched for *Chained Male* on the nightstand. It and *Glenda's Forbidden Daddy* were autographed copies borrowed from Steve Footer's private collection.

Five minutes into the book, and five pages into an obscenely grisly fist-fuck, Cord laid the book aside in disgust not only for the author of such perverted garbage, not only for the readers who regularly bought such filth, but for himself having unbelievably regained his erection during the reading. There was no way, after the relief he'd found in the bathroom but minutes before, that he should be hard again. For him, quick penile resurrections were relegated to a distant past when boners and sex had been new and exciting. At twenty-six, he was an old hand at fucking, and he was certainly no virgin to become so turned on by *forbidden reading* smuggled into the privacy of his bedroom.

He tossed the book to join the other, this time making a perfect dunk-shot into the wastepaper basket without even trying. Witnessing the complete disappearance of the offending book into the garbage, exactly where it belonged, gave Cord an immensely pleasurable feeling.

He turned off the bedside light, scooted deeper beneath the lone sheet covering his body, and tried to deal with an erection that wouldn't go away. There was one sure way to take care of it, but it wasn't a viable alternative. It was one thing jacking off like a damned adolescent because of some old man screwing his nubile young daughter in the pages of a straight fuck book, quite another to beat off after reading how some muscle man was taking another stud's fist and arm up his rectum. Masturbation now would insinuate something about Cord's psyche that he wasn't about to concede. If just because it wasn't true.

He folded his hands behind his head to get them out of temptation's way. He ceased all movement, because even the slightest shift of his body against the overlying sheet increased his awareness of the phenomenon he was trying his damnedest to ignore.

Morgan Kent had to be sick! *Really* sick! Who else but a sick person could have pumped out as much pornographic crap as Morgan had? Over 150 of the disgusting books, each filled to the brim with 160 pages of downright perversion: daughters fucked by fathers, sisters fucked by brothers, brothers fucked by brothers, asses fucked by fists, women fucked by dogs; crocodiles and at least one goat fucked by men. How many of those rich socialites at the *Equus,* thinking it was so chic to be hobnobbing with an ex-porno writer, had ever sat down and taken the time to read any of Morgan's literary contributions from before the time he graduated into publishing big time? Cord shuddered, disappointed when the chilling was less than ardor-dampening.

What made Morgan Kent tick? Somehow the answer had become almost as important to Cord as who killed Horton Lendland, and that realization wasn't one Cord easily endured. He particularly didn't savor the idea that he'd somehow become just another piece of human flotsam or jetsam caught up in the mad whirl round Morgan. Cord wasn't a queer hot for Morgan's body. He wasn't a jaded old fart out to explore new environments. He wasn't a masochist who got his jollies off by being mind-fucked by a bastard who thrived on sadistic games. He was a cop out to solve a murder, and Morgan should have been *just* another suspect.

What Cord wanted to do was fall asleep. Asleep, it would hardly matter whether his cock was hard or soft. At the moment, it was hard, and *that* mattered. What mattered even more was his almost uncontrollable urge to take hold of his hard prick and beat it to climax, knowing there was a box of Kleenex underneath the bed to take care of the resulting mess. He wouldn't even have to go to the bathroom. Afterwards, he could get the badly needed rest he wasn't getting nearly enough of these last few days.

It wasn't as if he hadn't had more than his share of hard-ons lately, which he attributed entirely to his separation from Cheryl. Usually, however, he successfully ignored them. God knew, he had enough other things to occupy his mind and time. That he hadn't given in to frequent masturbation, with the exception of this evening's excuse given by reading the straight fuck book, was because of the nature of the Horton Lendland murder case. Cord didn't want to become confused by associating his involvement with queers with even self-induced pleasure. Granted, he had greater faith in himself than such paranoiac behavior indicated, but it was better to be safe than sorry.

The phone rang. Thank God for the phone!

"Maxwell here!" he answered into the mouthpiece, listening before assuring his caller he'd be right there.

He hung up and hurriedly dressed. He had difficulty zipping up his pants, but that was only because not even the news that Bobby Jordan had been found murdered was negative-enough stimulus to make his cock lose its painful erection.

CHAPTER FIFTEEN

JACK

"WELL, THE CALL CAME in while we were checking out the guys who were cruising the ladies and gentlemen of the night on Pike Street," Jack said. "We were the closest unit, so...."

"Lab boys finished?" Cord asked, nodding greetings to officers on all sides.

"Not yet, but you can take a look."

"Right," Cord agreed, steeling himself for the chore. No matter how many dead bodies he saw, he never got used to it, especially the ones that had resulted from violent deaths, especially the young ones. Twenty-one, old in street terms, *should* have been mere beginning.

"Doesn't take a genius to take one and one to make the two for this one, does it?" Jack observed. Bobby Jordan was bound, hand and foot, blindfolded and gagged. He'd been blown away by a bullet to the base of his skull.

"An execution," Cord said, more to himself than to Jack who wouldn't have needed any such obvious edification.

"Oh, it was that, all right," Jack agreed; no bones about it. "Drug-related. And, what's more, we've a witness to prove it."

"A witness?"

"Seems Bobby boy was shacked up here with another young hustler," Jack assured. "Kid by the name of Timmy Dean, rhymes with *Jimmy Dean*. You know, like the sausage? Only fourteen, *our* Timmy Dean, and he has a series of arrests as long as your arm: loitering, prostitution, possession, petty theft...you name it. His old man turned up missing about four years ago. His mother is serving time in the Gig Harbor lock-up for extortion. Foster parents, a long line of, keep throwing in the towel."

"And he *saw* the killing?"

"Sat right over there," Jack said and motioned toward a chair by the door. "Tied and gagged but *not* blindfolded. They didn't plug his ears either. *Hear and see* was the name of their game. They wanted it to go down as nothing else but what it was: punishment for sticky fingers, Bobby having played drug courier for quite some time. Our key witness remains a little vague on the specifics. Not that I can blame him. You can bet you ass he was promised a little something by way of retribution should he remember more than he was supposed to."

"How many in the goon squad?"

"Two, probably pros brought into and already out of our area. No one saw them enter or exit the building. No sign of a struggle. A silencer kept the noise down. The rope you can buy in any Seattle hardware store but was probably brought in from out of town, too."

"Descriptions?"

"Business suits, full head hoods, gloves. Think that's good enough for an A-1 All Points Bulletin?" Cord knew it wasn't.

"What exactly did they say?" Cord asked.

"We've some people back at the station trying their damnedest to help Timmy Dean remember."

"I'm surprised the Captain could spare anybody," Cord said facetiously. "This reminds me: congratulations on lucking out on that Hefty-bagged woman. Someone told me there's a similar M.O. in Portland."

"Right!" Jack confirmed. "Wasn't that *just* luck, too?" Before the press had gotten wind of the latest corpse in Seattle, someone in Portland had remembered a similar case of a Hefty-bagged corpse down there. Cord had been too busy to get all of the specifics, but some Portland housewife had apparently been killed and bagged before Seattle's *Dint Slough* killer had even dumped his first body. Anyway, the Portland woman and a girlfriend (still missing), had disappeared while grocery shopping. Neither had had a record of prostitution, not even the suburban variety, leading to the conclusion that the Seattle corpse, when identified, wasn't apt to be a whore, either. Besides, the Seattle woman had been a long-time dead, compared to the ladies of the night being dropped off by the *Dint Slough* killer. And, it was still the *Dint Slough* killings monopolizing the public's attention and the police's time. The *baggie* murders, numbering an insignificant two by comparison, one of those in Portland, relegated to the back burner. After all, there was no reason to suspect the *baggie* killer was still in the area. From Portland to Seattle to *God-only-knew-where-by-now!* The *Dint Slough* killer, on the other hand....

Cord returned his attention to the case at hand. If he would have rather been back on the *Dint Slough* task force, or even investigating the *baggie murders*, he was stuck with the Horton Lendland killing (and the Bobby Jordan murder—*if related*), for better or worse. "What kind of drugs are we talking?" he asked.

"Coke. Bobby's little friend said they'd been snorting a few lines of the misbegotten gains just before the execution went down. Found a couple of bags, plus some grass, in a dresser drawer. Both top-quality."

"I would have given anything for ten minutes with him before they killed him."

"You figure this is tied with Horton Lendland's murder?"

"Not exactly the same M.O., is it?" Cord argued. "Doesn't fit the way the lawyer and that other hustler bought it, either."

"Wouldn't it wrap things up nicely, though, if that's Horton Lendland's killer right there, dead and gone?" Jack asked, nodding toward the body being strapped to a gurney for transport to the morgue. "Think of the taxpayers' money saved by your killer having been taken out by a couple of his own kind."

"Yeah," Cord agreed. However, he didn't believe in miracles, especially that one.

CHAPTER SIXTEEN

Timmy

"I'VE GONE OVER IT a thousand times," Timmy Dean bemoaned. He looked ragged around the edges. What's more, he looked familiar. The kid in the can with Cord at Alki?

"Your other tellings of the tale were for *them*," Cord explained, referencing the two officers who were leaving the room. "This time, it's for *me*."

"Jesus!" Timmy exhaled in seeming helplessness. "What a fucking mess!"

This wasn't the kid in the restroom at Alki: just as young but more handsome. "Murder is never pleasant," Cord assured. "So, why don't you go back to the beginning and start there?"

"Where in the hell is the beginning?" Timmy wanted to know.

"How about your first meeting with Bobby Jordan?" Cord suggested.

Timmy eyed him warily. "Maybe I need a lawyer?" *he* suggested.

"That's your right," Cord agreed. "However, you're hardly our prime suspect, since you were bound and gagged at the time of the murder."

"Right."

"You have any idea who called the police?"

"All I know is that one of the guys...."

"One of the *killers?*" Cord interrupted.

"Right. He said I shouldn't worry; there'd be someone around before I died of fright, thirst, or starvation."

"Describe the man who said that."

"Again?" Timmy protested.

"Please," Cord cajoled.

"Tall," Timmy said.

"How tall?" Cord pressed.

110

"Maybe six-feet. Maybe more. Both of them were taller than Bobby, and Bobby was five-eleven."

Actually, Bobby would measure out, at the morgue, at a little above five-ten. "How much taller?" Cord asked, "An inch? Two inches?"

"The blond guy had to be *at least* six-feet, the dark-haired guy only a tad shorter."

"How do you know the colors of their hair?" Cord asked. They'd supposedly worn full-head masks and gloves.

"Eyebrows and lashes," Timmy said. "The masks had big eye holes."

"How about eye color?"

"Blue and brown, except it was the blond with the brown eyes."

"Other distinguishing features or marks?"

"Gloves and masks. That's about it."

"How about voices?"

"What about them?"

"Would you recognize them?"

"They didn't say much."

"It was my understanding they said plenty," Cord begged to differ.

"About my *spreading the good word to other greedy punks with sticky fingers?*"

"Right!"

"That was all prerecorded," Timmy said. "On one of those small pocket-size recorders the blond had. It came out sounding like Alvin the Chipmunk. Same thing when I was told to expect rescue: that from the recorder, too. Otherwise, it was all grunts; but, believe me, I had no difficulty getting the gist."

"So, which one pulled the trigger?"

"The blond."

"Was he nervous?"

"He was as cool as a cucumber, as if he blew people away every day of the year." Timmy shivered.

"And Bobby was killed because he short-changed somebody in the drug department?"

"That was the message. Loud and clear."

"There was no indication he was killed for some *other* reason?"

"Like what?"

"Oh, I don't know," Cord admitted. "Make a guess."

"All I know is what they said," Timmy assured. With a leftward sweep of his right hand, he rearranged the blond hair banging his forehead. Who else did that *hair-thing*? Rolin Holdsett, that's who.

"*Had* Bobby short-changed anyone?"

"He said *no*. He said they *should talk about it*."

"What else did he say?"

"Nothing else. They gagged him."

"And you?"

"I was already gagged by then and trussed up like the bottom man in an S&M session. I was doing no talking, too busy pissing my pants." Timmy wasn't talking figuratively, either.

"You mention S&M," Cord probed. "Did any of this come across with sexual undertones?"

"You shitting me?" Timmy asked. If he wasn't surprised by that suggestion, he was certainly playing the part damned well. "Some guys may get their jollies by S&M game-playing, but *these* dudes were all business."

"How about their guns?"

"Handguns. Other than that, what do I know about guns?"

"Aside from these having had silencers, you mean?"

"I've seen enough TV to know a silencer when I see one. Besides, there was no more noise than the opening of a champagne bottle, maybe even less."

"The guns weren't *Lugers*, though," Cord persisted. "You've seen enough TV to know a *Luger* when you see one, haven't you?"

"They weren't *Lugers*."

"How about revolvers?" Cord queried. "Did the guns take bullets in a chamber, or were they fed by clips?"

"God, ask your people!" Timmy insisted. "They've got the damned bullet, don't they?"

Cord had already asked ballistics. What he was doing now was checking Timmy's powers of observation and memory. A lot of people blacked out in a crisis. Also, Cord wanted to catch signs of lying. If Timmy lied about the little things…. "So, let's backtrack to your first meeting with Bobby."

"You want a timetable, I can't give it to you," Timmy said. "I knew who and what Bobby was long before I ever met him."

"And just who and what was he?"

"Bobby Jordan: another face and body on the street," Timmy said.

"Another *cock* on the street, don't you mean?" Cord suggested.

"Yeah," Timmy agreed without batting an eye. "A big cock it was, too"

"Bobby was your competition, then?"

"Right."

"But he was twenty-one, wasn't he? Twenty-one is kind of *over the-hill* in your business, isn't it?"

"I didn't know how old he was."

"Surely, you made a guess," Cord insisted. "Surely, there had to have been talk."

"Twenty-one or not, Bobby was doing pretty well for himself," Timmy argued. "Some of us *chicken* should have been so lucky at turning as many tricks."

"A lot of johns used Bobby's services, did they?"

"With Bobby, it was quality rather than quantity," Timmy explained.

How do you mean?"

"For one, he had an open-end marriage with John Berd."

"Owner of *The Playground*?"

"One and the same and, admittedly, quite a catch."

"By open-end marriage, you mean…?" Cord paused, waiting for Timmy to fill in the blank. This he did.

"John gave Bobby spending money, food, a place to crash when he needed it, free booze. Bobby gave John occasional good sex. Anyway, I guess it was good. Rumor had it that John put up with a helluva lot to get it."

"Like Bobby playing house with you?"

"Wrong, smart-ass cop!" Timmy disagreed, less the frightened mouse, more the street-wise smart punk.

"Okay, what *did* you mean?" Cord asked, prepared to give the benefit of the doubt.

"John didn't give a fuck that Bobby screwed on the side. That was part of their *arrangement*."

"So, John didn't care Bobby was fucking you *and* Horton Lendland?"

"Me and who?" Timmy asked, having waited too long to sound genuinely spontaneous.

"Come on, Timmy!" Cord encouraged. "Bobby must have mentioned Lendland."

"Lendland was that barbecued gallery owner with the pole rammed up his ass, wasn't he?"

"Actually, it was a spear," Cord corrected.

"Whatever," Timmy waved off. "You think there's a connection?"

Cord would give a week's pay to be handed one. "Horton and Bobby were lovers. They were gay. They were murdered," Cord pointed out. Not the connections Cord wanted, but they'd have to

113

do. "They snorted coke," he added as an afterthought and watched Timmy's reaction. "They *did* snort coke, did they not?"

"Maybe you've got a different source than I do," Timmy said.

"Maybe I do," Cord agreed. "Was your source Bobby?"

"You think Bobby and I spent our time talking about his other tricks?" Timmy asked, sounding defensive." We had better things to do."

It was time to put the little prick back in his place. What Cord wanted were answers not conversation. "*Better things* being co-caine?" he suggested. That would get his message across. "You know, there were a couple bags of the stuff left at the murder scene. Was it yours?"

"Bobby's!" Timmy countered quickly getting the message.

"A controlled substance," Cord emphasized. The little bastard might as well know where he stood, or, at least, where Cord could put him. "And you've been picked up for possession before, haven't you, Timmy?"

"*Just* a little grass," Timmy protested.

"*Just* a little grass?" Cord echoed, but made it a question. With facts and figures at his fingertips, he didn't have to take Timmy's word for a goddamned thing, and the kid knew it.

"Okay, some pills," Timmy admitted. "Some uppers and down-ers. No hard stuff."

"Well, there's always a first time," Cord said. "It's the grass and the pills that lead down the merry road to the hard stuff, isn't it? Maybe you took that road."

"Look, Bobby got blown away because he was helping himself, didn't he?" Timmy argued. "You think he needed me to supply him?"

"I'm pointing out alternatives, here," Cord said. "You were found with a dead man and some high-quality coke. You and the dead man were snorting prior to the murder."

"I was tied and gagged when Bobby bought the farm," Timmy reminded.

"So you say," Cord agreed. "However, certain aspects of this case would behoove you to cooperate."

"Who says I'm *not* cooperating?"

"Certainly not I," Cord protested, all innocence. "Especially since you were telling me about Bobby and Horton Lendland, weren't you?"

"Bobby didn't kill Lendland," Timmy said.

"You were there when that murder occurred, too, were you?" Cord asked facetiously.

"Hell, no!" Timmy denied.

"Then, you couldn't know if Bobby did or didn't do it, could you? That is, unless...."

"Unless what?" Timmy fed into the pause.

"Unless you and Bobby were having fun and snorting coke the night of Lendland's murder, too. Were you?"

Timmy seemed seriously to consider his reply. "No," he admitted finally.

"Where were you the night of Lendland's murder?"

"I never even met the man!" Timmy complained.

"Which doesn't answer my question, does it?" Cord reminded.

"Look, I could have lied and said I was with Bobby, right?" Timmy reasoned. "Bobby's dead and isn't about to say otherwise."

"This is all leading to an answer to my original question?" Cord asked with evident impatience.

"I was walking the streets, like every other night," Timmy said. "You want the names of the guys I went down on, or who went down on me? Hell, I can't even remember their faces."

"Did Bobby ever tell you where *he* was the night of Lendland's murder?"

"He said he was walking the streets, too."

"Here in Seattle?"

"Yeah. He'd been back a few days when Lendland was killed."

"Back from where?"

"Los Angeles. He'd go there regularly on business."

"On *drug* business?"

"He never went into details," Timmy said. "Really."

"When he got back from these business trips to Los Angeles, he had a few bucks to spend, did he? Maybe a few bags of top-grade coke to snort?"

"Maybe."

"I'm not after *maybes,* hotshot!" Cord warned. "I want definite *yeses* or *noses.*"

"Bobby *always* had plenty of cash. I already told you that John Berd gave him an allowance."

"And coke? What about Bobby's cocaine supply? Did John Berd give him that, too?"

"I don't know. I *only* know he always seemed to have plenty of it."

"So much of it, in fact, that it was common knowledge he was a courier, right?"

"I don't know about that," Timmy denied, his eyes sparking the fear found in those who'd witnessed a tragedy in which they could yet become another victim. "All I know is that the two guys who killed him seemed to think he'd had access and had taken advantage. Bobby and I never discussed any business but selling our cocks."

"You *did* discuss his relationship with Horton Lendland, though?" Cord said. It was a good time to make the transition. It was doubtful anyone was getting anything out of Timmy about Bobby's drug dealings, even if the kid *did* know something. Leaving behind a witness to put out the word that *skimming* had its consequences was one thing, but leaving behind someone who would likely really complicate matters by *telling all* was another thing altogether.

"Bobby had a love-hate relationship with Horton Lendland," Timmy said, obviously glad to be off the subject of drugs. "I always suspected it was more love than the other."

"Why?"

Timmy shrugged, appearing on shaky ground. "Bobby always had nice things to say about Lendland, you know? How Horton *tried* to save him. How Horton persuaded him to see a shrink. How Horton gave him a job at the gallery. How Horton cared. Things like that."

"So, where did the hate come into it?"

"Horton sucked Bobby's cock, and Bobby hated anyone who used him *like that*."

"But cock was what Bobby was selling, wasn't it?"

"Jesus, ask his shrink," Timmy pleaded. "We're all of us, on the streets, a little fucked up. Bobby was possibly more fucked up than most of us. I couldn't make heads or tails out of it."

Cord had all intentions of talking to Doctor Ellen Riley once again. She might rave on about doctor-patient confidentiality, but Bobby Jordan was beyond caring. If Riley gave him static, Cord would subpoena her ass *and* her records. "Do you know anything about Bobby calling Horton the week prior to Horton's murder?"

"Bobby called him a couple of times from the hotel," Timmy admitted.

"Did you overhear any conversations?"

"He never seemed to get through."

"You mean, he never said anything during these phone calls?"

"Isn't that what I said?"

It wasn't what he'd said, but Cord wasn't about to go into semantics. "So, why don't you explain what you and Bobby had going if he was so involved with John Berd *and* Horton Lendland?"

"I was just a little fun on the side," Timmy admitted.

"Who paid whom for this fun?" Cord wanted to know.

"I don't know what you mean."

"Two hustlers, each selling cock for a living, get together for a bit of fun and games. We talking busmen's holiday?"

"Bobby had a hang-up about getting old," Timmy said. "A lot of gays have it, but it's worse when you're out on the street. How old did you say he was?"

"Twenty-one."

"He *said* he was eighteen," Timmy said with a shake of his head. "I guessed nineteen, maybe twenty."

"Well, he was twenty-one, going on a hundred, and he isn't going to get any older now," Cord confirmed. "But while he was alive, he had this thing about making it with hustlers younger than he was, like you. It made him feel young. Right?"

"Right."

"But it didn't really work for him unless he was doing *it* with you for free. Because any old, broken-down faggot can take even the youngest hustler home for a price. Right?"

"I suspect it was something like that, yes."

"And since everyone knows all prostitutes, male and female, have hearts of gold, you said, *Hey, I'll help poor old Bobby through his mid-life crisis by giving him a few freebies.* Is that how it was?"

"I suppose."

"Nah; that isn't how it went at all, is it, Timmy?" Cord contradicted. "Bobby might not have paid in cold cash—" Anymore than Horton Lendland would have put out $100 in cash for that New York hustler. "—but Bobby *did* pay." Just as Horton Lendland never counted the gifts, the dinners, or the trips as payments in full. "He paid by the cum-dripping coke-snowy spoonful, didn't he?"

CHAPTER SEVENTEEN

SHARON

SHARON TAYLOR GROANED. Cord almost missed hearing it, distracted as he was by the resounding smack of English cane against hard *English-public-schoolboy* ass again up on the theater screen.

Sharon had obviously fucked in a theater seat before, her contortions down to a science, including her using the arms of the seat as fulcrums to lift her rhythmically and sit her back down.

Cord was required to do nothing but remain motionless beneath the riding of her cunt over his cock. He *had* ventured his hands up her blouse, his palms dented by the hardness of her nipples. "Easy," he instructed. It had been a long time since he'd had sex other than masturbation, and he was already hovering on the brink of orgasm. What perverse coincidence, though, coordinated his raging surge of pleasure with this particular part of the movie *Another Country*? Certainly, it couldn't have been planned. Cord couldn't have known this point would be reached just when the main character of the movie, an English gay, was getting his ass caned. Or could he? Cord had seen the movie often enough to know what followed what. He was familiar enough with his body, too, to have estimated, albeit subconsciously, how long it would take for the theater manager to get him off. And Sharon hadn't made her move until she'd been perfectly clear of his invitation.

"Feels good," Sharon whispered, punctuating with another moan. She dropped her head forward, her blonde hair cascading over her face. Her ass gave a sensuous torque against Cord's open zipper.

On the screen, the actor's ass was hit again; Cord responded with a shiver that fed his inner fires rather than quenched them.

He should have fucked Sharon *before* the movie. Even *after* the movie. Not *during* the movie. Not when his watching the film invariably cemented what was happening on the screen with what was happening in the almost deserted theater. Some guy getting his ass whacked shouldn't have added a sexual element inseparable from Cord's fucking. Since it did, this simple guy-fucking-gal sex became less normal than it might have been under different circumstances. If Cord could stop, if he hadn't committed himself too far to pull back or pull out, now, he would have aborted. Knowing he was a helpless puppet of the moment didn't ease the horror with which he must face the ramifications when it was all over and done.

"I'm close," he warned, burrowing his lips against the back of Sharon's neck. She smelled of lilies and female perspiration.

Cord had lost track of how many times the length of cane had connected loudly with the bruised buttocks on the screen, but he might still go off exactly when the last whack resounded from the sound track.

"Yes, yes," Sharon encouraged. Cord thought he'd already counted her having had orgasms twice. Would she have a third to match his first?

"Oh, God!" he exclaimed with a low and throaty moan, suspecting Sharon would have less to do with his orgasm than either of them would have liked. He was close now, very close. And he knew from the duration of the caning scene that the butt-whacking was just about over, too.

And why was he suddenly thinking of Morgan Kent, except that Morgan's repeated attendance at this movie had pulled Cord back to it? Why did such thoughts make Cord's pleasure and his guilt intensify?

There was an ear-splitting crack of final cane struck against damaged ass, and it was accompanied by a riptide of ecstasy released inside Cord's body. Cord squeezed Sharon's tits as if they were raw dough, he the baker. He opened his mouth against her neck and grunted a breathy sigh.

It was all he ever dreamed sex with a woman should be, tied up with all he'd ever feared about his sexuality.

CHAPTER EIGHTEEN

ELLEN

"I GAVE YOU EVERYTHING," Dr. Ellen Riley protested, her blue eyes accusatory from behind *Nina Ricci* fashion-framed lenses so thick they made her eyes too big for her heart-shaped face.

"I'm hoping you can help me put all the words into perspective," Cord said, dropping the file folders on her desk. The resulting wind caused a sheet of notepaper to become airborne and flutter to the floor.

"What's wrong with *your* deductive reasoning?" Ellen asked, turning her swivel chair and bending to retrieve the stray paper. Her full breasts plumped the severe cut of her plain cotton blouse. Back to a sitting position, she anchored the recalcitrant paper beneath the leading edge of a square cut-crystal paperweight.

"*My* reasoning tells me I'm not reading the files of two men but of twelve," Cord said, taking a chair that hadn't been offered.

Ellen shrugged, continuing to look hostile. "Nevertheless, I've discharged my legal obligations," she reminded. "You've what you wanted, so make the best of it."

"Why?" Cord asked, his voice condemning.

"Why?" Ellen echoed, her psychiatric training obviously having instilled within her an automatic need to answer any question with a question.

"Why *shouldn't* I ask your assistance?" Cord elucidated. "How can I possibly be a threat to two of your patients beyond helping? In fact, had I had access to Bobby Jordan's file sooner, I might have gotten to him before his killers did."

"And I don't believe *that* for a minute" Ellen contradicted, and her smirk indicated *she* was the pro a mind games.

"Maybe not," Cord retracted. "Then again…." It was his turn to shrug.

"I'm not overly fond of policemen," Ellen said, sitting back in her chair, her eyes unblinking behind their magnifying lenses. "In

Chicago, I had the grave misfortune of having been married to one of them."

"I know."

Ellen looked momentarily surprised but quickly recovered. "Of course, you know," she granted, leaving it at that.

"Somebody has to solve murders," Cord reminded.

"You think you're going to solve these two?" she asked, nodding toward the file folders on her desk.

"You sound as if you have your doubts," Cord observed.

"I do," Ellen admitted. "Bobby was killed by men who make it a business of killing and not getting caught."

"And Horton Lendland's killer or killers?"

"Your department doesn't have a very good track record as regards killers of gay men," Ellen accused. Whether true or not, the observation was one Cord was damned tired of hearing. "Shall I tell you why?" she surprised.

"By all means," Cord encouraged, unable to keep out a trace of sarcasm.

"Because street people are transitory. They're here today, gone tomorrow, remaining anywhere only for as long as it takes to become yesterday's bargain. Horton's murderer has now moved on to some dark street in Los Angeles, New York, or New Orleans."

"I've a helluva lot more suspects than *here-today-gone-tomorrow* street people," Cord reminded.

"I thought we were discussing killers, not suspects," Ellen argued with a condescending smile.

"You think Horton picked up one of these street people who killed him?"

"He had a penchant for *rough trade*," Ellen said. "You're familiar with that street vernacular, are you, Detective Maxwell? Rough trade: young men with sex for sale who haven't graduated from Harvard, or Yale, not even from the U. of W. Theirs are the schools of hard knocks. Boys unrefined, with sometimes dangerously sharp edges. Youth exposed to none of the advantages money can buy. Kids who won't have a next meal if they can't *get it up* for the next buyer. Near animals from which the veneer of civilization can easily be totally stripped."

"Killers?" Cord asked.

"Life is cheap on the streets," Ellen reminded.

"There were over two-thousand dollars worth of twenty-four-carat gold found melted down with Lendland's body," Cord said. "Whoever set fire to the man left him all his jewelry."

"Uneducated minds easily panic," Ellen assured. "Suddenly gone too far, they can't reason beyond the moment. Survival impulses take hold, and gold is forgotten in lieu of destroying incriminating evidence and making a quick getaway."

"The motive for murder so quickly forgotten when the deed is done?" Cord queried doubtfully.

"And if the motive wasn't gold?" Ellen conjectured. "If it was born of deeper psychological demons? If a kid, forced to survive by selling his body, hating the buyer for degrading him, hating himself for allowing the degradation, suddenly cracks?"

"Is that how you see it?"

"There'll never be a complete picture without all of the pieces," Ellen parried. "Will you ever have all of the pieces?"

"You've dealt with hustlers who could murder because of self-loathing and loathing for their johns?"

"We could all murder if put in the right circumstances," Ellen argued.

"What about Bobby Jordan? Could he have killed?"

"Killed Horton Lendland? You've read Bobby's psychiatric file," Ellen challenged. "*You* tell *me*."

"I think he could have killed him, but I'd like an expert's opinion."

"This expert says, *no*."

"Why?"

"Because Bobby saw Horton as a father figure. Having been traumatized by seeing himself responsible for his real father's death, I don't foresee him having willingly submitted himself to the additional trauma of a repeat."

"I'm a little confused by his sexual involvement with his father," Cord admitted. "Your transcripts later have Bobby professing his first homosexual experience was in reform school."

"And it might well have been," Ellen confessed. "All I can tell you is that his father *did* commit suicide. If he did so because of guilt compounded from continual sexual abuse of his son, who knows? Maybe Bobby's mother could shed some light on the matter, but where's she? I can't find her, and I've looked."

"But there's the possibility Bobby wasn't sexually abused by his father? That his old man bought the farm for other reasons than guilt?"

"Yes."

"This suddenly means Horton Lendland becomes less a father-figure and more just another *dirty-old-man-on-the-make*."

"You know, Detective Maxwell, a psychiatrist is really an archaeologist shifting through piles of mental debris, coming up with conflicting evidence from which he or she is required to make educated guesses. Actually, we're less lucky than the archaeologist, because we seldom have anything tangible to work with. Meaning, the information upon which we must base our guesses is supplied by patients who might be lying through their teeth. Thus, we can end up with the two conflicting stories of Bobby's indoctrination into male-male sex: via his father sexual abuse; via a gang-rape at the boy's reformatory. I count on my expertise to tell me which is correct, and I've told you my opinion."

"Why the two stories to begin with?"

"Because I deal with emotionally disturbed people," Ellen reminded. "That they've come to me may mean they recognize a problem, but it doesn't mean they're going to spill their guts to someone they don't yet know they can trust. Trust takes time, and sometimes it's never strong enough for the truth to emerge. Or, if the truth *does* come out, the patient attempts to protect his psyche by camouflaging it with out-and-out lies."

"You did or didn't have Bobby's trust?"

"We were working on it."

"This means, *all* of it might be bullshit?" Cord said, indicating Bobby's file with a tap of his finger.

"That's correct," Ellen agreed. "However, like the truth lurking in dreams, the truth invariably lurks within the fabrications."

"What about Horton? Did you have his trust?"

"At the time I was treating him, yes, I think I did. When he died, I hadn't treated him for quite some time, as you well know. If I saw him at all, in recent years, it was in conjunction with Bobby's treatment. If Bobby didn't show for a scheduled appointment, I'd call Horton. And, of course, Horton signed all of the checks for Bobby's sessions."

"Did Bobby miss his appointments very often?"

"Sometimes for months in a row, but Horton would always persuade him to come back again."

"A pseudo father persuading his pseudo son to get well?"

"A little more complicated than that," Ellen chided.

"Was Horton cured, that's why he quit seeing you?"

"Cured isn't applicable," Ellen argued. "What Horton managed was to deal with his homosexuality, to recognize those impulses behind his need to befriend men from the streets. He never altered his life-style, because he never intended to. He merely became more comfortable with it."

"What *was* this *thing* he had for *rough trade?*" Cord asked, knowing what Ellen would answer and not be disappointed.

"You've read his files," she insisted.

"I'd like you to put all the data into summation," Cord encouraged with what he hoped was a winning smile.

"For starters, Horton had an inferiority complex," Ellen said, surprising Cord by offering no argument. "It was deeply ingrained during a sickly childhood, reinforced by a father who wanted a jock and got a ninety-nine-pound weakling, by a younger brother who excelled in sports and got all the attention and glory. The brother went into the *manly* profession of Chevrolet dealerships, and Horton went from one low-paying job to another. Finally, Horton took on selling art which, no matter how much money it eventually brought in, never quite seemed the *kind* of work in which a *real* man should have been succeeding. To oversimplify, Horton preferred rough trade, because he could always come out of such relationships feeling superior. He could further bolster his ego by offering opportunities to these kids and watch them fail. That proved to him that not everyone could achieve what he had, no matter what his father might have thought to the contrary."

"Why was he homosexual, do you think?" Now, *that* was something Cord would genuinely be interested in hearing.

"Why was he homosexual?" Ellen repeated with addition of a sardonic laugh. "The jury is out on why *anyone* is homosexual, Detective Maxwell. Take your pick of proposed reasons: gene damage, mutation, reversion; environment; dominating mother; submissive father; the lure of forbidden fruit; the natural bisexuality of the human animal; on and on."

"He didn't want to be cured of his homosexuality?"

"In my profession, we no longer look upon homosexuality as a disease to be cured. It might surprise you to know there are some well-adjusted homosexuals, quite content with whom and what they are. That you and I come into contact with them so seldom is a measure of their complete adjustment and integration into society. That Horton was gay was never his problem. Had he been straight, he would have likely frequented prostitutes."

"I'm a little unclear as to both Bobby and Horton's relationship with Morgan Kent."

"It's all in the…." She paused, apparently deciding her argument wasn't likely to be any more effective this time than the other times. She sighed. "Quite frankly, I remain uncertain of Mr. Kent's relationship with either Horton or Bobby."

"Why's that?"

"When Morgan Kent appeared on the scene, Horton was no longer my patient. I was, therefore, deprived of discussions with Horton as an information source. On the other hand, Bobby was evasive. If I had to take a guess, though, I'd say Morgan Kent was the one person Bobby wanted and couldn't have. Whether he could have him or not, however, his *desire* for him was a problem for someone who didn't consider himself gay. You find it amusing that Bobby considered himself straight," Ellen said, and it wasn't a question. Cord realized he was venting his disbelief *in just that* notion with a wry smile. "Well, I can assure you there are many hustlers who firmly believe they're straight," Ellen assured. "What they do they do because they must do it to survive, or so goes their reasoning. Sex for them, gay sex, isn't an emotional act but a mechanical one. Some hustlers won't kiss, because that's emotion above and beyond the call of survival. Some insist upon always being dominant; *i.e.*, no *real* man would let another man ever use him like a woman."

"In your opinion, did Bobby and Morgan Kent ever have sex together?" he asked, ignoring her previous indication to the contrary.

"Bobby never showed up for his last three appointments," Ellen said. "So, I can't say anything for sure about what happened all that lately."

"But how about any time before the last time you saw him?"

"I think not," Ellen said. "I think it would have come out if he had, one way or another. Bobby, I think, would have been noticeably changed by the experience, because Morgan wouldn't have been content to service him without reciprocity, would he?"

"Wouldn't he?"

"I'd say, no. Though that's purely a guess, you understand. Morgan after all, has sex with women, doesn't he?"

"Does he?"

"That's my impression, having been given meager facts and having never met the man."

"Bobby told you that Morgan fucked women?"

"You've read the files," Ellen reminded for the umpteenth time, not in the least affected by Cord's use of the *f*-word. "Or, did you miss that?" she smiled sarcastically. "Shall I tell you something else you might have missed?" she asked. She didn't wait for his reply. "Morgan fucking women was part of the attraction he held out for Bobby, because Bobby, as much as he liked to swagger and pretend otherwise, couldn't *get it up* for *any* woman. That he chose a pregnant woman as his hostage when he robbed that grocery store was no accident. She represented his mother who'd run out on him. The mother he blamed, along with himself, for his father's suicide, she having threatened her husband with exposure for child molesting. Morgan Kent was everything Bobby wanted to be: socially and sexually at ease with *both* men and women, a success in the gay *and* straight worlds, rich, a friend of people like Horton Lendland without *having* to be their plaything. Morgan was sophisticated, educated, clever, a genuine *user* where Bobby, more often than not, was merely *used*."

"Used *by Morgan?*"

"Used by *everybody,*" Ellen emphasized. "But, as I've already said, or at least insinuated, the problem was compounded by Morgan not paying enough attention to Bobby, sexually *or otherwise*. Love and hero-worship directed toward someone who looks right through you can entail disconcerting emotions difficult for even a well-balanced individual. For Bobby, it was worse.

"So, if Morgan would have noticed Bobby enough to ask a favor of him, Bobby would have gladly complied?"

"I would think that would well depend upon the favor," Ellen hedged.

"How about if Morgan asked Bobby to act as courier on a drug deal?"

"Bobby was very closed-mouthed about his association with drugs."

"But you knew he was somehow involved with them?"

"Bobby was very closed-mouthed about his association with drugs," Ellen repeated with finality.

"What about his tendency toward violence?" Cord asked, deciding upon tact when confronted by a stone wall.

"Manifestations of his hatred for women."

"But he...."

"...beat up on gays?" Ellen interrupted with a wave of her hand. "Bobby looked upon most gays as surrogate women. You'd be in a better position to check, but I'd imagine his gay victim were mainly effeminate."

"Is that Jim Holdsett's problem, too: a hatred of women?"

"We are not discussing Jim Holdsett," Ellen said, coming to her feet in obvious conclusion. "Nor are we *going* to discuss him. Now if you'll excuse me, I have people more needy of my time than you are."

"Back to doctor-patient confidentiality, are we?" Cord asked, staying seated.

"Look for your killers disappeared into some big city other than Seattle," Ellen said. "Jim Holdsett didn't kill anyone, and I'd testify to that in any court of law."

"You just might have to," Cord said cryptically, still not getting to his feet. "Now sit down, because we're not finished!"

CHAPTER NINETEEN

GEORGE

"DID HE PROVIDE YOU WITH anything helpful?" George Genlic asked, Cord re-joining him at the bar.

"Did you tell him I was a cop?" Cord asked, in condemning disbelief. "Did you?" George was a faggoty lawyer who should have known better.

"He wouldn't have talked to either of us if I hadn't told him," George replied, very little apology in his voice. "We're not his type."

"You're a jerk-off!" Cord informed, slipping off the bar stool and heading for the door. Without looking, he knew George was in his wake. Cord had almost bodily forced the bastard into the *Ball and Chain*. It wasn't likely George was staying on without him.

"So, I'm sorry," George conceded only after they were on the dark sidewalk heading for the unmarked police car. "I have difficulty handling that scene, okay?"

"No; damn it, it's *not* okay!" Cord informed. "What good is a gay liaison that can't liaison for shit?"

"You wanted to talk to him," George rationalized. "I arranged it."

"By telling him I was a cop, for Christ's sake!" Cord accused disgustedly. "Hell, I thought you just *might* know the guy."

"Hardly," George protested with a shiver. Cord had about had it with this prick. He could have gotten as good results, if not better, by *hitting* the bar on his own. "I've only been in the *Ball and Chain* this once," George informed.

"Great!" Cord exclaimed, although George's admission wasn't so much news that Cord hadn't guessed as much. "I have the murder of a gay possibly involved in Seattle's B&D scene, and my liaison to the gay community wouldn't know a bullwhip from bullshit."

"They're a close-knit group," George protested. He was in the car but going nowhere, except down on Cord's shit list. "As well they should be," George added. "I can't imagine anyone getting their cocks off by being tied up, can you?"

"What you or I can or can't imagine has nothing to do with it," Cord concluded. "I'm a police officer, assigned to a case and gone undercover to investigate, my cover blown by the guy who supposedly has been assigned to help me. How much pertinent information did you think that freak was going to give a policeman?"

"When I volunteered for this job, I didn't know you needed entrée to the leather scene," George rationalized. "Had I known, I…."

"You would have what?" Cord persisted, not about to let it go unsaid. What he needed was some leverage to get this jerk off his back without being accused of being anti-gay. He thought he knew the key when he'd found it.

"Leather isn't my bag," George said. "Leather bars, and the people who frequent them, make me nervous."

"So, maybe I'd be better off with someone more comfortable in the gay haunts that Horton Lendland frequented. Right?"

"Maybe so," George agreed.

"And there's someone you recommend as less uptight than you are?"

"I'll have to think on it," George parried.

Yeah, let the bastard think all he damned well pleased. The longer the better. "You did know that Horton was into B&D, didn't you?" Cord queried, as if George had become the biggest disappointment in Cord's entire career as a police officer.

"How could *I* have known?" George argued.

"Horton was a highly visible member of the gay community, wasn't he?" Cord challenged. "The very same gay community of which you're a member."

"We hardly frequented the same segment, though," George insisted. "Remember, I never met the man."

"And few of *your group* ever met him, either?" Cord asked with obvious sarcasm. He shook his head and started the car. "What conceivable good did you think you could do me on this case?" Cord asked pulling the car out into traffic. "You're nothing but a bloody ball and chain around my neck!"

CHAPTER TWENTY

Sean

"IT WAS A FIGURE OF SPEECH!" Sean Wilshire insisted
"But you did say you *could kill the bastard!*"

"I was drunk and angry, okay? But saying and doing are not one
and the same thing. Besides, I have an alibi." This was true; however, for the moment, Cord was ignoring it.

"Why didn't *you* mention you threatened him?" Cord asked.
"Why did *I* have to stumble across the fact in the grapevine?"

"In my place, would you have mentioned it?" Sean challenged.
"Besides, despite everything, Horton and I remained friends, all
right? I helped him out in good times by buying paintings. He
helped me through some lean times by feeding some of my art collection back onto the market."

"Nevertheless, he was put out by the way your landscaping of
his yard went over budget."

"We had a communications problem, that's all," Sean explained. "He wanted things done at the last minute, and he didn't
fully understand the accumulated cost of them."

"And it wasn't your job, as landscaper, to set him straight?"

"I tried to. The problem being that all those little costs he approved piecemeal eventually added up to the total he disapproved."

"He did an awfully lot of bad-mouthing you, didn't he?" Cord
fished.

"There were unforeseen problems during the landscaping of his
place," Sean continued, apparently preferring not to comment on
how Horton's derogatory remarks had or hadn't affected his reputation and business. "It rained and didn't stop for two weeks, putting
my crew knee-deep in mud. We hit some underground electrical
wiring no one could have known was there. On and on."

"Tell me about your little *difficulty* of a few months back that
had you needing Horton to sell off some of the paintings in your collection."

"I had a temporary financial set-back. That's all."

"Because of a lawsuit instigated by a Mr. Severson? Something about a botched landscaping on his beach property?"

"We settled out of court," Sean reminded.

"As you and Lendland settled out of court?"

"Yes."

"Lendland said he should have been forewarned by the Severson lawsuit, instead of having to find out for himself that you were incompetent."

"Horton thought he could get dollars' worth of work from a friend by putting out mere pennies. God knows, it did turn out that way. Everything considered, I ended up doing the job for less than cost."

"All of which left you and Lendland less than the very best of friends?"

"Granted, it left our friendship at a decidedly low ebb," Sean admitted, "but not down and out for the count."

"Despite Lendland broadcasting to anyone who'd listen that you *couldn't dig a hole and piss in it for less than twenty-five thousand dollars*?"

"Horton was known for his over-exaggerations," Sean argued. "It was his way. Anyone who knew him took his outbursts with a grain of salt."

"His criticism didn't affect you financially, then?"

"Oh, I suppose it might have, to a degree," Sean admitted, apparently not about to paint himself into that corner. "But I did seven jobs between my trouble with Severson and my misunderstanding with Horton. There were those seven satisfied customers balancing Horton's complaints. You can't please everybody all of the time, and I think most fair-minded people realize that and take it into consideration."

"You're not going to mind if I recheck your alibi for the night of the murder?"

"Of course not."

Why should he? He'd been in a bar with at least six friends. Still, the murder *threat* had been a new twist that Cord was obliged to check out.

CHAPTER TWENTY-ONE

WINSTON

"SURELY YOU DON'T WANT to hear it *again*?" Winston Jones bemoaned, not needing a *Who's Who of the Seattle Police Department* to identify the man on his doorstep.

Jones' alibi for the night of Horton's murder wasn't as good as some. Wives had been known to lie to protect their husbands. "Just one more time," Cord cajoled. In truth, he thought he was grabbing at straws by backtracking, but going over and over the facts often turned up new leads. He could use a few new leads about now.

"Maybe if I put it on tape, you could replay it whenever?" Winston suggested.

"Who is it, Winston?" Deidra Jones asked, appearing behind her husband in the doorway. "Oh, Detective Maxwell," she identified, answering her own question with obvious disappointment.

"This will only take a few minutes, Mrs. Jones," Cord assured.

Halfway through Winston's *tired-from-the-telling* story, Cord's intuition warned this return visit was useless. He continued listening, anyway, to the tale of Lendland and an expensive Mark Toby painting he'd sold to Winston Jones on a monthly payment plan, with the provision that should Jones resell the painting before he'd completely paid for it, he would make good on his outstanding account with the *Lendland/Holdsett Gallery*. Jones *had* resold the painting but had refrained from telling Horton or Jim. Instead, Jones had continued to make the standard monthly installments. This Horton, quite haphazardly, had discovered, pressing Jones for total payment. Jones had contended that the balloon-payment provision was illegal and, thus, invalid. Horton had sued. Jones had countersued. In the subsequent *long-drawn-out* legal battle, Horton won, but only after a complicated maze of appeals and decision reversals that ended up in the State Supreme Court. Court costs and *all* legal fees had been dumped on the loser (AKA Winston Jones), the liability computed to over five times the original value of the Mark Toby painting in question.

However, Jones killing Horton didn't eliminate Jones' responsibility to pay his debt to Horton's estate, to the court, to Jim, and to the lawyers.

CHAPTER TWENTY-TWO

PETER

"WERE YOU FOLLOWED?" Father Peter Margaux asked, nervously checking the empty hallway.

"Not that I know of," Cord assured curiously. He was surprised to see the Father in such obviously good health. A barrage of the *Retreat* lawyers and doctors had been insisting the Father too ill to be interviewed in connection with the Lendland murder case. Cord's insistence to the contrary had produced very little more than signed affidavits from five Fathers of the *Retreat St. Julian*, stating the Father Peter Margaux had been with them, in prayer, when Horton Lendland was murdered.

"It's only a matter of time before they find me," Father Peter Margaux said, leaning against the shut door. "Not that I blame them. The scandal, you know?" He looked far younger than Cord had expected him to be, no matter the Catholic Father's snow-white hair.

"Of course," Cord agreed, although he wasn't sure *which* scandal, since there were several possibilities.

"Well, let's sit," the Father insisted, leading the way into the hotel room. *The Presidential Suite* of the *Seattle Sheraton* hardly seemed the most inconspicuous meeting place. "I've taken the liberty of warming some cognac," the Father said, smiling in the direction of two large snifters tilted in wire contraptions over candle flames. "I hope you like *Grand Marnier*," the Father said, lifting one glass and handing its warm bowl of liqueur to the policeman. "It's one of my favorites." He claimed his own glass and, then, snuffed both candles with his un-dampened thumb and forefinger. "To cleared conscience!" he said, raising his glass in toast. He sipped, while Cord tried to survive the heady fumes emanating from his own glass. The liqueur tasted of oranges.

"Am I to understand that the Fathers at the *Retreat* don't know you're here?" Cord asked, taking the chair the Father offered. The Father sat on the facing couch and crossed his legs. His pale eyes

134

looked pink behind the pink-tinted lenses of his eyeglasses. His lips seemed entirely too sensuous for a man of God.

"Oh, I suspect they know I've gone," the Father admitted, "but they would be most disturbed to hear I've gone to meet you. Oh, *most* disturbed," he emphasized with a sounding that verged on a belly-laugh. He put his brandy snifter on the coffee table between them and used a white handkerchief to clear tears of amusement from his eyes. "The scandal, you know" the Father assured, his wink insinuating Cord and he were privy to the same delicious secret."

"About this scandal…?" Cord said, attempting to maneuver the conversation with an open-ended question.

"Yes, I suppose it would behoove us to get on with it," the Father said. "They could arrive at any time and interrupt, couldn't they?"

"*They?*"

"The lawyers, the doctors, the Fathers, the Bishop, the Cardinal, the Pope," the Father said with a breezy wave of his free hand. With his other hand, he raised his glass and sipped more cognac. "Ah!" he exclaimed, smacking his lips. "Exquisite!"

"The Pope would be disturbed, would he?" Cord asked, deciding to join in what the Father seemed to think was some kind of game. Frankly, Cord was a little confused. The clandestine summons by the Father had come completely out of left field.

"The Pope *will* be most disturbed," the Father affirmed, looking very sober. He eyed Cord over the edge of his glass. "Though which is more important: Holy Church or the cleansing of a man's soul?"

Under the circumstances, Cord thought he could correctly venture a guess. "The cleansing of a man's soul?" he suggested.

"Exactly!" the Father congratulated. "Scandal be damned!"

The two sat in silence, Cord getting the impression they were in temporary limbo. "Well?" he asked. "Shall we begin?"

"I thought you would be reading me my rights," the Father said with a frown. "Isn't that how they do it on television? Not that I watch that much television, you understand? It rots the brain. Do you think that would be an adequate defense? *TV made me do it!*" He chuckled and had a sip more of brandy.

Cord read him his rights, although there was something definitely *off* about the whole thing. Rather like a picture somewhere askew in an otherwise well-ordered room.

"Yes, I suspected so," the Father said, a nod of approval in accompaniment. "It wouldn't do for you *not* to follow correct procedure," he continued. "Criminals do sometimes get off because of such oversights, do they not? But I'm not one of those to sneak out any backdoors. One can't be cured without taking one's medicine, can one? Bitter as that medicine might be."

"You want to make a confession?" Cord suggested, the scene still slightly off balance. He automatically checked the paintings on the wall, two of which were slightly atilt. His impulse was to align them, but it was an impulse he resisted.

"Yes, a confession," the Father admitted. "To cleanse my conscience and hope Dear Jesus will see fit to cleanse my soul."

"Maybe you'd prefer doing this down at the station?" Cord suggested. "We could have someone get it down on tape and paper."

"Oh, I'll repeat it in front of your witnesses, to be sure," the Father promised. "So, let's just stay put for the moment, shall we? Too soon I'll be deprived of even these creature comforts." In emphasis, he held up his glass and twirled pale amber liquid to coat the inside curve of the snifter.

"Very well," Cord conceded.

"Or, maybe, you'd prefer asking particular questions first?" the Father suggested. "I hear you're curious about my relationship with Jim Holdsett. Perhaps, we might start there?" He proceeded without pause. "I was Eve to his Serpent," he said. "Appropriate analogy, under the circumstances. Referring to *penis* as *serpent,* I mean."

"Your relationship with Jim Holdsett, then, was a sexual one?" Cord asked, hardly sure he'd heard correctly.

"Not at first," the Father protested. "Initially, I was aesthetically motivated. His beauty appealed to me. You'll admit he *is* an exceptionally beautiful young man."

"Hmmmm," Cord commented noncommittally. Everyone, the Father included, was entitled to his opinion.

"A *demon fruit plucker—or something that therefrom rhymes— in angelic disguise!*" the Father chanted rather loudly. He sat back with a sigh. "And I was fruit ripe for the plucking—or whatever. I'd gotten as far as I had in the church by mere charm and bravura, not unmitigated religious conviction."

"You met Jim Holdsett how?"

"At a *Save Venice* dinner. And I shall never forget it. So like a heavenly visitation: this attractive young man suddenly sitting beside me. *I'm Jim Holdsett,* he said. *And you're the Father Peter Margaux of St. Julian.* He took my breath away." The Father got up and went to the bottle of *Grand Marnier* on the side table. He pantomimed an offer of more liqueur which Cord declined. The Father refilled his empty glass and came back to his place. Without bothering to warm the liqueur, he took a sip and smiled. "I should have more regrets, you know?" he said. "I fear I'm not as repentant as the Good Lord shall require of me."

Cord said nothing, deciding to let the Father proceed at his own pace. In the meantime, Cord tried to pinpoint what made it all seem unreal.

"When I was very young," the Father said, "I carried around in my BIBLE a picture postcard of one of the Bernini angels on the *Castel Sant'Angelo* in Rome. Have you ever been to Rome?" Cord shook his head. "Jim *was* that angel," the Father assured. "Alive. Blond hair. Blue eyes, White teeth." He visibly shivered. "Temptation personified, and I was weak," he said. "And he enticed with paintings, my original passion. So, I began buying supplements for the *Retreat*'s meager collection. Of course, I was less interested in the paintings than in the seller, but the one was my rationalization for the other."

"Jim Holdsett was hustling you?"

The Father looked positively pained. "He was a consummate salesman, not above using seduction to sell a Callahan or a Toby."

"And where was Lendland all of this time?"

"Ah, Horton!" the Father exclaimed with a sigh. "The Grand Puppet-Master, pulling all our strings."

"Your strings? Jim's strings?"

"Horton, of course, recognized my feelings for Jim from the start. Before I did and before Jim did. But, then, Horton had experience in such matters, didn't he? It was all new to me, a man over fifty who hadn't an inkling of male-male love beyond the love of God."

"Jim didn't know what was happening?" Cord asked dubiously.

"Jim wanted to prove himself to Horton and to himself by selling paintings. When it finally hit him as to what was happening between us, I think he was genuinely shocked and surprised by it. Of course, by that time, the end warranted whatever the means, and neither of us could retreat. Nor was I above putting a price tag on my continued patronage of the *Lendland/Holdsett Gallery*. Have you ever been in love, Detective Maxwell?"

"A little," Cord said, remembering Cheryl.

"Oh, that wasn't love, then!" the Father disagreed. "Real love is never *a little*. Love is a virtual glut. An overflow that pushes all reason into oblivion. Heaven and Hell combined. Euphoria and despair united. Wonder and awfulness converged into one ball of wax. Pleasure and pain." He sipped his drink, eyeing Cord strangely. "Shall I tell you about the pain?"

"Jim physically abused you?"

"Only where it wouldn't show," the Father admitted, seeming not in the least surprised by Cord's correct guess. "It would have been ill-advised for a Father of *St. Julian* to arrive visibly black and blue from each and every session with the *Retreat*'s art consultant."

"You let Jim beat you?" Cord asked. One act of brutality might have resulted from the Father being unable to defend himself. Multiple beatings insinuated something else again.

"Ritual flagellation," the Father said. "Scourging by way of penance for the sins of the flesh. Deserved retribution for degradation. Punishment for putting my love of a young man above and beyond my love of God. In the end, though, the beatings weren't enough for either of us. After all, Jim wasn't totally blameless, no matter how he liked to pretend *I* seduced *him*, not vice versa. How many times, I wonder, in all the sordid affairs that do and don't come to light, is it the *child* who seduces the helpless *adult*?" *Shades of Gary Green!* "We forget mere babes are born into original sin, don't we? Innocence tainted from the outset."

"The Fathers at *St. Julian* know about your relationship with Jim?" Cord asked. The Father seemed momentarily reticent about continuing. No wonder the good Fathers had attempted to keep their spiritual leader under wraps.

"Artwork doesn't come cheaply," the Father said after a lengthy pause. "Neither do pleasures of the flesh," he added wryly. "My passion for the one quickly depleted all official funds for the other. So, I began diverting funds. Except, my inventive bookkeeping wasn't clever enough to pass close scrutiny. Questions were asked. Not that anyone could complain that the *Retreat* didn't suddenly have a fine art collection. In fact, the collection, at the moment, even surpasses that of Mr. Kent who had a decided head start."

"You know Morgan Kent, then?"

"A voyeur of the first magnitude!" the Father said, and Cord wasn't sure whether it was a compliment or an insult. "I'm sure he viewed our performance as a comedy played out for his personal amusement."

"He knew about you and Jim?"

"Horton would have told him," the Father informed.

"Why?"

"Because Horton told Morgan everything. Morgan was friend and confident. He was an anti-Christ to be truly amused by Horton's manipulations of a horny man of God and a sexually insecure young man."

"And Horton was able to laugh with Morgan about *you* and *Jim*?"

"You're really asking if Horton was jealous."

"Yes," Cord admitted.

"Is a pimp jealous of his number-one lady prostituting herself for profit?"

"So, why exactly did you kill Lendland? Because he manipulated you and Jim into an unbearable situation?"

"Kill who?" the Father asked in what seemed genuine surprise.

"Horton Lendland. You did kill him, didn't you? That *is* what this is all about?"

"Horton dead?" the Father asked. "No major loss, you understand. In the final analysis, he was not a very nice man." Cord was confused. "No, I killed Jim," the Father confessed. Cord was more confused. "I *had* to, don't you see?" the Father insisted. "I couldn't go on. We'd become abominations in the sight of man and God."

"You killed Jim Holdsett?"

"He didn't want to let me in, of course," the Father said. His glass was empty, but he made no attempts, this time, to refill it. "He said the man was still there cataloging Horton's things, but I knew that was done with. Besides, Jim *wanted* me to come in, no matter what he said. He liked getting his serpent tamed. It was only afterwards that he felt obligated to confirm his masculinity by beating up the poor, old, offending queer who'd worshiped at his priapic shrine."

CHAPTER TWENTY-THREE

JIM

"DO I *LOOK* DEAD AND BURIED?" Jim Holdsett challenged. "No! This tells us both that Father Peter Margaux is certifiably crazy. Why else do you think the good brothers at the *Retreat* tried keeping him under lock and key? I saw this coming. He had two nervous breakdowns in the short time I've known him."

"None of his story about the two of you is true, then?"

"You seem determined to make me out a fag!" Jim accused. "So, make me out one, even if you *and* the Father are full of shit."

"Those who lie down with dogs get fleas," Cord said, not sure that was the saying he was after but certain it would get his message across.

"You want to believe that sick old man, you believe him," Jim said. "But he said he killed me, and I'm not dead, am I? He said he went to bed with me, and he didn't do that, either."

"You merely acted as a consultant for the *Retreat*'s art acquisitions?"

"Correct."

"You *do* know Father Margaux bought paintings from you with monies misappropriated from *Retreat* funds?"

"I know that now. I didn't know it at the time," Jim insisted. "He said there were special resources set aside at the *Retreat* for just such purchases. I'm going to believe a Father is lying and cheating through his teeth?"

"You're Catholic, aren't you, Jim?"

"What's that got to do with the price of tea in China?"

"It must have come as somewhat of a spiritual blow to find a man of God, a Father in the Catholic faith, no less, coming on to you."

"Isn't that what they all do, these days?"

"But *if* he did, what, I wonder, would have been your reaction to learn Horton had known all about what the Father really wanted from you all along, Horton even arranging for you and the Father to spend so much time together? You think that might be your once-missing motive for murder?"

"And do you think a more logical motive for murder might be found for a poor deranged Father who has already been proved to have fantasies of killing me?" Jim countered. "Brethren of the faith who would lock up a deranged man to conceal a scandal involving embezzlement of church funds would stop at lying to cover up the scandal of murder, would they?"

Once again, Jim Holdsett proved to Cord he was anything but stupid.

CHAPTER TWENTY-FOUR

JACK

"**FEAST OR FAMINE;** famine or feast!" Jack Sudlow proclaimed, his body finally showing the results of his daily workouts. If he sucked in his gut, he could even see his penis. Not that he ever seemed to consider his cock the big deal some people did. "We're feasting now," he informed. "On bodies and on the people claiming to be the suppliers of those bodies. Your and my bad luck is that none of this glut of confessions is easing *our* case loads."

A department store manager, Phil Kendrigs, had walked into Police Headquarters the night before and had confessed to killing the gay hustler and the gay lawyer who'd been on the police books prior to Horton Lendland's murder.

"It *would* be nice if Kendrigs accepted responsibility for Lendland and Bobby Jordan while he was at it," Cord admitted, pleased his own recent visits to the gym had restored some of the long-missing firmness to the muscles of his body. He could still afford to shed five more pounds, but he'd momentarily stalemated his battle of the bulge.

"Maybe if you explained to Mr. Kendrigs just how very much he would influence people and make friends if he added Lendland and Jordan to his hit list," Jack recommended. He was belly-down on the massage table, awaiting the ministrations of the masseur presently working the muscles on Cord's *body-made-pliable-in-the-sauna*. "While you're at it," Jack suggested, "have him confess to the *Dint Slough* killings, too. We might as well wipe the slate even cleaner while we're at it."

"He's way too modest to claim credit for what's not his," Cord insisted and punctuated with a low groan as the masseur popped an errant vertebra into proper alignment. "I even suggested his friend, Max, after all a hustler, had somewhere along the line made it with Lendland and/or Bobby Jordan."

"He wouldn't buy it?" Jack asked, resting his chin on folded and hairy forearms. "Shame! Real shame!"

"He killed Max because the kid was supposed to have given up polygamy for blissful monogamy with Kendrigs, which the kid hadn't. He killed Wilson because the lawyer was regularly getting into Max's pants when Kendrigs was supposedly looking the other way. Kendrigs didn't know Lendland or Bobby Jordan, and he'd spied enough on Max and Wilson enough to know Lendland and Bobby weren't anywhere in that picture, either. And since Kendrigs has *never* fucked a woman, you can wave good-bye to any chance he'll accept blame for any dead prostitutes. End of unlucky-us summation."

"Well, at least we've improved the department's record of solved gay murders, haven't we? I hope you boasted that up to your gay lawyer friend. What's his name?"

"George Genlic," Cord supplied.

"*He* should be especially pleased by our having rounded up the murderer of a fellow gay lawyer. Right?"

"He says we'd still be looking if Kendrigs hadn't walked in and given himself up. What's more, he's probably right. We didn't have a clue on either of those murders before Kendrigs obliged with a confession. We didn't even know Kendrigs and Max, *or* Max and Wilson, were an *item*."

"We would have gotten around to all of that in time," Jack assured. "Kendrigs knew he'd be caught and merely decided to save himself the inevitable knock by us on his door. It's as simple as that, and if Genlic—or whatever the hell his name is—doesn't want to see it that way, well, we've had to put up with an unappreciative public before."

A few seconds passed, Cord luxuriating in the strong fingers at work on the corded muscles of his back. He had a hard-on, but he always had one during a massage. Jack did, too, Cord having seen it more than once. The masseur, married and with three kids, seemed to take his clients' arousals as a matter of course. Boners were apparently natural side effects of his trade. Nothing *gay* or even *sexual* about it.

"What about this Father character?" Jack asked languidly, his hairy ass making a mountain of the sheet thrown over it.

"The Father Peter Margaux of the *Retreat St. Julian*, you mean?" Cord asked; he was sorry the masseur had finished with him and had moved over to Jack

"The old coot really crazy?" Jack asked after telling the masseur, *I'm not goddamned bread dough, and you're not a goddamned baker, so take it easy.*

"Crazy like a fox, maybe," Cord granted. "The Father has a motive. Unfortunately, he, also, has an airtight alibi."

"Think a cabal of Holy Brothers is lying to protect one of its own?" Jack shut his eyes, better to enjoy the massage's pleasure/pain.

"Thou shalt not kill!" Cord reminded. "As cynical as everyone might be these days about commandments from God, I've got affidavits from five priests who say the Father was praying. *Five!*"

"The church is just another fraternity and/or lodge," Jack said. "You ever read *The March of Folly* by some broad named Tushie?"

"No," Cord admitted, surprised if Jack had. Jack reminded Cord more of the pulp fiction, blood-and-guts type reader.

"Read it," Jack instructed. "Those Popes weren't above knocking off a few people here and there."

"That was a few centuries back, I'll bet," Cord decided, enjoying his hard cock firmly wedged between the padded tabletop and his hard belly.

"Yeah, well, history has a way of coming around and biting itself on the ass, doesn't it?" Jack observed. "If I were you, I'd check out those praying priests. I figure the Father Margaux regularly browned his sanctified cock up some unsanctified asshole and came down with a bad case of the guilts, bumping off the primary cause."

"Wouldn't that have seen him killing *Jim?*"

"Nah!" Jack disagreed. "How could it be the kid's fault? Holdsett is as much a victim as the Father, see? He couldn't help himself, any more than the Father could. On the other hand, who could have stopped it, or at least slowed it down? Lendland, that's who. Lendland, backstage all the while, writing out his scenarios in which the two helpless players were thrown together again and again."

"The DA won't buy that with five priests saying otherwise," Cord reminded.

"So, we've solved two gay murders this week," Jack rationalized with a smile of contentment. "Who can expect us to bat a thousand every time?"

"Right!" Cord agreed without much enthusiasm. "Maybe my weekend off this case will let my subconscious filter all the shit and put things in perspective."

"You're taking a weekend off, are you?" Jack asked, sounding surprised. He opened his eyes and cussed the masseur for too vigorously kneading a particularly sore group of thigh muscles.

"My cousin is getting married," Cord lied. His only cousin was already married, with three kids. "I thought I'd fly down to LA and play best man." His only cousin lived in Spokane.

"Any best man worth his salt would tell the potential bridegroom that marriage will lead to nothing but trouble and grief," Jack said cynically. "Take that from an authority on the subject."

"Ted is one of those old-fashioned guys who likes to make his fucking on-paper official when the right girl comes along," Cord said. He hadn't seen his Cousin Ted in ten years and never *had* liked him. Cord couldn't remember if he'd even sent a gift when the bastard got married. He sure as hell hadn't attended the nuptials.

"Well, the inevitable nasty divorce will cure him of any marriage number two," Jack promised.

"A divorce didn't seem to keep *you* from tying a second knot," Cord facetiously reminded.

Jack twisted his head in the masseur's direction. "Tenlin, do you hate cops or something?" The masseur ignored him. Jack grunted submission and turned his attention back to Cord. "LA is a cesspool!" he announced emphatically. "The only place more so is New York City."

Tenlin coaxed Jack to his back, exposing a hairy chest and belly, *and* a visibly hard ridge tenting the sheet from Jack's crotch to his navel.

CHAPTER TWENTY-FIVE

REGGIE

"YOU'RE SURE THE NAME is *Sarah* Robinson?" Reggie Turner of the Portland, Oregon, Police Department asked, shaking his head. "Licensing doesn't have any readout for any such animal."

"Yes, Sarah Robinson," Cord assured from his chair beside Reggie at the computer terminal. Cord was disappointed. "Maybe her girlfriend drove them to Seattle."

"Got a name for the girlfriend?"

"Tess."

"That's not much to go on," Reggie said when it was apparent Cord had given him all there was. "You checked the phone directory under Robinson?" Reggie asked in alternative.

"One Sarah. Age: eighty-three this week."

"Any daughters or granddaughters or great-granddaughters?"

"Four daughters, sixteen grand kids, nine great-grand, ten of that total daughters. One named Sarah, age three. Besides which, grandma claims connection with most of the Robinsons in the Northwest, none of whom seemingly fit the bill."

"Well, I ran the name through *arrests and convictions*, and there's nothing there, either. Your Sarah Robinson, besides never having driven a car, boat, train, or plane, never snitched grapes in any Portland supermarket, either."

"Maybe it was S-a-r-a?" Cord said, suggesting the different spelling.

"Thought of that," Reggie boasted. "No S-a-r-a, no S-a-r-r-a, no S-a-r-r-a-h, or any variation thereof, either."

"Well, what can I say but, *thanks?*" Cord said, getting to his feet. His stopover in Portland had rewarded him with zilch. On the other hand, what had he expected? If he had any guts, he'd admit he was here at all out of purely prurient interest. He'd wanted to meet the woman Morgan Kent supposedly had fucked while Gary Green was being terrorized by a supposedly cock-hungry Tess.

"Sorry I couldn't be of more help," Reggie apologized. "Always ready to help Seattle Police."

Cord saluted his thanks. He'd intended to stick around Portland long enough to *interview* Sarah Robinson, but there was a plane for LA he could just about make if—

"Couldn't have been *Tara* Robinson, could it?" Reggie asked, bringing Cord up at the door.

"You've something on a Tara Robinson?" Cord asked, turning back. If Steve Footer had been unsure of Tess's name, how could he have been so positive of the other? Robinson, maybe, since there *had* been a popular song from the movie *The Graduate* about a Mrs. Robinson. But Tara *sounded* an awfully lot like Sarah.

"I coordinated the Tara Robinson case with an inquiry from a Sudlow out of your department in Seattle a couple of weeks ago," Reggie said.

"Jack Sudlow?"

"Right. You guys had a *baggie* murder and were looking for similar M.O.'s. We had one."

"Name of *Tara* Robinson?" Cord asked. Had he ever heard or seen the murdered Portland housewife's name? If he had—*surely, in* passing, from Jack—it hadn't registered. But, then, the *baggie* murder wasn't Cord's case, and he had been more than a little preoccupied, hadn't he?

Reggie punched up Tara Robinson on the computer and watched the neat white letters appear one at a time on the green screen.

"Does that say she was married?"

"Husband: Charles B. Robinson, school teacher, Washington High. Seems he identified the body. Rather, he identified personal belongings. Dental X-rays did the final ID."

"Mr. Robinson have a current address?"

"There's this one that's listed. Current? Your guess is as good as mine."

"What else can you tell me?"

"Not much. It's still officially an open file. Mrs. Robinson and a friend disappeared while shopping. Robinson's body, wrapped in a baggie, turned up a couple of years later. Her friend never turned up."

"This friend have name?"

"Let's see," Reggie said, scanning the visible data and punching up more. The lines of white letters rolled on and off the screen like the credits of a movie. The motion stopped. "Here we go," Reggie informed. "Opalline E. Sinclair. Jesus, can you imagine being stuck with a handle like Opalline?"

Cord was disappointed. So far, the wanted connection just wasn't happening. "What's the *E* stand for?" he asked. There would have been a *MIO* if it were *middle-initial-only*.

Reggie punched in the request, and the screen momentarily blanked before responding. "Opalline *Elizabeth* Sinclair," Reggie announced.

"Elizabeth?" Cord echoed. *Beth?* Or was Cord grabbing at straws? And did Beth sound enough like *Tess* to have been confused by Morgan Kent's junior-high-school buddy, Steve Footer, in the telling of his tale of the woman Morgan had summoned to Seattle from Portland to terrorize Gary Green who'd belittled Morgan's first attempt at writing a fuck book? Morgan having gone upstairs to fuck *Tara*, not *Sarah* Robinson? The woman Morgan had fucked ending up dead in a *Hefty* bag in Portland, like some other *Hefty*-bagged dead woman who was unidentified in Seattle? Beth (Tess) Sinclair dead, too? Signifying what, for Christ's sake?

"You think you've found your Tess?" Reggie asked, his thought process apparently just as facile as that of the Seattle detective.

Cord wondered aloud if the tragedy of Tara Robinson's murder had driven her husband, Charles, from the Portland area.

CHAPTER TWENTY-SIX

CHARLES

"MORGAN KENT AND TARA? An item?" Charles Robinson asked with a laugh. "Jesus, you must be kidding, right?"

"You find that so inconceivable?" Cord asked.

"I don't know who your source is, Detective Maxwell, but Morgan Kent is gay. Anyway, he was when I knew him."

"You and he, ah…? Cord suggested.

"God, no!" Charles protested. "A couple of circle-jerks in high school were my brief excursions into homosexuality."

"But you're certain Morgan is gay?"

"We met him in a gay bar," Charles informed, as if that were proof-positive. If it was, it labeled Charles as gay as Morgan. Whether gay or not, whether bisexual or not, Charles wasn't Morgan's type, at least the way Cord saw it. Charles was too skinny, the guy looking as if he hadn't had a decent meal since his wife failed to come back from the super market. "Besides, Tara said he was gay," Charles added as a verifying afterthought. As if Tara, if fucking around with Morgan, would ever have confessed to Charles that the supposed faggot was a better cocksman than her husband. "She knew him well enough to know," Charles assured.

"You say you and your wife met Morgan in a gay bar?"

"Place called the *Happy Stud* by the Multnomah Stadium. It's not there any more, but we used to go there all of the time, because Tara liked to dance." *Shades of Jim Holdsett!* "Though dancing has never been my bag," Charles clarified, "Tara could never seem to get enough. We'd go to the *Happy Stud* so she could dance with gays, and I wouldn't get all bent out of shape by her shameless flirting. I mean, she could flirt all she wanted in a place like that, couldn't she, and it was never going to go any farther, was it?"

"Morgan asked her to dance."

"Tara asked him. Say, if this is about him being somehow involved in her murder, the authorities already checked, and Morgan was on some Pacific cruise when Tara disappeared. With some new-found granny friend hot to show him the world."

"But you doubt he ever fucked this granny friend?"

"Hell, not only was she a woman, but she was in her eighties, wasn't she? Anyway, I heard she was. At the time, I'd pretty much lost track of him. So had Tara for that matter."

"It was my impression that your wife and someone named Beth…. Would that, by chance, be Opalline Elizabeth Sinclair?"

"Good thing Beth isn't around to hear you call her Opalline," Charles said, waxing nostalgic. "She couldn't stand the name. Not that I can blame her, can you? She wasn't overly fond of *Elizabeth,* either."

"Your wife and Beth drove up to Seattle to see Morgan a couple of times, did they?"

"*Exactly* two. The second time, though, was a dry run, because Morgan and his friends had moved without leaving forwarding addresses. The way I figure it, he was already involved with this older woman."

"Morgan didn't bother keeping you or Tara informed of his whereabouts, then?"

"Well, *I* was never as close to him as Tara. Tara, though, was a little hurt when he dropped out of her life so completely, because the two used to spend an awfully lot of time together when he lived in Portland."

"What exactly did the two of them *do* together? Besides dance."

"Tara loved the beach. She had skin that tanned overnight. So does Morgan. Me? Well, I don't tan, just burn lobster-red and peel. I went with them a couple of times to *Rooster Rock*, but broiling all day in a hot sun was never my idea of fun. Still isn't. In the winter, they were always driving to this Indian reservation south of Mt. Hood. Some kind of a resort there boasts an Olympic-size pool filled with hot water from a hot springs, plus three-hundred-and-some days of sunshine every year. Tara and Morgan always came back brown as Indians. They'd tell everyone they'd been to Hawaii for the weekend."

"Did you know Morgan was in the Army all of the time he was here in Portland?"

"He worked at the *Armed Forces Enlistment and Examination Station* (AFEES), right? Specialist Four or Five; I can't remember which."

"You never found it incongruous that, considering the military's abhorrence of homosexuality, that Morgan apparently had no qualms about flaunting his?"

"Hey, Morgan never flaunted anything, let me tell you," Charles protested. "Just looking at him, you'd have thought he was as normal as the next guy. Sometimes he could *act* effeminate, but those times were few and far between. That he passed so well for straight was one of the reasons Tara liked going places and doing things with him. She wasn't too enthused about being labeled a fruit-fly, even if she was one."

"Morgan never appeared in the least apprehensive that his frequenting of gay bars was a threat to his military career?"

"It wasn't as if he had to check in every night with a commanding officer," Charles reasoned. "The closest military accommodations to Portland are Vancouver Barracks, and those aren't convenient for the AFEES personnel. So, Morgan had his own apartment. Half the time, I'd forget he was in the Army, his hours so much like the rest of us poor schmucks punching nine-to-five time-clocks. I seldom saw him in anything but civvies. He was a damned snappy dresser, too." The last was said as if that, too, verified Morgan's *gayness*.

"How did you first discover he was in the Army?"

"How?" Charles mused with an obviously slow recall.

"Did you discover it by accident? Or, did he tell you?" Cord led.

"Can't say," Charles admitted after a bit more thought. "Not that I ever had the impression it was a secret. Although Tara told me they knew at AFEES that he was spending a lot of time with her."

"Knew? How?"

"Can' remember that, either. I only remember we had a good laugh over it. Not that Tara or I objected to it. I mean, we knew it was harmless. And the gossip had to have helped Morgan."

"Helped him, how?" Cord asked, knowing the answer. Morgan Kent had an uncanny way of maneuvering people and situations to his advantage.

"A queer wouldn't be spending so much time with a woman, would he?" Charles confirmed.

"And you weren't in the least jealous?" Cord pressed, continuing to find the three's relationship unusual, to say the least.

"I wish you could have met Tara," Charles said, sounding as if that would have made all explanations unnecessary. "She was a vibrant and active woman. Her need to be constantly on the go could run me ragged. Morgan was a welcome diversion for her, as far as I was concerned. He was safe. He was charming. And he could take care of himself *and* Tara, because he was an expert in some kind of kung-fu he picked up when he was stationed in the Orient. I was sorry when he got his discharge and decided to pull up stakes for Seattle. I *know* Tara missed him."

"What about Miss Sinclair? How did she fit into the picture?"

"Oh, Beth and Tara were good friends. They worked at *Tectronics* and, before Morgan, it was always Beth who went out on the town with Tara whenever I wasn't up to it—which was most of the time. At first, Tara, Morgan, and Beth were an inseparable threesome, but that didn't seem to last long. Not that Beth acted rejected or left out, but I think Morgan and Tara, between them, simply succeeded in running Beth ragged."

"Beth was with your wife when she visited Morgan in Seattle?"

"I didn't like for Tara to travel on the road alone. Hell, anything might have happened with the car between here and Seattle, and..." He paused, looking out the picture window at a well-manicured lawn. "Funny how I *should* have, instead, worried more about her when she went to the goddamned grocery store!" It took him a few moments to regain his composure. "After Morgan left," Charles resumed, "Tara and Beth got back into their pre-Morgan routine. There were a couple of gay guys with whom Tara occasionally went places—but no one as steady as Morgan had been. I tried to take up the slack for a short time after he left, but I'm just not up to being *on* every damned night of the week. At first, I thought Tara decided I was too much of a stick in the mud and just pulled up and moved out on me. Except, she hadn't taken anything with her. Then, they found her car abandoned in the parking lot of *Albertson's*. Jesus!" he said, burying his face in his hands. "After all of this time, you'd think I'd be through with the pain, wouldn't you?"

"I'm sorry I have to put you through all of this again," Cord apologized.

"Why *have* you put me through it?" Charles asked, looking up. "I don't know if you really ever made that clear," he accused.

What did Cord say to that? That Morgan had, also, known the woman found dead in the baggie in Seattle? Hell, Cord wouldn't even know if that hunch was correct until Jack Sudlow could get back to him. Even then, it might be untrue. No sense, either, in bringing up how a lot of the men and women Morgan *might* have fucked were dead and buried. Charles would never believe Morgan had fucked Tara. It was surprising how many people put gays on one side of some mystical line, straights on the other, refusing to accept the possibility of crossovers. Before this case, even Cord had been less inclined to believe that there were some people who definitely didn't seem to care who or what they fucked as long as they got their rocks off. "There's been a murder," Cord managed. "A friend of Morgan's in Seattle."

"And you think Morgan did it?"

"He's merely one of several suspects."

"This murder has some connection with the murder of my wife?" Charles asked hopefully.

Cord only wished he had the answer. "I wouldn't want you to get up your hopes, Mr. Robinson," Cord warned. "All of this is merely routine. We're trying to check out every angle."

"They never found the bastard who killed Tara," Charles reminded. "They never found Beth, either," he added. "They thought Beth might have murdered Tara, but *I* never thought so. Some sick freak got them both, and Beth will, one of these days, wash out of some shallow grave, all neatly tied and wrapped in her own personal *Hefty,* to prove it."

Cord didn't ask if Beth and Morgan might ever have had sex. A husband who wouldn't consider being cuckold by a guy met in a gay bar wasn't likely to believe Morgan had been slipping hard cock to Opalline Elizabeth Sinclair, either.

CHAPTER TWENTY-SEVEN

Cord

INTUITION. INSIGHT. INSTINCT. Premonition. Presentiment. Clairvoyance. Sixth Sense.

HUNCH.

Whatever, was it merely coincidence that *Ka-Nee-Da,* the Indian resort in north central Oregon where Tara Robinson and Morgan Kent spent so much time one winter, was, also, as Cord remembered it, one stopover made by Gary Green and the youngster, Andy Sacks, during the ill-fated trek that ended with Green arrested and charged (if not convicted) of pederasty?

Cord sat in the manager's office, oblivious to the sunshine and steaming Olympic-size pool just outside. Splayed pool-side, like pink salmon fillet on the grates of a barbecue, men and women baked in one state of undress or another.

Cord flipped through the card file, quickly finding *Green, Gary.* There would be no *Sacks, Andy,* because the kid was a minor at the time and traveling with Green. So far, that was nothing Cord hadn't known all along.

He began a slow search of the *K*'s, approaching any vindication of his hunch via a maze of Kachin, Kadrik, Kaelus, Kaffinger, Kah, Kallis, Kambri, *et al.*, to *Kent, Morgan.*

Cord flipped through the *L*'s to *Lendland, Horton.*

"Green, Sacks, Kent, Lendland, all at *Ka-Nee-Da* on the very same day of the very same week of the very same month of the very same year. What, if anything, did *that* mean? Neither Kent nor Lendland had been called by the prosecution *or* the defense to testify at Green's trial; Cord was sure he would have remembered if they had.

CHAPTER TWENTY-EIGHT

HARLEY

"**HORTON AND JIM** were the proverbial rats deserting me, the proverbial sinking ship," Harley-Gransen Davis accused. He'd obviously seen better days. His Los Angeles apartment was a dump. Cord hadn't seen the like since he'd stopped by Boris Cousel's pig-sty earlier in the investigation. Like Boris, Harley looked as if his physical condition wasn't all that hot, either. He was pale beneath the darkness of his California tan. However, he would probably have looked worse, and been in even less pleasing surroundings, if his misappropriation from a *family* trust fund hadn't finally been smoothed over by the intervention of a bevy of relatives apparently having become far more distraught by all the attending publicity than by a missing few of their millions.

"And Morgan Kent?" Cord asked.

"Was never on board," Harley informed. "I never blamed him for my mess. Not even for his taking Curtis to one side and explaining the facts of life. He was right: I *did* treat Curtis like a doormat."

"Come on, Harley," Cord cajoled non-threateningly. If he didn't play Devil's Advocate, who would? "You really *did* resent Morgan's interference, didn't you?"

"Oh, I never said I didn't resent the social-climbing bastard, did I?" Harley reminded. That he was drinking milk, and obviously not enjoying it, seemed to say a good deal. "I always marvel at how Morgan so successfully manages to look down on so many people, myself included, when *he's* the from-nowhere ex-pornographer. But, at least, I knew where he and I stood from the very first meeting. Horton and Jim were supposedly my friends. What they were, of course, were hustlers out to make a fast buck. You think they cared where my money came from, as long as I was buying paintings? It was only when they realized the well was running dry that they decided to cover their collective ass."

"*Did* you ask Lendland to cover for you?"

"Harley looked wary. "According to Lendland, his first indication of my financial problems was when I approached him with a request to perjure," Harley said. "Not saying I ever did any such thing, I *do* say it would have meant very little sweat off his balls to say that I'd spent considerably less on paintings than I had, but he insisted the bookkeeping of saying *that* was impossible. As if he or that shit-for-brains Jim keep accurate records! Jim can't count to twenty-one unless he drops his pants and brings his little digit of a pecker into play."

"If you could refresh my memory on why you were in Seattle at the time of Lendland's murder," Cord prodded.

"Can't be content in just seeing how far I've sunk?" Harley accused, eyes flashing. He waved off any efforts of Cord to deny it. "Oh, hell, what does it matter at this stage of the game? I was there to borrow some money from Curtis," Harley admitted. "It's not been easy to adjust to the small stipend my family gives me to live on these days. They gather daily to chant incantations to make me drop dead of natural causes, the only thing making them save me from starvation is the threat of more bad publicity."

"You flew to Seattle, met with Curtis Hurt—" Cord knew from Curtis that Harley got his loan. "—and flew directly back to Los Angeles?"

"Insert one night on the town," Harley instructed. "Not a very enjoyable night, mind you. There's a certain celebrity about losing a good deal of money, but it doesn't attract as much as does inheriting a bundle."

"You didn't see or contact Lendland or Holdsett the whole time you were there?"

"Why in the hell would I want to see or contact either of those two sons-of-bitches?" Harley asked with a dismissing sniff. "But in answer to your question, *No*. As," he added with a smile of snide satisfaction, "Curtis would have confirmed without your having had to waste the Washington State taxpayers' money by flying all of this way."

Cord didn't bother telling him he was in LA unofficially. This was just the first stop of three on Cord's list of extracurricular activities.

CHAPTER TWENTY-NINE

COOPER

"**A MURDERER?**" Cooper Reynes asked in obvious disbelief. "You're shitting me!"

"Killing *is* part of being a good solider," Cord reminded. "Morgan *did* enlist. No one shanghaied him."

"He was a Personnel Management Specialist, for Christ's sake!" Cooper protested. "He spent his time with a typewriter not an M-16."

"He couldn't know he was going to spend his whole enlistment behind a desk when he enlisted," Cord pointed out. "The Army could have shipped him off to a war zone at any time."

"Do you know how many college grads, with two years ROTC under their belts, enlisted in those days and opted to come into the Army as lowly privates, bypassing a commission or warrant-officer status, *and* Officer's Training School? So few that Morgan was the instant darling of a helluva lot of non-commissioned officers who saw him as the rarity he was, an educated man who apparently preferred their life-style to that of the brass and, thus, deserved their protection. Every time a commissioned officer came around to try and talk Morgan into signing up for OTS, each time Morgan said *no thanks,* his rating went up in an awfully lot of NCO score books. And it's the NCO's who pull all the strings in the military, no matter what the brass would like to think to the contrary."

"Morgan got expert medals for shooting, two years running," Cord said, moving the conversation back where he wanted it. Not that Morgan's expert gun-firing status automatically labeled him a killer all these years later.

"He did it without firing a shot, too," Cooper assured. "Look Detective, when you work in Army Personnel, having someone *fix* the paperwork for an expert badge is a piece of cake. In Morgan's job slot, he could have gotten a helluva lot more for the asking."

"What exactly *was* his job slot?"

"Transportation clerk. Not local point-to-point travel, either. The long haul, like deciding which enlisted men *and* officers came out of the Orient on which plane and on which boat. As no one wanted a boat, believe me, Morgan *was* in a position of power. Besides which, he prepared the rosters requesting all reassignments. One slip of his pen, and a guy asking for State's-side duty could end up in Timbuktu. Another slip and the same guy could be there today instead of tomorrow."

"Morgan never actually killed anyone, then, during his whole term of service?"

"Well, there was Sergeant Rodríguez," Cooper said, sounding anything but serious. He smiled. "But we could hardly count him, could we?"

Cord knew a leading question when he heard one, and he was tempted to refrain from playing straight man to whatever joke Cooper had up his comedic sleeve. However, he had come all of this way to LA to achieve certain insight. "What about Sergeant Rodríguez?" Cord asked.

"One of the exceptions to the rule about no one wanting to go to war in those days. He was one gung-ho mother-fucker, anxious as hell to kill the enemy for quick promotion."

"So?" Cord asked when it became apparent that Cooper was waiting for encouragement.

"Cord couldn't stand Rodríguez," Cooper said. "So, he pulled some strings to get the Sergeant what they both wanted: Rodríguez's reassignment to a war zone. Since Rodríguez was sniper-shot, disembarking at his reassignment destination, you might say Morgan was responsible, by proxy."

"You and Morgan were stationed at Orient Headquarters Command?"

"Correct."

"You'd been there three months when Morgan arrived." It wasn't a question.

"Word was out about his arrival before his plane even touched down. We had requests coming in from all sides for him. He was Regular Army and educated: an unbeatable combination in an Army known in those days more for grunts without high school diplomas. Headquarters had first grabs, though, and Kirkbaum wasted no time in reeling in the prize."

"Kirkbaum?"

"The warrant officer in charge. He and Morgan hit it off right away. Morgan hit it off with most people. Even with the officers who looked on him as a traitor to his education and potential."

"Sergeant Rodríguez, then, was some kind of an exception?"

"That, indeed, he was. There are always exceptions but, for the most part, they were few and far between. Morgan had a certain calculating charm. I remember when our new First Sergeant came aboard, fresh from a teaching stint at Fort Ord, California. Morgan was the orderly on duty that night and signed Finley in. As soon as Morgan found out First Sergeant Finley had been at Ord at the same time Morgan had been there, Morgan fed him a line of bullshit about having taken several of the First Sergeant's Advanced Individual Training courses. Of course, Morgan didn't *really* remember the old fart from shit, but it all paid off dividends at promotion times."

"The First Sergeant looked out for Morgan, did he?"

"Our company had a review board for every promotion," Cooper said, obviously warming to his subject. "A rinky-dink quizzing about Chain of Command, General Orders, the parts of the rifle, shit like that. Morgan refused to be bothered. He was put up for SP4 twice and declined to go before the board both times, saying the new rank and advanced pay grade weren't worth the effort. So, Finley got together with the First Sergeant at one of the Military Police companies attached to Headquarters. The MP's didn't require review boards. Morgan was made an MP for a day, just long enough to fill an available SP4 slot, before being transferred *back* to Headquarters. All neatly done on paper, without Morgan *physically* going anywhere. Was that VIP service, or wasn't it? Of course, later, our First Sergeant and the one at the MP company got reassigned early and, you can bet your ass, they went back to the States by plane. Morgan repaid favors and debts."

"How'd Morgan take care of his enemies?" Cord asked. "Sergeant Rodríguez ended up dead, but what about the others?"

"Who did you have in mind?" Cooper asked.

Cooper had been Morgan's friend during their time together in the service. The two still kept in touch. Cord really needed somebody more neutral on the subject. Someone not biased in Morgan's favor.

"Surely, there had to be more *exceptions* who hated his guts," Cord insisted. It had been his impression that most people either loved Morgan or hated him. Who were the other haters during his time in the service?

"My guess is that they went home by slow boat," Cooper ventured. "A fate worse than death, and you can take that from someone who spent some before-Morgan time on one of those sardine cans. I would have sold my soul for an airline ticket out." Had he?

"Morgan always went by plane, did he?" Cord guessed. Knowing what he did about Morgan, Cord figured he already had his answer. What's more, he was right.

"When he arrived in the Orient, he was the only private on a plane otherwise loaded with brass and noncoms," Cooper confirmed.

"How, I wonder, did he arrange that?"

"Morgan said that *anything* could be arranged if you knew the rules of the game in play."

"Morgan looked upon the Army as a game, did he?" Cord asked. It wasn't his first indication that Morgan considered pretty much *everything* a game."

"He might have, at that," Cooper granted. "He was in the Army, to hear him tell it, because it was *the thing to do*. Serving God and one's country could still look good on a résumé."

"So, why did Morgan risk the possibility of dishonorable discharge?"

"I'm not following," Cooper confessed curiously.

"Your overseas assignment had quite a gay underground at the time you and Morgan were there, the way I hear it," Cord elucidated. If he'd been unable to do in-depth research, he'd come up with a few basic facts long the way. "A bunch of gays were shipped home just before Morgan's arrival and another lot were rounded up and shipped back to the States shortly after he left. Morgan seems conveniently lucky to have been safely sandwiched in between."

"He wasn't gay, if that's what you mean," Cooper argued. "He just knew an awfully lot of *that* crowd. So many, he was told it might be better for him to leave early and avoid even a hint of guilt by association."

"Told to pull out early by whom?"

"Hell, he had his connections everywhere. He once arranged for an application from a corporal for marriage to a local to be processed in two days, when six months was the usual minimum. The intelligence officer assigned the case dropped by personally to tell Morgan that the girl in question was a known prostitute, but Morgan and the potential bridegroom already knew that. So, that was that. Certain papers were discreetly pulled, and somewhere in the good old U.S. of A. today, there's an ex-hooker happily married to her ex-GI because of Morgan's connections."

"That happened often: soldiers marrying locals?" Cord knew where he was taking this. He hoped Cooper would follow along.

"Usually, we just fucked them," Cooper said. "Some guys, though, did, occasionally, get carried away, their cocks ruling their brains."

"How about Morgan? Did he get carried away on occasion?"

"How do you mean?" Cooper asked, not making it easy. Apparently if Cord wanted information, he had to work for it. As usual.

"He have any special local lady he might have considered taking home to mom?" Cord asked putting it in black and white.

"Jesus, no! You didn't enlist in the Army as part of any long-run plan and, then, blackball yourself by trying the knot with Miss Orient."

"He kept away from whores, then?"

"Oh, I see where you're heading—once again," Cooper said with a nod of enlightenment. "But you're way off base."

"Where *am* I heading?" Cord asked.

"Morgan *did* like girls," Cooper insisted.

"You're sure about that, are you?" Cord pressed. Cooper certainly seemed a lot surer of his facts than most.

"*Everybody* was sure," Cooper assured. "How else do you think Morgan managed to associate with those gays and come out with his rank and honorable discharge intact? Had there been any question, there would have been no saving him."

"But just *how,* I continue to wonder, can anyone—can *you*—be so one hundred percent sure?"

"One, because I set him up with one whore. Two, I got a cut from the gal's pimp every time Morgan fucked her, which gave me an awfully lot of pocket money at the time. Three, I saw Morgan take the broad on, plus another whore, in tandem, leaving them both begging for more."

"You *saw* him fuck two prostitutes?" Cord asked. Surprised? Hell, he'd known all along there had to be some reason for Morgan so successfully escaping the noose of the purges. The military still shied away from any association with homosexuals, and there had been even more paranoia in the Army of Morgan's day. "Tell me more about this prostitute you set him up with."

"What can I tell you? Miss Kim was but one more whore among thousands. She and the girl with whom I was shacked up at the time, plus several other *ladies of the night,* shared digs owned by their mutual pimp. Very informal-like, you know. Hell, more than once I was in the middle of a screw and one of the other girls, or the pimp, would come strolling in without knocking. At first, it was a bit disconcerting, let me tell you. After awhile, though, I got used to it and just kept right on fucking. Voyeurs didn't bother Morgan, either.

In fact, he turned in some of his best stud-man performances before those impromptu audiences."

"You wouldn't know where I could find this Miss Kim, now, could you?"

"Hardly! Morgan once told me that when he'd shipped out, he'd left her with her legs splayed and her feet aimed at the ceiling, offering up her cunt to some lieutenant."

"Would you be at all surprised to hear she ended up getting herself killed?" Cord asked, grabbing at straws. This was the first he'd heard of the woman.

"No, it wouldn't surprise me, at all," Cooper dismissed. "Those dizzy Oriental broads were always getting knifed or knifing one another. They called it *cutting down the competition*."

CHAPTER THIRTY

SCOTT

"SO, WHAT BRINGS A SEATTLE police detective all of the way down here to sunny LA?" Scott Jesse asked, shaking Cord's hand before motioning him to a chair in the cluttered office. In the main studio, beyond the closed door, two attractive young men, naked as jays, beneath terry-cloth-robes, were awaiting a photo shoot.

"A murder investigation," Cord informed, taking a snapshot of Bobby Jordan out of his inside coat pocket and handing it across the desk. "I thought maybe you knew him." If Bobby Jordan were Cord's excuse, not his *real* reason for being there, it wasn't so far-fetched an excuse. Bobby *had* been in LA. He *was* an attractive young man who'd known Scott Jesse, having once broken an expensive camera of Morgan Kent that Scott had literally been flashing around Seattle gay bars.

Scott checked the picture and shook his head. Not necessarily unusual, considering the camera breakage *had* been a long time back in Scott's possibly fuzzier and more drunken past. "So many attractive young men pass through here in the course of any given day," he apologized, buzzing for his assistant who was coordinating activities in the next room. "Michael, would you come in here for just a minute," he instructed, then turned his attention back to Cord. "Michael has a memory for faces," he said. The next interruption was the entrance of the attractive blond who had ushered Cord into the office in the first place. Michael accepted the photo Scott handed him. "Recognize this one?" Scott asked.

"Bobby *something*," Michael identified, and to say Cord was surprised by the positive ID was an understatement. Cord's main purpose for seeing Scott Jesse was to pump the man about the photographer's relationship with Morgan Kent. Cord had arrived with no preconceived suspicions that his ruse for this interview would turn up such unexpected pay dirt. "I think we used him for that *Stop Pollution—Pick up a Faggot* card."

"Oh, yes!" Scott admitted as if a familiar chord had finally been struck. "Pull that file, will you?" He smiled apologetically at Cord. "Before Michael, this place was really pure chaos," he admitted. Michael handed Scott a file from a cabinet near the desk, and Scott opened it. "Right," Scott confirmed. "Bobby *Jordan*." He handed Cord one of the greeting cards which had resulted from the photo shoot. On the front, a bluejeaned Bobby, naked to the waist and sporting a bulged crotch that looked too obscene to be believed, was hitchhiking on a lonely country road. *Stop Pollution—Pick up a Faggot* was the attending caption. "You say the kid was murdered?" Scott asked.

"We think his death might have been drug-related," Cord said, deciding that the Scott-Bobby connection definitely needed more probing.

"Of course, you know more about it than I do," Scott said, his attention momentarily back on the file, "but the boys Morgan recommends to me are usually clean as newly fallen snow."

"Morgan Kent?" Cord asked automatically, grateful it had been Scott, not Cord, who'd brought up Morgan's name; although it, also, brought in a few new aspects to Cord's investigation that the policeman could have done without.

"You know Morgan?" Scott asked curiously. Cord had to be careful to keep Scott's defenses down.

"Isn't he a writer or something in Seattle?" Cord suggested vaguely.

"That's Morgan all right," Scott agreed. "He and I go back a long ways. Actually, we were in the Army together."

"*You* were in the Army?" Cord asked and immediately moved forward with his *God-am-I flustered* routine. "I guess I merely assumed.... Well, I am aware that the bulk of your work, and...." Even a retard could take it from there.

"My Army days preceded my official exit from the closet," Scott admitted with a smile. "It was only after I was in the military that I finally realized I was *truly* liable to get my balls shot off by the enemy before *I* shot them off in more friendly male territory."

"Your Army job slot was...?"

"I shot pictures for the *Stars and Stripes*."

"And you met Morgan Kent *in the service?*"

"Yes."

"Morgan Kent, likewise, in the closet?"

"Well, at the time I met him, he was availing himself regularly of the services provided by one particular prostitute of the *female* persuasion. However, the rumor had it that he had more than his share of gay friends and, then, I *did* run into him in Seattle at a gay bar. So...." He shrugged. "Actually, Morgan remains somewhat vague about his sexual preferences, at least around me. And since we've never *made it*, together, I'm sure as hell no authority. I do know he's never had anything against gays. As a matter of fact, he advanced me a sizable sum to start up this business, knowing I'd be catering to the homosexual marketplace. Of course, that was before either of us realized there would be such a lucrative boom of women libbers interested in exploiting the male body. I'd like to see the ex- pressions on a few thousand female readers of the presently popular male-exploitation magazines were they to learn that two-thirds of those hunky centerfolds, with whom the horny broads fantasize sex, are actually too busy putting *it* to men to pay all that much attention to pussy."

"You said Morgan referred Bobby Jordan to you?"

"That *is* what it says here," Scott said, tapping the file folder but sounding as if he couldn't be sure.

"What exactly did Morgan say in the letter of introduction?"

"Oh, it's never that formal," Scott explained. "Some kid in Seat- tle lets drop that he's heading for LA and, if he has potential, Mor- gan gives him my name and number. I certainly don't need any kind of background info on these guys, except to know they're over eighteen and preferably hung like a horse. Photographs deal with externals, unless you adhere to the theory that externals reflect the inner man. A theory which, considering some of the genuine jerks I've photographed who came across on film looking like a million bucks, I'd be happy to debate with you."

"Are you familiar with the name Horton Lendland?" Cord asked.

"Not right off hand," Scott said, sounding apologetic. "But I'm worse at names than I am with faces. Is he someone I *should* know?"

"He was a friend of Bobby's in Seattle who happens to have been murdered, too."

"Another drug-related killing, was it?" Scott asked.

"Some people do think so," Cord said, failing to add that the majority thought not.

"Well, I really wish I could help you, Detective," Scott said, sounding sincere, "but I run a clean shop. Considering the sexual connotations of most of my work, I have to be extra careful to avoid police harassment. No reflection on you, or on the local authorities, you understand, but cops, in general, do tend to be homophobic."

Cord wondered if Scott had explained away, as just another exception, the case of the *dead-from-an-overdose* muscleman, Grey Matthews, another *model* who'd appeared on one of Scott's cards.

"Did Bobby have a local address?" Cord asked for the moment.

"None that I see here," Scott said, checking the file, "but Michael might have something. A lot of my models live on the streets, or shack up for the duration with whomever Tom, Dick, or Harry is available for any one evening."

"It must be inconvenient when you want to round your models up for a shoot," Cord observed.

"Tell me about it," Scott agreed. "However, that's just one of the facts of life I have to deal with in my business. Despite all those fictitious bios you'll see accompanying male centerfolds. You know the ones: *Bill is an architect who, in his spare time, enjoys eating blintzes and listening to Wagner on his stereo with that one special lady.* Most guys with good jobs aren't pulling down their pants for the prices I'm paying. So, I make do. I let a model know when I want him and, nine times out of ten, he shows up, because he needs the bread."

"So, Bobby Jordan just showed up here one day, said Morgan Kent sent him, after which you photographed him, and he dropped back out of sight," Cord summated.

"That's pretty much it in a nutshell," Scott agreed.

"What about Bobby's royalty payments for sales of the card? Where'd you mail those?"

"All of my models sign up-front all-rights releases for which they're given a one-time lump payment for their session," Scott explained. "It saves me paperwork, and they don't know where they'll be from one moment to the next, anyway."

"What about the time Bobby broke that expensive camera of Morgan Kent that you were using to snap pictures of Seattle queers?" Cord dropped on him. "Did you carry around any long-lasting grudge?"

CHAPTER THIRTY-ONE

MICHAEL

"**DETECTIVE MAXWELL,** Seattle Police, may I introduce detectives Fairchild and Wentlin, LAPD," Michael Moore said, Cord's paranoia obvious. "They and I work narcotics," Michael continued. "Our question to you: What in the hell do *you* work?"

Cord was in Michael's apartment. Rather, he was in *the* apartment to which Michael had given Cord the address earlier at Scott Jesse's studio. *"Let me check around about Bobby Jordan and see what I can come up with for you,"* Michael had said. *"Drop by my place tonight, why* don't *you, and I'll fill you in with whatever."*

"So, Cord had dropped by. For this! "You're a cop?" Cord said, having taken Scott Jesse's assistant for *anything but*. He watched detectives Fairchild and Wentlin holster their guns which had kept Cord pretty much rooted to the spot on the couch since the two men had materialized unexpectedly from the bedroom.

"My ID," Michael said, displaying his badge and giving Cord plenty of time to read the attending small print. "We've already confirmed you're who you say you are, although you have us and one Seattle Police captain confused as to why you're busy screwing up one of our operations when you're supposedly at a cousin's wedding. You even have a cousin in LA, Maxwell?"

"I hate weddings," Cord said lamely. "So, since I was in the neighborhood, I thought I'd check out a few leads I had on a kid blown away recently in Seattle."

"And there's going to be shit to pay if, by not bothering to check in with us first, you fucked up a collar we've been working on for one helluva long time!" Michael warned.

"Scott Jesse?"

"Bigger fish to fry, here, than Jesse," Michael said. "We could have picked up that queer's ass a long time ago if his was the only one we wanted. Now, we have to sit back and see if you've scared off the really big whales by barging in and broadcasting to a mere minnow about possible police awareness of a drug link."

"Maxwell, you are an A-one fuck-up!" Detective Morris Fairchild condemned from across the room.

CHAPTER THIRTY-TWO

JACK

"**CAN'T I LET YOU LOOSE** in polite society without you ruffling feathers?" Jack Sudlow chided from Seattle.

Cord adjusted his position on the hotel bed and shifted the phone from his right to his left ear. "I was told the *good* news beat me back to Seattle," Cord observed, disgruntled.

"Speaking of beating it back to Seattle," Jack said, his voice not totally without amusement, "I have a message to you from the Captain that, if delivered verbatim, would be misconstrued as an obscene phone call. Suffice it to say he requests the pleasure of your company at the very earliest convenience."

"I'm scheduled out of here at six o'clock on *Northwest.*"

"Yeah, well, I hope you're traveling with a suitcase full of answers."

"The Captain was ticked, was he?" Cord asked, knowing his question superfluous.

"Not *just* because you screwed up some LAPD sting, by the way. Some guy down there by the name of Jesse—got that?"

"Scott Jesse," Cord confirmed.

"—called Morgan Kent to find out what in the hell was happening that had a Seattle detective nosing around. Not only did Kent go to some bigwig in the Mayor's office to complain, but he had Judd Kleverton— You know that dude from Kleverton Lumber?"

"I know the one."

"—and Robert Lasalo—*that* ring any bells?"

"Just get on with it, Jack! This call isn't likely to be expense-account deductible."

"—call the Mayor to suggest you're spending an inordinate amount of time—albeit, unbeknownst to them, your *free* time—trying to pin the Lendland murder on Kent when Kent doesn't even have a motive. Does that, or doesn't that, they're wondering aloud—*very aloud*—to our captain, constitute harassment?"

169

"Look, this photographer, down here, knew Bobby Jordan, in LA *and* in Seattle," Cord argued. "What's more, there were bad feelings between the two in Seattle. Not to mention an awfully lot of dead and/or missing people who Morgan Kent knew once upon a time."

"We talking *Biblical knew,* are we, good buddy?" Jack asked suggestively.

"Circumstantial evidence could paint it that way," Cord admitted.

"Kent didn't screw Sue Parring, did he?" Jack asked.

Cord's insides did a slow roll. Sue Parring being the woman Tony France had insinuated was fucking not only Tony's one-time lover, Russ Tompson, *but* Morgan Kent, a few years back. Though Sue was missing, Morgan had had a wild hunch as to where she just might be at the moment, and he'd asked Jack to check it out. With any results? "You have something on Parring, then?" he asked, fighting for calm and cool.

"I've saved the best until last, haven't I, Detective Maxwell?"

"Come on, Jack! What do you have for me?"

"As you suggested, Sue Parring turned out to be a certain Seattle lady in a baggie. A lady very dead from *homicidal violence of an undetermined nature*. We got the positive ID on her just this afternoon, based on dental records."

"Jesus!" Cord's exhalation of held-in breath was loud and long. Sue, dead and bundled up in a baggie, just like another potential fuck-mate of Morgan Kent—Tara Robinson—was dead and had been bagged in Portland, Oregon. Opalline Elizabeth Sinclair dead and bagged somewhere, too? Russ Tompson definitely dead! By the sounds of it, Morgan Kent fucking you was paramount to buying the big farm in the sky. The bastard's sperm was lethal! Or was it all, albeit unbelievably, merely coincidental?

"Is that surprise I hear?" Jack asked. "I mean, you *did* give me the choice of this Parring dame or Sandra Wheems, didn't you?" Sandra Wheems, one-time fruit-fly on the Seattle gay scene, now dropped out of sight (of her own volition?), was another missing lady who might have opened her legs for Morgan Kent's fat cock. Now another corpse somewhere? Jesus! "Granted, I would have bet on *Wheems* being the one in the baggie," Jack continued. "Not only was she a fruit-fly, but she turned a few tricks in her time. And we know how some people do like to make it with prostitutes and then drop them by the wayside."

"See you soon, Jack. I've a plane to catch."

"Do remember to bring those answers for the Captain, Cord!" Jack insisted. "I would have greedily claimed all of the credit for the Parring ID, but I don't have a clue as to how I might have pulled her name out of the hat. Neither the Captain nor I have a clue as to how *you* managed to come up with it. From Portland, no less, wasn't it?"

"Do you recall your little talk with someone out of Portland about M.O.'s when you were out to shift Seattle's *lady-in-a-bag* out of the *Dint Slough* killer's ballpark?"

"Affirmative. Cop named Turner, right? Reggie Turner."

"Right. Well, Portland's *dead-lady-in-a-bag,* who supplied you with the magic M.O., was, at one time, a very, very close friend of Morgan Kent. As close, maybe, even as Sue Parring and Sandra Wheems were close to him."

"Back to talking *fucking* close, are we, good buddy?"

"It all depends upon to whom we talk."

"Well, I have heard of a switch-hitter or two in my time. Matter of fact, a guy I once knew even professed to have fucked a dog, that having been all that was available at the time. Can't say, though, as I believed him. You think Kent might be a real-live honest-to-goodness bi?"

"Frankly, I don't know what we have."

"Better think of something," Jack warned. "The Captain isn't going to be satisfied with any ifs, ands, or buts on this one."

"Thanks for that word of encouragement," Cord said, breaking the connection.

CHAPTER THIRTY-THREE

VICTOR

"**YOU'RE NOT EVEN ASSIGNED** the Bobby Jordan case," Captain Victor Smith, Seattle PD, reminded. "Yet, supposedly in Los Angeles for the wedding of a cousin—who, by the way, turns out to live in Spokane, married already—you're flashing pictures of Jordan to some faggot photographer."

"Scott Jesse was an Army buddy of Morgan Kent," Cord explained. "Kent is a suspect in the Lendland murder."

"Morgan Kent has more important friends that *just* some LA fag photographer," Victor said. "Be forewarned."

"I heard you were getting pressure from the Mayor's office."

"We're possibly not talking unwarranted pressure, you know?" Victor suggested. "Maybe we're talking a valid complaint, huh? Because going all of the way to LA, premeditatedly behind my back, just to ask questions about Morgan Kent from his old Army buddy, does seem a bit overzealous."

"I didn't figure the department would carry the extra expense."

"And you figured right. Nonetheless, even detectives are supposed to go through the chain of command. It's worse that you didn't come back with anything. You didn't, did you?"

"I identified the Parring woman," Cord pointed out, waiting for the captain to point out how that had been accomplished out of Portland, not out of LA.

"You weren't assigned *that* murder, either," Victor said instead. "You weren't assigned the Bobby Jordan murder. You were assigned to find Horton Lendland's killer. Tell me, did you do that?"

"Look, there are missing persons and bodies all over the place, Lendland's included, that connect to Morgan Kent. Russ Tompson, a guy Morgan might or might not have fucked, dead of a hit-and-run. Sue Parring and Tara Robinson, women Morgan might or might not have fucked, murdered and stuffed into baggies. Sandra Wheems, part-time fruit-fly and part-time prostitute, who Morgan might or might not have fucked, missing. Mary Bjorn, a woman Kent lived with, and might or might not have fucked, dead…."

"Come on, Maxwell," Victor interrupted. "I know for a fact that Mary Bjorn was not only in her eighties, but she died in the hospital after an operation for gallstones. You're blaming Kent for that, for Christ's sake?"

"Mary Bjorn was almost run over by a car a matter of weeks before her operation. She was pulled out of the way by a passerby who broke her collarbone during that successful rescue. Her weakened physical condition, due primarily to that collarbone injury, was part of the reason she didn't make it through the operation for gall-stones."

"And Morgan Kent was in Europe at the time," Victor stated. Obviously, he hadn't gotten where he was without keeping tabs on what was and wasn't going down around him. "He was in Los Angeles when Tompson got it via a hit-and-run. He was on a cruise of the South Pacific when Robinson disappeared. He was at a party here in Seattle when Bobby Jordan got his. You think Kent is some kind of magician who can be in two places at once?"

"He doesn't have an alibi for the night Lendland was murdered," Cord insisted.

"And don't you think someone clever enough to be responsible for all the murders you want to place at his doorstep would, once again, be sure he had an alibi for this one?" Victor asked patronizingly. "Hell, he could have *said* he'd stayed to see that movie another time, and who would have said differently? He'd already seen it so many times, why *not* another?" Victor pushed himself back in his chair and folded his arms. "I think you've possibly become too involved in the Lendland case, Maxwell," he criticized.

"Too involved?" Cord echoed. How in the hell could a cop get *too* involved in an investigation?

"It happens sometimes," Victor consoled. "When it does, it's easy to lose perspective."

"You think I've lost perspective?"

"Either that, or, for whatever the reasons, you have it out for Morgan Kent."

"That's shit!" Cord challenged, regretting the retort the moment it was out. He wasn't reassured by the red that flushed Captain Smith's features from Prince Charles' ear to Prince Charles' ear. The Captain's bald head suddenly appeared sunburned: an obvious illusion, since it had been raining steadily in Seattle for the last week.

"Do you want to repeat that last comment, Detective Maxwell?" Victor asked; his voice was noticeably strained. "I didn't quite catch it."

"I said you were mistaken," Cord amended, knowing a second chance when he heard one, and not too proud to take it. He respected the Captain for maintaining his cool. "It's just that everywhere I turn, Kent's name keeps popping up."

"The gay community is an incestuous community," Victor remarked, his face still a shade pinker than normal. "Though it isn't as large as some homophobes like to think it is, it does have a crime rate way out of proportion to its size. That's because of the nature of the homosexual animal, rampant promiscuity breeding strange bedfellows. The more strangers you sleep with, the more you're apt to meet up with a weird one. Your odds not helped by a segment of that subculture which is devoted to whips, chains, and other accouterments of torture. By *you* and *your,* I'm figuratively speaking, you understand."

Cord felt his skin flush, and he mentally replayed the Captain's last comment. "I'd like to continue my investigation," he said, deciding he was being paranoid for no reason. If he *had* been too long with queers, he wasn't a quitter.

"Wouldn't you prefer coming back over to the *Dint Slough* task force?" Victor invited. "Sudlow could take over for you, since he pretty much seems up on the Lendland case."

"I'd like to remain on the Lendland investigation," Cord repeated. He had *something,* even if he hadn't nailed it down. With a little luck, he'd get it all pulled together.

Victor sighed. He came forward in his chair and leaned across his desk to insinuate sincere bonhomie. "I wouldn't want your head all fucked up over this one," he said, friend-to-friend, priest-to-acolyte, father-to-son, captain to detective. "Gays live in a world all their very own, with mores and manners which straights, like you and I, can't possibly begin to fathom."

"I don't know what you mean, sir," Cord said, hoping against hope that he didn't know.

"Broke up with your girlfriend recently, did you?" Victor asked. Cord knew there had been no real change in their subject of conversation, although it might have appeared that way to any just-arrived-on-the-scene eavesdropper.

"Yes, sir," Cord said, admitting the well-known but taking it no farther.

"Amicable breakup, was it?"

"Yes, sir."

"Good," Victor said, sounding genuinely relieved. "I've known men who had a falling out with a wife or a girlfriend and came out of the ordeal questioning their manhood. I'd hate to think I dropped you into a gay sewer if you had any such festering wound. People like Morgan Kent are difficult to understand under the best of circumstances, you know? I met him once at a charity thing to which my wife insisted upon dragging me. Kent had just come back from the final shooting of that World War II miniseries they'd made out of his book. Though my wife doesn't approve of homosexuality, she though Kent was *charming*. Actually, she thought him *fascinatingly exotic,* and my wife isn't one for hyperbole."

"I'm afraid I'm losing you, sir," Cord insisted, refusing to follow through the verbal maze.

"It's *I* afraid of losing *you*," Victor admitted, "to some kind of vendetta you may have against Morgan Kent. A vendetta the likes of which you, or I, or anyone else is likely to sort out for you."

What in the hell *was* he saying? "I have no intentions of incriminating an innocent man!" Cord insisted, with as much indignation as he could muster.

"Just remember, Maxwell," Victor said, pulling back to lengthen the distance between them, "that no one really expects miracles as regards the Lendland killing. It's too obviously one of those crimes that tells you from the beginning, as if it has a goddamned voice of its own, that it's going to be sitting in the active files for one helluva long time. That you've managed to come up with identification on the Parring woman is a bonus for which you can be proud when the time comes for you to move on to something with more priority. Failure, in a case like the Lendland murder, isn't something that's going to be held against your record. In fact, I'll see to it that—" He was interrupted by a ring of the phone, his frown saying more than anything that the sudden stringent sound was unappreciated. "Captain Smith here!" he answered quickly and brusquely. A few seconds and a short conversation later, he hung up and turned to Cord. "I wouldn't plan any more trips to LA in the very near future, Maxwell," he said, looking less pleased than when he'd answered the phone. "Scott Jesse was just found murdered—executioner's-style—by a bullet to the back of his head. This leaves you with very few friends in the LAPD at the moment."

CHAPTER THIRTY-FOUR

Matthew

"**I CAN'T SAY I UNDERSTAND** the connection," Matthew J. Rears of *Peterson, Torquen and Rears* said once Cord was settled in, "but Jack said it *could* be important, and I've known Jack Sudlow for a long time. So, how can I help?"

"During the trial, your client, Andy Sacks, professed...."

"*Professed?*" Matthew interrupted. "I remain firmly convinced, Detective Maxwell, that Gary Green *is* as guilty as hell. That the jury somehow came in with a not-guilty verdict, assisted by a lot of well-meaning witnesses who thought they were coming to the aid of a much-maligned innocent teacher about to be martyred in the recent gamut of child-abuse cases, doesn't change my opinion. You know, Green's sister as much as told me he fooled around with both of her two kids. Of course, she wasn't about to testify to that in court, or let her kids put Uncle Gary behind bars—which is where the son-of-a-bitch very well should be." Cord didn't interrupt. It was obvious the lawyer wanted to vent. "Smartest thing Green ever did," Matthew continued, "was keeping his hands off his own students and restricting his perversions to Sacks whose life was so fucked up already that the kid wouldn't come off as a reliable witness in court. Yes, oh, yes, but Green did come out the Good Samaritan betrayed by the fatherless boy he tried to befriend. Befriend, my ass! All that Green gave Andy Sacks was cock every which way from Sunday. Our problem was in how long it took for the tale to come out. Whatever the physical damage, it was healed. And Andy had been catapulted into puberty during the interim. Suddenly, he was a young man the jury couldn't see being physically forced into anything. Even I found it ludicrous seeing Andy and Green side by side. Andy was a foot taller, making the raped and the rapist look like Mutt and Jeff, the levity of which didn't help our case, you can bet your ass. Jesus, listen to me!" he exclaimed with a disgusted shake of his head. "It sounds like so much bitter grapes, doesn't it?"

176

"I'm interested," Cord admitted.

"You don't think Green killed Lendland, do you?" Matthew asked, his disbelief evident in his tone. "Lendland was too old to tickle Green's fancy."

"Lendland and his killer didn't necessarily have sex prior to the killing," Cord reminded. "Evidence of sexual intercourse, other than by spear, is inconclusive, due to the state of the body after the fire."

"Green has a motive, does he?" Matthew asked hopefully. Unable to send Green up on a charge of pederasty, he apparently would settle for a murder conviction.

"Actually, there's little evidence to support Green even having known Lendland, except in passing."

"Oh!" Matthew punctuated with a grunt of disappointment. "So, why sift through the ashes of a dead-and-buried court case?"

"I don't now about you, but when I get stymied in an investigation, I begin looking just about anywhere for new leads," Cord explained. "Since the obvious avenues have dried up, I'm looking farther field. Green is a good friend of someone who's a suspect."

"That would be Morgan Kent, I suppose," Matthew successfully identified. He must have read Cord's surprise, because he immediately added, "I've a contact in the Mayor's office who keeps me informed."

"Were you aware that Kent and Lendland were at *Ka-Nee-Da* at the same time Green and your client were there?"

"You think Lendland saw something happen between Andy and Green that might have brought a retrial had Lendland ever decided to tell it?" Matthew ventured.

"Is that possible?" Cord reacted, ready to jump at just about anything.

"I don't think so," Matthew said. "I knew Lendland and Kent were there. The way I heard it, Kent and Lendland were out for some mere fun in the sun. Lendland, Kent, Andy and Green all got together for dinner one night, but that was it. Andy didn't see either Kent or Lendland anywhere near a bedroom."

"Kent and Lendland being there didn't come out in the trial, did it?" Cord had read all the pertinent articles, although specifics had been often left out because Andy was a juvenile. Lately, Cord had given the *pilfered-by-a-friend* file a once-over. He couldn't find Kent or Lendland mentioned.

"No," Matthew admitted. "Frankly, their testimony would have been of little use to us. In fact, it could have been downright detrimental if either had testified Andy, for having been raped in Spokane, Boise, Idaho Falls, Yellowstone, Salt Lake City, Reno, *and*

177

Medford, didn't look any the worst for wear by the time he and Green checked into *Ka-Nee-Da*. Testimonials of the kind I could anticipate from *any* friend of Gary Green. Besides which, neither could have seen much, even if he'd been willing to give an unbiased recount, because Andy says, surprisingly, Green didn't do anything to Andy in *Ka-Nee-Da*. What Green *did* do was jack-off, making Andy think the raping was finally over."

Cord didn't bother asking why Andy might have mistakenly given the impression to Morgan, Lendland, or to anyone else, that he wasn't being *put upon* by the time he'd reached *Ka-Nee-Da*. The victim of multiple rapes should have been looking at least a little under the weather by that time. "However, no such luck!" Matthew continued. "Once in Portland, Green took up the sexual molestations again as if there'd never been the short respite."

CHAPTER THIRTY-FIVE

KENDALL

"FOR TWO REASONS," Kendall Franklin of *Stevens, Westshall, Franklin and Lambert*, explained. "One, my client asked that neither be called on his behalf. Gary felt there was little point in publicly linking them to the scandal. Kent's somewhat sordid past was behind him, and Gary, innocent as he was, just didn't feel any possible tainting of his friend's hard-earned respectability, even by unsubstantiated insinuation, was worth it. Not that Gary's wishes would have stopped me from calling *any one* if I'd personally thought it necessary. However, by the Sacks boy's own admission, there'd been no sex between him and my client at *Ka-Nee-Da*. So, we didn't need collaborating testimony. Nor did we need Kent as a character witness, since we already had plenty of those. In fact, Gary is such an A-1 teacher, we had grateful parents and students lined up for blocks to testify the Sacks kid's accusations were a bunch of slanderous bullshit. Don't ever let anyone tell you justice, in the good old U.S. of A., doesn't win out in the end, more often than not."

CHAPTER THIRTY-SIX

OLIVE

"YOU REALIZE GREEN'S HOMOSEXUALITY, *per se*, was never in question?" Olive Wexler, MD, PS, said and bit the erasure of her pencil. "Green never did deny it. What he denied was the *nature* of his homosexuality. Pederasty versus sex with men above the age of consent. Laws against sexual discrimination pretty much shielded him from prosecution or persecution for the latter in a school district of above-average income families, where heads of households are considerably more liberal than their counterparts in average, below-average, or lower-income situations. Green's case was helped by his exemplary performance as a teacher for so many years without incident or scandal. When the accusations came, they came not from any of his students, past or present, but from an unknown outsider of low-class origins. Those accusations were a reflection not only on Green's reputation but on the judgment of parents and students who had already found Green above reproach. Educated, fair-minded people couldn't believe they'd been duped. Ergo, the Sacks boy was judged vindictive not because he'd suffered a series of sexual assaults but because he hated his father who'd discarded him, an unfortunate Green having become the detested *father-figure* via the *Big-Cousins* program. Green's case was, also, helped by *John Doe v. Lieftworth* and *John Doe v. Jones,* both of which reversed the heretofore universally accepted premise that small children can't lie about *such thing*s but only *report* what's happened. Besides, Andy Sacks was no small child when the alleged molestations occurred. He was, in fact, so near adolescence that puberty occurred before the case reached the courtroom. Judge and jury were confronted by a physically changed young man who not only looked capable of defending himself against any unwanted physical advances by Green but probably *was* able to do so by that stage of things."

"You completed a psychological profile on Green for the prosecution."

"That's correct."

"In which you reached the professional conclusion that he *could* have been guilty as charged."

"In all fairness, I must point out that psychiatry and psychology are subjective, as versus objective, fields, Detective Maxwell. No more fully illustrated than by my learned colleague for the defense, Dr. Grownal, who believed Green totally innocent of the charges. Our conclusions were so contradictory, they cancelled each other out, the defense and the prosecution deciding to omit any psychiatric testimony altogether."

"I have an appointment to see Dr. Grownal later this afternoon."

"Then, I'll refrain from offsetting my comments with his, letting him argue his points himself."

"I remain confused as to how, if Green were sexually drawn to children, there were no reported incidents of his molesting any of his students. Weren't they the most logical as his potential victims?"

"It's a misconception, Detective Maxwell, even held by some within my profession, that sexual drives *always* operate to the detriment of all rhyme or reason. Granted, that *does* sometimes happen. As in the case of the man who assaults the neighborhood boy collecting for the newspaper, or the man molesting the *Camp Fire* girl selling her cookies. Such actions are taken despite the danger of discovery, because there is little or no conscious control by the initiating individual over his sexual impulses. However, in my opinion, most people, even those with a predisposition toward sexual release outside the accepted norm, aren't so much the puppets of their unnatural urges as even they are want to believe. Why? Because they've been programmed to the contrary since birth, knowing what is right and what is wrong. They've become cognizant of the punishments for deviation: prison; ostracism; loss of prestige, reputation, job position; et al. They have the capacity to balance consequences against actions, calculating risks. It's only when risk is seen as minimal that the scale tips in favor of an otherwise unacceptable-to-them course. Why do you think so many cases of child abuse occur within the family? It's because the instigator feels himself in charge of that environment. Green molesting one of his students would have had attending threats of all kinds of dire consequences. Had that remained his only alternative, he might have gone through life with certain unnatural needs kept in check. However, *Big Cousins* provided a situation wherein he was put into close contact with a boy whose own problems, resulting from desertion by a father, alcoholism by a mother, and a poverty-level existence, made Andy Sacks an easy victim with minimal risk. Having had one father desert him, Andy could be cowed by the threat of being responsible for the desertion of a father-figure. Having suddenly been exposed to the material things of life—gifts like the stereo, the tape deck, the television that Green gave, *not as a lover but as a surrogate father*— the boy could be made distraught by the thought of losing what other boys his age got as a matter of course. Needless to say, Dr. Grownal interpreted things differently."

"He put more weight on Andy having been homosexually active prior to Green?" Cord suggested, having done his homework.

"Whether or not Andy was *knowledgeable in the carnal sense* prior to Green's arrival doesn't eradicate the fact that the boy *was* underage. Consenting *adults* means just that."

It came out during your interview with Green that, when a minor, he had been molested by his own father. Isn't that a typical catalyst for role reversal as an adult?"

"Yes and no," Olive said. "More vaguely: sometimes, sometimes not. Many child molesters *have* been sexually abused as minors. On the other hand, there are people molested as children who, through strength of character, or whatever, manage quite well within the normal sexual boundaries imposed upon them by society. Therefore, I can say, yes, Green's molestation by his father was likely a contributing factor to his aberrant behavior, but Dr. Grownal can as easily sight valid examples of his own to support his deductions to the contrary."

CHAPTER THIRTY-SEVEN

RICHARD

"**THERE IS NO DOUBT IN MY MIND** that Gary Green was the victim of a very disturbed and malicious young man out to punish a *father-figure* for the crimes of the father," Richard Grownal, MD, PS, said with firm conviction. "There was no indication that Green's homosexuality exceeded normal bounds."

"*Normal* bounds?" Cord questioned.

The Doctor's patronizing expression told Cord that Richard Grownal looked upon the cop as something of an extinct creature—or one that very well *should* be extinct. "Homosexuality isn't a disease," Richard said patiently. "And what two consenting adults do in the privacy of their own bedroom should be nobody's business but their own, or don't you agree?"

"It has been suggested that children are often the victims of sexual abuse not because they're genuinely epitomized as sex objects, but simply because they're all that's available," Cord said, ignoring the Doctor's question.

"I'm familiar with that line of thinking," Richard admitted.

"What if what Green *really* wanted wasn't available?" Cord suggested.

"But, it *was* available, Detective Maxwell!" Richard emphasized with the seeming patience of Job. "Available to him from any one of a number of Seattle gay bars, gay steam baths, and/or gay cruising areas. Sex without the necessity of prolonged courtship. Sex, in most instances, without cost. Sex certainly more convenient and risk-free than sex with Andy Sacks."

"Green doesn't exactly remind me of someone who'd have much success in attracting any takers through the usual gay outlets, the marketplace infamous for placing such high stock and demand on superficialities like good looks and good body," Cord said, watching Richard—no example of prime manhood himself—wince at the observation."

183

"Beauty is in the eye of the beholder, Maxwell," Richard reminded, retaining his professional composure, "and maybe you just have a jaundiced eye. It has been my professional experience that the sexual preferences within the gay community are as varied as those within the straight community. I have one gay patient who weighs in at over three-hundred pounds and is dearly beloved by another man attractive enough to be a movie star. Nor do you have to be a great beauty when you're on the paying end; the streets of any big city, these days, Seattle no exception, are filled with sub-teens out peddling their asses for a few bucks spending money."

CHAPTER THIRTY-EIGHT

ELLEN

"**I WASN'T BORN YESERDAY,** Detective Maxwell," Ellen Riley, MD, PS, said. "I *do* read the newspapers. This let's-pretend case of yours bears a striking resemblance to that of a man named Green, who was cleared by a jury of his peers."

"All I want is for you to tell me which of the two conflicting psychiatric opinions that I've come up with is the one with which *you* agree."

"I've never met Green, and I have no intention of passing judgment on the man from afar."

"Did I say it *is* Green?" Cord objected. "Even if it is, is it too much to ask for your impartial professional opinion? How is a layman, like I, supposed to analyze two such thoroughly contradictory reports?"

"Both analyses are based on valid psychological and psychiatric premises," Ellen said, coming to her feet. "Now, if you'll please excuse me…."

CHAPTER THIRTY-NINE

GARY

"**MORGAN CALLED TO SAY** he'd be a few minutes late," Gary Green said. "Can I get you a cup of coffee or something?"

"No thanks," Cord declined.

"Then, if you don't mind, I won't wait with you," Gary apologized. "I've some work to do on the computer before Morgan checks in."

"Your book?" Cord asked. Morgan had suggested they meet at Gary's apartment, because Morgan *had work to do there on* his and Gary's *book-on-the-trial* project. Cord, since talking to several authorities about Gary's problem, or lack thereof (depending upon the doctor), had welcomed the chance of seeing Gary again.

"Yeah, my book," Gary agreed. "I'm behind in my part of the work, and I'd like to catch up. So, if you'll let Morgan in when he gets here...." He headed out of the room but turned back before completely leaving. Eyeing Cord strangely, he was more Buddha than child molester, his chins layering the entire space where his neck should have been. "*You've* been working out," he said, surprising Cord with the observation.

Cord was pleased and embarrassed. His regular workouts with Jack Sudlow had gotten results, but he hardly thought they were noticeable to anyone but himself. Then again, gays were known for putting an inordinate amount of emphasis on externals; Gary, an exception, having shamelessly neglected his own. "I was getting a little thick around the midsection," Cord alibied.

"Yes, you were," Gary agreed, placing the palms of his hands flat over his own ballooned stomach. "Which is rather like the pot calling the kettle black, isn't it?" he said, his smile revealing tiny white teeth. "And, this pot would do well to make a few trips to the gym himself. However—" He shrugged. "—I only seem able to crowd so many things into any given day, stuffing myself with food taking precedence."

Dr. Wexler suggested Gary's weight problem was another indication of the teacher's sexual penchant for children. Overeating was a defense mechanism, making Gary so repulsive that the kids would keep their distance. If, as according to Nelton Manson, Gary had always been heavy, he *really* started putting on the weight after the charge of pederasty had been leveled against him. *Cleared of the charge, he continued to layer himself with protection,* said the doctor, *in order to keep temptation farther at bay.*

CHAPTER FORTY

MORGAN

"YOU'VE BEEN WORKING OUT!" was the first thing Morgan Kent said. "Looking good!" was the second.

Cord's resulting flush of pride and embarrassment was far more intense than what he'd experienced because of Gary's similar comment. "I was getting a little thick around the midsection," he could only repeat.

"But you've always had a good musculature, right?" Morgan said, heading for the coffee and pouring a cup. Cord was too ill at ease to answer, but Morgan didn't seem to mind. "Genes play a key roll," Morgan said, sipping coffee and leaning against the kitchen counter. He smiled his brilliantly white teeth made whiter by his tan. "But you didn't meet me here to discuss your new exercise program, did you?"

"No," Cord admitted.

"You came to hear my reaction, firstly, to Scott Jesse's death, *and* secondly, to the discovery of Sue Parring as a body in a garbage bag." He didn't wait for confirmation. "Well, Scott had a tendency toward excess. The step from alcohol to drugs isn't a very big one."

"You think his murder was drug-related, then?"

"Don't you?" Morgan said, still looking too young to be over forty. Cord had seen more lines on the face of an eighteen-year-old. "Not that Scott was ever candid with me," Morgan continued. "He knew how I feel about drugs."

"You disapprove of them?"

"Oh, don't get me wrong. I'm certainly no saint. I've *done* grass, now and again, usually in a brownie, since I don't smoke. I *dropped* a tab or two of acid and took my share of mescaline, purely to expand my awareness, you understand?" He *did* have a winning smile. "I've *snorted* a few lines of coke, but an abhorrence of hypodermic needles keeps me from mainlining the hard stuff. But, in answer to your question, it's the excesses of which I disapprove."

"You do recognize the possible connection between Scott Jesse's execution in Los Angeles and Bobby Jordan's similar death here," Cord said, wishing Morgan didn't make him feel so god-damned uncomfortable. Cord hadn't seen Morgan for weeks (purposely, just because there was something about Morgan that Cord found so disconcerting?). "I mean, you know the Jordan kid was seeing Jesse whenever he was in LA, didn't you?"

"Did I?" Morgan evaded, sounding innocent, whether he was or not.

"Jesse said it was *you* who sent Jordan to him in the first place," Cord informed.

"I suppose that's possible," Morgan backtracked. "Scott was a photographer, and Bobby *was* photogenic."

"Except, Jesse and the Jordan kid went back a long ways before you introduced them," Cord said, wishing he could read something other than amusement and curiosity in Morgan's expression.

"Oh?" Morgan encouraged, his cheeks dimpling as he took another sip of coffee.

"That comes as a surprise to you?" Cord asked.

"Shouldn't it?" Morgan replied, a question for a question.

"Didn't Jordan one time break a camera of yours, lent to Scott, during Scott's Seattle days?"

"Right!" Morgan agreed. "Anyway, I was *told* Bobby did it. Frankly, I do remember the incident, but I never quite make the connection, even now, with Bobby. I'm not that good with faces. Nor, for that matter, was Scott. With all the models and would-be models in and out of his life, I'm not surprised he misplaced the specifics on one. Especially since his Seattle days were seen through an alcoholic haze."

"Unstable, was he?" Cord asked, wondering if Morgan worked out regularly and, if so, where. A guy Morgan's age didn't keep in good shape without expending the effort. "I mean, his alcoholism in Seattle and his possible drug involvement in LA," Cord elucidated, wishing he could keep his mind on business and off Morgan Kent's impressive physique.

"Like many military veterans, Scott never quite recovered from combat," Morgan explained. "That he recorded much of the horrors of war on film, being exposed to it not only on the battlefield but later in the darkroom, took an additional toll. Besides, it was in the war zone that he realized he was gay, and that was best handled by him in an alcoholic stupor. While he grew more comfortable with his sexuality, he continued with war nightmares. If he was taking drugs, I understand why, even if I wouldn't have condoned it."

189

"And Bobby Jordan's reasons for drug involvement?" Cord queried.

"I really didn't know Bobby all that well," Morgan reminded. "Horton was the one who could have filled you in on Bobby. I *can* *guess* that Bobby's life-style was part of his problem. It's a very fast lane out there on the streets."

"You know, I find it a bit of a coincidence that it was only a short while after Jesse gave you a call, informing you that I was *nosing around in LA,* that he ended up dead," Cord said, deciding it was just as good a time as any to backtrack and drop that bombshell on the battlefield.

"It would be *more* of a coincidence if the LAPD hadn't called the Seattle police about *your nosing around,*" Morgan countered, obviously up to the attack. His smile widened. His teeth were too perfect *not* to be capped. "I'd say it was no big secret you screwed up an LAPD sting operation," he continued, "only God knowing who might have leaked *that* to organized crime, either here, or in Los Angeles. Not all cops are honest, as much as you and I might like to think to the contrary." He turned slightly to lift the coffee pot and refill his cup.

Cord didn't regret having dropped the bomb, even though he wasn't pleased by how easily Morgan had disarmed and re-aimed it. Had Cord expected Morgan to break down and confess to a return call made to Los Angeles to demand a permanent solution be found to a *possible problem,* AKA Scott Jesse? "Let's see if you can as easily parry your involvement with *two* women murdered and stuffed into garbage bags," Cord challenged.

"Sue *and* Tara," Morgan identified. "That, I'm afraid, I'm less able to explain away," Morgan admitted. Cord would have been happier if Morgan's inability to come up with something could be construed as meaning anything. Because if Morgan had no explanations, neither did Cord or anyone else. This left Morgan in the clear. "Coincidence doesn't seem adequate, even from my standpoint, but what other explanation is there?" Morgan asked, holding the steaming cup poised before his full and sensuous lips.

"Could you clarify your personal relationship with both women?" Cord pressed. So far, all he had on *that* subject was hearsay.

"I was their friend," Morgan conceded.

"Did you go to bed with either-or?" Cord pressured. Enough beating around the bush!

"Do gays go to bed with women?" Morgan responded, and his left eyebrow arched quizzically.

"Which doesn't answer my question, does it?" Cord reminded. "A simple *yes* or *no* would be more sufficient."

"Do I look like someone who'd kiss and tell?" Morgan asked, still sounding more amused than put-upon."

"I hardly think the ladies in question are going to mind any such reflection on their reputations," Cord said angrily. "On the other hand, I felt my question pertinent, or I wouldn't have asked it."

"See me as some kind of bisexual black widow, do you, Detective?" Morgan asked, and there was no amusement in his accusation. "Fuck them and kill them, is that what you think I do?" It *had* crossed Cord's mind, especially since Dr. Wexler had admitted there were rare cases in which men looked upon their semen as a vitally important part of their body that was stolen during sexual congress: a throwback to medieval fears that a witch could cast disastrous spells when in possession of the victim's fingernail clippings, hair, or whatever. *More likely, though,* Dr. Wexler had concluded, *more sexual murders have less to do with stolen sperm than with the simple expedience of concealing a crime.* "I might remind you, Detective, that I was in the middle of the Pacific when Tara disappeared," Morgan informed. "Fucking and murder are difficult from such a great distance; especially the fucking, unless you're hung like a trans-oceanic cable. Which, big as my cock may be, just in case you're interested, I'm not."

Cord ignored the reference to Morgan's cock size, except for the cop's suddenly gone-pink cheeks. "You'll admit that a good many people with whom you were intimate, and not just Tara Robison and Sue Parring, are no longer with us," Cord challenged. "Would you like me to run down the list?" He didn't wait for permission. "Russ Tompson who, according to his old lover and owner of the *942,* was enjoying sex with you *and* Sue Parring: dead of a hit-and-run. Sandra Wheems, with whom you were reported to be so friendly that she once boasted that you were *the best cocksman around*: missing. Bobby Jordan: dead. Horton Lendland: dead. Scott Jesse: dead. Mary Bjorn: dead."

"You think I killed Mary?" Morgan asked, looking and sounding incredulous. "How? By injecting her with a lethal dose of gallstones?" he asked sarcastically.

"Before her gallstones were diagnosed, she was nearly the victim of a hit-and-run. Russ Tompson was killed by a hit-and-run."

"I was in Europe when Mary broke her collarbone," Morgan said, sounding angry. "I was in Los Angeles when Russ was killed. Or, are you suggesting I hired someone to do my killing for me, making sure I had alibis at the time?"

"That's certainly a viable option, wouldn't you agree?"

"So, why wasn't I just as clever with an alibi the night Horton was killed?" Morgan asked.

"That you even see your lack of an alibi as a possibly recognizable reflection on your cleverness makes me wonder if you didn't purposely plan to be without one. Maybe I was supposed to think a killer would have, after successfully covering himself on every other occasion, never slipped up on something so obviously needed. Then again, maybe you figured you didn't need an alibi, because no one could be expected to have witnesses to his whereabouts every given minute of every given day."

"And maybe the sun won't come up in the morning," Morgan commented dryly.

"That's certainly the case, Mr. Kent, for an awfully lot of your former friends," Cord replied. "In fact, I'd say being a friend of yours can be downright deadly."

"My only consolation in putting up with your bullshit this long is in knowing that I'm not the only one not buying it, or you'd be here with an arrest warrant," Morgan responded smugly. "However, even that consolation is wearing thin."

"Maybe you'll file another complaint with Judd Kleverton or Robert Lasalo?" Cord suggested resentfully.

"You might be right," Morgan said, his eyes shooting daggers. How did he remain so goddamned attractive, no matter the emotions played out upon the features of his handsome face?

"On the other hand, wouldn't it be easier for you to cancel my suspicions, regarding you, by personal cooperation rather than by you exerting pressure through the Mayor's office?" Cord suggested. "Especially since the latter proves only social connections, not innocence."

""Funny, but I was under the impression that, up until now, I'd been the epitome of cooperation," Morgan challenged. "Cooperation which you've abused to the point where I think all further conversations between us should probably take place with my lawyer in attendance. Or, better yet, relayed to me *through* my lawyer."

Cord sensed having possibly gone too far, when he needed the attractive man's cooperation more than ever. "I say we forget your lawyer and work together to discover who killed Horton Lendland," he suggested.

"Together?" Morgan echoed, exuding disbelief.

"Why not?" Cord argued. "You've something you can give me to help find the killer. If you're as innocent as you say, why not volunteer to share it?"

"And I suppose that's my cue to ask what in the hell *it* is?" Morgan said, putting his coffee cup on the counter and eyeing Cord warily. He crossed his arms defensively across his chest, looking very butch. "Well, I'm not sure I'm interested enough to bother asking," he informed.

"Then, I'll tell you, anyway," Cord said, not about to be brought up by the curly short hair after coming this far, not even if he wasn't completely at ease with what he was about to suggest. Ill at ease not *just* because people close to Morgan showed an above-average chance of ending their lives violently…. "You can give me heretofore unavailable access to a segment of gay life I think deserves closer scrutiny in this case," he said.

"What's *that* supposed to mean?" Morgan asked, obviously belligerent enough to make Cord spell it out.

"Lendland ran with a certain group of people, especially in Canada. You know the group I mean?"

"Why don't *you* tell *me*?" Morgan suggested.

"The bondage-and-discipline set," Cord obliged. "For the most part, difficult to track, let alone pin down. Firstly, because of their lifestyle. Secondly, because they're nationals of a foreign country and not easy to get to if they've a mind to be uncooperative. There are legal ways to ferret them out, of course. Canada and the U.S., for the most part, have friendly relations. However, legalities take time and, I don't know how much time I have." Was that something he should confess to someone who might be up to his ears in the killings? "Finding Lendland's killer doesn't have much priority about now," Cord continued. In for a penny, in for a pound! Besides, he probably wasn't telling Morgan anything a man with connections didn't already know. "The department can boast the recent solutions to two gay murders, no matter that the killer walked in off the street with a guilty conscience. All that matters is that, with our present track record on gay murders, Lendland is now even farther on the back burner, while the *Dint Slough* Murders get more and more press. I figure it's not long before I get transferred to the *Dint Slough* task force, and who's going to complain?"

"I thought you already had a liaison to the gay community," Morgan argued.

"Mr. Genlic, you mean?" Cord asked with an accompanying laugh he hoped relayed his opinion of that jerk-off lawyer. "Have you ever met him?"

"Not that I recall," Morgan admitted.

"And he's never met you, never met Lendland, and doesn't know Jim Holdsett, Darold Keshmont, or the Father Margaux. In fact, I'm not sure who Genlic *does* know in the gay community. He certainly has no access to the people I want to meet and talk to in Canada."

"If you think those people in Canada are going to take any more kindly to *my* being the one to drag a cop up there and dump him in their midst, you're sadly mistaken," Morgan informed.

"What if I didn't approach them *as a cop*?" Cord suggested.

"Undercover?" Morgan asked in a way that said the idea stunk. "Pardon me if I point out that your record as an undercover agent, at least in LA, didn't impress a whole lot of people."

Having his nose rubbed in that, once again, Morgan struck back. "Maybe you're just not interested in who killed Lendland," he accused. "What's his death to you when you can have so much fun playing gallery owner with Jim Holdsett?"

Morgan pursed his lips and rolled his eyes, obviously unimpressed with Cord's latest argument. "Come over here for a moment, Detective Maxwell," he said finally, crooking an index finger in additional invitation. "Come on," he insisted. "I want to illustrate a point."

So, why was Cord feeling so damned funny inside when he did go closer, stopping at a spot where he could have reached out a hand and touched Morgan's square jaw line, or the outline of Morgan's sensuous lips? "This proves something, does it?" Cord asked, aware that sweat was gathering in his armpits. He shifted uneasily from one foot to the other.

"What would you do if I groped you, here and now?" Morgan asked, smiling at Cord's expression. "I mean, like, copped a feel, cupped my hand over your big basket and gave a friendly hi-there squeeze?"

"I know what a *grope* is," "Morgan insisted, put no more at ease by his admission.

"Well?" Morgan queried. "What if...?"

"Why don't you try it and find out," Cord warned. What *was* this wise-ass trying to prove?

"I won't try it, because I wouldn't want to get belted and then arrested by a cop paranoid with his homophobic fears that his being touched by another man is somehow destined to rob him of his masculinity," Morgan said. "Nor, I can assure you, do I plan to risk the reaction I'd likely see should the same paranoid cop haul off and slug someone in a Canadian gay bar, just because of a harmless grope possibly encountered in passing." His smile was decidedly mocking. "You'd stand out like sore thumb in a gay bar," he condemned. "*Any* gay bar. You might as well tattoo *COP* across your forehead. My suggestion is to stay in Seattle, because that'll give you as much information as you'd end up getting in Vancouver. Why waste your time or mine? Conversation ended?" He shook his head as if he hardly believed the conversation had occurred in the first place. His smile was no less mocking or any the less attractive.

"So, grope me," Cord invited, surprising himself by getting it out before he could think twice about it. He knew what thinking would do: paralyze him and strike him dumb.

"You only *think* you can handle it," Morgan warned, and his gaze casually drifted over Cord's right shoulder. "Doesn't he, Gary?"

Cord did an abrupt about-face, embarrassed to see Gary Green only a few feet away. Gary looked as embarrassed as Cord felt. "I could go back for a couple of minutes and come in again," Gary said finally, making Cord feel more like a fool.

Morgan only laughed. "No need," he assured. "Whatever Detective Maxell has started here, he and I can always finish in Canada. He's jut invited me up to Vancouver to see the sights, and I've accepted."

Cord couldn't think of anything to say. He was blushing and could feel the uncomfortable heat. His pulse was a Buddy Rich drum roll. Worst of all, his cock was painfully hard.

CHAPTER FORTY-ONE

DON

"FASCINATING, ISN'T HE?" Don Richards commented, refer-ring to Morgan who was talking to an attractive, fair-haired young man.

"Certainly that," Cord agreed, trying to *seem* at ease and suc-ceeding; trying to *feel* at ease and failing. The Vancouver bar smelled of sweat, sex, leather, and crushed amyl ampoules. Male bodies, all in one state of undress or another, were open invitations for perversions. No exception was the enticing way Morgan's mus-cled chest and stomach were exposed by the unfastened zipper of his *Gucci* jacket.

"Morgan tells me you and he enjoy many of the same things," Don said, sounding English and looking it in tweed. "Some people here will be sad to hear that," he added. "Look at poor Clarence there." Don's nod isolated the blond talking to Morgan. "He remains hopeful Morgan will see the light, but Morgan has bypassed more enticements than Clarence to run true to form. Personally, I've al-ways been a *doer,* my best on center stage."

Cords wasn't saying much, fearing he'd get it wrong and prove himself the failure at charade that Morgan predicted. However, he was there to get certain information, and he shouldn't waste any op-portunity when it was presented. "Was Horton Lendland a doer?" he ventured. He might have felt less at ease with the question if Morgan hadn't already paved the way by having explained to Don how Cord had become interested, like so many others, in Horton when the art dealer met his horrible end.

"Horton was a case all his own," Don observed, apparently not put off by Cord's query. "I always sensed a kindred spirit lurking there, but he never seemed able to loosen up. I'm afraid, in the final analysis, he was pretty square. You would have likely been disap-pointed. Then again," he amended, patting Cord's hand in a surprisingly nonsexual way, "you might have been just the catalyst Horton needed."

"Morgan doesn't believe Horton was killed by a member of the B&D fraternity," Cord said, deciding to go on for as long and for as far as Don would let him.

"Oh I agree," Don admitted. "Anyone who knew Horton as did Morgan and I did would tell you the same thing. The police have such a distorted way of looking at things, thinking Horton would have ever willingly allowed someone to tie him up. Horton wasn't in the least bit trusting, and only the doers trust." He smiled and sipped his beer. "It's a lack of trust that keeps both you and Morgan on the sidelines, isn't it?"

"I suppose," Cord said, not sure to what he'd just agreed.

"See!" Don exclaimed, again isolating the blond-haired boy with a nod. Morgan had left the young man for the latrine, reminding Cord of his own need to piss which had demanded his attention for the last twenty minutes. There was no way he could see his way clear to urinate in the bar restroom. "Clarence is as frustrated as I predicted he would be," Don observed with a shake of his head. "Although you can't blame him for trying. Morgan is about the sexiest thing around, isn't he?"

"Yes," Cord admitted, although undeniably reluctant to make even that much of a commitment.

"And Morgan sees *what* in you, I wonder?" Don mused. He laughed, delivering another reassuring pat on Cord's hand. "I'm afraid that came out sounding less complimentary than it was," he apologized. "It really wasn't meant to insinuate *only* Morgan could find you attractive. I'm merely fascinated by the criterion Morgan used to single you out of so many."

What Cord understood was how he wouldn't have been there if he'd had to count on Morgan's like, sexual or otherwise. No wonder Don was curious. "I haven't figured it out, either," Cord said, opting for feigned humility.

"You know, you're the only person I've ever seen him *with*?" Don said. "*Officially* with," he corrected. "There was always the occasional young man drummed up for this occasion or that, by one of us trying to provide Morgan that magical individual who would spark more than polite forbearance. Horton always tried his hand at the *let's-attempt-to-please-Morgan-once-again* game, actually sending out talent scouts to comb the countryside. I remember this one *Mel-(when-he-was-younger)-Gibson* look-alike. Are you at all familiar with Mel Gibson?"

"Drunk celebrity denigrating the Jews."

"Right," Don agreed. "He's getting long-in-the-tooth now, but when he was younger, wow, what a stud! And didn't Horton congratulate himself on coming up with someone who was a mirror-reflection of that younger Mel. Not a regular street person, either, *our* Mel. None too keen on going to bed with just *anybody,* mind you." Don laughed merrily. "What we ended up with," he began between chuckles, "was a Mel Gibson look-alike who was hotter to get laid by Morgan than Morgan was to lay him." Don looked up as Morgan rejoined them. "Ah, there you are!" Don exclaimed. "I was just telling Cord about your adventure with that pseudo Mel Gibson we found for you."

"You mean, Mr. Parker Schaffer?" Morgan commented with an indulgent grin.

"Was *that* his name?" Don asked. Apparently if he'd ever known, he'd since forgotten.

"The only reason *I* remember is because it sounded like two ink pens," Morgan confessed. "Whatever did you and Horton end up doing with him?"

"Fucked him every which way but Sunday and then sent him back into relative obscurity," Don confessed merrily. "I've never seen anyone quite so hot for your body and so disappointed in ours."

"What exactly was wrong with him?" Cord heard himself asking. If he hadn't been so curious, he might have been more embarrassed by his question.

"One can like someone's look without wanting to go to bed with them," Morgan said. "I liked how Mel Gibson looked when he was younger, still do. I liked Parker Schaffer's looks. It just doesn't naturally follow, however, that I wanted or want either in my bed."

"And what about Cord?" Don asked. "What does he have that Gibson/Schaffer doesn't/didn't?"

"Who says he has anything?" Morgan asked, casting Cord just the trace of a bemused smile.

"I can't say I fancy being talked about as if I'm not here," Cord criticized, acutely aware of the heat generated by his blush.

"Nevertheless, you must have something Morgan sees as special," Don insisted, undeterred, "or Morgan wouldn't have you here, would he?"

"I haven't quite decided *what* it is about Cord that I so much like," Morgan said, his smile more pronounced. "That's possibly why I'm so captivated. Of course, he and I *do* like a lot of the very same things."

"He's as sexually limited as you are, you mean?" Don defined.

"Hmmmmmm," Morgan was noncommittal; Cord blushed redder.

"So, what do two voyeurs do in bed?" Don queried.

"Watch one another?" Morgan suggested.

"Is that true?" Don asked Cord, who was tongue-tied.

"Sex isn't everything, Don," "Morgan said, obviously enjoying Cord's discomfort. "Surely the ideal relationship surpasses the sordid nitty-gritty of cock in hand, mouth, or ass."

"I know you and Horton never made it," Don said. "I know you never made it with anyone Horton or I rounded up for you. But I can't believe you and *this handsome stud* exist purely on some ethereal plain that precludes even touching."

"Oh, we touch," Morgan said, covering Cord's hand with one of his own, smiling when Cord reflexively jerked his away. Where Cord had endured Don's hand-patting, he found Morgan's touch disconcertingly electric. Don eyed them both with unabashed curiosity. "However, as you see," Morgan continued, pulling back *his* hand and pretending to examine it thoroughly, "touching isn't really Cord's thing."

"What a waste!" Don insisted with a shake of his head.

"Only from *your* standpoint," Morgan assured. "Cord and I cope."

"And I say, you're full of bullshit," Don said. "Then again, possibly not. It's that uncertainty that lets me find you so fascinating. Horton, more than once, commented virtually the same thing."

"Poor Horton," Morgan said, tipping back his chair to balance it on its rear legs and to rest his head against the wall. A deep *V* of serrated pectoral cleavage and ridges of deeply scalloped abdominals were sexily parenthesized by the black-glove leather of his open jacket. His indented navel was haloed by a growth of dark pubic hair that tapered to disappearance beneath his belted waist. "Have you ever heard any scuttlebutt as to whom was responsible?" he asked easily.

"Not a goddamned whisper," Don disappointed. "And I should have heard something had the killer been *one of ours*. Mistakes of that magnitude aren't easily concealed within our admittedly inbred and tight-grouped community."

"You know," Morgan said, locking his gaze with Cord across the table, "Don's right."

CHAPTER FORTY-TWO

MORGAN

"A PIECE OF MEAT?" Nah!" Morgan Kent disagreed. "We were talking about you like a prize stud stallion discussed by two avid connoisseurs of prime horseflesh."

"Well, *that* makes me feel so much better," Cord informed facetiously.

"Actually, it's Don who deserves to be bitching," Morgan argued. "He thinks you're my lover, not a crazy cop from Seattle brought along for the ride. And what about *my* complaints? Everyone here suddenly thinks my sexual preferences suddenly run to frigid studs with big cocks and hunky bodies."

"Very amusing," Cord said, refusing to admit he was hard-pressed not to smile at Morgan's *aren't-I-put-upon* delivery.

"I guess our only recourse is to sit here and bear it," Morgan summed up. "Unless you'd like to dance." His accompanying smile preceded Cord's expected decline of the offer.

"I only know how to lead," Cord replied sarcastically. There was a slow-playing song on the jukebox; Don Richards was dancing, grinding belly to grinding belly, grinding crotch to grinding crotch, with the attractive blond to whom Morgan had been speaking earlier.

"I've been known to follow a real man's lead," Morgan said, continuing to look amused and too attractive for his own—and for Cord's own—good.

"That's not the way I hear it," Cord responded, wishing he hadn't.

"Oh?" Morgan asked on cue. "What did you hear?"

"You really do look upon all of this as some kind of game, being played out for your personal amusement, don't you?" Cord accused.

"It just might be my hope that dancing will make the time go faster," Morgan rationalized, "because my definition of fun isn't showing the gay side of Vancouver to a straight Seattle cop, believe me."

"I'm not dancing with you or with anyone," Cord said with finality. "And don't tell me I have to, in order to fit in, either, because there are plenty of other guys in here who haven't set foot on the dance floor."

"Horton used to dance," Morgan said by way of insinuating Cord was there to follow in Horton's footsteps. "Though, he did sometimes look like a kangaroo during the fast dances," he added with a wide smile.

"What's this little *get-together* Don has planned for later?" Cord asked, changing the subject. Don was okay for small talk in a public place, but continuing *any* kind of a relationship with him elsewhere could make an albeit curious Cord downright apprehensive.

"Where's your sense of adventure?" Morgan chided. "I'll protect you."

"I find that reassurance somehow less than reassuring," Cord complained. He wasn't at all sure it was smart (especially for his own well-being) to be in Vancouver with Morgan. He might be meeting Horton's Canadian friends, just as he'd intended, but he wasn't learning much of anything, so far, to help him unmask a murderer. What's more, he was, as Morgan had predicted, uneasy in the continuing performance of his ongoing charade."

"Don is part of that special gay world you wanted to see up close," Morgan reminded. "Stick with him, and you'll meet others to pump cleverly for information. Now, then," he said, shifting his beer to one side and leaning across the table, "ask what's going on in back room." There was a constant stream of foot traffic entering and exiting one dark rear doorway.

"I *know* what's going on in there," Cord informed. He wasn't born yesterday.

"Horton spent a lot of time back there," Morgan said. "It would help you get a better insight into the man by taking a closer look at one of his preferred environments."

"As a writer, you should know that some things can be just as easily grasped from afar," Cord reminded, feeling particularly clever. "Or, did you live each and every perversion you've ever written?"

"*Touché*," Morgan conceded winningly. "I'm only trying to help. It's not as if there's a vortex back there that sucks you up and refuses to spit you out. Nothing happens but what you allow to happen. There are polite ways of saying *no thank you* without ramming a fist into someone's face. You'd be surprised by how much you can accomplish by merely taking hold of a wandering hand and diplomatically moving it elsewhere."

"Sure," Cord said, sounding unconvinced.

"I go back there all of the time and don't do anything," Morgan assured.

"And if I believe that, you've some swampland you'd like to sell me in Florida?"

It was an old turn of phrase, but Morgan smiled at it nevertheless.

"It's a misconception on your part that every gay here is uncontrollably hot for your body," Morgan said. "There are plenty of willing participants without having to force an unwilling you."

"You'd love to see me back there making fool of myself, wouldn't you?" Cord accused.

"Make a fool of yourself how?" Morgan asked, sounding genuinely offended. "I certainly wouldn't relish seeing one paranoid, and probably homophobic, cop show his true colors on schedule. I just thought you might be up to the adventure, but obviously you're not. You're still Cro-Magnon man preferring to solve every assumed threat to your manhood with fisticuffs." Morgan's observation had echoes of something Cord had once said to Jim Holdsett. Cord didn't like anyone, Morgan included, lumping him with Horton's sexually uncertain one-time partner. Cord had parried more than one gay sexual advance in his time without resulting to King-Kong tactics. "Have you *ever* been propositioned by a man?" Morgan asked, as if having read Cord's thoughts and not having believed what he'd found.

"I haven't spent my life in a goddamned monastery," Cord informed, wondering if he would have been less insulted if Morgan had thought he'd been propositioned more often.

"And you know you're attractive, don't you?" Morgan delivered with just the right inflection to make it less the compliment it might have been.

"I know I don't have to hide my face," Cord said, uncomfortable with compliments, jokingly delivered or not, from another man. "I'll tell you something else that isn't two," he added, deciding to broach a subject already almost too overdue. "I have to piss like a racehorse, and there's no way I'm going to manage that in here. So, if you have any *less-than-wise-ass* suggestions...?"

Morgan laughed, all dimples, white teeth, and flashing eyes. He still didn't look over forty. He still didn't act over forty. Most of the time, he made Cord feel the older. "My suggestion," Morgan managed finally leaning closer so Cord became more aware of Morgan's

4711 cologne, "is that you take a few minutes to check out the rest-room before you risk arrest in the alley for indecent exposure. You may find that some people, like you and I, who don't get their jollies off by displaying our pricks over the urinal, have our pick of not one, not two, but three toilet stalls. The one on the far right having only one glory hole conveniently neutralized by standing with your back to it while you unzip your pants and haul out your thick hose for fire-dowsing pissing."

"Had you been less a sadist, you'd have made that explanation a few minutes earlier and briefer," Cord said, deciding to take Morgan at his word, although pissing in the alley still wasn't to be completely ruled out. He scooted back his chair and got up. Passing across the dance floor, Cord maturely ignored three gropes before he locked himself in the far right toilet stall and let go a flood of pale-yellow urine. His accompanying sense of relief was decidedly sexual.

Morgan wasn't waiting at the table but at a spot where people constantly decided on entering the toilet or detouring into the back room. "Surely, after mastering a piss, you're up to an even more daring reconnaissance," Morgan suggested.

Well, he had another thing coming if he thought Cord was so easily led by the nose. "I'll pass, but you feel free to go ahead," Cord said, stepping to one side and giving Morgan all the space needed to access the doorway into moan-filled darkness.

"Coward," Morgan whispered stepping by. His body was all hard muscle as it touched Cord briefly before gliding by into the all-accepting gloom.

CHAPTER FORTY-THREE

CORD

"FOR GOD'S SAKE, you have to be kidding!" Cord said after seeing what Morgan selected for him from one of several closets.

"Who would expect a cop to dress like one?" Morgan argued. "It's perfect."

"I don't understand the need for any of this," Cord said. "Why dress up like it's Halloween, anyway?"

"Because you *want* to understand," Morgan insisted. "And dressing up is part of it. Besides, Don has someone here tonight who I'm sure you'd like to quiz about Horton. It's this way, or no way."

"Who are we talking about?" Cord asked, still hoping to delay the inevitable. Having come this far, he wasn't prepared to turn back *or* go forward. No matter that he'd feel right at home in a cop's uniform. He'd worn one plenty of times before becoming a detective, although he'd never done so under such extenuating circumstances.

"You'll see," Morgan assured, dropping the uniform on a bench that would have looked right at home in a school locker room. In fact, the whole place resembled a locker room. There were two private showers and a large, communal one. There was a urinal, three toilets, and a bidet, all lined up military style, and a couple of enclosed toilet stalls. Pretty extensive a setup for some guy's basement.

Cord watched Morgan who, obviously knowing where things were, conjured motorcycle boots, a helmet, a billy-club, handcuffs, and what looked like a genuine police-issue revolver and holster.

"Oh, yes, the gun *is* real," Morgan guaranteed. "Don is a stickler for authenticity. It isn't, however, as you've probably noticed, loaded. Don can't know, as I do, that you won't get carried away and shoot up the place in a fit of orgasmic excitement."

"I still think you might get me something a bit less conspicuous," Cord objected.

"Trust me," Morgan parried. "Anything else will make you feel and look even more uneasy than you already feel and look."

"What if it doesn't fit?" Cord asked, still stalling. He could tell, just by looking, that, if possibly a little small, the uniform wasn't all that far off.

"It'll fit," Morgan promised, again sorting through the collection of available costumes, many of which Cord couldn't readily identify. "I called ahead with your measurements," Cord informed.

"Where'd you get my measurements?" Cord asked; Morgan responded by tapping a forefinger to his right temple.

"We gays have this thing for male bodies," Morgan reminded. "After closely examining so many, I have this knack for guessing correctly nine times out of ten."

"Yeah, well it looks as if this is a size too small," Cord criticized, wondering what he was feeling about Morgan having, at least once, given Cord's body a thorough appraisal.

"Maybe," Morgan agreed, "but that's because you wear your usual clothes too loose."

"What in the hell are *you* planning to wear?" Cord asked, changing the subject. Morgan's scrutiny, past and present, remained inexplicably unnerving.

"This, I think," Morgan said. "A German Army: Tank Crew Member, *Gefreiter,* 1940," Morgan identified. "It's black so it doesn't show the oil and grease stains for which armored vehicles are so well-known. The jacket is short to afford ease of movement in tight quarters. It's double-breasted to give extra protection during cold weather. No cuffs, no external buttons; shoulder straps stitched flat on the shoulder: all to prevent the uniform from catching up on anything inside the tank. None of which seems to have helped its original owner all that much," he said, pushing his right index finger through a hole in the front of the jacket. "I'd say, from the bullet's angle of entry, our man didn't have a very pleasant exit from the reality at the time."

Cord shivered, once again having second thoughts. There was something about all of this, about the strangeness of it, about the macabre aspects of a dead German's uniform about to be worn again in some kind of weird charade, about the unknown that awaited Cord beyond how many *as-yet-unopened* doors, that made the young policeman more and more apprehensive.

"Besides, I look good in black," Morgan offered in final analysis, "and while Don has a couple of exceptional genuine *SS* uniforms, I don't want to get you all flustered by seeing me in one of those this first time around."

Morgan was right: Cord was sure he would be put off by Morgan, or anyone else, in *SS* black. He wasn't sure he even approved of tank-crew black. It being German. Even harmless fantasies concerning the Nazis seemed uncomfortably kinky and obscenely perverse. And what was all this Morgan bullshit about *this first time around*?

"So, I suppose we should get to it," Morgan said, checking his wristwatch. "Don will be wondering what's keeping us."

"Where *is* Don?" Cord asked. He didn't want to be overly long here, alone with this man, in this place, surrounded by these closets filled with these uniforms of which some had been purloined from dead men from another time and place.

"He has some preparations of his own," Morgan replied cryptically, sitting down on the bench next to Cord and pulling off boots that would soon be replaced by another pair, the latter calf-high, black, and spit-polished to a mirror-like sheen.

Morgan unzipped the *Gucci* jacket he'd been wearing without a shirt. He peeled off the soft leather, revealing a muscled beauty highlighted by a thin gloss of sweat. The seeming perfection took Cord's breath away, and Cord quickly rationalized it was the circumstances, not Morgan's partial nakedness, causing Cord's labored breathing.

Morgan's chest was hairless, except for a halo of dark silky hair surrounding each dime-sized nipple. His pectorals were chiseled rectangles, separated by a deep and serrated cleavage that opened onto a scalloped stomach. His navel, like his nipples was haloed by hair, its black curls running in a straight line down his belly to disappearance beneath the waistband of his pants. When his belt was unbuckled, the crotch of the trousers unzipped, additional black hair came into view.

Cord looked away as Morgan, again standing, dropped his pants. Cord was acutely aware that Morgan wore no underwear. By turning to look now, those pants peeled down over Morgan's muscled butt and firm thighs, Cord could have seen Morgan Kent completely naked. It was something he wanted but didn't want to see. It was something he anticipated but feared. Deriving pleasure from another man's naked body was acceptable only under certain prescribed conditions, none of which Cord believed existed there and then. Morgan wasn't a marble sculpture in a museum. Morgan wasn't a model for an art class....

On the other hand, maybe Cord *should* look, if just to verify Morgan Kent's nakedness was no big deal. After all, Morgan was over forty, for Christ's sake! Except, conceivable or not, Cord had seen no flaws in the way Morgan's chest muscles and stomach muscles, bronzed by the sun, had flowed, one into the other, in at least the illusion of perfect harmony. Could what existed below Morgan's waist be any less perfect?

Cord turned to the business of getting himself dressed, disgruntled that he should have even the hint of *love* handles when Morgan didn't have any. Why should Cord's gut look puffy when Morgan's stomach was rippled and solid as rock?

Thank God, Cord *was* wearing underwear! By turning his back to Morgan, while dropping one pair of pants and stepping into the other, Cord could even conceal his embarrassing erection. Its bulge, though, was obvious to him and not disguised by the tight-fitting trousers of the policeman's uniform. In contrast, Morgan's tank-uniform pants were loose, showing no trace of what Cord had missed by not having given in to the temptation of looking when he'd had the chance.

"You *do* look sexy," Morgan complimented. It was what Cord had been thinking about Morgan but would never have said. Even admitting to himself that Morgan *looked* sexy was traumatic enough. Women were sexy—to men. Normal men were many things, but *never* sexy to other normal men. That Cord had momentarily removed himself from the normal world didn't make it easier for him to accept the anomalies of this one.

Cord tugged on his last boot, watching Morgan use blousing rubbers to secure trouser cuffs low over black boots. A silver corporal's chevron on Morgan's left sleeve said his uniform was no more an officer's than the one Morgan had worn throughout his entire three years in the U.S. Army. Telling Cord what?

Morgan's lapel insignias were piped with violet. His silver belt buckle echoed the silver of a tank-corps badge pinned lower left on the breast of his jacket. Morgan put on field-gray steel helmet, fastening the strap beneath his cleft chin.

"Ready?" he asked.

Ready for what? There were a helluva lot of things for which Cord, strapping on his holster and empty gun, wasn't ready. No matter how butch and invincible he looked in the reflections danced back to him from several well-placed mirrors in the room, he was in unfamiliar territory. His adrenaline rush was that of a traveler about to see unexplored, and possibly booby-trapped, territory for the very first time. A wayfarer who knew he might somehow have miscalculated distance and come too far to ever get safely back again.

CHAPTER FORTY-FOUR

TERRY

"COWICHAN," **TERRY SEABEAR** answered, identifying his tribe only after the riding crop again connected with his naked ass.

"Very good," Don Richards congratulated. "Except, we forgot the *sir,* didn't we?" He whacked the young American Indian's ass again.

"Cowichan, sir," Terry obliged.

Cord watched from inside a seeming nightmare. He wanted to stop what was happening, but the otherworldliness of it kept him in check. Not to mention his doubts that he could do much, since Don, Terry, Morgan, and he weren't the only ones in the room.

Jesus, what a room it was, too. Straight out of a horror movie. A gloomy castle dungeon, complete with weepy walls glistening dark stones through moist slime. A torture rack, a pillory, a stock. Tables indented for the human figure, holes drilled where a man's ass or cock would fit. Ropes, chains, and attending paraphernalia webbing the ceiling, dangling at intervals. Winches and other controlling mechanisms punctuating the walls. More chains linked to metal eyelets protruding from the cold stone slabs on the floor. Metal bracelets and leg irons. A shelf of riding crops, like the one Don wielded. Whips, switches, canes, paddles. Implements Cord's imagination couldn't begin to grasp.

"You knew Horton Lendland?" Don asked the Indian. His arm rose and fell. Leather-sheathed stick connected hard against firm young ass.

"Yes, sir, I knew Horton Lendland, sir," Terry admitted.

Cord couldn't possibly be seeing what he was seeing, because Don was too ludicrous in a leather vest opened over a chest more bone than flesh. Bare arms like toothpicks. A prick pathetic, jutting from its bushy nest of gray hair at a crotch naked and parenthesized by the leather chaffs encasing two skinny legs.

Terry came off less ridiculous, only because he was stark naked. He'd given his age as eighteen, after whack number two of the riding crop, but he looked twenty. There was nothing unusual about that. He was a street person, after all, and that life, even in Canada, wasn't conducive to the young staying young. This didn't keep the kids from hustling the streets where it was apparently no big deal to drop one's pants for a couple of bucks.

"Tell the policeman here, Terry," Don instructed, referring to Cord who had been assigned *policeman status* and a chair close— too close!—to the proceedings, "what Horton liked to do when you were alone."

There was no answer until the obligatory smack of the riding crop. Only then did Terry manage to reply, "He sucked my cock, sir." The kid was bent so far over a sideways sawhorse that he looked back through his own legs—at Cord. His hair fell to a black puddle on the floor, his ass crisscrossed with welts swollen in angry scarlet through natural pigmentation and tan.

"You liked Horton going down on you, did you?" Don asked.

Cord didn't want to watch, but he couldn't help himself. The riding crop was hypnotic as it raised and lowered, violated flesh vibrating beneath each assault.

Terry cried out. And why wouldn't he? These weren't love taps. Nothing here was indicative of the love with which Cord was most familiar. In fact, as fascinated as Cord was, he was equally repelled. It made no difference that he'd been assured by Morgan that everyone was willing. Cord couldn't believe Terry Seabear could have possibly known what he was getting into. The kid's erection wasn't evidence enough for Cord, because to have accepted it as such would have meant analyzing Cord's own distasteful penile arousal.

"Yes, sir, I liked Horton going down on me," Terry said, his voice strained and breathless.

Morgan stood off to one side, his arms crossed at his chest. Watching. There were two other men. Weight-lifters, by their looks. Wearing very little else but leather jockstraps and sandals, the latter laced up to bulged crotches. Cord couldn't see them at the moment, because they'd faded into the deeper darkness. He felt their cool scrutiny, though. Did they have him pegged for the phony he was? Were they Morgan's insurance that Cord wasn't going to cause a scene?

Don smacked the kid's ass three times more in quick succession. Cord cringed at the resulting whimpers emanating from the brutalized young man.

"*You* gave Horton the *Cowichan* spear that someone fucked up his ass, didn't you?" Don asked.

Cord's ears perked.

"Yes," Terry confessed, his ass striated with welts, blood oozing from the junctures of several.

"*Sir!*" Don emphasized, his displeasure evident by a whack so forceful it threatened to topple the kid and the sawhorse.

"Sir!" Terry managed.

"Why the spear?" Don asked. Another whack. Another whimper.

Cord was sweating dark stains under his arms. He drew his forearm across his forehead, soaking his shirt sleeve with his perspiration.

"He wanted it, sir," Terry said. "He saw it in my apartment and wanted me to trade it for a trip to Hawaii. It had been my old man's. I didn't use it, and I'd never been to Hawaii."

The riding crop raised and lowered. Again. Again. Again.

Cord tensed. The ongoing mutilation of Terry's butt, and the kid's increasing whimpers, were more and more a strain. Refusing to believe Terry could be enjoying his beating—Cord didn't care what *anybody* said—Cord wanted it to stop. It was unnecessary. It was vicious and cruel. It was sick. How did these people get so fucked up as to equate pleasure with pain?

"Went to Hawaii, did you?" Don asked, running one leather-gloved hand over Terry's ass and transferring a smear of the kid's blood to Don's bird-like chest.

Cord felt sick.

"Yes, sir," Terry said. "I gave him the spear, and he took me to Hawaii."

"Although later you wanted the spear back, right?" Don prodded, using the lash of the riding crop as further incentive.

Cord wanted to jump up, tear the riding crop from the sadistic bastard's hand. He wanted to strike out at Don's ugly face. Better yet, at Morgan's handsome face. This whole scene was fast becoming more and more repulsive. Cord felt violated in having been tricked into witnessing it. Yes, by God, tricked! Somehow—by Morgan Kent. Clever Morgan. Standing there in the shadows, thinking what? Enjoying it all? Certainly enjoying Cord's discomfort.

"Noooooo!" Terry protested. Whether in reply to Don's last question, or in pleading for Don to stop the beating, Cord couldn't tell. *"Sir,"* the kid added, but was so much an afterthought that Don delivered five more punishing whacks before pausing.

Don's eyes were glassy. The bastard was literally salivating, gnashing his false teeth, and looking like a rabid dog drooling over bloody meat still on a bone. Revolting! Sickening!

"I didn't care about the spear, sir," Terry said, barely audible. Blood trickled the backs of his thighs. His leg muscles gave uncontrollable jerks. Unbelievably, his cock was still hard.

"So, where were you the night Horton was killed?" Don asked. "You have an alibi, my little Indian brave?"

More whacks, each more wet and mushy than the last. Blood splattered and Cord was unable to stand much more. For the life of him, he couldn't understand it. He didn't *want* to understand it. He felt put upon for having been given verification that such obscenities existed.

"I was here, sir. With you, sir," Terry said. "The night Horton died, sir."

"So, you were," Don confirmed, giving Cord a twisted smile. He dropped a finger into the blood on Terry's ass and, then, licked retrieved blood from his fingertip.

Cord, physically sick to his stomach, pushed himself to his feet and hurriedly stumbled from the room. It was either leave or make an attempt to smash somebody's goddamned face in.

CHAPTER FORTY-FIVE

MORGAN

"**ANYTHING WRONG?**" Morgan asked, folding his arms and leaning against one of the closed closet doors. His faint smile was all amusement and mockery.

"That display—of whatever it was—was more than a little sick," Cord accused. He wished Morgan hadn't followed him out. As it was, Cord had only managed to pull off his boots. Once again having to drop his pants in front of Morgan, even if just to change into another pair, wasn't something he'd enjoy. Especially not in his present state of arousal that would undoubtedly cause comment from the observant bastard.

"Come on, now, Detective Maxwell," Morgan chided. "I would have thought your job had conditioned you to far more horrendous sights."

"All of what I heard in there could have been summed up in one short interview," Cord condemned, "instead of making a porno production number out of it." He'd probably be dreaming about Terry's bloody ass, and Cord doing nothing to prevent it, for years to come.

"But why deny Terry and Don their little fun, when they were doing you a favor?" Morgan cajoled.

"Not to mention *your* fun," Cord criticized. "And don't bother denying it."

"I always enjoy other people enjoying," Morgan said. "More often than not, anyway," he qualified with a cheek-dimpling grin.

"You really expect me to believe Terry Seabear was enjoying himself?" Cord asked. He wanted to change his clothes and get the hell out of there, as quickly as possible. He kept hoping his cock would soften to a more presentable state. It was too much to hope that Morgan would pass up the chance to comment on it.

"You don't think Terry was enjoying?" Morgan asked.

"No!" Cord said with finality.

"I'd say the evidence was otherwise," Morgan protested. That cryptic reference to Terry's hard cock, throughout, meant it was only a matter of time before he got around to noting how Cord's cock had responded. Well, Cord was ready for him, by Christ!

"Just because hanged men die with erections—" Who'd told Cord that? "—doesn't mean they're getting off on having their necks stretched," Cord said. Giving Morgan *that* to chew on, Cord dropped his holster with its empty gun on the bench beside him. He unfastened his trousers and dropped them, too. Morgan's spurt of laugher was the price Cord was prepared to pay for getting away as quickly as possible.

"Do, please, remember that *you* came to *me,* begging for a glimpse of what Horton did in Canada," Morgan reminded, blessedly not commenting, for the moment, on the bulge in Cord's pre-cum dampened underwear.

"Yeah, well, I've seen more than enough to know why Horton turned up dead," Cord said, having trouble with the zipper of his pants. He was suddenly afraid he wasn't going to get his fly closed.

"Surely, you're far too intelligent for such an asinine statement," Morgan accused.

"Flattery will get you nowhere," Cord insisted, finally succeeding with his recalcitrant trouser fly. Thank God! Now for his shirt and his boots, and it was good-bye to all these sickies—Morgan Kent included.

"I *am* disappointed," Morgan said, tsk-tsking like Cord's mother who'd once caught her son playing with himself in a hall closet.

"Well, tough shit!" Cord said. He'd buttoned his shirt wrong, but he decided to leave it. "I saw what I saw."

"You saw a game," Morgan begged to differ. "A game willingly played."

"Willingly?" Cord refused to believe it.

"Would you like Terry personally to tell you what a good time he had and is having?" Morgan invited.

"I've heard more than enough, for one evening, from Terry Seabear," Cord insisted. The last thing he wanted was to hear Terry confess to having a good time. That would have gone against all that was believable. No one could get off on having his ass beaten bloody. Even the faggot in *Another Country* didn't *enjoy* getting his ass caned.

"Do think twice about running out on this opportunity for exploration with minimum involvement," Morgan said. "You might be surprised by possibilities approached with a more open mind."

"Thanks, but no thanks," Cord said, tugging on his last boot. He was ready to go, and none too soon.

"Don't you wonder, as I do, if you might be protesting just a mite too much?" Morgan asked, smiling more widely. "After all, Terry was the one getting his butt whipped, not you. If anyone should be making a row, he should. I don't know about you, but I've seen gorier special effects on TV."

"We're not talking special effects, though, are we?" Cord said, wondering why he was taking the time to argue. All he wanted was out, wasn't it? "This isn't fantasy."

"Oh, but so much of it is *just that*," Morgan protested. "Don isn't *really* a dungeon master. Terry isn't *really* being held captive. Nor is Terry being *forced* into divulging information that could as easily have been had from him, as you've pointed out, during a dull and short-lived interview. After all, what does Terry have to hide that needs beaten out of him? The spear was a gift. How could he know what some madman would do with it? Terry has an alibi. Don has an alibi. It's all a game, Cord," Morgan insisted. "Why make some nonexistent bogeymen one of the game pieces?"

"Horton Lendland is dead, and I don't have time for games," Cord said, heading for the door. He wasn't sure how Morgan managed to get there before he did.

"I'm a pretty good judge of character, Cord," Morgan said, blocking the way. "I think you're passing up a chance to explore aspects of Detective Cord Maxwell, the man, which you're not likely to get again any time soon."

"What in the hell is that supposed to mean?" Cord asked, not wanting to know. What he wanted was out, and if Morgan didn't move, Cord would move him. "On the other hand, don't bother trying to explain *your* ideas about me," Cord insisted. "*I* know what's best for me."

"Do you?" Morgan asked, sounding doubtful. The handsome prick! Who in the hell did Morgan think he was talking to?

"The name of the game is *pleasure*," Morgan said. "Death means a botched game, and pros don't botch."

"So, maybe Horton was playing with an amateur," Cord ventured.

"I think Horton's murder had nothing to do with B&D or S&M sex," Morgan said. "You're barking up the wrong tree, and I think you've known that all along."

"Excuse me, if *I think* what *you think* isn't worth shit," Cord said, determined to end this, here and now, while he still could. He could handle Morgan Kent any day of the week, but if those two hulks came in from the other room, Cord would be up a creek without a paddle. Was Morgan stalling for reinforcements?

"You've come this far," Morgan said, "so why chicken out now? Why spend the rest of your life wondering if you missed out on something just because you wouldn't take the few additional steps to get it?"

"All I want is Horton Lendland's killer," Cord said. "Although for the moment, I'll settle for just being out of here."

"Maybe you'd prefer whipping my ass and fucking it," Morgan ventured.

"You're sick!" Cord proclaimed, surer of that than ever.

"I could whip *your* ass and fuck it," Morgan suggested in alternative. And Cord fought down strange, unhealthy, and exhilarating emotions simultaneously swelling inside of him.

"You fucking queer pervert!" Cord accused, lunging, only to find Morgan somewhere other than where the bastard should have been. Cord turned quickly to confront the shit, who'd moved, and tried his damnedest to wipe the condescending smirk off Morgan's face with a backhand. Once again, Morgan successfully sidestepped. Although this time, Morgan executed a graceful pirouette that lifted and extended a leg whose leading foot struck Cord hard against the side of the head.

Cord went down—to his knees, then farther. He felt all Jell-O, and darkness was an ocean suddenly threatening to drown him. He struggled to maintain consciousness, wondering who told him Morgan was an expert *in kung-fu or something*. Charles Robinson had told him, that's who. It had been one reason Charles had felt his wife so safe with Morgan. That poor, deluded son-of-a-bitch!

CHAPTER FORTY-SIX

CORD

IT WAS A WET DREAM GONE BAD. A confused collage of darkness, immobility, clanking chains, and wet sounds.

It wasn't any woman's mouth hot and hungry between his legs, because he'd had Cheryl down there enough times to know. This was pure, masculine aggressiveness, not needing Cord to coax or cajole. This guy knew about suction, tonguing, and supplementary nuances, like creeping a finger up the crack of Cord's butt.

It was a man's large hand clamped hard on Cord's right thigh.

There was a hood over his head. No eye holes or mouth hole. Silk rather than wool, because the material was soft and slick. Nor was it suffocating, even though the clingy material stuck to his mouth and nose whenever he breathed in.

He was partially dressed, in that his pants had been yanked down to where they were chafing his lower legs, his shirt stretched up along his chest.

His arms were lifted and held there. When he moved, he heard metal rattling. A pressure around both wrists told him he was probably manacled, although there was no irritation of hard metal against tender skin. He could swing, but not freely, weights seemingly anchored his ankles.

"No," Cord mumbled. He wasn't gagged; his voice sounded high-pitched and strange.

Whoever it was didn't stop doing what he was doing.

So, it was finally happening. Something Cord had imagined more than once. Oh, he'd never imagined himself tied and hooded, but there had been times when he'd wondered how it would be to drop his pants and let some queer have at him. The closest he'd ever come to making the daydream happen had been when the kid had propositioned him in the Alki can. *You look like you have a big cock,* the kid had blatantly said, *and I'd really like to suck it.* Well,

Cord hadn't succumbed to temptation then, nor had he ever planned to. It had been taken entirely out of his hands.

"I'll kill you once I get down from here, you bastard!" Cord threatened. Not exactly the kind of talk to be coming from someone who wasn't going to get down from anywhere without somebody giving him a hand. It had to be said, though. There was no way this should be mistaken for willing acceptance and enjoyment. Cord wanted Morgan to know that.

If it *was* Morgan. The assumption that it was Morgan was logical, considering the lead-in. But Cord, unwilling to admit his precarious position in the least erotic, could make it less enjoyable by thinking it was Don's mouth down and over Cord's straining erection.

"Goddamn, let me down!" Cord insisted, jerking his chains, increasing the strain on his shoulders. "Don't keep this up until it's too fucking late, either, you bastard!" he warned.

As if it wasn't *already* too fucking late. All that remained was for him to shoot his wad, and it was nit-picking to think no orgasm would make a difference. No matter how far this already was, it was *too* far. When he got down, if he got down, there was going to be hell to pay, and Morgan would exact the payment. Jesus, Cord would pound that faggot bastard to a pulp. There'd be no one saying Morgan Kent was handsome after Cord was through with him. A plastic surgeon wouldn't' be able to put Humpty Dumpty back together again.

So what if Morgan was a *kung-fu expert of some kind*? Cord knew a few tricks of his own. He just hadn't been expecting Morgan to broadside him. Morgan had had the advantage of surprise, but that wouldn't be the case the next time. If there was a next time. Cord had to get free first.

"Let me down, bastard!" Cord commanded. "I'll pretend none of this ever happened." Fat chance! How did any guy forget the very first time another guy went down on him? An invisible hymen had been broken, never to grow back again. It made no difference that Cord was here against his will. Tied up or not, forced into submission or not, the damage was done. Whoever was sucking his cock was fucking his mind as well. Cord didn't like that.

"I'm warning you," he said; telltale shivers told him things would have to stop damned fast if they were going to be stopped at all.

So, he begged, making no more of an impression than when he threatened. Obviously, he wasn't dealing with anyone compassionate or understanding. This was a pervert whose screwed-up perspec tive saw a latent homosexuality existing in Cord's need to search out Horton Lendland's killer in whatever perverted nook and cranny. By God, Cord wasn't queer! Getting his cock sucked by a queer didn't make him one, either.

So, why had he so diligently resisted male-male experimentation in the past? He didn't want to think about that right now, because it only further muddied murky waters.

He tried addition: one plus one equals two; two plus two equals four; 408 plus 617 equals what? 1,025? He tried multiplication: 109 times 1,602 equals?

"Stop it, faggot!" he insisted, nothing keeping him diverted for long from what was happening to him. He wasn't dealing with a novice. When this guy wanted all of Cord's attention, he knew just how to swallow all of Cord's cock to get it.

Cord couldn't believe his own lack of control. It was bad enough, being strung up like a side of beef, but to have an erection in the bargain? There should have been nothing about this rape—yes, rape!—that was erotic. That his subconscious somehow thought otherwise wasn't something safely dealt with at the moment.

Cord *did,* now, at least, have an inkling of what might have flashed through the mind of Horton's killer when that bastard had decided the queer gallery owner wasn't fit for living among decent human beings.

"Stop it, goddamn you!" Cord protested, determined to resist to the very end. He'd ignore the finger snaking up his asshole and driving him wild. He'd control his helpless grunting and groaning. He wouldn't shiver when firm lips gummed the base of his cock, or whenever tongue languidly wrapped the bulbous tip of his prick. He'd stop comparing this sex with all the other, denying that there had never been a cunt to pleasure him quite as much as he was being pleasured now.

He teetered precariously on the verge of losing even his modicum of control. Then, it was completely gone. Stolen from him.

He bellowed loud and undecipherable, simultaneously spewing his seed. Seemingly being turned inside-out by the suction that greeted his jettisoning semen.

He jerked on his chains, a fish out of water, a leech-like mouth drinking its full of his life's man-juices. His pleasure bordered on pain, and Cord hoped the balance would tip toward the latter. Disappointed once again.

He gave his final shudders, fearing it would all begin again, as if he were but some nectar-bloated ant, playing living storage vat, for whatever other insect might decide to come around for the next sample.

No one in Seattle knew he'd unofficially come to Vancouver on the Lendland case. Not even Jack Sudlow knew, because Cord hadn't wanted his need to explore the darker side of Horton's sex life to be misinterpreted *by anyone*.

Morgan wouldn't likely tell anyone Cord's present whereabouts. Nor was there anything in Cord's luggage at the hotel to point the way. He was using fake ID, picked up on the Seattle streets. Would anyone make the connection between a cum-drained body, found in Vancouver, and a missing straight cop from Seattle? Jesus, it was doubtful.

He was thinking the worst when his hood was pulled off. Despite the small difference in lighting, between before and after, it took him a full minute to focus.

Terry Seabear was there, wearing a loin cloth and moccasins. His glossy black hair was braided and decorated with two up-jutting eagle feathers. He was one-time muscle going to fat. He needed more workouts in a gym, less in this dungeon.

"Hi," Terry said, looking as if he hadn't just done what he'd so obviously done; Cord's spent cum was still wet on the Indian's lips.

It had been Terry, then, not Morgan, not Don. Cord knew that now, and he wondered why he was feeling disappointment in it not having been Morgan.

Hadn't the self-confessed-voyeur Morgan at least stuck around for the show? Maybe he was off in the darker shadows with Don and those muscle-bound freaks.

"I want you to let me down," Cord told Terry Seabear, sounding calm, cool, and collected but being none of the three.

"Sure," Terry said, as if he'd just thought of the idea himself.

Cord didn't believe him. The kid would be a fool to let Cord down, no matter how much Cord wanted down. The cocksucker knew what he'd done. He knew Cord knew what he'd done. He knew Cord wasn't pleased by what had happened. Or, had Morgan tricked Terry by telling him differently? It made no difference to Cord. Not at the moment. Not when Terry was there and Morgan wasn't. Bastard Morgan! Shithead Morgan! Morgan who would have had more sense than to let Cord down, here and now. Where this poor slob was playing *thank-you-dear-God Cord-thought* stupid.

Cord was hung above the floor, his ankles bound with fur-lined manacles. The manacles, in turn, were attached to chains anchored to the floor. Terry removed the manacles, leaving Cord suspended from fur-lined bracelets. The bracelets, in turn, were attached to chains anchored to a wooden support beam raised or lowered by a winch. Terry lowered the wooden support until Cord's feet touched the floor. Cord was weak, his legs threatening to collapse beneath his weight.

His pants were still down, bunched around his ankles and feet. Cord's remaining chains hadn't been given enough slack, yet, for Cord to pull up his trousers.

Cord didn't *really* think Terry was letting him free. The kid had to see the fury in Cord's eyes. Any idiot would know Cord was a raging fire only waiting to burn brighter.

Terry released one wrist bracelet, but there was still the still-attached other. Cord could do some damage, as-he-was, but …

The second bracelet snapped loose, and the very first thing Cord did was pull up his trousers. His puffy cock was obscene evidence that Cord wished to have quickly out of sight and mind. Besides, mobility was difficult with his legs bound by fallen pants.

Terry stood, taking no advantage of his last chance to escape. Did he know he was tempting fate? Had Morgan brainwashed him into thinking Cord would accept everything as a matter of course, even be grateful for the degradation? Had Cord sounded anything at all like a man playing games when he'd threatened and begged Terry to be set free? He shouldn't have climaxed, because *not* doing so would have been the ultimate proclamation that his protests had been for real. So, why *had* he spoiled it with an orgasm, for Christ's sake?

Terry remained a target too tempting to resist. Cord was too frustrated, confused, embarrassed, and ashamed, not to take out his pent-up emotions on somebody. Terry was the one handiest, Cord deriving a physical pleasure in the brutal contact of his fist against the young Indian's jaw.

"Fucking Indian queer!" Cord accused, kicking the bastard who'd gone to the floor. No fancy footwork from Terry, as Cord had witnessed from Morgan. Terry was down and vulnerable. Cord's indignation spilled over even more. Each kick Cord delivered to the folding and unfolding body was a release from some of the demons that possessed him.

Except, the Indian wasn't the one Cord wanted. Terry was merely the proxy for *Morgan-the-even-more-perverted faggot.* Morgan whose dirty work the kid had done and now must suffer the consequences. Damn, how had Terry been such a stupid-ass pawn? Why wasn't he putting up a struggle, now? Granted, Cord had caught him off guard. Or, had he? Cord couldn't believe, even now, that his anger hadn't been anticipated. It had to have been obvious, all along, that Cord hadn't been just pretending when he'd told Terry to stop.

Terry, taking on the responsibility of playing the game, should have known real from pretend. What other protection was there from a game going too far? Amateur playing might have caused Horton's death. That Morgan might have left Cord in the hands of a know-nothing made the young cop even more furious.

"Ignorant shit!" Cord accused, kicking Terry again. It was Morgan, though, he was seeing and kicking.

It was a while before he got back some reasonable mental and physical control. When he did, he stopped kicking, breathing hard, his ears ringing. His vision was blurred, his eyes stinging from sweat drooling into them from his wet forehead. He wiped his arm across his eyes, blinked several times, and told himself somehow to get calm.

He thanked God when Terry moved. That was something, considering the damage Cord had probably done. He wasn't even certain how long it had been since he'd been released from his chains. His shirt was wet with perspiration, the soaked material sticking to him like glue.

He thought of calling an ambulance, but that was out of the question. Cord wasn't up to making explanations.

Terry looked up, his lips cracked and bleeding. His nose bleeding. His right eye puffy and beginning to discolor. He looked like shit, and Cord was responsible. Liberal Cord who'd always felt so damned superior around jerks like Bobby Jordan and Jim Holdsett who took such sadistic delight in beating up queers.

What was Cord seeing in the young Indian's dark eyes, Terry slowing dragging his bruised and battered body over to Cord and taking hold of Cord's legs. Jesus, what *had* Cord done?

"Don't stop," Terry begged, and Cord couldn't believe what he was hearing. "Beat me. Kick me. Piss and shit on me. Sir!" Terry pleaded.

Jesus, he was licking Cord's boots! The horror and disgust took Cord's breath away, leaving him empty inside, except for the sickness building there.

He kicked free, as if dislodging himself from a piece of crap. Hell, the kid *was* a piece of crap. Or, more likely, strange and alien offal that Cord couldn't begin to fathom.

Cord stumbled to the door, surprised to find it would open. He hurried through the empty locker room, someone having removed the police uniform Cord had discarded earlier.

He headed up the stairs, at any moment expecting someone to try and stop him. Take him back to that nightmare downstairs. Witness what he'd done to Terry Seabear. No one here caring what the kid—and Morgan Kent—had done to Cord.

The kitchen was empty. The dining room was empty. The living room was empty. If Morgan or Don were still in the house, they weren't sending off any *here-we-are* vibes. Not that Cord wasn't tempted to conduct a room-by-room search, anyway. He would have loved getting his hands on Morgan and beating the shit out of him. However, he needed time to get all of this into perspective. The way he felt now, he would kill Morgan if he found him now. Murder, delivered in response to a blowjob by Terry Seabear, not Morgan Kent, was an exchange too violent for any judge and jury to buy as warranted.

He went outside into a night hot and sticky. He headed across a lawn of overgrown grass, through the hedge and between two cars parked on the street. He had to get away and think. Thank God he had had the foresight to drive his own car, having followed Morgan to this hellhole.

His car was still there, too, although Cord had feared it would be gone. Just as he'd feared Terry wouldn't unfasten the chains. Just as he'd feared the dungeon door would be locked, the house door bolted shut. The only explanation was that Morgan must have had sense enough to know that any attempt to keep a cop permanently on ice would truly have dire consequences. Smart guy. Or, maybe not-so-smart. Because, Cord had every intention of finding that prick and making him pay far worse than Terry ever had.

So, where in the hell was his car key? His mind flashed an image of the key having fallen out of his pants while he was strung up and being sucked off. Key later kicked into darkness during Cord's rampage. Key taken by Morgan to make the game more interesting.

Easy, easy, Cord told himself. His key was where it should be. Right there in his pocket. All he had to do was take it out, and, Jesus, almost drop it. His hands were shaking like it was the morning after a major drunk. He could hardly get the key into the lock. A lock that didn't work. The wrong key, maybe. No, the right one. The wrong car? He stepped back, actually suspecting Morgan of having plotted this latest sadistic twist. Except, everything looked right. He merely had to get his shit together.

The lock *finally* unlocked.

He hadn't seen the sedan pull out down the block. He didn't see or hear it until it was at top speed and almost on him. Its bright lights came on suddenly, holding Cord as firmly transfixed in their glare as any startled buck ever hypnotized by a poacher's spotlight.

Too late, Cord's reflexes tried to get him out of the way.

CHAPTER FORTY-SEVEN

JACK

"LET ME GET THIS STRAIGHT," Jack Sudlow said, turning from the hospital window and facing Cord on the unmade bed. Jack's newly slimmed figure made his old clothes look baggy. His late-night drive up from Seattle had left him looking even more rumpled. "You followed Morgan Kent here to Vancouver without the Captain's approval and without Canadian authorization. This after you'd gone off on your own in Los Angeles and seen the repercussions of stepping on all the wrong toes. While up here, Kent tried to have you snuffed. In order to make him think he succeeded, you pulled in some markers and somehow arranged for the hospital to write up Cord *Hexell,* your alias, as a *Dead on Arrival.* You're now proposing to go underground to keep Kent under surveillance. Still not telling the Canadians or the Captain. Please feel free to add anything I've left out."

"You know the department is prone to leaks," Cord reminded, ignoring the Canadian question. "With Morgan's connections, he'd soon know I was alive." He stiffly shifted his position, aware of the damage the hit-and-run had done. Jack had said it all: *"Hell, man, you look like shit!"* No matter that Cord had been damned lucky. Far luckier than Russ Tompson. Not to mention luckier than Mary Bjorn who, while having been rescued from the guy trying to run her down, had ended up with a broken collarbone that fatally complicated a later gallstone operation.

"You don't think the Captain can keep his mouth shut?"

"I don't think the Captain would go along with my plan," Cord admitted.

"I think you're right, Maxwell. I'm not sure *I* go along with it, either."

"All I need is for someone to be there when the Captain starts wondering where I've gone. Tell him I mentioned a break on the

Lendland murder that might suddenly require my going underground for a few days."

"Which will go over like a lead balloon," Jack prophesied. "You know standard operating procedures."

"I really need you as my insurance policy in case I *do* disappear," Cord explained, remembering how he'd felt hanging in that dungeon with no friendly face knowing he was in Vancouver under an assumed identity.

"You're sure it was Kent who tried to run you down?" Jack asked. He didn't sound convinced.

"Even if it wasn't, I can't watch him as well *alive* as with him thinking I'm dead and out of the way," Cord argued.

"You may really fuck up your career by taking this route, Maxwell," Jack warned. "You got burned in LA, so why head off to another stove equally as hot?"

"It's a chance I'm willing to take," Cord assured. *He* knew the hit-and-run had been no accident. Whoever had been behind the wheel, if not Morgan, then someone Morgan had hired, had had all intentions of leaving Cord a dead man. That Cord wasn't dead was no fault of the driver.

"I don't like it," Jack said frankly. "We're not talking any real evidence here, are we?"

"Nevertheless, I'm convinced Kent is responsible for my hit-and-run, for Horton's death, and maybe for a few more murders thrown in for good measure."

"You *think*," Jack emphasized. "Disappearing by playing dead is kind of drastic measures on a mere hunch, isn't it? Out on your own again, no one but me knowing this time that you haven't dropped off the edge of the Earth. You've no proof against Kent, for Christ's sake, Maxwell! You didn't *see* who was driving that car. I'd bet my ass Kent has an alibi that'll stand up in any court." Cord didn't doubt that, either.

Cord could have made things clearer to Jack by detailing what happened in Don Richard's dungeon, but that wasn't something he was up to telling at the moment. He only knew he'd been used and abused, and he was going to get the bastard who'd set him up for degradation *and* attempted murder.

"I just wish I had a better idea of where in the hell you're coming from, Maxwell," Jack said, shaking his head. "In my opinion, you've let yourself get too involved with a bunch of freaks, when the Lendland cases could have been swept under any convenient rug. It still can be swept there, for that matter. So, why don't you just sit back and let things slide? Kent will hang himself, sooner or later, if he's guilty of anything."

"Well, I'm not as sure about that as you might be."

"Look, if I tell you something...." Jack looked ill at ease, actually nervous.

"Something about Kent?" Cord pressed.

"What it's about, Maxwell, is some guys in LA who put in a lot of overtime after you screwed them up on the Scott Jesse thing. They get wind you're apt to fuck them over again, and I wouldn't want to be in your shoes for all the tea in China."

"Fuck them up, how?" He wasn't going to let Jack leave it. "I'm talking Canada."

"Rumor is LA has someone ready to spill his guts," Jack said. "And if you tell *anyone* I said so, I'll deny it. Remember that."

"LA has someone tying Kent to what?" Cord pried, determined not to let Jack stop now. "Narcotics? Murder?"

"The point is: no one knows for sure what this stoolie has," Jack said. "He's running scared, afraid his ass is about to be blown away by the big boys. He's promising a lot, but he's not about to come across until he's damned sure he's protected, now *and* tomorrow, and I can't say as I blame him. Until he's satisfied with arrangements, LA asked the Captain to make sure there were no waves from this end. Meaning, I presume, *from you*. This surveillance you've planned for Kent is just liable to be the unwanted wave that starts here but breaks all of the way down in LA."

"This snitch has implicated Kent in what?" Cord asked again, wanting to know.

"It's Robert Lasalo who supposedly has the possibly really dirty hands. With Lasalo and Kent so chummy, what does that tell you?"

"We talking drugs?" Cord asked, wanting Jack to pin it down.

"Major shipments out of the Orient and Afghanistan. A network distributing the stuff via Mexico all of the way up here into Canada. Sound familiar?"

"*The Belgium Connection*. Deep involvement of a Lasalo-controlled spice company in Bruges. Two executives arrested who might have implicated Lasalo. Both killed by unknown assailant and/or assailants before they spilled much of anything. Lasalo squeezed through, clean as an ass after an enema."

"Kent was in the Army at the time of *The Belgium Connection*, wasn't he? Stationed in the Orient?"

"Yes," Cord confirmed.

"And Scott Jesse? He got around slant-eye territory about that same time frame, too, didn't he?"

"The Orient *and* Afghanistan."

"So, Kent and/or Jesse might have been in key places at the right times for Lasalo looking to reroute pipelines interrupted by *The Belgium Connection* busts, wouldn't you say? Kent, especially, was well-placed for recruiting military personnel for courier duty. He got around among the Orient locals, too, from what I understand, dispensing favors here, and favors there. More than one prostitute ended up in the US on the arms of a grateful American GI, compliments of Kent's wheeling and dealing. Kent's present life-style takes him from the dregs of society (the sellers), to the crème de la crème (the big buyers), without drawing any large amount of suspicion. He travels extensively, five times to the Orient in the last five years. Winters in Mexico. Even now, he's here in Canada for not the first time this year. Never any question about Jesse's involvement. LA was holding off pulling him in only in an effort to snag some bigger fish. Maybe LA will get lucky with this new snitch where Jesse didn't pan out for them." He didn't mention Jesse hadn't panned out *because of Cord*.

"But there's no guaranteeing either Lasalo or Morgan will take the fall on this one," Cord reminded. It wasn't a question.

"Jesus H. Christ, Maxwell!" Jack exploded. "Hell, no, I'm not giving any guarantees! I'm giving a warning that by fucking with Kent now, you just might somehow be fucking up something that can put him away for a long time. Make him paranoid, and you're apt to make others paranoid. Those others might start checking around to see why you're supposedly dead but nosing around, and… You want one dead stoolie in LA laid on your doorstep?"

"Kent thinks I'm dead," Cord reminded. The only person Cord could trust to see that Morgan paid was Cord. He couldn't count on the mere chance of some guy in LA *possibly* implicating Morgan in a major drug bust. Because, whether or not Morgan was implicated beyond a shadow of a doubt in narcotics, in Cord's hit-and-run, in the death of Horton Lendland, or in the death of all the others, the bastard, by God, *was* going to pay for what happened to Cord in Don Richard's dungeon.

"Whatever Kent *thinks,* you're not going to be invisible for long, Maxwell," Jack reminded. "If he spots you, he'll know for sure something is up. So will everyone else, even as far away as LA."

"I'll be careful," Cord promised.

"What *is* it between you and Kent?" Jack asked.

"He's a menace to society," Cord deflected, unprepared to take it any farther.

"Take my advice and lay off for the time being," Jack suggested. "If nothing comes of this development in LA, *then* make your move."

No matter what Jack said, Cord couldn't sit on his butt, waiting for someone else to pin Morgan to the wall. What's more, Cord knew better than to pin any hopes on some stoolie in LA. If Morgan *was* involved with the big boys, as Jack was suggesting, or if Morgan *was* one of the big boys, the stoolie had about as much chance of making it to the courtroom as a snowball had of surviving in hell. "You going to give me some long-distance cover with the Captain or not?" Cord challenged. If he had to, he'd bring up some favors Jack owed him, but he was hoping he wouldn't have to conjure past debts Jack should have remembered on his own.

CHAPTER FORTY-EIGHT

GREGORY

"**HAVE YOU A PAPER AND PENCIL HANDY,** or are you committing this to memory?" Gregory Salson asked, his voice sounding static-free despite the distance between Vancouver and San Diego.

"Shoot!" Cord instructed.

"It's quite a little jigsaw," Gregory said. Cord couldn't tell if the man were complaining or bragging. Knowing Gregory, he decided it was the latter.

"I knew it would be, Gregory. That's why I asked you to look into it for me," Cord flattered. "I knew if anyone could make heads or tails of it, you could. Some mighty good people have failed before you."

Cord and Gregory went back to the Kellelsy murder. Cord had needed someone who could meaningfully wade through the piles of paperwork resulting from corporate maneuverings by three supposedly competing Seattle-based companies. He'd needed a motive for Tom Kellelsy's murder. Gregory, a professor at the University of Washington at the time, had come highly recommended by Jack Sudlow. It had taken Gregory months to detail in-depth big-business machinations which Cord still wasn't sure he fully understood. The prosecutor, however, had evidently had a better grasp of business, because he'd moved for an indictment of three executives from Montip Electronics and two from Kellelsy, Incorporated. A judge had ruled for convictions on the same evidence. Gregory had since transferred to the University of California's Los Angeles campus. Los Angeles was only a commuter plane ride away from San Diego.

"Honey View Press is a subsidiary of J. Ryon Publications," Gregory said, "which is under the umbrella of Hendrix, International, namely as its communications division incorporated as Daniel M. White, Inc. Daniel M. White, Inc. has three major stockholders: John Mexlic, who's also President of Honey View Press, as well as Vice President of J. Ryon Publications and Vice President of Daniel M. White; Swendon F. Shifton, who's Vice President of Honey View Press, as well as President of J. Ryon Publications and Vice President of Daniel M. White, Inc.; Freddie Foley, who's Vice President of Honey View Press, as well as Vice President of J. Ryon Publications and President of Daniel M. White, Inc. Follow so far?"

"Right!"

"Foley is major stockholder with thirty-four percent."

"I follow that, too."

"He's, also, Vice President of Jackson-Reason Restaurant Supplies with twenty-five percent of the stock. Control of Jackson-Reason is in the hands of Ferdale, Incorporated. Ferdale, Incorporated is a company wholly owned by Valerie Creston. Valerie Creston is married to Peter Creston, nephew of Sylver Creston, who's married to Ruth Creston (AKA Ruth Carlson). Ruth is the daughter of Sam and Helen Carlson. Sam's a junior partner in Johnson Amalgamated with Simpson Shakiny who just happens to be Robert Lasalo's third cousin by marriage."

"Bingo!"

"Albeit a very tenuous *bingo,* but it's the best I could do on such short notice. Actually, it's even more convoluted than I've painted," Gregory added, sounding as if it might have come across too straightforwardly over the phone. "I can forward the computer readout if you'd care to leave your current forwarding address. Your office relays the distinct impression that they either don't know where you are, or they're not talking."

"Undercover," Cord alibied.

"Ah!" Gregory accepted at face value. "You interested in any of the other inter-connections now, then?"

"What other interconnections are we talking, Gregory?"

"I only came up with Lasalo on the one, but a lot of the other names appear regularly on one helluva lot of corporate boards for those purely dummy-variety companies with Grand Cayman post-office mailing addresses."

"I'll get back to you with where to mail the readout," Cord assured. "Until then, do you have any sources in New York?"

"A frat brother teaching at Columbia."

"I'd like a look at the power structure behind Coliseum Books."

"A prestige house," Gregory said. "I can tell you that much without even bothering Hector. They're into *publishing tomorrow's literary greats today.* The young Hemingways, Steinbecks, Bellows, *et al.*"

"I need a Lasalo connection, if there is one."

"It's quite a step from Honey View Press to Coliseum Books."

"Yeah, well, I know at least one person who's made the trip," Cord said cryptically.

"We talking the author of *Bomber*?" Gregory asked, an expert, after all, in cutting the crap. Then again, anyone with even a modicum of knowledge about current literature knew where Morgan Kent had come from, where he'd gotten, where he was likely headed.

"Just see what you can do for me, will you, Gregory? I'll get back to you in a couple days time."

"It might take more than a couple of days on this one," Gregory warned.

"A couple of days may be all *I've* got," Cord said, leaving it at that. No need explaining he couldn't stay holed up in Vancouver forever. Sooner or later, he was going to resurrect and be forced into making explanations to his captain. His only consolation was that one queer bastard was going to be as surprised as all hell by Cord's *Second Coming* (no pun intended).

CHAPTER FORTY-NINE

CORD

HAD HE NOT KNOWN how careful he'd been, Cord would have suspected he'd been spotted. Morgan had gone through some pretty fancy footwork geared, as far as Cord could tell, toward losing any tail. Twice that morning, Cord thought Morgan had slipped by him. Once, it was only Cord's consummate skill, born of long hours of on-the-job training, which saved the day. The next time it was sheer luck and a keen eye that had Cord spot Morgan headed down an *up* escalator.

Morgan was now seated at the window inside a small Vancouver café. Cord was across the street, going over possible mistakes he'd made that might have tipped Morgan that Cord was alive and well. No matter how often Cord went over it, he couldn't fault his precautions.

Not that Cord's efforts had produced results. Morgan's activities had been inane, up until now, to say the least. Had Cord actually expected to catch him in the act of killing someone or dealing cocaine on the streets? Possibly Cord was muffing his best chances of nabbing Morgan by continuing to stay undercover. Apparently wanting Cord dead and buried, Morgan might have been less careful had he been forced into making a second attempt.

Don Richard's pulled his car up in front of the café.

Morgan came out and got into Don's car.

Following Morgan and Don was no piece of cake. They changed to a taxi at the *Bayshore Inn*. Next, they disembarked at a downtown street corner, walked a couple of blocks and, then, got into a cab hailed for them by *The Mandarin Hotel* doorman.

Taxi two dropped them at a *Budget Rent-A-Car*. Cord watched from an adjacent side street as the two men picked up the gray *Toyota Tercel* that the maintenance boy drove around front for them.

The *Tercel* headed south on 99 out of Vancouver. Cord needed one of those James Bond gadgets to track via electronic grid-screen.

Unfortunately, he only had two eyes. He dropped farther behind as the lessening traffic made his continued presence more conspicuous.

They were headed for the Canadian/US border, but they turned east on a private dirt road before they got there. Cord pulled to a safe stop on the edge of the highway. A dust cloud marked the *Tercel*'s progress as far as a distant farmhouse. If and when the *Tercel* started up again, there'd be more telltale dust. As long as Cord kept the farmhouse in sight, he was momentarily sitting pretty.

It was fading daylight that finally persuaded him he was going to have to move closer. The *Tercel*'s dust would be harder to spot after nightfall, and there were no guarantees there was only the one road leading in and out of the farm. First, though…

Cord dialed his cell phone.

"Sudlow here!" Jack's voice boomed suddenly from the other end of the line.

"Guess who?" Cord asked. That would be enough. Jack's response was a long pause into which Cord injected, "I thought I'd check in to let you know I'm alive and well. How are things at your end?"

"This is not the best time," Jack said. His voice had gone so low that Cord could barely hear it. "But I *do* need to talk to you. A certain stoolie in LA has been shot but seems intent upon pulling through. A few people are running scared about his eventually regaining consciousness, which could be at any time now. Several concerned people have already dropped out of sight. Give me an hour and ring me back. Don't you *dare* do anything foolish until we talk."

The connection went dead just as Cord heard the plane. He thought it was a crop duster, except there was too little visibility for dangerously low crop-dusting passes. The plane was definitely making an approach, though, for somewhere (an airstrip?) just on the other side of the farmhouse.

Cord started his car and floored the gas pedal. He sped down the dirt road, skidded around the gray *Toyota* in the driveway of the farmhouse. He continued to drive toward Don and Morgan who stood knee-deep in wheat stubble a few yards from him.

He sped by them, delighted by their *my-God-how-did-you-get-here-?* expressions. He braked to a stop in the middle of hard-packed ground marked out for the approaching airplane. The plane converted its landing into a low pass and proceeded to regain lost altitude. It began circling.

Cord got out of his car, flushed as hell with the adrenaline rush. "Going somewhere?" he called to Morgan and Don.

"Just what in the hell are you trying to prove?" Don asked, red-faced and indignant. "You could have gotten someone bloody killed!"

Morgan seemed calmer. Cord would have preferred him more visibly impressed by Cord's resurrection. "We were just heading north for some fishing," Morgan said by way of greeting. "Were you hoping to get an invitation to tag along?"

Don proceeded to give the plane some *for-God-sake-stick-around* waves of his spidery arms.

"You don't seem to be traveling with much fishing gear," Cord observed. "How long were you planning on being away?"

"Oh, a couple of days at most," Morgan answered. "There's plenty of gear already at the cabin."

"They've arrested Lasalo," Cord said. It was probably a lie. Jack's message that *several had dropped out of sight* undoubtedly *could/would* have included Lasalo. Cord had to resort to *something,* though, to make Morgan tip his hand, since Cord couldn't actually come up with anything substantial on which to hold either Morgan or Don. If that continued to be the case, Morgan could and *would* raise all kinds of a holy hell.

"*Robert* Lasalo?" Morgan asked, looking all innocence. He was in a faded Levi jacket, faded jeans, scuffed cowboy boots, and a blue tie-dyed T-shirt. The informal costume seemed as made for him as had the German tank crewman's uniform in the dungeon. Cord refused, though, to be impressed by the man's natural good looks as they were farther flattered by the rosy twilight.

"Get that damned car of yours out of the way!" Don commanded. He headed in the direction of Cord's car.

Cord dangled the car keys. "I've the keys, and I wouldn't suggest you doing anything foolish to get them," Cord warned.

The plane, having completed another circle, began yet another.

"Why ever was Robert Lasalo arrested?" Morgan asked coolly. He still sounded innocent as hell, but Cord knew a class-act liar when he saw one.

"Seems some snitch in LA is recuperating from a bullet hole that should have left him dead but didn't," Cord obliged. "He's decided to spill his guts about the men he figures were responsible for trying to book him a one-way ticket to oblivion."

Cord was well aware that the wounded stoolie in question might not have said anything, might *never* say anything. If Lasalo had dropped out of sight, if Morgan and Don and anyone else involved were preparing to do the same, that didn't mean one and all couldn't come back wide-eyed and bushy-tailed from their respective *fishing trips* once the existing threat was successfully neutralized and/or removed.

"Get your bloody arse out of the way, and do it now!" Don ordered. Too late, Cord realized the man was accompanying his latest demand with an unholstered gun.

Foolishly, Cord's preoccupation with Morgan's responses had had him considering Don as merely incidental. After all, this was between Cord and Morgan, wasn't it? It had been something between them from their very first meeting. Cord resented the intrusion of this pseudo-Englishman shithead who got his rocks off by beating ass in his makeshift basement dungeon. The sooner Cord got Don out of the way, the sooner Cord and Morgan could get on with *their* business.

Morgan started chiding Don about knowing *the difference between bluff and the real thing* as Cord went down and, drawing his gun, commenced a roll. Cord took Don out with one shot. Reflexively, seeing Morgan go for a gun, Cord took him out with the next two.

* * * * * * *

THERE WAS NO SIGHT OR SOUND of the plane, but Cord didn't remember it leaving the airspace above.

The moon was up, glorious and full, but Cord didn't remember it rising. Nor did he remember the sun setting in a dazzling display of color.

He was busy replaying whatever it was that had left him alone with two dead men in a Canadian wheat field. He had no problem remembering the gun in Don's hand, nor a determination to take Don and Don's weapon out of the picture. He could be pleased with the coordination he'd exhibited in accomplishing just that.

It was Morgan's death that bothered him. The reason for it was less clear. Had Morgan *really* been going for his gun? Granted, there *had* been one for him to go for. Morgan wore a loaded pistol couched in the leather holster at his left armpit. But, would he have gone for it after having just insisted—*"My God, Don, can't you tell a really pathetic bluff when you hear one?"* Yes, he would have, if Morgan had suddenly thought, Don shot, that things had gone too far. Yes, he would have, if he'd weighed his alternatives and felt the one that made the gun-firing Cord dead, as Cord *should* have *already* been dead, was the best choice at hand.

Supplementary, however, there were Cord's attending wild suspicions that maybe it had been *Cord* who had thought things gone too far, *Cord* who had weighed alternatives, aimed his gun at Morgan, in direct result, and pulled the trigger. Maybe Cord had so *wanted* Morgan to go for a gun that Cord had *imagined* it was so, and now used that as his rationalization for having killed the man who had so fucked up Cord's life. Killing Don, whose dungeon had been the site of Cord's humiliation, might have been incomplete without killing Morgan who had not only engineered Cord's humiliation, there, but hadn't even bothered to stick around long enough to swing from Cord's hard cock.

Cord *had* wanted Morgan dead. Not only because Morgan was probably up to his ears in drug trafficking that ruined countless of lives each year. Not only because Morgan had possibly been responsible for the deaths of Horton Lendland, Mary Bjorn, Sandra Wheems, Sue Parring, Russ Tompson, Tara Robinson, Opalline Elizabeth Sinclair, and God only knew how many others. Not only because Morgan had maneuvered Cord into exploring a darker side of sexuality.... Although any and/or all of *those* might suffice as damned good reason for Cord having shot the bastard even if Morgan *hadn't* been making a move to draw a weapon.

Cord tried desperately to fight his unacceptable suspicions that Morgan had died in that wheat field *primarily* because Cord had wanted him *sexually,* and Morgan would have remained unattainable to the end. Such *wanting* had made a living and breathing Morgan a continual threat to Cord's well-being. The policeman had realized just how much of a threat that was when the silk hood had come off his head in that dungeon and he'd experienced his tremendous disappointment in discovering it hadn't been Morgan sucking his dick. *Had* it been Morgan feasting between Cord's legs, Cord might have made the necessary mental adjustments to combat the guilt the policeman would have felt in Morgan being there. However, having fought his darker passions for so hard and for so long, Cord had felt cheated in having been forced into finally surrendering himself not to Morgan but to Terry Seabear.

Morgan had held a power over Cord that no one man should ever be able to hold over another. Especially not a man like Morgan who wasn't kind, wasn't good, wasn't caring, wasn't appreciative of what Cord might have been persuaded to willingly give. Morgan was a taker without feelings, without genuine emotions, without scruples, without morals. Killing such a manipulator of men and women didn't just save Cord. It saved countless other potential victims who might have been enticed into Morgan's deadly games, Morgan appearing the desirable prize that could never be had in spite of all the indications to the contrary.

"Why did you go for your gun?" Cord asked, over and over, rocking Morgan, as handsome as ever, even in death, against Cord's tear-stained lap.

CHAPTER FIFTY

GARY

"JUST KEEP ON COMING INSIDE, Maxwell," Gary Green surprised, "and, then, kindly push the door shut behind you."

Cord hardly recognized Gary who had gained even more weight. Layers of new fat overflowed old in cascades that puckered Gary's shirt and folded over his pants' waistband. Seemingly part of the chair on which he sat, his chubby right arm extended his chubby little fingers that held the *looking-mighty-small-in-comparison* gun.

Cord had been taken by surprise, and he had only himself to blame. He spent too much time, recently, lost in a world of rehashing what had happened in that Canadian wheat field. His superiors had noticed just such preoccupation and had insisted he take *a leave of absence for rest and recuperation*. They wanted him out of the office for other reasons, too. Like, so the Captain wouldn't be constantly reminded of how Cord's violations of SOP had left Morgan Kent and Don Richards dead. Even more pissed off, if that was possible, were the Canadian authorities, even though Cord's defense of self-defense had been helped along by the testimony of the LA stoolie whom had finally gotten around to surviving his bullet wound and spilling his guts. Morgan, Tony France, Judd Kleverton, Curtis Hurt, Scott Jesse, Bobby Jordan, and Don Richards, had all, finally, been implicated in an extensive drug network. Robert Lazalo had been implicated, too, but he was last reported in Brazil.

"The best place for those fish of yours would be in the sink," Gary instructed, referring to the trout that had seemed determined to commit *seppuku* on Cord's fishhook. Fishing had been Cord's ruse to make him appear part of the scenery. Not that anyone had been looking. China Lake was an isolated pocket of alpine water, and Cord's nearest neighbor was three miles father along the rugged shoreline. It was the ambience of being on the lake, alone, with his thoughts, in a boat, which had coaxed him to come there.

Gary's pistol followed Cord's every movement from door to sink. It stayed aimed securely at Cord's midsection when Cord turned slowly and wondered silently about the possibilities of reaching one of the rifles in the gun cabinet. He doubted he could. Gary doubted Cord could, too.

"I'm admittedly not the best shot," Gary confessed, "but it wouldn't take too much talent to hit you from this range."

Cord agreed.

One of the four hardy kitchen chairs once carpentered by Cord's father was now positioned beneath one of the cabin's rustic roof beams. A chain was draped over the beam, equal lengths dangling metal links almost to the seat of the chair. Handcuffs were attached to each end of the chain. Another chain was intricately weaved around the bottom of the chair and locked into place, manacles attached.

Gary smiled, his teeth looking small within the hole revealed above his cascading chins. His neck was lost in a sea of skin-flow.

Déjà-vu filled Cord's mind with images of the chains and manacles in Don Richard's dungeon. Simultaneously, he mentally chided himself for having walked into *this*. A man Gary's size didn't tiptoe anywhere without leaving squashed plants and dented cement behind him for anyone who was seriously looking. Unless, that is, he took extensive precautions.

"I'd really like to know what this is about," Cord said, making no moves to get any closer to Gary or to the specially rigged chair.

"It's about destiny," Gary obliged. "Fate, karma, kismet. Now, sit down in the chair I've so carefully prepared for you, or I'll have to shoot you, here and now."

Reluctantly, Cord went to the chair and sat down on it.

"Manacles to your ankles, first," Gary instructed. *Handcuffs* first wouldn't have given Cord enough slack to affix the manacles. *Handcuffs* first would have meant Gary would be required to step on over to either unfasten the cuffs, so Cord could begin again, or to fasten the leg manacles himself. Either way, there would have been a chance, albeit slim, for Cord to deliver a quick kick to Gary's groin or head. Gary obviously knew that, too. "Manacles first!" he repeated.

Cord hesitated, beginning to sweat. His fingertips painted moist prints on one manacle's cool metal surface.

"Do it, *now,* please!" Gary commanded, sounding none too friendly.

The resulting snaps of manacles and handcuffs were far more ominous than any sounds Cord had heard in Don Richard's dungeon.

"Why did you shoot Morgan?" Gary asked, his pupils beady little pin-pricks.

"Self-defense," Cord rationalized, for not the first time. His chain rattled as he shifted uneasily. "Morgan was going for his gun." He *did* believe that, didn't he?

"I figure you blew him away, because his fucking your ass was a threat to your notion of personal macho," Gary offered in alternative.

Cord spontaneous reaction—additional shaking of chain—must have come off as Samson attempting to topple the temple, because Gary pulled back as if he were dodging falling masonry.

"Maybe Morgan even let *you* fuck *his* ass," Gary suggested, once apparently reassured that neither Cord nor the roof was going anywhere.

"You're sick!" Cord diagnosed when his anger gave him his voice back.

Gary scratched one middle chin with the barrel of his pistol. Cord wished the gun would go off, a bullet penetrating blubber and brains.

"Of all the others, you came closest to Morgan's physical ideal," Gary said. "And didn't you suspect just that as you hurried off to the gym to get even more so!"

"Our Captain doesn't approve of *any* of his policemen being out of shape," Cord informed. Cord's workouts with Jack Sudlow had had nothing whatsoever to do with Morgan Kent. They were to get Cord back in condition before he, like Jack, received an ultimatum *from on high* ordering him to do so or else.

"I *saw* the sparks, Maxwell," Gary begged to differ. "You two in the same room generated a storm of crackling sexual electricity."

"You're mistaken," Cord insisted.

"I'm *not* mistaken," Gary contradicted. "But it's always nice to find someone as fucked up about his sexuality as I am."

He put his gun on the end table adjacent his chair, revealing a large sweat stain at one armpit as he did so. He gave a massive sigh that started a chain reaction of vibrating flesh that should have shook the cabin but didn't.

"I first met Morgan when he was going through debriefing for eventual discharge from Fort Lewis," Gary said, seeming to think Cord was interested. "He'd come into Seattle regularly to visit his one-time school buddy Steve Footer with whom I was rooming at the time. Steve and I had been brought together by a mutual friend who knew each of us was looking for a bigger place to live but couldn't individually swing the payment. Together, Steve and I got a good deal on a three-bedroom rental on Twelfth Avenue East. There was nothing sexual between Steve and me, you understand, although Morgan injected a bit of sexual tension into our little household, because Steve had had the hots for Morgan for a helluva long time. However, at that time, Steve was dating some guy who put out for him far more often than Morgan was ever going to do. So, Steve couldn't complain too much at *my* obvious infatuation for his old school chum.

"You're wondering about this *attraction* I had for Morgan," Gary intuited. "Well, no more than I wondered about it at the time. That was before I knew Morgan was a chameleon able to be anything to anybody. Back then, I only knew I wanted him, and he wasn't anything like my standard sexual ideal. He was too old for starters. His voice had changed. His balls had dropped. He had hair beneath his arms, around the base of his cock, and a whole line of fuzz running the crack of his butt. Oh, he looked younger than he was, even then, but no way could he have passed for a tender pre-adolescent. Nevertheless, there was no denying that I *was* literally giddy when he agreed to move in with Steve and me once his discharge became final.

"I would have been far better off, of course, had I never met him. I know that now. I've known it for ever so long. Knowing, though, has never made any difference. So, you'd better believe love is blind, because I did love him. He was easy to love in that he went to excruciating bother to find out people's needs and cater to them. At least, he obliged *some* of those needs. Others he sidestepped with consummate skill.

"Morgan and I had long talks whenever Steve was out of the house with *his-man-of-the-hour*. Morgan was oh-so easy to talk to. He had a way of making me think he and I were the only two people on Earth. I used to look forward to our evenings alone on the couch, having a few drinks, discussing things which interested me and which I'd assumed interested him. All the while, like a technician in a lab, he was methodically dissecting lab-rat me to see what made me tick. Charmingly, he coaxed me into confiding more and more about myself, all my deepest secrets. I was frankly flattered he was interested. I was excited, too, by his actually being someone my own age with whom I contemplated sex. He was the only *man* I'd ever wanted *that way*. I saw him as a kind of Savior sent to lead me out of the world of Lilliputian desires into acceptable adult gay sex. Acceptable in that you do know even gays frown upon pederasty. It seems even aberrant sex has definable boundaries. Step over the boundaries, and you give queers a bad name."

He folded his hands upon one of the three great folds of his stomach. He was the creature from a poster Cord had once seen for some character, he forgot which one (Jabba the Hut?), in the movie *Star Wars*.

"Morgan pried it all out of me," Gary said. "My penchant for young boys, Morgan being the unique exception to the rule. He never exactly out-and-out refused to consummate our relationship, merely convinced me it wasn't *wise to rush something of such importance to the both of us*. In the meantime, the touch of his hand became one of the most sensuous things I can remember."

Gary actually sighed.

"He started writing his first porno book for some San Diego smut publisher. I didn't think he was serious. He was a college grad, wasn't he? A college grad didn't make his living writing porn. He read me passages about some guy fucking a goat on the edge of a cliff. I laughed. He laughed. I thought he was amused by my amusement. How was I to know that he was already contemplating porno as his launch pad for bigger and better things?

"He hinted that, come a certain Friday, we might finally go to bed together. It was all bullshit, but I believed him. I went around for days with a perpetual hard-on and, for once, it had nothing to do with the little darlings flocking around my desk at school each day."

He punctuated with a loud grunt and scooted in seeming effort to redirect his flow of fat into any stray chair crack or crevice that might have previously escaped suffocation.

"When that Friday finally arrived, I couldn't wait for Steve to go out for his customary evening of rutting. But even before Steve left, those two women arrived for *a little visit*. I was furious by their intrusion, hurt that Morgan seemed so delighted by it. I was more distraught when it came out later that Morgan had known they were coming all along."

His fingers still locked, he turned his knuckles-toward-his-belly and extended his arms straight out. Eight little piggy joints crackled in unison.

"Morgan took Mrs. Robinson, not me, upstairs," Gary said. His shudder was a visible thing, his flesh a storm-tossed sea. "He fucked her, too. No denying that! She wasn't quiet about it. She moaned. She groaned. She squealed. She begged him for more. It should have been me up there. He'd as much as promised, but he was a liar along with everything else. A liar who flaunted his preference for goddamned cunt instead of for me. Leaving me with a bitch who got hornier with every squeal the other broad made."

"You could have walked out," Cord reminded.

"I thought Morgan would come down at any moment. I thought it was a mistake, a practical joke. I couldn't believe he was up there, actually doing what he was doing with a woman when he liked men. *When he liked me.* Female moans and groans didn't fit. The aggressive come-on of the bitch he'd left with me didn't fit. None of it fit. It was a living nightmare in which hate blossomed and grew. Hate for both of those cunts. Monstrous hate for Morgan."

He punctuated with a piggy little smile.

"Oh, yes, I hated Morgan," he emphasized. "For the first time, I saw him for the unfeeling bastard he really was. All the illusions were gone. He'd used our evenings together to coax out of me how he might best degrade the feelings I had for him. On the other hand, he'd worked his spell well, because I still loved him, despite his betrayal. It's true that love and hate are closely related, you know, although I don't think he ever realized how much hate he was responsible for focusing that one night. The intensity of it surprised even me."

"Enough hate for you to kill?" Cord asked, and he wasn't just asking about the fate of Tara and Beth. In his mind's eye, he was replaying the scenario in the Canadian wheat field. Not the shooting this time. Rather, how Morgan hadn't seemed nearly as surprised as he should have to see a supposedly dead Cord resurrected. Had Morgan even ever thought Cord was dead? Or, had he, knowing Terry Seabear had freed Cord from the dungeon, assumed Cord had been hiding out somewhere and licking his violated sense of machismo? Morgan not having known anything at all about Cord's potential killer having waited in ambush outside Don's Dungeon in that car? Morgan might never have looked for or seen the resulting short newspaper statement about the DOA hit-and-run victim Cord *Hexell* (Cord's phony name on Cord's phony ID for Cord's phony death notice). Even Cord, purposely looking for his own phony obit, had had a hard time finding it where it had been buried on one of the back pages of the Vancouver paper.

"Morgan told me later he'd fucked that gal as kind of a fond farewell," Gary said, proceeding at his own time and pace. "She was part of his life in Portland, and he had no intentions of making her part of his life in Seattle. In truth, by the time I killed those two cunts, they'd long been dead by Morgan's way of thinking."

"But if he'd already tired of them...."

"…why did I bother killing them?" Gary finished for him. "I killed them, because I'd discovered hate as an aphrodisiac more powerful than my lust for either preadolescent boys *or* for Morgan Kent. Planning the murders was an even *more* powerful turn-on than the hate. Committing the murders was the *most* powerful sexual stimulant of all. Not even Morgan could know the irony of how his fucking that one broad, and leaving me harassed by the other, *finally* turned me on to women, albeit in a very specialized way."

He smiled, and it wasn't a pleasant thing to see.

"Oh, but I had both of those cunts moaning and groaning in the end," he boasted. "My, but they did squeal and scream up holy storms. Not, however, begging for more."

"You picked them up in that supermarket parking lot?"

"Easy as pie," Gary admitted. "I just pulled up and remarked on the lucky coincidence of my having spotted them both there, of all places, since I was on my way to invite them for drinks with *you-know-who*."

He shook his head in apparent wonder.

"Morgan Kent: a magical name!" he exclaimed. "More success-ful an incantation, by far, than ever was, *Want a candy bar, little boy, little girl?* The mere mention of Morgan brought them all to me, like bees to honey. That's the power he had over them. And I would as eagerly been a similar fly to succumb to any spider entic-ing *me* with promises of the same."

"*All of those brought to you* included more than *just* those two women," Cord suggested. It wasn't a question. The Lendland case was still open, although it had been delegated to a *really* back burner, what with recent escalation of the *Dint Slough* killings. Cord had tried his best to pin Lendland's killing on Morgan, but there'd never been enough evidence to manage it to anyone's satisfaction, Cord's included. Here was the best of all reasons why. "Horton Lendland?" Cord threw out for discussion.

"Oh, Horton Lendland, by all means!" Gary said, accepting the pass. "And don't forget Sandra Wheems, Russ Tompson, and Sue Parring. Mary Bjorn I have to share credit for with gallstones. Yes, I killed them all, because Morgan fucked them all in preference to fucking me. In the end, his screws gave me infinitely more pleasure than I'm sure they ever gave him."

"Morgan and I never made it together," Cord insisted, now knowing why it was very important he get Gary to believe that.

"It's a moot point," Gary said, surprising Cord and certainly not making Cord's life any easier, "and I'll tell you why." Cord was sweating buckets. "One of my students came up to my desk just yesterday," Gary continued after a short pause. "I asked him to stay after class to discuss a poor score he'd made on a science exam. When he did, I locked the two of us in my classroom and had him watch while I wrung the neck of the class's pet guinea pig. I told the kid if he told anyone what I did next I'd kill his parents and him just as easily as I'd killed *little Freddie*."

Cord shuddered.

"Before Morgan," Gary said, "I counted on my good sense to keep my passions for young boys in check. I was careful. If I played around with my nephews, neither they nor my sister would be turning in *Uncle Gary*. Maylene is a divorcee, with two kids, struggling to make ends meet. I'm the only helping hand she can expect whenever she gets in too deeply. I'm the only one promising to help her get her kids through college. At times, I risked the streets for a tender morsel or two, for my sexual enjoyment, but I didn't go that route too often. The police are always cracking down on the really young ones, and I didn't want to get picked up with one. I liked my job, and I didn't want it fucked up on a morals charge. Then, Morgan came along. At first, he merely held out hope of my someday having an *acceptable* sex life with another consenting adult. Later, he afforded me those other, more complex, diversions, like jealousy, hate, murder, and the *real* sexual gratifications those provided.

"I can't go back to where I was before Morgan," he said. "Doing without is always best achieved when you've never had it in the first place. My pleasures had through Morgan, albeit vicariously, were too vivid not to be missed. If I contemplated murdering some common hitchhiker, or a prostitute, I quickly realized my joy in killing was never *just* the planning of the murder and/or just committing it. It encompassed other vital ingredients. Like, Morgan inadvertently selecting the victims. Like, the accompanying jealousy and hate for which Morgan was, also, responsible. Without Morgan as a catalyst, I succumbed to older desires, far less able to contain them than I'd once been. I won't be forgiven for succumbing to them, either, because the youngster in question isn't a little nobody with a runaway father and a booze-addicted mother. His father heads an important bank, and his mother chairs a very prestigious charity. Even if the kid keeps his mouth shut, there'll be others. Certain boundaries are more easily crossed the second time. I'll be found out, and there won't be any reprieves like with Andy Sacks."

"What about Andy Sacks?" Cord challenged, little encouraged by what he was hearing. "Morgan alive didn't see you keeping your hands off Andy, did it?"

"Surely you're not equating Andy Sacks with one of my students!" Gary protested. "What I did with Andy Sacks should never have been a risk at all. Who gave a shit about Andy? Not his father. Not his mother, until she thought she could get something out of it. Nor was the kid any innocent when I came along. Many other dirty old men had had him before I got there. If he was young, it was only in the *legal* sense of years he'd spent on Earth. He knew exactly what I was proposing when I suggested our little trip. Our very first night on the road, *he* climbed blatantly into *my* bed, not vice versa. He was as happy as I was about the whole thing. It wasn't his fault or mine that Nelton Manson opened his busy-body mouth at the wrong place and at the wrong time. Even then, the resulting trial was more inconvenience than anything else. It seemed inconceivable to the liberal, well-educated, upper-middle-class parents of my students, past and present, who flocked en masse to my defense, that Mr. Green could have possibly bypassed their little darlings for a little nobody like Andy, if I'd *really* been the sort of pervert the prosecution was trying to paint me. And bypass their little darlings was exactly what I *had* done, don't you see? And that's what saved me. This time, though, I've sunk that particular lifeboat."

He tented two pudgy index fingers and poked them into the lower folds of one chin.

"However, in retrospect, you may have something," he conceded. "Andy Sacks might well have been the writing on the wall, harbinger of my life without Morgan in it. Because, my *thing* with Andy came about as the direct result of an exceptionally long stretch in which Morgan never seemed to be around. He'd taken up with Horton, who I'd, by the way, already marked for death. That Horton wasn't dead sooner was because he was forever heading off on trips to Paris, London, Hong Kong, or wherever, Morgan in tow. I wasn't about to kill him in some foreign country where the death of an American would have sent everyone scurrying for the culprit. Far better to do it on Horton's doorstep, where he was known, and where the local police would view it as just another killing of just another promiscuous old faggot. In the ever-extending interim before the killing, I used Andy Sacks as *filler*.

"Morgan and Horton got back from one of their trips, and Morgan heard from Steve that I was off traveling with Andy," Gary said. "Steve was keeping my houseplants from dying at the time. Morgan called me while Andy and I were stopping over in Medford. He suggested meeting us at *Ka-Nee-Da* for a day of sunshine."

Gary wrung his hands like a little old lady warming her arthritic knuckles.

"He brought Horton along, of course," he condemned icily, "Morgan obviously pleased to see how he could still hurt me. I think he was only there to check out the competition. To Morgan, everything was a game to be played, and he was *ever-so-damned* good at playing it. He got me off to one side, pretending Horton coming along hadn't been his idea. *Christ, Gary, how could I tell him to just bug off when he just got me that fantastic deal on a Toby?* He kissed me. He said he wanted me, and I believed him. He said there wasn't time to do much there, though, since he'd promised Horton to be in the room early. Horton was afraid the goddamned place might catch fire without Morgan around to wake him. *We don't want to make our first time a quickie, do we, Gary? It should be special, with plenty of time to do it all.* Andy thought my hard-on was because *and for* him. The kid wanted to party. All I wanted to do was jack-off and savor my latest anticipatory fantasies of Morgan."

Gary getting up took awhile to accomplish. His chubby arms hardly seemed up to the chore of launching his large bulk. Once standing, he stretched, hands above his head, producing no notice-able elongation of his torso. He shuffled over to the sink and spent an inordinate amount of time staring at the dead fish Cord had put there.

"I went to a doctor once," Gary said, Cord assuming he was re-ferring to a shrink. Cord was wrong. "I wanted to lose weight," Gary said. "I knew what kind of body attracted Morgan, and mine wasn't it. The doctor said I should eat less red meat and more fish. Trouble was, I can't abide fish." He chuckled, and the chuckle erupted into a full-bellied laugh. He turned back to Cord who had to look sideways to see him. "Do you find it the least Freudian that in certain vernacu-lar *fish* equals *woman*?" he asked with an accompanying shuddcr. "I didn't *really* want to be thin, because it would have made no differ-ence to Morgan. I wasn't his type, fat or thin."

He proceeded to the nearest window, using stubby fingers to hold back a section of curtain. It was still daylight, a slash of motes-infected sunshine cutting its way into the room.

Had Cord opened the drapes when he'd left that morning? If so, trudging up the hill from the dock, he should have noticed someone had closed them. Where had he lost his intuition, his sixth sense, his basic instincts for survival?

"I called the *Lendland/Holdsett* late one afternoon when Horton was there alone," Gary said. "I told him Morgan had arranged a spe-cial birthday gift for him. Magic name again: *Morgan*. Of course, Horton's actual birthday was nowhere close, but that didn't make any difference. Morgan had once told me that Horton had several birthdays during the course of any given year just on the off-chance of getting extra presents. I asked Horton if he'd mind sticking around the gallery a few minutes after closing. The gift—which I led him to believe was a hustler—was flying in from San Francisco, and I'd be picking *him* up at the airport any minute. I could deliver *him* to Horton at the gallery, where Horton often did his sucking after hours, compliments of Morgan, at such-and-such an hour."

He turned from the window, letting the curtain fall back into place. He sniffed his fingertips, all of the while rubbing them together. He wrinkled his nose which did little more than rearrange the fat lines in his face. Cord suspected Gary smelled the fish, since fishy smells were becoming more and more evident in the room.

"The spear was extemporaneous theater," Gary said. "It was behind Horton's desk, and it seemed ideally suited for symbolically saying it had been Morgan's cock up Horton's asshole which had *really* killed the art dealer."

He moved to a spot where Cord could better see him.

"I later regretted torching the gallery," Gary said. "Morgan was upset about the loss of some paintings that would have been his. He certainly was more upset about their loss than he was over losing Horton. Probably because he'd tired of Horton, by then, keeping close to him only for the paintings Horton could get for him at bargain prices. I'm sure Morgan going into partnership with Holdsett is just a way of assuring Morgan of those continued dealer discounts."

"Morgan never knew what you were up to?" Cord asked. Morgan's death would have been easier for Cord to accept if the answer was that, *yes, Morgan knew*. Gary, though, wasn't obliging.

"It wasn't as if I left a trail for either Morgan or the police," Gary boasted. "The body of Mrs. Robinson's friend hasn't turned up to this day. Mary Bjorn seemingly died of her gallstone operation, Russ Tompson of a hit-and-run, Horton Lendland of a still-unidentified someone. You *should* have died of a hit-and-run. Imagine my surprise when you didn't! I must say, I got double the pleasure, double the fun, out of planning your demise, not once but twice. Though I'd say that was only fair, since it's *because of you* that we're here, at the finish of everything, isn't it?"

"There are places that people like you can go for help," Cord argued. He didn't deny his sexual involvement with Morgan this time around, because it had become evident that it was as much the fucking that went on *in Gary's mind*, as it was the real thing, which had condemned all this bastard's victims.

"I'm not up to being sequestered within any little boxes with bars," Gary said. "I'm not up to getting my cock shocked every time the picture of a prepubescent boy is flashed on some video screen. I want things as they were. I want to be a good teacher. I want to be in charge of *things* going on inside of me. I, at least, want the *illusion* of some kind of control. Can you understand that?"

Maybe Cord *could* understand. Maybe he, too, longed for a return to a time in his life before Morgan Kent. A return to a time in which he was in charge of things inside *him*. A return to a time of no recurring nightmares about a Canadian wheat field; nightmares in which Morgan Kent never once went for his gun. A return to a time when Cord didn't helplessly find himself wondering how things *might* have been *if* only....

If only he hadn't desired Morgan Kent!

If only he hadn't been afraid of what those desires were doing to him, and where they were taking him!

If only he hadn't pulled his gun and shot Morgan in a Canadian wheat field!

If only Gary Green weren't standing in the open doorway of the cabin, lugging in a five-gallon container of gasoline and wheezing all the while!

"Don't do it, Gary!" Cord pleaded.

But the can was already open. The floor and Gary and Cord were soon soaked with gas, the room shimmering in an undulating shroud of noxious fumes.

"I *have* to do it," Gary argued, producing a lighter and, with a sad smile, flicking his *Bic*.

ABOUT THE AUTHOR

WILLIAM MALTESE was born in the Pacific Northwest. He has a B.A. in Marketing/Advertising and spent an honorable tour of duty in the U.S. Army, achieving the rank of E-5.

He started his authorial career writing for the men's pulp magazines and has since penned more than 150 books, both fiction and nonfiction. According to queerhorror.com, this included the first gay werewolf novel ever published. He also has written a number of bestselling women's romances under the name "Willa Lambert" for houses such as Harlequin and Carousel, including the internationally acclaimed Harlequin SuperRomance #2 (*Love's Emerald Flame*), which is being reprinted by Wildside Press along with many of his other novels.

He encourages his fans to visit his websites:

www.williammaltese.com
www.myspace.com/williammaltese